FLIGHT through FIRE

Based on a true aviation love story

CAROL FIORE

Flying Kea
Press

www.flyingkeapress.com

For Eric

Here, finally, is my promise

This is a work of fiction in that the author, after a decade, had trouble remembering exact conversations, descriptions, and chronology. Unintended errors are likely in reference to medical terminology. Most of the events are real. Most of the characters are real. All of the grief is real.

INTRODUCTION

W hy have I decided to list this book as fiction when the events that happened are real?

Primarily due to reconstructed dialogue. Did the characters say those exact things? No. I did not have a tape recorder when the events transpired, and although I have a good memory for conversations and wrote much of it down, it isn't accurate—it can't be after more than a decade. Therefore, this book is fiction.

During the decade of writing this book, I've tried to be as truthful as possible. However, I may have altered details, dialogue, and chronology. Physical descriptions of the many medical people are especially prone to error after so many years. I didn't write down things like hair and eye color, body shape, and other descriptors, so I've had to invent some details.

I've also omitted facts that would add unnecessarily to the length of the book. For instance, although I am the oldest of five children, only one of my siblings appears in the book (the others did not play a part in the events I describe).

I take the contract with my reader seriously, and I don't want to mislead with even the smallest details, which may be quite important to some. The people are real. The events are real. However, I have taken small liberties with the writing. It has been difficult to piece the story back together after so many years—another reason I can't list this book as nonfiction.

After much agonizing, I've decided to change every person's name except for family members, Eric's best friend RB, my university friend Linda, and names on e-mails (reprinted with permission). I randomly chose fictitious names. I also changed the name of the hospital. The sheer number of medical people would have been confusing for the reader, necessitating the omission of some and the combining of others to make a composite character.

The journals I kept at the hospital were indispensable in helping me recall facts and conversations years later. My sister Patty (love you, P!), a medical doctor, spent many painful hours going over exact details with me, helping to analyze over sixteen hundred pages of medical records. Errors in interpretation are quite likely, despite our care. I am, after all, not a doctor and likely made mistakes in the writing of medical information, possibly leaving out significant details.

I steadfastly praise the treatment my husband received at the hospital. In no way do my observations of the personalities of medical people reflect on the excellent care they gave.

Allow me to stress once again that conversations in quotation marks are intended to capture the flavor of people's speech, not exact structure and wording, which would be impossible after so many years. As stated previously, the reader should consider this a work of fiction, particularly concerning dialogue. I constructed several medical conversations directly from the medical records; they did not actually take place.

I thank all the amazing people who made this book possible, particularly my talented editor, Kate Eleanor, and my dear friend, the late Darwin Swett, who set me on the path from science geek to writer. I also thank my beautiful daughters, Tia and Robin, for their constant support—they never once stopped believing in me.

I'm grateful to the members of my writing groups and college classes for their unflagging encouragement. Thanks to my incredible friends Janine Crick and Stephanie Stinar for letting me talk incessantly about Eric.

Thank you to the kind and generous people of Wichita who donated to the Challenger Fund, which allowed me, with the help of my friends at the Kansas Cosmosphere and Space Center in Hutchinson, Kansas, to establish a scholarship and erect an impressive exhibit of Eric's flying memorabilia.

To all the people who came to the hospital—particularly the caring Bombardier folks—I thank you. If you sent flowers or food or helped our family but didn't receive a note, allow this to be my sincere thanks for your kindness.

Lastly, I thank my husband Eric, who always told me I could do anything, be anything, become anything. I will *always* be your little redheaded girl.

Day 1
Tuesday, October 10, 2000

*"Shit happens, and it doesn't mean
it's somebody's fault."*
– Eric

Cappuccino. Laughter. A quick kiss and good-bye with a call of "I'll see you at dinner."

It should have been raining—maybe a thunderstorm or a tornado. But it wasn't. He'd driven his sports car, top down, because the day promised to be sunny. Maybe we should be afraid of the ordinary days. They have the power to sneak up and mutilate us.

Eric took great delight in his cappuccino. He'd laughed while enjoying it. Eight hours later, my life, that life, ended. My identity would quickly disappear, leaving only a brittle casing. I would become like the dried-up exoskeleton of a beetle I once found deep in a rainforest.

My story begins on this promising day with my older daughter, Tia, a cheery teen, always laughing and delivering witty jokes, surrounded by friends. She has seen a black column of rising smoke off to the southeast, in the direction of the airport.

"Mommy, look at the smoke!"

As my eyes followed Tia's finger across the monotonous wheat fields of Kansas, Robin, always the intense but talkative child, launched into a bubbly stream of chatter from the back seat of the car.

"I'm glad you're going to teach at my school on your days off from the zoo, Mommy. And I'm glad you're teaching fourth grade and not Tia's yucky seventh-grade class 'cause I want you to be my teacher. I liked having lunch with you today, and my friend Lindsey said..."

We quickly forgot the smoke.

I would always wonder why I hadn't felt something other than the sameness of another ordinary day. It would take me years to understand that Eric and I were separate people.

After we arrived home, I switched on the television while preparing dinner. There had been a crash at Mid-Continent Airport—a small plane, the reporter said. I felt a sudden, odd flutter in the bottom of my gut.

The announcer's voice rang through the kitchen: "A plane from Bombardier hit the runway..." I felt myself exhale when a spokesperson for the company said the plane was a Challenger. Eric didn't fly that plane; he flew the Canadair Regional Jet that held more than fifty people. I reached for the phone anyway and dialed Eric's work number. The answering machine picked up.

A few minutes later, our British next-door neighbor, grandmotherly looking Sandy, called to say she was coming right over. Sandy had watched Robin frequently over the years, and occasionally Tia, when I was at school or work. Robin still liked baking bread and having tea parties with Sandy. Her husband, Phil, was a manager and one of Eric's bosses at Bombardier's Learjet Test Flight Division in Wichita.

There was a knock on the door. I don't remember opening it, but then Sandy was there, her arms around me, and I was trying to wrestle free of her grasp.

"Carol. I'm so sorry. Phil called. Eric was on the plane that crashed."

Sandy's face was puffy, blotched, her voice cracking as she continued in her British accent, "There were two pilots onboard. Phil should be calling soon."

"But...Eric doesn't fly small planes. The news said it was a small plane."

"He was on the plane. Phil's positive."

"No...No...I don't believe you. You made a mistake. Eric flies the Canadair—"

The ringing phone shattered the air. I could feel my nails digging into my arm as Sandy picked up the phone. After hanging up, she took my hands. "Phil said one pilot is dead and the other is being taken to the hospital. He didn't know which one was Eric, but he'll call back as soon as he knows."

For some of us, there comes a moment that shapes the rest of our lives, an instant when everything changes. I knew undeniably—this was that moment. From this point on, I would define everything that happened according to one simple timeline: before the accident or after the accident.

I heard myself screaming, shouting that I needed to go to the hospital, running to get my car keys. It seemed strangely unreal, like watching a movie. I was moving toward the door when Sandy grabbed me.

"Carol, you can't go. Please, love. We have to wait for Phil to call. We don't know if Eric was the one."

"Eric isn't dead. I can feel it. He's not dead. I would know."

Then Sandy was standing over me, telling me I needed to get up because I was scaring the girls. I didn't remember how I got on the floor. Tia and Robin stood near the stairs, clutching the railing, completely still, their eyes staring widely. Sandy whispered to them, and they quietly slipped upstairs. I tried to get up, but I couldn't move—everything was spinning. The phone rang, and Sandy answered: Phil again.

"Phil is on his way to the hospital," she whispered. "We still don't know who it is."

I sat up and rocked back and forth, back and forth, clutching my knees to my chest, sweating, unable to think. Then I remembered the hugging monkeys. I raced up the stairs, hitting my knee on one wall, my elbow on the other, in my rush to our bedroom.

* * *

"Why would you send me stuffed monkeys?"

I could hear the confusion in Eric's voice as I thought of a lame excuse.

"My mom thinks it's weird," he added.

The phone began to slip in my hand, my excitement over the gift fading quickly.

We'd been going steady for close to a year, and I wanted his twenty-first birthday gift to be special even though money was tight. Since I was in Arizona and he was in New York, I mailed the gift to him: a pair of plush pale-brown monkeys, a boy and a girl, their arms tightly wrapped around each other.

Eric dubbed them the hugging monkeys, and despite his dismay at the gift, he kept them. They were on his bed, then on our bed. Eric even became a bit superstitious about those monkeys, getting upset if I took them apart. Once, I rearranged our room and put them on separate night tables with the girl on mine and the boy on his. The look of alarm on his face convinced me not to separate the monkeys—ever. All he would admit was that he thought they looked better together.

But I knew.

Another time, I'd separated them on purpose because I was furious at him about something, throwing them on opposite sides of the room, the monkeys making soft thuds as they slammed into walls before dropping silently to the carpet. He'd grabbed them and said he loved me, we were a team, there was nothing we couldn't work out together, and don't ever separate the monkeys.

* * *

I couldn't remember having seen the monkeys recently, but almost immediately I spotted them in the corner of the bedroom, dusty but together. When I picked them up, the boy monkey fell; the Velcro had broken, and the boy monkey's arms had come undone. I yanked the elastic out of my hair and quickly fastened his arms back around the girl monkey. A wave of nausea flooded me, and I leaned against a wall. I felt my essence seep out—all that I was, all that Eric had helped me become, leaking out through thousands of tiny holes.

Clutching the monkeys, I walked slowly down the hallway, past the closed bedroom door. I paused. What could I say to Tia and Robin? I raised my hand to the doorknob, stopped, pulled it away. *Get it together, Carol. Don't scare them.* I put my hand back on the doorknob and paused, finally pulling my hand away.

I continued down the stairs, stumbling back toward the kitchen, frightening thoughts flooding my mind.

I heard the knock.

A priest stared at me as I flung the door open. "Mrs. Fiore? I've come to take you to Saint Cornelius Medical Center. Your husband is there with serious injuries."

As I grabbed my purse, Sandy took the priest's arm. "Are you sure it's her husband? Eric Fiore?"

"I'm positive."

"My husband hasn't called back yet to confirm—"

"There was a positive identification. The man they took to the hospital is Eric Fiore."

I thought of the girls, our babies. Tia had turned thirteen eight days ago, and Robin had turned ten in September. Just babies. Our babies.

The girls appeared, and as I hugged them tightly, I rallied my strength. "Pumpkins, Mommy has to go to the hospital right away. There was an accident. Daddy needs me."

Tia looked at me, her espresso-brown eyes—Eric's eyes—filled with tears. "Is Daddy dead?"

"No, honey. He's at the hospital. I have to go. Be good for Sandy. Take care of your sister."

My talkative Robin didn't say a word as she stared down at the floor.

As the car pulled away, I saw Tia and Robin at the front window, their frightened faces pressed tightly to the glass, Robin clutching her Harry Potter book, Tia wrapping her arms tightly around herself.

The nineteen miles to the hospital seemed to take forever. Why did we hit every red light? Why was the traffic moving so slowly? I said nothing until we were almost there. "How bad is my husband?"

"I don't know, Mrs. Fiore. I was told his condition is serious, and I should bring you immediately."

I clutched my purse and the monkeys. Why was he driving so slowly? And why did they send a priest to get me?

When we arrived at the emergency room entrance, I leaped from the car. Strangers surrounded me and led me to a private waiting room. I felt trippy as I watched myself, someone else. This was not my life.

A middle-aged woman with a short bob cut wrapped her arms around me as she told me Eric was critical. She asked about my parents.

"I don't want my parents to come." Gripping the monkeys, I said, "I want to see Eric."

"Your husband is in surgery. You can't see him right now. You need someone with you. If not your parents, who should I call?"

"Eric's parents."

Two nuns came in as the woman left to retrieve a phone. One nun explained that a priest had given Eric his last rites. I gripped the sofa.

At that moment, I thought only of Eric's life. Last rites meant death. It wouldn't be until much later that I'd question the ethics of performing a religious ceremony on someone without family consent.

The nuns sat next to me, one on each side. I drew my shoulders in and away from them. "What faith are you, dear?" one asked softly.

I wiped roughly at the tears that wouldn't stop. I didn't want to talk about my Catholic parents. I didn't want to think about my father's drinking, about my mother shunning me when I wasn't perfect, and how, as a child, I'd turned away from a religion I saw as hypocritical.

I remained silent.

"We'll pray for you, my dear," one of the nuns said.

I felt myself mumbling again. "Can I see Eric?"

The woman with the bob cut returned and handed me a phone. It took several tries to get the numbers right. My father-in-law answered.

I couldn't get it all out. I could hear my father-in-law yelling to my mother-in-law that Carol was on the phone and there was an accident. I could hear her panicked voice in the background. "Is it Tia? Robin? Has someone been hurt?"

"It's Eric…a plane crash…you have to come…" The woman who'd handed me the phone took it from my trembling hands and walked out into the hallway, talking quietly. She returned and put her arm around me again. "They probably won't be here until tomorrow. You still need someone to stay with you. Who else can I call?"

"My sister Patty. She's a doctor in Colorado. I don't know her number."

Before long, she handed me the phone again, and I heard Patty's voice. "Carol, they told me what happened. I'm on my way."

"I love him, Patty. You know I love him."

"I know. I need to go so I can catch the next flight. OK? I'll be there tonight even if I have to drive. Hang in there."

Patty was coming. She was a doctor. She would fix this.

I sat next to the woman with the bob cut as nuns and various medical people came and went, reassuring me everything was being done. Eric was still in surgery, and no, they didn't know what had happened, only that the plane had crashed.

A police officer came in and sat across from me. He told me he'd been with Eric when they brought him in.

"What happened? Why did the plane crash? Who was in it with him?"

The officer opened a small black notebook. "Here are the facts I have. The plane was a Challenger 604 aircraft that crashed on takeoff. It burned in the middle of Tyler Road. There were three crew members onboard—"

"But Sandy said there were two."

"My notes say three. Your husband was the only survivor. He was sitting in the right seat of the cockpit. The rescue workers had to cut him out of his seat restraints. The other two men appeared to have died on impact."

"Who were they?"

"A Mr. David Riggs and a Mr. Bryan Irelan. Their families have already been notified."

"Why was my husband in that plane? That's not his plane."

"I'm sorry, Mrs. Fiore. I don't know the answer to that question. Your husband's company can probably answer that." The officer shut his notebook and handed me a sealed plastic baggie, saying, "Here are the items he had on his person."

I took the baggie. It had the word "biohazard" marked on it, but other than that, it was just a plain see-through plastic bag. I placed it on my lap and stared at it, wishing it would disappear. They didn't think he would make it through the surgery. That was why they had given it to me. The officer said again how sorry he was and left.

I wanted Eric, but all I had was a baggie with his things in it. I continued to stare at it. People kept coming in and out, occasionally patting me on the shoulder, asking me if I wanted anything to eat.

I poked at the bag with one finger. It wasn't going away. I turned it over. I could see what was inside: his wallet, his sunglasses, his watch. And his pocket-knife—the one he always carried in his flight suit. He said it was for emergencies, for cutting himself out of the harness. I put my hands over the bag. I didn't want to open it, but I knew I would. I had to.

Carefully I opened it and took out Eric's wallet. I tried to close my nostrils and breathe though my mouth, as if I had a head cold. I didn't want to smell it, even though I had an underdeveloped sense of smell. Once, while I was working at the zoo, a skunk got in the bird barn. No one could stand to be in there with the smell, but I barely noticed it.

I knew I would smell this.

I spread all the credit cards on the couch. I looked at the one photograph he carried, the one of me. I took out the money—sooty and blackened, the edges damp. Panic rose inside me. There had been a fire.

I pulled out Eric's watch, a gift from me years ago when he'd become a test pilot. A large crack ran through its face. Eric had told me it was indestructible, but now my hands were black from it. Something round was on the band. Eric's wedding ring. He wore it on his watchband like many pilots and mechanics. "Don't want to risk getting your finger caught in machinery," he'd said.

The watchband wouldn't open; I couldn't get the ring off the band. Taking the corner of my shirt, I wiped at the ring. I struggled to open the clasp of the watchband. Then I wiped again at the blackened ring, then pulled at the clasp. With a sob, I set it on the couch next to the contents of the wallet. Then I took out Eric's glasses, amazingly free of soot, and set them on the couch too. I picked up Eric's license and pressed it to my chest.

A nurse from the burn unit came to get me. Eric was out of surgery, and I would be able to see him. I collected my things and, in a daze, followed her to a conference room on the floor of the burn unit. She told me the doctor would be in soon to speak with me.

The noise of heavy footsteps seemed amplified as my head began to pound. I looked up at a man about my age, forty-one, with cobalt blue eyes. He extended his hand, introducing himself as the ER doctor. I promptly forgot his name as he gave his report.

"Your husband is out of surgery and is in a room down the hall. You can go in to see him soon." He sat across from me, looking tired, with wide sweat stains under his arms and across his chest. "First of all, Mrs. Fiore, let me tell you that your husband's injuries are quite severe. His prognosis isn't good."

"Is he going to die?"

"We're doing everything we can." After a long pause, he began. "The most critical damage to your husband is a severe inhalation injury. We performed a procedure called a bronchoscopy that allows us to look into the lungs. He's on a ventilator right now to help him breathe, but the damage to his lungs is extensive. Additionally, he has burns over approximately forty-five percent of his body with about half of them being third-degree burns. We're not sure yet how deep the burns are."

"The burns…what do you do…I mean, about… the…burns…"

"That's Dr. Knight's field of expertise. He's the head of the burn unit. He'll handle your husband's care. Much of the skin is beyond repair; we performed a debridement on some areas. The burns to the face are extremely deep, likely down to muscle and skull on the left side and down through the fat on the right side. The hands are in bad shape."

"Does he have a brain injury?"

"He was taken for a CAT scan, or CT, of his head, and it appears to be negative, so I would say probably not. There are other injuries besides the burns and the lungs."

How much more could there be? I looked down at my bleeding left arm where I'd dug my nails in too deep.

"We performed a CT of his chest that showed right rib fractures, and he has a pancreatic contusion. He also suffered a significant L3 vertebral fracture with spinal canal involvement—"

"My God, is he going to be paralyzed?"

"At this point we aren't sure."

The room was moving. Spots of twinkling white light converged in front of me. I could hear the doctor talking, but his face was blurry.

"Do you have any questions, Mrs. Fiore?"

"What's…what's…a debridement?"

"It's a procedure in which the dead skin is surgically removed."

Horrible images swirled in my mind. I pictured doctors using a device like a potato peeler to take off the dead skin. I didn't want to know how they did it; I didn't want more shocking images. I asked about the pain.

"We're giving him morphine. Right now he's still asleep from the surgery, but a nurse will be in to get you shortly and you can see him." He patted me on the shoulder and left.

A nurse, young and pretty, blond hair in a high ponytail that bobbed when she moved, came in and sat beside me. "You can go in to see your husband, Mrs. Fiore. Did the doctor explain that all the instruments and tubes look scary? His burns are very bad."

I followed the bobbing ponytail down the hall, and the nurse paused at a sink. "Please wash your hands thoroughly here, and I'll get you a gown."

Room 29.

Shaking, I approached the still form on the bed. I saw his feet first and knew it was Eric; the perfectly shaped toes could only have been his. I could see burns on part of his chest, but the nipples were there. Bandages surrounded his arms and hands. I moved closer, avoiding his face, as the doctor's words played in my head: "The burns to the face are extremely deep, most likely to muscle and skull on the left side and deep down through the fat on the right..."

Slowly, I looked down. It would be another defining moment. My physical pains would forever seem trivial compared to this. It was a moment that would make me braver and redefine my concept of beauty.

Only his teeth were recognizable. I thought the burns would be red, but his face looked like meat burned black on a grill. A foul-tasting substance forced its way up my throat. I held it there a moment before I was able to force it back down.

"Can you give him more pain medicine? Please. He must be in so much pain."

There were two nurses in the room. One said, "Honey, see this bag? There's a lot of medicine in it. I promise you he doesn't feel anything."

I looked back down at Eric. His left ear was gone; a small, ragged piece of black tissue hung in its place. That perfect, kissable ear. And his nose. It wasn't Eric's nose anymore. His scalp was black; fuzz here and there. Around the left eye everything was black too, the skin puckered and the eye area misshapen. I could tell where Eric's beard had been, where his mustache had been. Both gone. His lips…

I turned away.

I couldn't be afraid. I wouldn't be afraid. He was still Eric. He was my guy. I began to talk to him, babbling, telling him I loved him; we were a team; we'd make it.

One of the nurses brought the news that Patty was at the airport. She'd be here soon.

*   *   *

When Patty first met Eric in January 1979, he and I had been dating for a year and a half and living together for one semester while we both attended Parks Air

College of Saint Louis University.* My religious parents had made it clear that "shacking up" was wrong, but it seemed right to me. I wouldn't tell them, but Patty knew, and she kept my secret.

Patty had heard everything about Eric, and he'd heard me go on and on about how smart Patty was, how fast she could run, and how perfect she was. I even confided how the guys always liked Patty best. I was clearly worried. Though Eric assured me I was being silly, it was with a bit of trepidation that I introduced them.

Flipping her long dark-blond hair, Patty said, "You're short."

"Really? Well, you're a bitch," Eric countered.

And so their relationship began. Although it remained cold, they learned over the years to respect each other. Eric came to admire Patty's medical skills, but he thought she was trying to break us up (she later admitted she was). Patty admired Eric's intelligence and abilities, but she thought he was trying to keep me away from her (he later admitted he was). I was stuck in the middle but slowly started to side with Eric. Before I met him, Patty had been the hero in my life. Now he wanted to be my hero, and I was forced to choose.

I picked Eric.

* * *

---

* Now Parks College of Engineering, Aviation and Technology of Saint Louis University

Patty arrived. I'd never been so thankful to see anyone in my life. She had canceled her patients, called her babysitter, and flown from Denver to Wichita without hesitation, on her wedding anniversary. Patty the doctor was here now.

"Patty, I can't understand what they're telling me—"

Her face was full of concern as she interrupted me, her voice steady, reassuring. "Eric is the toughest person I know."

Eric would be glad she was here because he thought she was a good doctor, and Eric hated doctors. With a few exceptions, he thought they were all incompetent.

We walked slowly to room 29. The same two nurses were there, looking at me sympathetically. After they left, Patty was all doctor. She seemed to memorize every instrument, every reading. She walked slowly around the bed, not speaking for a few minutes as she looked intently at everything. Then she started to explain what she was seeing and what she had learned in earlier conversations with the medical people.

"His lungs are in bad shape. Inhalation of toxins frequently happens in a fire, and that's the doctors' main concern right now—"

"But…the burns…his face…"

"I know, Carol. They tell me the burns are really bad, especially on his face and back. Look at how they're worse on the left side, but his chest is completely free of burns. So are his legs, and his feet are perfectly fine."

"I think his flight suit protected him. It looks like the fire came from behind and from his left."

"Where was he sitting?" Patty asked.

"He was in the right seat. He was the copilot. I know he wasn't flying. The plane wouldn't have crashed if he were flying." I felt my teeth clenching, a bad habit during stress.

Patty asked about the pilot.

"I can't remember his name. He died. He was sitting on the left. I'll bet there was ballast on the right side of the plane."

"What's that?"

"It's a big tank of water that adds or redistributes weight. It must have ruptured when the plane crashed. Maybe the water saved Eric. Could that be why his right side looks so much better?"

"That makes sense. You're the pilot."

"But look at…" I tried to force the words out, but they wouldn't come. I pointed helplessly to my own eye.

Patty didn't say anything for a long time. "The left eye may be gone, but the right eye looks all right. People can see with one eye. Uncle Bill has lived for most of his life with one eye. You remember his glass eye, don't you?"

Eric was so fussy about his eyes. He always wore safety glasses when he mowed the lawn and worked with power tools. He'd told me he wouldn't want to live if he couldn't see.

Patty looked tired. I asked her if I should call someone to take her to the house. She shook her head vigorously. "No way. I'm not leaving you. You forget, I was a medical student; I'm used to sleeping on the floor. I'll find some blankets and pillows for us."

As we walked slowly to the conference room, I grabbed her tightly by the arm and sputtered, "Patty, Eric isn't going to—"

"I didn't bring any black clothes. None. I didn't because I know Eric. He's stubborn and he's tough, and he never quits anything. He's not going to die, Carol."

I willed myself to believe her.

Day 2
Wednesday, October 11, 2000

"Never marry a girl who pukes in your plane."
- Eric

I got up repeatedly to look into Eric's room, and as the night wore on, I grew increasingly panicked. I'd never experienced such overwhelming feelings of exhaustion, fear, and hopelessness.

I watched Patty sleep. Her hip-length, dark-blond hair lay across her face, partly hiding her eyes. Her longish face, sharp nose, and athletic frame were all quite similar to mine. People assumed we were twins, despite my pumpkin-colored hair, but I was older by a year and ten days.

"Wake up, Patty," I wanted to shout. "Tell me everything is going to be all right." I knew it wouldn't be OK ever again, but Patty would still say what she thought I wanted to hear. I quietly left the conference room, shutting the door behind me.

I hurried to Eric's room and peered in. How many times had I done this so far? As soon as I walked back to the conference room and crawled into the mound of blankets on the floor, I imagined something was happening and I'd be back down the hall once again.

I was pacing when Patty woke. The corners of her mouth dropped slightly. "I hoped I was having a bad dream." There were dark circles under her eyes. "I'll talk to Eric's nurse and see what I can find out."

Returning, she shrugged. "They're getting ready to change shifts, and the doctor will be in. I'll be able to find out more in about an hour. It's best not to bug them during a shift change."

The minutes dragged by. I couldn't sit still and paced around the conference room, looked down the hallway, went to the drinking fountain, looked at my watch. At about 8:00 a.m., two people entered Eric's room. I ran back to the conference room to tell Patty. She held her hands up in a slow-down gesture. "Wait. They'll come and talk to you."

I looked down the hall again. "The door's still shut, Patty. Why is there a priest lurking? I had to hide so he wouldn't see me."

Patty sighed. "I think you know the answer to that. It is a Catholic hospital."

I didn't want this man bothering me or being around Eric. I knew Eric wouldn't like it. Nuns, last rites, priests, prayers—Eric didn't believe in it. I didn't believe in it either. He'd said, "If I'm really sick or dying, don't let them stand over me praying." I hoped he hadn't heard those last rites. He'd have been pissed.

They finally came out.

I shot down the hallway, but a nurse on duty saw me. "Honey, the doctors will be down in a moment to speak with you."

I reluctantly walked back to the conference room.

Four people entered. One of them was the lurking priest, but not the same one who'd driven me to the hospital.

"Hi, Carol. Remember me from last night?" It was the woman with the bob cut. She introduced the priest. I mumbled a hello. "And this is Dr. Knight and Dr. Russell."

The male doctor was of average height, in his early fifties, slightly paunchy, with whitish hair, glasses, washed-out blue eyes. I took his extended hand.

"I'm Dr. Knight. I'm handling your husband's case. This is Dr. Russell, who will be assisting me."

Dr. Russell extended her hand. She was young and obviously a resident, her long brown hair pulled back into a ponytail, about my height—five feet seven inches, and extremely slender. She remained standing as Dr. Knight sat in the armchair opposite the couch. I could read no expression on Dr. Knight's face or in his eyes as he leaned toward me. "Your husband's condition is serious. We didn't expect him to make it through the night. There's a good chance he won't survive his injuries."

I hadn't expected him to say that. He didn't know Eric. What about hope? Years ago, doctors had said I was going to miscarry with Robin, and I didn't. Eric would show him. I looked at this man, this Dr. Knight, and narrowed my eyes.

I hated him.

Knight thought Eric was going to die. He wouldn't. Hadn't Eric promised he'd never leave me? Then I heard Patty's voice. She would tell this doctor a thing or two. She would explain that this was Eric; superheroes didn't die.

"Dr. Knight. Dr. Russell. I'm Patty, Carol's sister. I'm a rheumatologist in Colorado. Could you give me a synopsis of my brother-in-law's condition?"

Both Russell and Knight extended their hands to Patty. I got up to leave, but Knight spoke abruptly, his voice flat and emotionless. "Your sister needs to stay and hear what I have to say."

I fell onto the couch.

Knight looked at me calmly and explained in a voice that indicated he'd said this before. "His severe inhalation injury makes it unlikely the lungs will recover. We performed a bronchoscopy, bronch for short, where we look at the inside of the air tubes. There was lots of black tissue. A healthy lung should be pink in color. I saw no pink. If the lung lining starts shedding, it will be all over."

Patty quickly turned to me. "The lung is lined with cells that accomplish air exchange. They're burned. So the cells die and slough. Scar tissue can't exchange air, and air exchange is the whole point of the lining cells." She turned to Knight. "What are you doing for that?"

"It's a wait and see, but we have him on a pressure-control ventilator right now, and he's on a Keane bed. We'll be performing bronchs regularly. I'll need consent slips for that."

I asked Patty what a Keane bed was. She mouthed a "tell you later" as Knight continued. "He also has a severe burst fracture of the vertebra"—he pointed to his lower back—"and the spinal condition remains unclear."

He ignored my gasp as he repeated what the ER doctor had said the night before. Pancreatic contusion, laparotomy, drains, tubes, debridement, catheters, rib fractures—the words seemed to take up all the air.

Patty watched him intently. Dr. Russell gazed out the door, while the woman with the bob cut and the priest stared at me.

"Does anyone have any questions?" Knight asked.

Patty spoke up. "I know my sister will be staying at the hospital. I assume there won't be a problem with her having unlimited access to her husband's room."

Knight shrugged before Russell spoke. "That's fine as long as she's in the waiting room while procedures are performed and bandages are changed. I can speak to the nurse about finding you a room on the floor if you're staying overnight."

The middle-aged priest was the last to leave. "Would it be all right if I prayed for your husband?"

His collar was slightly askew, matching his noticeably asymmetrical features.

I scowled at him but said nothing.

"I'll be praying for you too," he added as he left.

Anger welled up inside me as I muttered to Patty, "What do you think he'd say if I asked him why his wonderful, loving God did this terrible thing to my husband?"

"Carol, don't."

After a few minutes of silence, Patty said, "You asked about the Keane bed. Think of it as a big air bed with the patient immobilized by pads that hold the body, legs, and arms in the same place. It's great for circulation because the substrate is air instead of a solid—no bedsores. It's sort of like that old idea of beating on the lungs to get things moving. I think the bed rotates about forty-five to sixty degrees on each side."

She paused. "Who should I call? Is there anyone Eric would want here? I know his parents are on the way and his brother and sister."

I couldn't think. I felt numb and willed myself to focus. "RB. He's been Eric's best friend for about fourteen years. They both flew F-15s. RB's an airline pilot now." I told her the name of his airline.

Patty wrote in her forest-green spiral notebook as I headed down the hall to Eric's room. A nurse pointed out the chair they'd put in the room for me. The priest was in the room, but he closed his book and left when he saw me eyeing him.

I tried to concentrate on Eric, who he was and how much I loved him, and not on the burns. There was a strange smell; I'd noticed it yesterday—sort of sickly sweet, mixed with a harsh disinfectant and bleach. The room was stuffy, the air felt heavy, crushing. Like death.

"I hate him," I said to Patty in a whisper.

"Dr. Knight?"

I nodded.

"He's a surgeon. Has the personality of a rock." She shrugged. "They all do. That doesn't mean he's not good. They hide their feelings pretty well, but it doesn't mean they don't have any. I'll try to speak with Dr. Russell. She'll probably give me more information."

The ventilator continued to make regular pulsing noises, but every so often, I could hear a slight hissing sound. I couldn't understand the readouts. It was frustrating to feel so helpless. I could see Eric's chest rise and fall. No red lights or flashing indicators, so I guessed that was a good sign. I looked at the many plastic bags hanging from tall stands.

Sunshine streamed through the window in the back wall. I peered out. Thin clouds hung like a whisper in an aquamarine sky. Several people were chatting in the parking lot. One woman was eating a sandwich while another gal with a bright-red shirt leaned lazily against a car. A young man threw his head back. It looked as if he was laughing. I wanted to scream at them, "Don't you know what's happening up here?"

Dr. Russell came in, looked at some monitors, nodded at me, and left. Patty followed her. I sat down in the chair, my chair. I was determined to learn about these machines. I could see what the blood pressure was. It seemed low, but I wasn't sure. Was that Eric's temperature? One bag said "Dopamine." What was that?

Patty came back in and patted me on the shoulder. "Russell is great. She sees hope, so you should too. She says it's not a sure thing Eric is paralyzed. According to her, Knight always gives the absolute worst scenario. He doesn't believe in giving patients false hope."

"But does he have to be so mean?"

"I don't think he intends to be mean, Carol. Russell tells me he's the best. He's the head of the burn unit. I think Eric would want the best."

Eric's nurse came in and addressed me. "Mrs. Fiore, I'm Brenna. I'm one of your husband's day nurses. Dr. Russell asked me to have you read and sign these two forms. One is consent for blood transfusions, and the other is an authorization for a daily bronchoscopy."

I read the forms. "Patty, can't I give Eric blood? I can be his blood donor."

Patty and Brenna looked at each other. Brenna shook her head as Patty said, "He'll need a lot of blood. You don't have that much in you."

Another nurse stuck her head inside the door. "Some people are in the burn center waiting room outside the double doors. They said they work with your husband."

Patty offered to see who it was. I quietly asked, "I don't have to see them, do I?"

"Not if you don't want to. I'll ask their names. Then you can tell me if you want to see them."

After Patty left, I continued to speak to Eric as I paced nervously around his room. I asked Brenna lots of questions, and she patiently explained the equipment.

Brenna was a no-nonsense gal, going about her duties confidently, with purpose. There was no aimless wandering, no lethargic movements. The shapeless light-blue scrubs couldn't hide her short but athletic figure, and her intelligence was obvious in her flawless grammar and use of language. Eric demanded competence; he would have been pleased with Brenna.

I glanced into the hallway. There was that priest again, hovering around like some great black vulture. Didn't he have anything else to do?

Patty returned, the forest-green notebook in her hand. "Somebody named Phil is here. He said his wife, Sandy, is taking care of your kids. He's here with Eric's boss, Tim Ryan. There's also a man named Stan. They're in the conference room, so you don't need to go to the main waiting room." She paused. "And I don't think you want to go to the main waiting room because reporters are trying to get to you."

"What?"

"Don't worry. The hospital won't let them inside the burn unit, and I'll make sure they don't bother you. So do you want to talk to the people in the conference room?"

I felt myself tightening. "I don't want to talk to Stan."

"OK. I don't need to know why. I'll tell them it's too much. Do you want to talk to Tim and Phil?"

"I'll be there in a minute." It was going to start— visitors. Stan was the safety officer, for God's sake. Where was he when the accident happened? Anger flared, but I remembered Eric's words: "Don't blame people if there's an accident. Don't be the whiny wife."

I could be angry inside. Stan was the safety officer, a former astronaut. He'd gone up in the shuttle. He was probably having tea with a bunch of old ladies when the accident happened, telling tales of his exploits as an astronaut.

Eric had always wanted to be an astronaut. As a test pilot, he was so close. He'd applied to NASA last month. Why was "Safety Stan" an astronaut and not Eric? I didn't want to talk to Stan. If that was being meanspirited, I didn't care. Stan should have done his job and made sure the flight was safe. Now Eric would never go up in space. Eric might die and Stan would still be here.

It wasn't fair.

As I stood over Eric, I wiped at my eyes with clenched fists. I tried to remember everything Eric had ever said about the possibility of a crash.

Sometimes, for no apparent reason, Eric would insist I pay attention while he explained where the important papers were or what I would have to do if something happened to him. It was obvious to him I wasn't listening as I shuffled papers and fidgeted. Irritated, he would say, "Pay attention. This stuff is important. What are you going to do if something happens?" I told him nothing would happen; it was boring; I was busy; he was being melodramatic.

Eric seemed to feel he would die in a plane crash someday, never considering the possibility of surviving one; perhaps he didn't think it was possible. About twenty-two years ago, Patty had asked him, "Aren't you scared? I mean, what if you die in a plane crash in twenty years? Do you ever think about that?"

Eric had smiled. "I'll have flown for twenty great years." Then he added something he often said: "Afraid to fly, afraid to die." He called death the "ultimate judge of a person's character." Honor was essential to him, and so was doing the right thing. He wanted to be a hero, remembered for what he had accomplished and what he stood for. He wanted the Fiore name to mean something.

I was sure Eric wouldn't want me raging at everyone and being a bitch. I knew he wouldn't like it if I were mean to Stan. He liked Stan. He liked him a lot.

I would keep my mouth shut.

"I'll make you proud of me, Eric," I whispered. "But you have to fight. I can't live without you. You promised you wouldn't leave me, and you never break your promises. Remember the Great Pastry Promise?"

* * *

July 30, 1986. I know the date because I still have the receipt. The ticket says one Sacher torte, one Indian pastry, two coffees, the name of the Vienna bakery, the price, and the date. The proof is on that receipt shoved in my pocket all those years ago.

When Eric and I dated in the late 1970s, his favorite line was "I'll take you to Vienna for pastries one day." I told him it was the world's corniest line. At the time, I was struggling to pay my tuition and come up with money for college texts. Flying to Vienna—of all the ridiculous places—seemed too silly to consider.

Still, that promise came up every time we stopped at a bakery. "The pastry I buy you in Vienna will be better," he'd say seriously. I started to call it the Great Pastry Promise. Seven years later, when Eric was stationed at Camp New Amsterdam in the Netherlands flying the F-15 Eagle, he mentioned it frequently.

"Now that we live in Europe," Eric would say, his voice full of promise, "we'll get that pastry in Vienna."

One rainy day in July, we left on a road trip to Vienna. Four days later, in Vienna at last, Eric sashayed into a small bakery on a tree-lined side street that had a scrumptious display of goodies in the window. Small wooden tables and chairs were arranged outside the entrance, which was adorned with purple-blue and vivid-pink fuchsia flowers, their teardrop-shaped petals draped gracefully over window boxes.

Eric danced his way to our table with his selections, coughing for attention, announcing loudly, with much flair and drama, "I always keep my promises. I promised you a pastry in Vienna, and here it is." His eyes shone as laughter poured from him. It was more like the giggling of a small boy. At first glance, it didn't match his personality or his dark features, but the giggles fit him perfectly if you knew him well.

He was quite insufferable on the drive home, humming to himself, reiterating how he would never ever break a promise to me, and asking me at least a dozen times, "Who's the best husband you ever met?"

* * *

As I looked at him in the hospital bed, I thought of that other promise: I will never leave you.

I walked to the conference room. Tim Ryan was the vice president of Flight Test; I'd met him four or five times. Eric always called him Mr. Ryan except around me, and although Eric had the utmost respect for Tim and claimed he was a consummate pilot, he'd said Tim could be difficult—picky, demanding, hard to please; he worked his pilots hard. Tim was an important person, so I remembered him. He was tall, thin, slightly balding, in his midfifties. He had a mustache and pale, stern eyes. He would have terrified me if he'd been my boss.

Phil Davis, like his wife, Sandy, was a British citizen. They'd been our next-door neighbors for about five years. Phil was short and cheerful, with dark hair and a full beard, in his midfifties like his wife. Had Phil's hair and beard been white, he'd have been a perfect Santa Claus. He was the manager of Flight Test. I assumed he was an engineer, but I knew he wasn't a pilot, which seemed strange to me. On several occasions, I'd asked Eric, "What does Phil actually do?"

Eric would grin, bend close to my ear, whisper, "Carol," pause dramatically, and then add, "nobody knows."

Tim and Phil were talking to Patty, but they stood up immediately and came over to hug me. They both said, "I'm sorry"—two words that meant your life would never be the same again. I was sure I would hear them for the rest of my life. At least they didn't say, "I'm praying for you."

We sat down. Tim's eyes were bloodshot, with dark, puffy circles beneath them. He spoke slowly. "Carol, let me say again how sorry we are. Eric is one of my best test pilots. The company is going to do everything we can to help you and your family. I've been speaking with your sister Patty, who tells me Eric is receiving good medical care. She updated me on his condition."

"Tim, what happened?" I wasn't about to call him Mr. Ryan. Eric had sacrificed everything for the company. He was damn well going to be plain old Tim.

"I knew you would ask," he said, motionless as he looked directly at me. "We don't know, but of course there will be an investigation. You're a private pilot, so you know the National Transportation Safety Board will be involved."

Yes, yes. I knew about the NTSB.

"The company will cooperate fully, but it may take some time to determine what happened."

"Do you have any idea at all?"

"The plane crashed on takeoff. An eyewitness saw the wing drop twice and then hit the—"

"Eric wasn't flying."

Tim raised his eyebrows. "Excuse me?"

"Eric wasn't flying. It wouldn't have crashed if he'd been flying."

Phil and Tim looked at each other, and then back at me. Phil cleared his throat. "Eric was the copilot, but we don't know at this point who was flying."

I crossed my arms and sat on my legs, defiant and contained. "Eric wasn't flying."

Silence.

Phil spoke first, a forced lift in his voice. "Sandy said to tell you she's taking good care of Tia and Robin. They understand what has happened. They also understand you need to be with Eric. Sandy wants to know if she should call someone to take care of the animals.

Maybe someone from the zoo. She says the girls insist they don't know how to care for the bird."

I looked at Phil without speaking. He began toying with his pen, clicking the head open, closed, open, closed.

So. Nobody wanted to talk about what happened. I was pissed. I had a right to be, but I tried to concentrate on Eric's wishes. After a long, uncomfortable silence, Phil asked again about the pets.

"What?"

Phil's face was red as he stammered, "Should Sandy call someone about the pets?"

"Can she call the education department at the zoo? I have friends there. I think Eric's going to be here for a long time, and I'm not leaving."

I thought of my babies, Tia and Robin. I wanted to hug them, hold them, tell them everything would be all right, but I knew it wouldn't. I needed them, but I had to spare them from as much pain as I could. Sandy had a gentle, soothing air and a charming British accent. She'd watched them many times over the years, so I knew they were being well cared for.

After more silence, I looked at Tim. "You can see him if you want." Tim should see; they should all see, I thought. After Tim left, I put my head down on one end of the couch and pulled my knees up close to my chin. Patty motioned to Phil, and they left.

I closed my eyes. Images swirled in front of me— Eric calling for me, flames, firefighters, screams…I sat up, sweating and gasping.

Patty, Tim, and Phil returned. Tim looked sick as he wiped nervously at his forehead. "Did you know there's a priest in there? I didn't realize Eric was Catholic."

I clenched my fists. Patty said to Tim, "He's not. The priest is starting to get on Carol's nerves. We haven't said anything because we're trying to be polite, and Carol and I were raised to respect priests."

I stood up. "I'm going to see Eric."

Patty quickly jumped up and grabbed my hands. "You can't right now. The doctors are doing a bronchoscopy. They'll give us a report. Meanwhile, I think you should eat something. And don't tell me you're not hungry."

Tim sat next to me on the sofa. "You can't help Eric if you don't take care of yourself. You don't want to get sick."

Tim and Patty exchanged worried glances.

"I'd like some coffee. But what I want is Eric's cappuccino." The words slipped out.

Phil headed for the door. "He loves his cappuccino, doesn't he? I'll be right back with that coffee."

While Phil was gone, Patty left to answer a phone call. "I'm sorry about the two other pilots," I said to Tim. "Tell me their names again."

It took a few seconds for him to answer, his voice cracking. "Bryan Irelan was the pilot, and Dave Riggs was the flight engineer. Bryan was single. Dave and his wife have three kids."

"I'm sorry. I think I met Bryan once. Was he young, tall, worked in Tucson?"

"Yes. He was at our Tucson plant."

"Did he fly the Challenger a lot?" I asked.

"Yes, he was experienced. Alec Sorrentino can give you more information when he arrives. He was out of town when the accident occurred."

"Yes, I've met Alec. He's Eric's boss, and you're Eric's big boss, right?"

Tim forced a smile. "I think that's essentially correct."

Phil returned with my coffee, Patty came back, and once more we sat in silence. Just sat. Nobody even picked up a magazine. No fidgeting. The three of them looked like inflatable dolls someone had let the air out of, limp in their chairs, doing nothing.

When Knight and Russell returned, Knight nodded to Tim and Phil and addressed me. "Not much change. Burned and blackened tissues."

Tim still looked pale as he and Phil hugged me and quietly left.

Later, in Eric's room, I asked Patty whether she thought Eric could hear us. She answered, "Let's find out. I'll see if I can get him to move. I don't think the vertebra burst means he'll be paralyzed. I talked to Russell, and she doesn't think so either." She jabbed at the vertebra on my lower back and shook her head. "I don't think that one would do it."

Patty moved close to the bed and in a strong and confident voice, she began. "Eric, it's Patty. I'm here to make sure everything's done right. The medical people are doing a great job. Carol's here. You know she won't leave. You can't talk. Your lungs took a beating, and you're on a respirator. Your eyes are bandaged, so you can't see right now. All your body parts are intact. You haven't lost anything, Eric."

She paused and looked at me, waiting. I couldn't let Eric hear doubt or fear in my voice. "I'm here, Eric. I love you. Listen to Patty."

"OK, Eric," said Patty, "move your right foot." We both held our breath and fixed our eyes on Eric's feet. His right foot moved!

"Eric, you did it," I practically shouted. "I knew you could do it."

Patty smiled. "Good job, Eric. Can you move your other foot?" Quicker this time, Eric moved his right foot again.

"No, try to move your other foot. Move your left foot, Eric." Nothing.

"What about your right arm or your hand?" It moved, slightly. Patty continued. "Great, Eric. Now if you want to get rid of me, you'll have to move your other hand or arm." Only a slight twitch.

I wondered how much I should tell him. I wouldn't tell him about the other two pilots, and I wouldn't tell him how bad the burns were. But there was something I knew he'd want to know. I whispered to Patty, "You've got to look."

She looked at me blankly. "Look at what?"

"You've got to see if it's OK, so I can reassure Eric."

A look of surprise crossed her face as she grabbed my arm. "Oh no. I'm not looking."

"I'm afraid to look. Please." I knew I was shaking.

She shook her head in resignation and slowly lifted the cloth. I shut my eyes tightly.

"It's perfectly fine. Look for yourself."

I opened my eyes. Not a scratch, not a burn.

"You are not going to tell him I looked," Patty whispered.

"You have to tell him. He'll believe it if you say it."

"Fine, fine." She cleared her throat. "Eric, all your boy parts look great. Not a single burn, everything is in order. Carol made me look, so you'll have to get better if you want to yell at me."

Eric's right foot moved slightly. I leaned over him and asked, "Eric, do you know where you are?" He nodded. "Do you know what happened?" Again, a nod.

A nurse interrupted. "This is not a dog-and-pony show. My patient needs his rest."

Patty motioned for me to leave with her. I crossed my arms over my chest. I was not leaving. She looked at me pleadingly as I shook my head no. I could see the impatient look on the nurse's face and the beseeching look on my sister's face.

Patty gently took my arm; I pulled it away. She took it again. The nurse started to speak as Patty said, "Thank you. We're leaving."

As Patty pulled me out the door, I called back, "Eric, I'm right here. I won't leave you, Eric. I'm right outside the door. I love you."

In the hall, Patty gave me a thumbs-up. "He's not paralyzed, and I don't think there's brain damage. The CT scan came back normal. I saw it earlier."

I wanted to feel thankful. I wanted to shout and smile, but the other injuries were so overwhelming, I couldn't celebrate.

As we walked down the hall, a nurse stopped us. "I've got a small call room for you in the pediatrics ward. It's down the hall. If you want to get your things, I'll show you where it is."

Patty got her suitcase from the conference room. I gathered up my purse, the baggie, and the hugging monkeys, and we followed her down the hall. I was relieved the room was so close to Eric's. It had a small bathroom, a bed, a dresser, and an oversized reclining chair. "Patty, I think maybe I'll lie down. You'll come get me, won't you? If anything changes?"

"Don't worry. I'll be checking on Eric, and I'll come get you when his parents get here."

I dropped on to the bed.

Patty stood over me, calling my name softly. "Eric's parents are at the airport, and Sandy is here with the kids."

"Is Eric…?"

"Eric's OK. No changes."

In the conference room, Tia and Robin ran up and hugged me, confusion on their faces. What was I going to tell them? Robin clutched me as Tia let go to ask, "How's my daddy?"

I turned away and quickly wiped at my eyes.

Sitting down on the couch, I put an arm around each of them. "He's not doing too well."

Tia looked around the room at the solemn faces. "Is he going to die?"

"I hope not, pumpkin. He's a fighter, that Daddy. He won't give up."

Tears poured down Robin's cheeks.

Tia folded her arms forcefully across her chest and glared at the wall. Her waist-length blond hair looked unbrushed; her brown eyes, framed by dark, thick eyebrows against olive skin, were so like Eric's. "Can I see my daddy?"

I looked at Patty. She saw my glance and nodded, then came over to the couch and squatted down in front of Tia and Robin. "Guys, of course you can see him. But before you do, I want to tell you what to expect. Hospitals can be scary. When you go in, ask me if there's something you don't understand. OK?"

They nodded. She explained to them about the tubes, the machines, the bandages, the burns. Their eyes opened wider and wider. When Patty finished, she stood up and extended a hand to each of them.

The four of us walked down the hall, toward Eric's room. As we put on gowns and washed our hands,

Patty calmly explained the precautions. She entered Eric's room first and motioned to them to come in. Tia paused but then entered.

Robin stood in the doorway looking frantically at all the instruments, at the figure lying on the bed. Even her honey-blond ponytail, normally worn high, seemed to droop. "Do I have to go in? Can I stand in the doorway? I can talk to Daddy from here, can't I? He can hear me from here, can't he?"

I put my arm around her and squeezed her rigid body tightly. "Of course, honey. It's fine. Daddy can hear you fine from here. Remember what Aunt Patty said, though. Daddy can't answer you because he has a tube in his throat that's helping him breathe."

Robin continued to speak in a high-pitched squeak, quite unlike her normal voice. "I love you, Daddy. I'm standing here in the doorway, Daddy. Mommy said it was OK to stand here." She began to back up into the hall, her blond ponytail sagging, her eyes—normally a brilliant blue—full of tears. Her fair skin, like mine, was all red and blotchy from crying.

Tia stared at Eric. "How do I know it's Daddy? I can't tell if it's really Daddy."

I quickly walked over to Tia and spoke loudly to Eric. "Tia's here. She hasn't seen all these bandages before, Eric."

"No, Mommy, I mean—"

"Tia is here. Robin too." I clutched Tia, put my finger to my lips, and shook my head.

"Daddy, I love you. You're going to get better. It's not so bad, Daddy. You'll get better, and then you promised me I could go with you when you race your car. OK, Daddy?"

No response from Eric. I glanced over at Brenna, who had returned and was checking one of the IV bags. She said to the girls, "I think your daddy is sleeping. He needs to get a lot of rest so he can get better."

Robin shifted nervously from foot to foot. Tia wrinkled her nose. "Mommy, what's that funny smell?"

Looking at Tia crossly from the doorway, Robin said, "Daddy just needs a bath."

Eric's sister Lisa arrived along with their parents—Mimi and Ba, as the kids referred to them. I had always called them Mom and Dad (in contrast to my biological parents, who were Mother and Father).

Tia flew into her grandfather's arms, and he hugged her stiffly. It was not the usual warm, smothering embrace. Immediately my mother-in-law spoke loudly and clearly. "Where is Eric? Where is my son?" Her cornflower-blue eyes blazed.

My mother-in-law's small, barely five-foot-tall frame belied her outgoing and aggressive, but loving, personality. People often underestimated her energy and determination. A generous woman, she was the quintessential Jewish mother, completely dedicated to the welfare of her children.

She stated her demand again. "Where is my son?"

Patty got up and steered her out of the room. I knew how awful it was going to be. My father-in-law released his grip on Tia long enough to squeeze Robin weakly, but somehow Tia managed to hang on. They all three sank down on one of the couches. Dad began, nervously, to pat down the few loose hairs on his balding head.

Lisa came over and sat beside me. I noticed her tic immediately—the same slight twitch of the head and neck that Eric showed in stressful conditions. Her eyes were the same rich shade of brown as Eric's and her hair the same dark black, the thick eyebrows identical. Except for her short height, Lisa possessed an almost model-perfect figure. She was, like Tia, a bit exotic looking.

Eric, six years older, always referred to Lisa as his "little sister." She was brutally honest and outgoing, like her mom. A Buddhist, Lisa had chosen her own path in life. Eric had wanted her to be successful in a more ordinary way, but he'd confided to me in the past year that he was "sort of proud of her."

When Patty and Mom returned, Mom sank into a chair, hugging her arms tightly to her chest. I didn't detect tears, but her aggressive stance was gone. She looked pale as she began to drone in a quiet voice, "My boy…my beautiful baby boy…"

Eric's only brother walked in. Two years younger than Eric, David was taller, with dark eyes, an athletic build, thinning hair, and wire-rimmed square glasses.

He was always so intense, so serious. Eric was often intense too, but with a playful edge. I never saw that in David. Released from his mother's grasp, he came over to give me the required hug. It was stiff, as it had always been with us. I was never sure why our relationship was a failure, but we didn't seem to connect. David was a doctor—family practice—and for that reason, I was glad he was here. The more doctor firepower I had, the better.

Sometime later, while everyone was out, Mom started to question me. She had regained some of her earlier composure and was tapping her foot nervously as she loudly threw questions at me: "Will he recover?" "Will he fly again?" "What's the company doing to help?" "Are the doctors good?"

I wasn't leaving the hospital, I told her. Eric needed me. She was frank about what she and Dad could do. "I hope you understand this is too difficult for us. We can't stay here, but we can stay at the house and look after the children. Dad can't deal with this."

Dad loved all his children, but Eric was special, different somehow. They had a bond, an understanding. Eric repeated stories about his father often: the hikes up Mount Marcy, the adventures at Cape Cod, the baseball games, the trips to Pittsburgh to see the Italian relatives.

Dad had classic Italian mannerisms. In the throes of a heated debate, his hands flew. With two degrees in English and many years of teaching, he was a cultured and intelligent man and a master of the art of debate, encouraging his children to express their opinions. The entire family was so argumentative that I began to refer to such behavior as "being a Fiore." Like Eric, Dad could sometimes be abrasive without realizing it; he had a tendency to yell about everything. If he couldn't find the scissors, if his favorite ball teams lost, if someone was late, he would yell. Everything was a major crisis. It was a habit Eric had picked up. Dad yelled at Mom, and for the most part, she didn't take it personally. When Eric yelled, I took it personally.

The most striking difference between Eric and his father was fear. Eric was careful but fearless. He was obsessive about safety, he used precautions, and when he'd covered all contingencies, he let it rip and never looked back. Dad's fears included tight, enclosed spaces; all things technical and electronic; and most of all, flying. I couldn't imagine the courage it had taken for him to board that plane in New York.

The first time I met Eric's parents, I was overwhelmed. I had never seen such chaos, so much activity, so much love, and I was immediately and without hesitation treated like their daughter. They loved me because their son loved me.

My own parents were different or, rather, indifferent. Eric's parents loved him for who he was, but my parents loved me if I made them look good in front of their friends. My mother wanted her children to be famous. I thought bitterly of all the press Eric's accident was getting. Now my name was in the paper.

After Dad, Lisa, and the girls came back from a walk, we went to Eric's room. Dad's hands were shaking as he washed and put on a gown. We entered the room and surrounded the bed, except for Robin, who stood in the doorway. David was already there.

Dad came to the head of the bed slowly. He stared at the floor for an uncomfortable length of time. Then, slowly, he lifted his head. He took his glasses off, rubbed at his mocha-colored eyes, and moved from foot to foot. He didn't look directly at Eric as he spoke, his voice badly cracking. "Ric, it's Dad."

Eric moved his right leg and rolled his body slightly from side to side.

"You know what I'm thinking," said Dad. He shuffled into the hallway, sinking into a chair across from the door.

Robin called out from the doorway, "I love you, Daddy."

Eric nodded and moved his leg vigorously.

Tia moved up to Eric's head. "I'm here, Daddy. It's your Tia-wee. I love you, Pocket Daddy."

Eric's body exploded with movement. His head moved rapidly, his leg rose up higher than I thought possible, his right arm shook, and his body rocked from side to side.

Tia burst into tears. "I love you, Daddy. You're my pocket daddy. Don't die, Daddy. Please don't die."

I felt my gut fall to the floor. My poor little girl. I wrapped my arm around her quaking shoulders.

David moved to the head of the bed. "Hey, Eric. It's David. I know how you feel about doctors, so I'll make sure they do it right."

Eric nodded slightly. Then a nurse came in and said, "I think my patient has had enough excitement."

Why had I said he could be a test pilot? I should have told him to stay in the Air Force. What if we hadn't moved to Kansas? What if he had missed his flight home from the conference in Amsterdam and had to stay an extra day or two? What if he'd had the flu and couldn't go to work yesterday? My mind raced with what ifs. I knew a religious person—like that hovering priest—would say God had a plan. I wanted my life back, the normal one I'd had with Eric, even his yelling, even some of the bad times. I wanted them back because I didn't think I could handle another minute of this.

The ancient Greeks believed there was no escaping your fate. Was this Eric's fate because he loved airplanes? Because I loved airplanes? Even our first date had been in an airplane.

* * *

Eric bustled into the Parks Air College cafeteria, license held above his head. It was October 27, 1977. "I got my private license last week. Who wants to go flying?"

There was a collective groan from the guys at the table, who all professed to be too busy to fly with "Crazy Fiore," but I was practically dancing in my seat. "I'll go."

Eric looked around the table, carefully making eye contact with everyone but me.

"I'll go," I repeated, rising up out of my seat and waving my hand.

Eric began to speak faster and louder as he addressed each of the guys. "Jeff? Rob? How 'bout you, Mike? It's a great day, Alan. I know you want to go." None of the guys appeared even remotely interested as they ignored him and continued with their lunch.

I'd been trying to catch plane rides since I came to Parks—the oldest aviation school in the country and part of Saint Louis University. I was eighteen years old and in my first semester. I was there because I loved airplanes and wanted to be a pilot. Now I had a chance to go for a plane ride, and I wasn't about to let this opportunity get away. "I'll go," I yelled.

He couldn't ignore me anymore and smiled unconvincingly. "Well…then…let's go."

I followed him out of the cafeteria, skipping, barely able to control my excitement. While he was doing the preflight at Bi-State Airport, I asked aviation questions in rapid succession. After answering them, he turned to me with a frown. "You're not going to puke in my plane, are you? The last girl I took up puked."

I laughed, tracing a line across my heart. "I promise I won't."

Eric pulled negative Gs: nosing the plane down, pulling up rapidly, and then leveling, making me float upward in my seat. He practiced stalls, causing the plane to lose lift by hauling the nose skyward. As we dropped quickly, the ground rushing up at us, I heard myself shriek.

During the next stall, with the warning horn blaring and the engine almost quiet, he pushed the rudder pedal down hard. The stall turned into a spin as the plane twirled around and around. "One turn…two turns…" he called excitedly. Shouting over the noise of the rushing air, he yelled, "Tell me how to stop the spin."

I called out confidently, "Opposite rudder to the spin. Hit opposite rudder."

Out of the spin, he commanded, "Now you take the controls."

I pushed the nose down and then pulled up. Letting the nose fall level to the horizon, I looked at Eric and shrugged.

"Were you trying to do negative Gs?" he asked. I nodded. "Try again, but be more aggressive."

This time I pushed down hard, almost redlining the airspeed indicator. I yanked up firmly. Then I pushed the nose level. We both floated upward, and I giggled.

"Shit hot. You're my kind of girl," he shouted over the engine noise.

I watched as he navigated around the sky, pointing out landmarks: a herd of cows, the Cahokia bluffs, the Saint Louis arch in the distance, the buildings of the main campus of Saint Louis University. I wasn't looking at the ground much. He saw me staring at him a few times and smiled back. His eyes held a deep happiness as he moved the controls around with grace and joy. Winking, he asked me if I'd like to see something really cool. I practically screamed a yes, nodding vigorously, and before I knew what happened, I was upside down in a barrel roll.

I was looking sideways at the horizon; then I was falling out of my seat. The seat belt was the only thing that kept me from hitting my head on the ceiling of the cockpit, which now felt like the floor. Then I was sideways in my seat, and he was grinning at me. "Well?" he asked.

"Do it again," I screamed. He did. This time I shrieked through the whole roll. Eric was only twenty, a private pilot already, and he could do barrel rolls. *Wow.* He told me he'd taken aerobatics lessons.

He landed the Cessna 150 on a grass strip at Columbia Airport—barely twenty minutes from Bi-State. When we got out, he asked if I wanted to have a picnic lunch.

He produced a bag of peanuts from his pocket, and we munched on them as we sat at an old wooden picnic table. I kicked at the fallen leaves as two squirrels frolicked a few feet from us. The air smelled of newly mown grass.

Eric took a pen out of his pocket, drew a face on one of the peanut shells, and presented it to me, saying, "Here's something to remember our first date."

"Our first date?" I repeated questioningly. Was this extremely cool and sweet man going to ask me out? Did he say "first" date, implying there would be more?

"Of course," he winked. "I've always liked you, and now that I know you're not going to puke in my plane, I like you even more. So what do you say? Wanna go out with me?" He leaned over and quickly and sweetly pecked me on the cheek.

I'm sure a silly giggle escaped as I pretended to watch the squirrels. I had seen him around campus; everyone knew who he was. I'd even remarked to a couple of the other girls about his good looks. They had laughed at me, saying everyone knew Fiore was odd. But I didn't think he was strange. I thought he was adorable.

I wanted to say yes, I tried to say yes, but the mumbled mess that came out caused Eric to lean over and gently pull my face toward him. "Well?"

This time I overcame my shyness enough to be coherent. "Yes, I'd love to."

I could feel my face reddening as I fiddled with my belt buckle. How could I be so lucky? I put the peanut in my pocket, then transferred it to a keepsake box.

I still have the peanut.

* * *

I introduced myself to the night nurse, Laurel. I explained where I'd be staying in the pediatrics ward and insisted she needed to get me immediately if anything changed. Laurel was quite ordinary looking, with short brunette hair and hazel eyes. She was someone you wouldn't glance at twice, except you did. There was something special about her: a kindness, a gentle touch, a soft, calming voice.

A few hours later, Patty came in Eric's room, and I quietly asked her, over in a corner, a question that had been plaguing me. "I heard some orderlies today. One of them said Eric was trapped in the plane for over twenty minutes. Do you think that's true? Why didn't the firefighters get him out faster?"

"I didn't hear that, Carol. Maybe we can ask David to find out. It'll give him something to do so he isn't bugging Knight."

"It couldn't be true, though. Nobody could be that incompetent."

Day 3
Thursday, October 12, 2000

"Real men fly tail draggers,
dream of owning sports cars,
know how to cook,
and aren't afraid of dirty diapers."
- Eric

The house was burning, and I was scream-ing. Eric called to me that he loved me, but I couldn't see him. There was the searing heat and the feel of my skin melting. Then I jolted awake and didn't know where I was.

From the big chair in the corner, Patty looked at me sympathetically. "You cried all night. I think you were crying in your sleep."

Slowly I collected myself enough to respond. "I'm sorry I kept you up. Tonight you sleep in the bed."

"I told you, we medical students—"

"I know, I know. You're used to it. But maybe you should sleep at the house."

"Don't be ridiculous. I'm not leaving you." She gave me the direct, in-your-face, don't-argue-with-me Patty look.

How could this have happened? Eric was always so safety conscious, practically fanatical, never forgetting his seat belt, wearing a helmet when he rode his bicycle and raced his car. He took care of himself, never took drugs, didn't smoke, and ate right.

Until we had kids, Eric, nicknamed "Mr. Safety" by me, had been obsessed with my safety. Then he transferred most of his safety obsessions to them—particularly their well-being around water. He was so frightened of them drowning that even at swim lessons I had to sit and watch; I couldn't read a book because I might not be paying close enough attention. He seemed to forget that I couldn't swim. When the girls were in the bathtub, I had to be right there. When Tia started to fight the rule, Eric came up with a creative solution: both girls had to sing loudly, and if the singing stopped, however briefly, I'd have to race to the bathroom. Only when Tia was in fourth grade did Eric reluctantly let her stop singing. Eric's fear was deeply rooted in an incident that happened as a direct result of a small child's fascination with a movie.

It happened when we were at Sheppard Air Force Base in Wichita Falls, Texas. Eric took three-year-old Tia to the base housing pool while I stayed home with newborn Robin. Tia was obsessed with the Disney movie *The Little Mermaid*. She didn't just like the lead character, Ariel, she wanted to be her. She spoke like Ariel, dressed like Ariel, acted out parts of the movie, carried around a stuffed Flounder, and insisted her daddy pretend to be Prince Eric. As Eric turned away for a split second to put his towel and keys down, Tia jumped into the deep end of the pool. When he turned back, she was gone. He looked around the pool area. No Tia. The lifeguard was sitting calmly in his chair.

Eric saw two tiny pigtails floating in the deep end. He yanked her out of the pool, shaking and more scared than he'd ever been in his life. He was so distraught they came home immediately.

Tia seemed fine, and I assumed he was overreacting (as usual) and tried to dismiss the whole thing. He put his hands on my shoulders and looked into my eyes. "She almost died, and it would have been my fault."

He woke up in the night crying, and it took him about a week to get back to his usual self. Over the years, he would mention the incident occasionally; the shock and the scare never left him. He felt it justified all the safety rules he imposed on the kids and sometimes on me as well. I often resisted. "We are safe. Why don't you worry about yourself? You're the one with the dangerous job."

"Yes," he would retort, "but I'm careful. I know what I'm doing in a plane. I have to worry about the other guys, but most of them are good. I won't fly with the ones who aren't." He feared a crew member would kill him by doing something stupid.

Eric had been excited about making the move from Cessna to the Canadian company Bombardier about a year and a half ago, and I had never heard him complain about the competency of the pilots. A thought continued to haunt me: I knew Eric had not been flying the plane when it crashed, so had Bryan, the pilot, done something unsafe?

Dr. Russell's morning report was brief and delivered quickly. She seemed to dwell on Eric's bowel functions, so I asked Patty about the significance.

"Didn't I ever tell you doctors are obsessed with poop? Seriously, it's the best way we have to tell if the body's working." She grinned, trying to be light.

In the conference room an hour later, Dr. Russell gave me an update; I was glad Knight wasn't with her. "Eric responded to my voice, nodded his head, and was able to move his arms and hands slightly. Here's some of what's going to happen today: at about nine o'clock he's going to receive a blood transfusion, later a bronch, and this afternoon the debridement surgery. We'll need release forms. He's still on the Keane bed. We're taking spinal precautions and calling in a specialist about the burst fracture."

"But he's moving," I insisted. "He can't be paralyzed if he's moving, can he?"

"We want to keep him moving, so we'll be consulting with a neurosurgeon. The respiratory people will be in and out, and the occupational therapy people will fit Eric for fist splints."

I told her I knew the burns had compromised Eric's skin, and he was in danger of infection. I wanted visitors limited. I could at least be the watchdog outside Eric's room and make sure nobody came in with a head cold or dirty hands. Now I had a job.

Patty explained that fist splints were used to keep the hands from curling up, as burns caused bad contractions of the skin. She seemed pleased, nodding, smiling, and assuring me they were obviously looking ahead to rehab.

"Tim is here again with somebody named Alec," Patty told me. "Do you know who that is?"

"Alec Sorrentino. That's Eric's boss. Tim is Alec's boss."

"There's also a woman named Candice. She says she knows you from the zoo, and her husband works at Eric's company. Apparently she's in charge of getting meals to your house."

"I'll be right there. Patty, can you make that priest go away?"

Patty rubbed at her temple. I detected a hint of exasperation. With me? Or with the priest?

When I walked into the conference room, Alec stood up and gave me a hug. "I was in New Orleans, Carol. I got here as soon as I could." Alec was a compact guy who looked as if he worked out. His demeanor was not tragic like Tim's. His brown eyes were not bloodshot, and his voice did not crack. Alec was in his forties, a few inches taller than Eric, and with the same olive skin. He was wearing black slacks and a beige button-down dress shirt—casual, collected.

Tim introduced the early thirtysomething woman in the room. I forced a smile; I'd recently met Candice at the zoo. She greeted me with a hug and a string of perky chattering. "Hello, Carol. I'm so sorry to hear about your husband, and everyone at the zoo sends good wishes. I'm setting up meals for your home. I have a whole list of people who want to help. Tell me anything you need, anything at all. I'm sure things will get better for your husband. Everyone is praying for him, and I'll help in any way I can. Here's a basket of goodies from some of the wives at the company…"

She went on and on. I was glad I wouldn't have to worry about meals for the girls, but she was so perky. I kept nodding until she left.

Alec and Tim insisted they didn't know what had caused the accident. I eyed Alec suspiciously. He was maintaining an expressionless face. He hadn't been there when the accident happened, but he was Eric's boss. He was the one who had assigned Eric to that flight, wasn't he? He left with Patty to see Eric.

Eric liked Alec, who, like him, was of Italian descent. Eric had gone flying privately in Alec's plane a few times. I think Eric missed his own airplane, the one we'd sold when we moved to Wichita.

* * *

We bought our four-place Cessna 170 in 1988. Since Eric was a licensed airframe and power plant mechanic, he could perform most of the inspections and minor repairs. He made seat covers and tie-downs. He washed the plane every weekend and treated "her" like a queen. She was white and electric blue, and in great condition for a plane built in the 1950s. She was perfect except for one thing: the third wheel was in the back. She was a tail dragger.

I'd wanted a Cessna 172, wheel in the front, stable. When I told Eric I preferred a tricycle-gear plane, his answer was that real men flew tail draggers. My sassy reply was that I was not a man. But Eric was so excited I couldn't say no, even though I was afraid to fly it by myself. "What if I ground loop your pretty airplane?" I asked.

The thought of dropping a wing on the ground and digging the propeller into the concrete was terrifying. It wasn't the thought of ruining an airplane that scared me but of wrecking Eric's plane. He would have let me solo it, but I wasn't confident enough to fly it alone. I didn't care because I preferred to fly with him anyway.

When I was pregnant with Robin and had to be on bed rest, Tia took my place in the cockpit. She would show me her logbook and tell me about the flying she'd done. Her favorite trips were the ones where Eric flew her to a grass strip across the road from a McDonald's. Tia wore a flight suit and told everyone she was going to be a pilot like her daddy. Eric was delighted. After

Robin was born and I could fly again, I often made excuses for not going so Eric and Tia could spend time together.

*   *   *

Patty returned with Alec. I looked at him closely for a reaction to what he'd seen, but there was none. Was he hiding his emotions?

Dr. Russell arrived soon after, saying Dr. Knight had postponed the debridement surgery until tomorrow. After she left, I told Alec about Dr. Knight, adding, "I think we should call him Dr. Doom and Gloom."

Patty agreed that it was an appropriate name but cautioned me not to let him hear it. She constantly reminded me to be on my best behavior with the medical people. As we talked, Eric's best friend, RB, arrived from Atlanta.

I hadn't seen RB in about a year. He and Eric had been friends for close to fourteen years, serving in the Air Force together. Eric wasn't fond of talking on the phone unless it was with RB. The two of them could talk for hours. RB seemed quiet, but next to Eric, almost everyone seemed quiet. RB was a classic Southern gentleman: standing up when people entered a room and addressing people by their formal title. Even his sandy-brown hair and light blue eyes contrasted with Eric's dark looks.

I told RB about the eye situation. His words were brief. "He's Eric. He'll pull through."

I found Patty at the nurse's station, bent over Eric's charts, intently concentrating. "I'm looking at some labs. Would you like me to go over them with you?"

I nodded politely and understood most of what she said. She talked about platelets and white blood cells. I asked her what it would mean if the white count got too low.

She bent low over the papers and put both her hands to her forehead. She paused for what seemed like a long time. I heard her take a deep breath. She looked up, but past me, as she said, "That would be bad. Systems in the body would start shutting down."

She paused and then looked directly at me. "But this looks encouraging today. His lungs are a bit better. He's a fighter. He's going to beat this one."

I clasped my hands together in a silent prayer, to a God I knew didn't exist. *Don't let the white cell count get low. Please.*

I walked back to Eric's room and stopped abruptly. The priest was there. Again. Instantly I was watching myself, another Carol, screaming at the priest. This Carol was not the polite one I tried to be, the one who was taught to respect priests. This Carol had had enough. The priest tried to tell her she was distraught, but she screamed louder for him to leave. She wanted him to respect her, to respect Eric. She didn't care about being tolerant anymore. When he hesitated, she screamed a third time. "Get out!"

When he left, the hysterical Carol followed him out into the hall, shouting to Patty to make him leave.

I knew I was acting inappropriately. I couldn't help it—the other Carol had control of me. Everyone in the hallway was staring. I was angry at the priest, at the world.

Patty steered me to the nurse's station and sat me in a chair. She whispered, "Carol, he's gone. I promise he won't come back. If you don't calm down, they'll make you leave. I know you don't want to leave Eric. Take a deep breath. I'll talk to the social worker about it, OK?"

I sat without moving for a long time. Eric needed me. I dried my face and walked slowly to his room. Several nurses looked down as I passed them.

America is supposedly the land of religious freedom, but it isn't the land where you can be free *from* religion. Eric had said many times he wouldn't want people praying over him. Why did no one respect that?

Day 4
Friday, October 13, 2000

"Teach children about all religions, unless you want them to grow up being intolerant."
– Eric

The surgery transport team arrived while I was reading to Eric.

I didn't know the operation, the first since the day of the accident, would be such a production, and I was unprepared for all the medical people, the urgency in their voices, the equipment beeping and flashing, and the tension. The more I watched, the more panicked I became. I knew I was pacing; I knew I was pulling at my hair. My hands felt clammy, my throat dry. It was another day in a series of nightmarish days that constantly caught me off guard, with no sense of control. I could feel the fear building inside me as I heard orders shouted: Lift him carefully. Watch out for the back. Hold the IV bags.

I felt myself hyperventilating as I gripped the corner of the bedside table. I could think of only one thing: he was going to die on the operating room table. I was never going to see him again. I could hear my cries of "Eric, I love you" and "Eric, I'm here" become higher and higher pitched as though the words were coming from someone else. Then he was on the wheeled stretcher with at least seven or eight people around him, including Dr. Russell. Dr. Knight appeared in the hallway, dressed in surgical gear.

An orderly had cleared the hall and yelled for everyone to move, a critical patient was coming through. The surgery room was at the end of a long corridor that snaked its way through the burn unit and several other wards. I followed, losing control.

As they wheeled Eric through the big metal surgery doors, I clasped both hands over my mouth in an attempt to stay the vomit. My stomach lurched as I sank to my knees in the hallway. The metal doors shut with a loud clang.

A nurse stepped in front of me, clearing her throat loudly. "Mrs. Fiore, please go to the waiting room, or I'll have someone escort you there."

I glared at the nurse, her blond curls perfectly in place, her makeup a bit too heavy. What was her name again? Rochelle. I sat in the hallway and glowered at her.

Patty and the social worker, Jennifer, tried to guide me back down the hall, but I pushed them away when they touched me and ran to the conference room, flinging myself furiously into a chair, refusing to look at anyone. David and Patty stepped out into the hall with the social worker. I knew what they were saying about me. I didn't care. RB leaned over and in a low voice asked if I would like some coffee.

"No," I heard myself snarl.

What if they didn't give Eric enough anesthesia? What if he woke up and felt the pain? What if...

Eric's parents, Lisa, Sandy, and the girls arrived, quietly, their footsteps silent. Her arms wrapped around each of the girls, Sandy said, "There's your mum, loves."

Tia and Robin came over to hug me while the rest fell into chairs. Tia tried to reassure me: "Daddy will be OK." I tried to smile and hide my tears as I held the girls tightly. Robin sobbed into my shoulder. Everyone heard the muffled cries but pretended not to, looking down at magazines, inspecting fingernails, flicking lint from the sofa.

I continued to stare at my watch. Another hour, then two. David began to pace and announced he would check on things, but was soon back to say Eric was still in surgery.

Dr. Knight entered, expressionless, followed by Dr. Russell. Knight stood in the center of the room, his white hair matted to his forehead, his scrubs drenched in sweat. "He tolerated the procedure well and left the operating room in stable condition." His tone was flat, even.

Knight continued, "I'll give some technical information for the doctors in the family." He looked at David, continuing in the same flat voice. "I debrided both upper arms, both hands, and the digits of the hands. Due to the significance and difference in the bleeding on each side, the viability of the left digits and hand is questionable...." He continued with the medical information.

He paused and looked around the room. "Are there any questions?"

"Is Eric going to lose his left hand?" I asked.

"It's too early to tell. Anything else?" He might have been responding to an inquiry about the weather. Nonchalant.

The people in the room had surprised looks. Tia dropped a book loudly, purposefully. Dad remained in his self-made cocoon, folded up as tightly as possible.

Knight and Russell left, and after several minutes of fidgety silence, quiet conversations began from various parts of the room: Dave's service this morning, meals that had been sent to the house, the many friends who had called the girls.

Tia helped herself to a large plate of cookies. Looking around anxiously to see whether anyone was watching, she slipped several in her pocket while stuffing one in her mouth.

Robin snuggled next to me. Her small hands shook as she wiped at my tears.

Patty handed me a Chinese takeout box. "Vegetarian fried rice," she announced firmly. Patty the boss was in the house. "Please eat something."

I stared at the box as the smell of sesame oil drifted through the air.

* * *

"How can you hate Chinese food?" Eric asked in amazement.

It was Saint Louis, 1977, and he'd just asked me out on our third date. I explained to him that Chinese food was nasty and soggy, and I didn't like it.

"Maybe they don't have good Chinese restaurants where you lived in Illinois. What did you order the last time you went to one?" he asked.

"I've never been to a Chinese restaurant."

Eric's eyes opened wide. "Never?"

"No, but my mom used to make it. I don't like it."

He tried to suppress a smile. "Please tell me your mom didn't feed you that La Choy crap."

"Uh...yeah. It was La Choy, I think. It came in a big can, and then she dumped it over rice." My nose wrinkled at the thought of that slop. "It's disgusting."

"That's not Chinese food. I'm going to take you to a real Chinese restaurant. It won't be as good as New York Chinese food, but you'll like it. I promise."

I was not happy with the sudden turn of events in our dating. The first date had been an exciting plane ride and the second date a wonderful pizza place in Saint Louis. Now Chinese food—ugh.

Off we went in a car Eric borrowed from a friend, driving to the part of Saint Louis known as University City. It would become one of our favorite places. Eric had heard the Chinese restaurant next to the repertory theater near Washington University was decent. "Let me do the ordering for you," he offered.

Throughout dinner Eric told me, with much drama and hand waving, about his semesters in Montreal studying art, his summers on Cape Cod, his English teacher parents with their famous friends, and the great literature he'd read. I couldn't stop staring at him, even spilling my tea and dropping a piece of pork onto my lap. "I love Chinese food."

He threw his head back and laughed. His gorgeous chocolate-brown eyes seemed to say that he was quite pleased with himself as he reached across the table to squeeze my hand. "You're enchanting."

He excused himself to pay the bill and came back with his hand behind his back. "I've got a surprise for you so you'll always remember your first time in a Chinese restaurant." He presented me with a pair of black wooden chopsticks inlaid with mother-of-pearl.

Over the years, I asked him what he'd ever seen in a sheltered small-town girl like me. His reply was always the same. "I saw potential. Anyway, you were so damn adorable."

* * *

Several visitors entered the conference room: Dave Riggs's sister and mother, his daughter, and a few other relatives whose names I didn't catch. Dad hugged them. I was shocked and continued to sit, unable to stand. Today was Dave's funeral, yet here they were, concerned about all of us.

Dad, tears in his eyes, turned toward me. "Carol…" His voice cracked as he reached over to grasp my hand. I pulled myself up and hugged one of the Riggses. "Thank you," I murmured.

Dave's daughter, about the same age as Tia, handed me a basket of yellow flowers. As they were leaving, she whispered something to Tia, who nodded slowly. I caught a quick but subtle flash of anger from Tia. After they'd left, she stood before me, arms folded tightly across her chest. "What good will praying do?"

I was in Eric's room when Patty stuck her head in the door. "Wow. It's hot in here." The family had all left but her, and RB had flown back to Atlanta.

"Eric's shivering."

"That's why they turned the heat up. His temp is only one hundred. They like it to be higher."

She motioned for me to step out in the hallway as a nurse piled blankets on Eric. "I've been looking at the medical records," she said. "I'll point out some stuff to you."

At the small cubicle adjacent to Eric's room, she flipped pages in his chart, narrating as she went. I'd signed releases for her and David to have access to the records and everything else. "Looks like the neurosurgeon was consulted about the L-3 vertebral fracture. He wants Eric immobilized."

Patty told me the white blood count was down. I remembered from biology class that human blood has three components: red blood cells, white blood cells, and platelets. She said something called creatinine was at 0.9 and steadily rising.

"What's creatinine?" I asked.

"It measures kidney function. As the creatinine goes up, the kidney function goes down. Dialysis is usually started at three or so, but if somebody has slowly declining renal function over many years, they don't usually start dialysis until the creatinine is six or seven."

I pointed to a column labeled "pH." "I didn't know they kept track of pH levels."

"Oh yeah," said Patty. "It's bad if the blood pH falls below 7.4. It means the patient is acidotic, a sign of a bad infection."

"This latest lab report says the pH is 7.49. That's high."

Patty shrugged and continued to point to various columns of numbers. "He just had surgery, so I wouldn't be that concerned. I'm sure Russell is all over it. Oh...here's the bilirubin. It's down a bit from yesterday to—"

"What's the bottom line?"

"Things are as good as can be expected. It looks as though the surgery went OK."

I went back in to sit with Eric. The room was stiflingly hot, and after a few minutes, I moved out to my chair in the hallway. The chair was a few feet from the door, directly in line with it, so I could see right in. I had left a journal on it. I opened it up and started to write.

Amanda was the nurse in charge for the night. She was a big gal with a big, kind voice. Her scrub top had cute puppies racing across it. I wished it were Laurel because I had become fond of her gentle ways, but Amanda seemed to know what she was doing. I liked the way she talked to Eric.

"Your husband is quite a fighter," she said. "How long have you been married?"

"Twenty years. We dated for three before that."

Amanda folded her beefy arms across her chest. "So how did you two meet?"

"We met at the oldest aviation school in the country." I wondered if I should leave out the part about the guy before Eric.

*　*　*

Parks Air College of Saint Louis University was every girl's dream—one thousand guys and fewer than thirty girls. I was eighteen when I arrived on campus in the fall of 1977. I had never dated. Oh, there was the boy

I had kissed on New Year's Eve, but except for that, I was naïve and totally inexperienced. I was shy, plain, and lacking in self-confidence. In high school, I had lamented that the boys didn't like me. Maybe it was because they knew I was raised Catholic and they had no possible hope of getting me into bed.

Even though as an adult I wasn't religious, there was no shaking that Catholic-girl upbringing. My mother, a devout Catholic who had tried to become a nun, raised her girls to be decent and proper. "Keep your legs together," she would say. "Boys can't be trusted. They're only after one thing. There's a name for girls who let boys get in their pants." She never told us what that name was, but we knew it was bad. The church preached abstinence until one was married, and then a couple was only supposed to do *it* in order to procreate, not to have fun.

My boy troubles vanished the minute I arrived on campus. I had so many dates I became cocky. There was the time I failed to show up for one promised date because I had a better offer—definitely not a kind thing to do. Perhaps my mother should have told me there was a name for girls who did that.

I met the bad boy of my dreams during the first week of school.

Marcos was incredibly good-looking, exotic, Puerto Rican. He told me he dropped acid; a previous school had kicked him out for drug use. I heard he had another girlfriend.

I knew from the start I shouldn't be involved with him, but I was too busy pretending to be bad and acting as if I were having fun. Marcos's idea of a good time was getting high, trying to get me high, and then trying to get in my pants. Not only did the Catholic girl inside me know it was wrong, the intelligent woman inside me knew what could happen. I remembered my mother's words: "It only takes one time." I knew he didn't love me, and even at eighteen, I knew the difference between a crush and real love. I wanted to save myself for the man I was going to marry.

Safe sex was not openly discussed in 1977. I'd never heard of herpes or AIDS. The thing that kept my legs shut was guilt. Someday I was going to find the perfect man, and I didn't want to explain or hide that I'd slept with a loser because my hormones got out of control. I was, admittedly, a prude.

Patty warned me about him. Marcos and I had driven to the University of Illinois to see her. Two other students came with us, and we ended up partying with Patty, her boyfriend, and his friend—the only boy I had kissed in high school (at a New Year's Eve party after having too many tequila sunrises). The three of them pronounced Marcos the biggest asshole they'd ever met after watching him stagger around the dorm, drinking, dropping acid, and making out with four girls—at once.

"What would our mother say?" Patty declared.

"Drop him," they all three shouted at me. "You're too good for him."

I tried. But he was cool and good looking, and I was tired of always being a good girl, with perfect grades and never a date. I was determined to be bad with a capital *B*.

One night a few weeks later, I was sitting in Marcos's dorm room waiting for him. I'd heard about his weekend tryst in Cincinnati. It involved several girls and guys and drugs and kinky sex. I was disgusted. We'd only been dating for six weeks, and though I didn't expect we would be exclusive, I wasn't going to put up with this.

Eric walked by and stuck his head in the open door. His room was down the hall, and I'd seen him occasionally since arriving at Parks, having breakfast with him once, discussing classes, seeing him at a few parties, and training together at the college radio station.

"Hey, Carol. What's up?"

"Waiting for Marcos," I said, throwing my back-pack on the floor.

Eric glided in and sat beside me on the bed. "What's wrong?"

I told him what I'd heard. I probably wouldn't have told just anyone, but I knew Eric, sort of, and he made me laugh when we worked at the radio station. I didn't think he could make me laugh now, though; I was so angry.

Eric was unusually quiet as I started to complain about everything Marcos had ever done, about what a jerk I thought he was, everything. The usually talkative and loud Eric didn't say a word.

"So…what do you think, Eric?"

"You know what I think of Marcos."

"You think he's an ass."

"I think you're too good for him."

"You do?"

"Of course. You're not fooling me. You try to act dumb around him, but I know you're bright. You're not like the other girls here. And you're not a pothead either, even though you're trying hard to be something you're not."

There was an awkward silence before he said, "And you're pretty." His black mustache twitched upward. I'd never noticed what a handsome mustache it was. His dark, unruly shoulder-length hair fell forward, partly covering his chocolate-brown eyes. Why hadn't I looked closer at his eyes? They were full of emotion and promised adventure. There was sweetness there too.

Even though Eric was short, he was good looking. If only he wasn't so uncool. It was the seventies, for God's sake, and he was always lecturing everybody about smoking pot.

"I don't think Marcos cares about me," I said. "I think he just wants to get in my pants."

Eric attempted to hide a smile, but I saw it. I was indignant.

"You don't think I'd let him, do you? Well? Do you? I'm not that kind of girl."

Eric's grin was so big there was no concealing it now. "Of course I don't. Anyway, he told us."

"What?"

"He told us he's been trying but can't get anywhere with you."

"He told you that?"

"Yeah…uh…he calls you 'the Eternal Virgin.'"

"He what?"

"At least he didn't lie. Think about it for a minute. It's sort of a compliment." Eric smiled broadly and tugged at the corner of his mustache.

Marcos walked in. "Fiore, why are you always in my room? Don't you have anything else to do?" He sat down in the chair at his desk and watched Eric walk out the door. "So what was that all about?"

I got up from the bed, disgusted with Marcos but mostly with myself for associating with him. I picked my backpack up off the floor, swinging it over my shoulder roughly. "Nothing. How was your weekend? Did you have a fun time? Do many drugs, did you? Sleep with many girls, did you? And how were those boys, by the way?"

Marcos leaned back in his chair, an arrogant smirk on his face. "You're such a prude, Carol," he said sarcastically. "Lighten up."

"Good-bye, Marcos. I can't believe you would do this to us."

As I walked out the door, I heard him laughing behind me. "There never was an us, honey."

It was shortly after this incident that Eric took me flying for the first time. That was when I realized he was the cool one with his sweetness and brilliance and passion for flying. Marcos and his crowd were the uncool ones. Defying the system and breaking the law didn't make them better than everyone else, it made them stupid. And I was stupid for trying to be like them. Why hadn't I seen it sooner?

One day at the start of the spring semester, after we'd been dating for a few months, I remarked to Eric that he was different from the other guys. He didn't just want to get in my pants.

"You know I care about you, Carol," he answered, grinning. "I hate to use the word 'love' because I don't want to freak you out, so I'll say that I really, really like you a lot. I've never felt this way about anyone before, but...." His eyes held a mischievous sparkle.

"Yes?" I asked coyly.

"But I would really like to get in your pants."

"You would, huh?"

"Yes, I really would."

He stared at me, pretending to pat down his mustache while actually hiding the big grin spreading across his face.

Day 5
Saturday, October 14, 2000

*"If you're bored, it must mean
you're boring."*
- Eric

I wanted the medical people to see Eric before the accident. That was why I decided to post a picture on his hospital door.

The picture David brought that morning was the one of Eric in his flight suit in front of Cessna's replacement for the T-37 Air Force trainer. Eric was the second person to fly the prototype of this brand-new jet dubbed the JPATS. Unfortunately, Cessna didn't get the government contract, and the jet never went into production. Things would have been different if they had: Eric wouldn't have moved on to Bombardier. He would still look like the Eric in that picture. He would still have a face. He would still have hair.

Eric had beautiful, thick, dark hair. Past tense. I used to joke with him that his best features were his deep brown eyes and his cute butt, which more than one woman had commented on. Eric always watched what he ate, but during the last half a year he had trimmed down, probably too much, getting a real cyclist body—140 pounds, lean and strong. At slightly under five feet and five inches, he handled his short height well, putting up with the inevitable jokes and being able to laugh about it. More than once he commented that he had to marry a woman taller than he was (I'm almost two inches taller) in order to get some height in the Fiore gene pool.

Eric had the olive complexion so common to people of Mediterranean descent. He also had a real Roman nose; it was his most prominent feature. He claimed Julius Caesar had a nose like his, one that roamed all over his face. Eric had delicate ears, and although his teeth were small, they were perfectly straight and white. I had endured years of braces to get my straight teeth, but Eric was born with his.

When I first met Eric at Parks College, he had a full, bushy mustache that was the envy of many guys. After he joined the Air Force, there were problems—it was against regulations to have a mustache extend past the corners of the mouth. Any attempt to cut it to meet the rules resulted in a tiny Hitler-looking mustache, so he gave up and cut it off. When he became an Air Force captain, he grew the mustache back and, at my urging, kept it. I was always after him to grow a beard, but he never would until he left for Argentina this past summer. When I picked him up at the airport at the end of July, he was sporting a trim beard. He had that college professor look, and it suited him.

By midmorning, I got some response from Eric—slight hand and feet movements. "Eric, please don't leave me. You're not going to leave me, are you?"

Eric shook his head no in a strong movement that shocked me, and I instantly felt horrible for having asked it. Then I couldn't focus my eyes at all, and although I continued to talk to him, there was no further response.

In the conference room, Patty read the company newsletter Tim had dropped off earlier. "What's this safety award they mention in the paper?" She pointed to the newsletter. "It says here that Eric got a prestigious award called the Tony LeVier Flight Test Safety Award. I wondered what it was."

I looked down at the floor, too ashamed to look her in the eyes. "I didn't go."

"You didn't go? Go where?"

"To Beverly Hills. When he got the award over a year ago."

There was an awkward pause before Patty asked, "Why didn't you go?"

"I'm sorry...I'm so sorry...I should have gone...he wanted me to go..."

I thought back to last September. The semester had started for me at Wichita State University, and as always, I was intense about my graduate studies. I was single-minded. I was teaching chemistry as a graduate teaching assistant and winding up my research and my degree. I could think of nothing else.

It was then that Eric had learned from the Society of Experimental Test Pilots (SETP) that he had won one of their most prestigious awards: the Tony LeVier Flight Test Safety Award. The society awarded it only to truly outstanding test pilots. It was an incredible honor, and Eric was ecstatic. He was going to receive the award at the big SETP banquet in Beverly Hills on September 26, 1999. He had a tuxedo all ready for the occasion, and he wanted me to go.

While Eric was at Cessna, he'd instituted an aggressive safety program and authored a flight test manual. I remembered because I'd helped proofread parts of it, and although I didn't understand it, I looked for grammar and spelling errors. The FAA's Wichita Aircraft Certification Office (ACO) eventually used the manual as a standard for safety procedures in the FAA Central Region. Eric had poured himself into the project. He deserved the award, and he deserved to have his wife by his side when he accepted it.

But I wasn't there.

Why didn't I go? I was so wrapped up in my life, in my job, in my schooling that I couldn't spare the time. I didn't want to miss classes, find someone to watch the girls, and locate an instructor to teach my chemistry classes.

Eric was disappointed. "Fine. I understand. You have school," he said dejectedly. After a long pause, his face brightened. "We'd have fun. We could go on a mini-vacation, and we could..."

I wouldn't budge. I told him I was sorry; I couldn't take the time off. Sorry. Have a nice time. Congratulations on the award. See you when you get back.

He came home from Beverly Hills with his award and presents for everyone. I was studying. I had a test. "That's great," I said hurriedly and went back to studying. I was busy—too busy to pay attention to my famous test pilot husband. All those times he had supported me in my work, helped me with my research, assisted me with my chemistry, listened to me ramble on and on about birds. He deserved better. If I could undo one thing in my past, it would be that. To hell with school. I should have gone.

One night a few weeks ago, Eric was working in the study. As I stood there looking at the award, he quietly said, "I wish you'd gone with me, Carol."

Jan, Eric's day nurse, was the first to see the picture I taped to the door. "You're right. He's quite handsome."

Knight and Russell headed toward us, and I recognized the medical personnel pushing the bronchoscopy equipment. They all paused when they saw the picture. Knight quickly glanced at it, but didn't say a word. The door shut behind them.

"The nurses are working on an essay about Eric to hang over his bed," Jan began. "It will tell medical personnel who come in the room something about him. Is there anything you can tell me about Eric and his hobbies?"

Jan was a stunning woman with wavy black hair and emerald-green eyes. "What does he like to do?"

"Eric has an unbelievable number of interests," I said. "He says life is too exciting to be bored."

"He's a smart man."

"Life with him is never boring."

Eric had a habit of throwing himself into something for several months and then burning out fast. Like golf. Eric had immersed himself in golf with a passion pros would have envied. He read books, he spent hours picking out clubs, and he bought the right clothes. He even took his clubs to Montreal in a special flight bag he'd bought for his gear. He played frequently for a good six months, and then he got tired of it. I thought of his clubs and bag sitting in the garage. It had been over a year since he'd touched them.

There was downhill skiing when we lived in Holland in the mid-1980s. We'd driven to Germany a couple times to ski for the day. Again, Eric bought equipment and clothes, and he read books on proper technique. Then he burned out, and the equipment sat in the closet. He purchased an expensive telescope over a year ago and lugged the huge contraption outside every night for weeks. For a couple months, he talked of nothing but astronomy. He bought new books, red flashlights, and star charts. He even began drawing the sky in exquisitely detailed sketches that he kept in a midnight-blue leather notebook. Then he stopped. Too much light pollution, he'd complained.

Over the years, there was the soccer passion, the racquetball craze, the Apple computers obsession. He would work intensely doing repairs and updates on our various houses; then he wouldn't touch them for years. I never minded all the obsessions because I enjoyed being married to someone who could always find something to do. I was sure I wouldn't like being married to a puppy-type guy who depended on me for all his entertainment. I had interests and hobbies too, so it suited our marriage. I never ever heard Eric say he was bored, and I thought of the reply he always gave to Tia when she complained of being bored: "You mean you're boring, don't you?"

Eric never counted flying and airplanes as a hobby. It was his life, a part of him, and classifying aviation in a category with his other hobbies would have been calling it a fleeting interest.

Sometimes it was difficult for him to find time for his hobbies because Bombardier worked him hard, with long hours being the norm. He was elated when he had time to attend a car race or take a fifty-mile bike ride. He was one of those rare people who seemed to be productive every minute of the day.

Eric's latest passion was autocross racing in his Miata. He read car-racing books with a fervor I had never seen outside of flying, remarking to me that he secretly wanted to be a race car driver. Exasperated, I'd blasted him. "Can't you pick something safe? Why do you like these dangerous hobbies?"

He'd gone into detail about how he wore his special racing helmet (more new equipment) and how he always put safety first. I was not thrilled with the race car obsession. Eric started to daydream about a Ferrari and bought shirts with the logo on it, talked about racing with anyone who would listen, and installed a satellite dish so he could watch the Speedvision channel.

Then there was the bicycle hobby. I was excited about that one. Eric seemed happy on his bike, so I encouraged it. He looked the part of a cyclist, and almost every weekend we'd go to the bike shop and he'd buy a jersey or a pair of biking socks. He'd begun to stare fondly at a titanium racing bike. It was, he told me yet again, all about the equipment.

I thought of the hobbies Eric would no longer be able to do. I tried to convince myself that he would find something new, but I was afraid for him. And for me.

Lisa, Mom, Dad, and the girls arrived. Everyone slumped quietly into chairs in the conference room. Dad, normally one for hugging and socializing, sat in the far corner, building an emotional cage for himself. One with no windows.

Knight came to the conference room to give his report. David and Russell were with him.

"Pinker, with a couple areas of ulceration." Knight paused. "Are there any questions?"

Tia and Robin were silent. They'd picked up on my nickname of Dr. Doom and Gloom, and they were both afraid of him. After Russell and Knight left, David asked his father if he wanted to see Eric. Dad hesitated, rising in his chair, and then falling back into it. His eyes were wide as he wiped vigorously at the perspiration gathering on his forehead. He nodded his consent, and we all trudged down the hall after David.

Dad stayed in Eric's room for only a brief minute. He tried to speak to his son, his face contorted in anguish. "Ric...it's Dad..."

Eric rocked his whole body. Dad fled from the room. Mom, following him into the hall, put a gentle arm around him as he fell into a chair, my chair, in the hallway. "It'll be all right."

He shook off her arm and angrily replied, "No, it won't. How can you say that? It will never be all right."

The family left and Candice returned, as perky as ever. She had attractive hair: shoulder-length, tan-colored with artfully placed blond highlights, curled down slightly on the ends. She was the woman I'd met recently at the zoo. I barely knew her, yet she seemed to be taking charge as though she were my best friend. Why was she doing this? She outlined all her plans for food delivery, assuring me "things could be worse" and managing to add in a few sentences about "God's plan."

I interrupted. "Gee, Candice. I don't see how much worse they could be."

She soon found a reason to leave. I felt bad for being snippy, but the perkiness was more than I could take. I probably should have told her—and everyone else—I wasn't religious, but the years of hiding my views came so naturally I didn't think about it. Until now. Maybe I needed to get some moxie and come out of the atheist closet. What was the worst that could happen?

"I know you've been anxious to see these," Sandy said in her British accent as she entered the waiting room. She handed me a thick package of pictures.

The photos were from Eric's trip to the Netherlands. I'd dropped off the film right away when he returned, October 9, only one day before the accident. He'd gone to Amsterdam to attend a conference on human factors in the cockpit, his latest project at work. I thought of the presents he had brought me, still sitting on the counter where I'd left them. I knew he'd visited our old houses in Holland (where we'd lived from 1985 until 1988), the hospital where Tia was born in 1987, and Camp New Amsterdam, where he'd flown his beloved F-15. As I held the photos, I had one thought: I needed to see a picture of Eric. I held my breath as I flipped rapidly through them.

I found it—a photo of Eric. There was only one. I held it up to Sandy.

"He looks blooming happy," she said.

In the picture, Eric stood next to the extremely tall Dutch owner of the shop where he'd bought his bicycle so many years ago. He was smiling, and the owner had his arm on Eric's shoulder.

Eric had become a proficient cyclist. It was difficult keeping up with him. I considered myself a decent rider; I'd won two biathlons and competed in several bike races. I was an accomplished runner, and I did not like to lose. I refused to let Eric know how badly he was beating me, and I'd cover it up with lots of excuses: the red light caught me; my shoe came untied; I had to blow my nose.

I started sending him off on his fifty-mile rides without me. I could have done that many miles, but not at his pace. I was slowing him down. I made excuses for why I was too busy to go, but he was on to me. I'd finished my degree and had much more free time. He knew I knew, and I knew he knew, but we both pretended nobody knew.

I suggested he think about competing. I owed him much for all his years of supporting my running, and I began to daydream about a joint effort in a biathlon. As a team, we would be invincible.

Last month I spoke with him about the titanium bike he'd been drooling over. "Buy that bike, Eric," I said. "What are you waiting for? You're good. If I wanted an expensive pair of running shoes, you'd buy them for me. We have the money. Buy it."

"Carol, I can't justify spending $3,000 on myself."

"You don't have to. I want to buy it for you. I have a job now."

He grinned. I could tell he wanted to say that on my seven-dollar-an-hour zoo salary, it was going to take a while. Instead, he said, "That's sweet of you."

Tim Ryan, the vice president of Flight Test, arrived at the hospital with Colin White, Mr. Big Important Head of the Company. He had on his suit and his power tie. His sandy-brown hair was impeccably combed. The Bombardier spokesperson followed them. They all took turns assuring me the company was going to take care of me. "Eric's salary will continue until he is back at work," they promised.

The Bombardier spokesperson towered over Tim and Mr. White. I could see why he held that position. You don't question a lumbering mountain.

Tim's voice cracked as he looked directly at me and said, "Eric will always have a job at Bombardier. If he can't fly, there are other things he can do. He's an important and productive part of our team. We'll make sure he has whatever special equipment he needs to do his job."

Had he received permission from Mr. Big Important to say that? But Tim didn't look at White, he looked at me. He didn't seem to be asking for approval.

I believed him.

I looked up at the three faces surrounding me. They were nodding. They were smiling. But they were giving one another glances, slight ones, that said, "We'll see what happens." Were they being generous because they didn't think Eric would live?

Everyone in the room knew Eric would never fly again. The silence lasted several minutes, almost as though we were paying our respects to the pilot in Eric that would never take flight again. Sadness spread through me. I was quite sure only a pilot could have fully understood what it meant to lose your wings. I wanted to tell the world someday, but I wondered if I'd ever be able. Did the words even exist?

I'd written a short letter to the company about how much Eric enjoyed being a test pilot, and about how much he liked the company. Mr. White informed me the letter had been sent to headquarters in Montreal and the entire company was pulling for Eric. White sat, leaning forward, looking at me as if I were the most important person in the world. Did he learn that in a management class? It was his job and nothing more.

I looked away. I hesitated. I started to say something, then stopped. The thoughts running through my head were wrong.

Wrong. Wrong. *Wrong.*

Eric loved his company. We both loved airplanes. Bombardier had shown nothing but kindness. I bit my lip until I tasted blood. I looked up and forced a small smile into my eyes. "Thank you."

I would keep my promise to Eric. I was not going to disgrace myself, and him, in front of the head of his company. And in front of Tim, his boss, a man he respected.

I said it again. "Thank you."

Tim stayed after White and the spokesperson left. He pulled at his mustache. "The company tries to be so safe."

I made a superhuman effort to keep my mouth shut. *They weren't safe enough*, I wanted to shout. But I didn't. Tim was devastated. It would have been mean to say what I was feeling. Eric's words echoed through my mind: don't be a whiny wife; make me proud.

After Tim left, I went back to sit with Eric. I was not looking forward to tomorrow—Patty was leaving. I understood, of course. She had a medical practice, patients who needed her, a husband, and two children.

That evening, as the night nurse Laurel was checking all the medical equipment, she started to ask me questions about Eric. "All the nurses love the wonderful stories you tell about Eric. We feel as though we're getting to know him."

"You're not tired of my incessant babbling?" Compassionate Laurel was quickly becoming my favorite nurse. I still couldn't describe exactly what it was that made her so special.

"Absolutely not. You're a great storyteller."

I began another story, one that started when I was a child.

* * *

"Carol Ann! Get out of that mud hole this instant. Act like a girl."

My mother's voice sailed across the yard so loudly I swore she must have had a megaphone. I froze, mortified. The grooviest boys in the neighborhood were at the dirt mound in the big empty field behind the row of enlisted housing at Grand Forks Air Force Base, North Dakota. They all turned to see my mom with her frizzy short hair and cat-eye glasses, hands on her hips, yelling at me.

I scrunched up my shoulders and tried to disappear into the ground. I was an honorary boy with this bunch, quite the prestigious thing when you're only seven years old. I was neat, I was hip, and I was groovy. The neighbor boy, Chuck, a year younger, had insisted I wasn't like those other girls. My mom ruined it for me in an instant.

I reluctantly picked up my three marbles and headed for the house. Nobody said a word as I left. I glanced behind me; they'd gone back to their game. When I got to my yard, I had to endure five minutes of lecturing about how a girl was supposed to act. My mom scared me, so I was afraid to say anything. I'd tried not to get dirty, really I did. There was only a little mud on my slacks and none at all on my blouse, the brown one with the buttons shaped like tigers.

The whole neighborhood had probably heard my mom. I hung my head. It wasn't fair. "Chuck gets to have marbles, and Chuck gets to play in the dirt hole,"

I said quietly. I thought it might make a difference. My mom was friends with Chuck's mom.

"That's because Chuck is a boy and you're not. Stop sassing and get in that house and wash up." Her usual stern voice was shriller than ever. Her small, close-set eyes appeared even smaller behind her cat-eye glasses.

I'd asked for marbles at Christmas but didn't get any. I knew there was no Santa; he'd have given me some. Chuck got a big jar with beautifully colored marbles. He showed them to me proudly. Why, there must have been every color ever made in that jar. He even got tiger's-eyes. Chuck got a shooter too. Now he had two of them. His new shooter was mint green with black spots. Sometimes Chuck let me hold it. I'd roll it in my fingers, feeling its smooth surface. I'd hold it up to the light and stare at it. Once Chuck forgot he gave it to me. I could have said later that I lost it, but I knew it was wrong to steal, even though the thing I wanted most in the whole world was a shooter.

I only had three marbles. Chuck had given them to me because he felt sorry for me. I never got a shooter, though. I stopped shooting marbles with the boys because I knew my mom would catch me. I remember sitting on the porch crying. More than anything, I wanted to be a boy.

When I got older, I realized I didn't really want to be a boy. I wanted to be able to do boy stuff, like flying, rappelling, weight lifting, kickboxing.

One time I told Eric about the marbles and the shooter. He was sympathetic and a bit horrified by the story. Liberal parents had raised him, and the thought of not being able to do something because I was female was foreign to his way of thinking. He'd stared at me with a pained look in his eyes. "I can't believe some of the things your parents did to you."

I shrugged.

Almost a year after I'd told Eric the marble story we went sightseeing in a quaint Texas hill town. Over lunch, Eric held out his closed fist and grinned.

"I've got a surprise for my girl who wanted to be a boy. I know it can't make up for what happened, but I want you to know how much I love you."

He opened his fist. In his hand, he held a round piece of black glass with blue swirls on it. It was the most fantastic shooter I'd ever seen.

Day 6
Sunday, October 15, 2000

*"Not everyone is lucky enough
to have a great childhood.
I had a great one because
I have great parents."*

– Eric

"What should I do with Eric's car?" Phil asked me in the conference room. "It's in the parking lot at Bombardier." He said it matter-of-factly, as if Eric were off on a trip. He reached for a pastry.

Phil was one of Eric's bosses. He and Sandy had been great neighbors—the best, actually. The girls thought he was funny; their daddy was lucky to work with such a nice man, they said. But what about Phil's job as Flight Test manager? Where was he when the accident happened? What was his part in all this? And what—

"Carol?"

"Oh…sorry…Eric's fussy about the Miata," I said. "Can you drive it to the house and put it in the garage?"

Phil swallowed a bite of pastry. "Maybe you better not tell Eric I drove his car." His British accent was faint, not nearly as pronounced as his wife's.

"I don't think he'll care about his car anymore," I heard myself whisper.

Eric's forest-green Mazda Miata Limited Edition convertible sports car was his baby. We'd bought it for his fortieth birthday, less than three years ago.

* * *

I hated that car.

I knew it wasn't fair of me; I should let Eric have his toy, but I couldn't seem to help it. I was so angry about that damn car. Why should a stupid car be more important than me? He loved to take me for rides, but he wouldn't let me drive it. We'd taken out a second mortgage on the house to buy it, and now I couldn't get behind the wheel.

It was unfair. Maybe I wanted to drive it too. Put the top down, turn the stereo up too loud, drive a little too fast…

Last winter Eric was out of town, and the car alarm went off. He'd insisted on arming it when it was in the garage. Who was going to break into the garage and steal it?

I called the hotel in Alaska where he was staying and left a message. A few hours later, the phone rang.

"Did someone accidentally hit my car?" he asked. He didn't sound mad; he sounded tired.

"Nobody touched the dumb thing," I shouted into the phone, over the noise of the blaring alarm.

"Have you driven it since I've been gone?"

"Of course not. You won't let me, remember?"

"I think the battery is low. When it goes completely dead, it'll stop," he said casually.

"How long is that going to take?"

"I don't know."

"Great. It's loud, Eric. This wouldn't have happened if you had let me—"

"I'm sorry. I'll take care of it when I get home. OK?"

"You know it isn't fair," I said, trying to lower my voice. "You never let me drive it. You trust me with the children, but you won't trust me with the car."

"I'm sorry. I will. I promise."

An hour later, the alarm was still going off, and I was madder than ever.

I hated that car.

When Eric returned from Alaska, nothing changed. He said I could drive the car, but he imposed all sorts of restraints on where I could and couldn't drive it, so the situation remained unchanged.

Eric drove his precious Miata in autocross competitions, winning ribbons and participating in the local sports car club. I was so mad that he wouldn't let me drive it, I refused to watch him compete. He took Tia instead.

* * *

I realized my life was going to be like this—dredging up and reliving every single unkind thing I ever said or did to him. This was what it meant when people used that old cliché about being eaten up by guilt. I felt as if all the bad things I'd ever said or done were crushing me. I'd try not to think about them, but odd memories, years old, would pop into my head.

I should have let him enjoy his toy.

In August, Eric's feelings about the car changed. He'd spent two months in Argentina, cold-weather testing "his" plane—the Canadair Regional Jet, or RJ for short. I don't know what happened, but something changed.

For the better.

One day in late August while I was getting ready for my web design class—something I had done on a whim after I graduated—he insisted I take the Mazda. I ignored him. About five minutes later, when I couldn't find the keys to the Jeep, I yelled up the stairs. "Eric, I'm going to be late for class. Where are the keys to the Jeep?"

"I've got them."

"Well, hello. Can I have them please?"

He appeared at the top of the stairs with a grin on his face. "Nope. Take the Mazda."

I was going to be late, and he knew I hated being late for class. "Give me the stupid keys."

"No. Take the Mazda," he said calmly.

"I'm not taking the dumb car. You don't want me to drive it, and what if I scratch it? Oh my God, it would be the end of the world."

He came down the stairs and hugged me. "I'm trying to be better, Carol. Please take the Mazda. I want you to drive it. If you wreck it, I'll fix it. It's only a car."

Did he mean it? Was he actually going to let me drive it? Maybe I didn't want to drive it now, the stupid thing. "It doesn't have a cup holder. I don't want to drive a stupid car without a cup holder." He'd been acting like a jerk, so I could too.

"I'll buy a cup holder."

I huffed loudly. "Still don't want to drive it."

"Please, Carol. I've been trying to be better since I got back. I love you, and I'm trying not to yell, and I really, really, really want you to drive our car." His always-expressive face looked sad.

"Yeah. OK…you have been better. It's like in that movie, *Sommersby*. Maybe you're not really Eric. Maybe the real Eric is going to come back and yell at me for driving his car." I paused, considering my options. "You really want me to drive it?"

"Yes, really." His voice was soft as he looked into my eyes.

"And you're not going to lecture me about the way I shift?"

"Nope."

He kissed me good-bye, and I reluctantly got into the driver's seat. As I was pulling out of the driveway, I yelled out the window, "Have you changed your mind yet?"

"Nope. Have a good class." He flashed me a big, sincere smile.

When I got home, he asked about class, but he never asked about the car. He didn't even go into the garage to check on it. From then on, I drove the car. That was less than two months ago. It was one of the many things that changed when he returned from Argentina. He was so much better, and more like the Eric I had fallen in love with.

What had happened down there?

Lisa, Eric's sister, said nothing happened. Being a Buddhist, Lisa believed Eric felt something terrible was going to happen to him, so he went about changing things and taking care of the people in his life. She seemed so sure of herself.

I didn't believe it.

It was a Sunday; visitors had been arriving nonstop, including some from the FAA. Patty spoke with an officer from airport security about the rescue. He claimed the fire was put out quickly, but according to one visitor, the newspaper had reported screams. Patty seemed to be getting conflicting information about the rescue, and though I refused to read the paper or watch the news, it was hard not to overhear all the whispering going on around me.

Nobody seemed to know what, if anything, Eric had said. I'd asked every medical person I'd met because there was talk he'd spoken in the emergency room. Knight and Russell weren't in the ER when Eric was brought in, but I wouldn't quit until I found someone who was there. Maybe someone would find me. I had to be patient. And continue asking.

In the conference room, Robin asked Tim if he knew about Rocket Day. Eric had taken off half a day of work to come to her school, surprising both Robin and me. It was the day before the accident; he'd just returned from Holland. I couldn't help but think how different things would have been if Rocket Day had been October 10 instead of October 9. I wouldn't be sitting here watching Eric suffer. What-ifs torment our lives and sometimes batter us until we break...

Robin had an amazing vocabulary for a ten-year-old, and Eric and I could already tell she was gifted. It wasn't long before she told Tim, in a grown-up and sophisticated way, the detailed story about Rocket Day at her school. Several people in the room listened as she spoke.

"And my rocket went the highest out of everyone's because Daddy made it."

The room was silent as she finished. She didn't notice the tears in Tim's eyes.

More and more people continued to file in, probably because it was a Sunday. I didn't know them; I was sure they didn't know me. I assumed they worked at the company. They brought cards, food, flowers, and sad faces. The conference room became somewhat loud as every chair filled and people flowed out into the hallway.

Dr. Russell came in to report on the bronch results and the grafts—both were as good as could be expected. They'd put Eric on a paralytic drug to prevent the overbreathing he had been doing on the ventilator. He would not be able to move at all. They would take him off the drug later, when things were better.

Knight wasn't with Dr. Russell. I'd nicknamed her "the Burn Lady," and that was what Tia and Robin started to call her.

My voice was a bit too shrill as I asked, "What about his eyes?"

"Dr. Knight will be addressing that."

Because the conference room was noisy, no one heard but Tim. He patted me on the shoulder, looking past me.

Patty came to tell me Alec was driving her to the airport. "Carol, I'll be back. I'll call several times a day, and I'll talk to Russell every single day and get reports. Do the knee exercises I showed you since you're blowing off your physical therapy, and please eat something."

I didn't want her to leave, but I couldn't say it; I couldn't make her feel guilty. It would be wrong. I tried my best to smile and said, "You're leaving me alone with…with…David."

Patty squeezed my hand. "Bye, Carol. I'll see you soon."

I followed her down the hall, watching as she left through the big steel doors. She hadn't left the hospital once; she hadn't left the burn unit at all—not once in five days. I slumped down in the chair in the hall across from Eric's door.

Spotting David talking to Dr. Knight in the hallway, I walked up to them. "What are you going to do about Eric's eyes?"

David gave me a hard stare as Knight looked over the top of his glasses and said, "Right now my primary concern is saving my patient's life. The eyes are what they are."

I flew into Eric's room and stood over him, trying not to cry. Why couldn't I get them to do anything about his eyes?

David came in the room. "Knight agreed to get someone in here in a day or two to look at his eyes. Let me take care of it."

"OK, David…I'm sorry…it's…"

He leaned toward me until his nose was practically touching mine. "I'll take care of it." Pointing at the paper hanging on the wall above Eric's bed, he asked, "Did the nurses write that?"

I nodded.

Hi. My name is Eric.
I am strong. I love life. I am a fighter.
I live here in Wichita.
I am originally from New York.
My wife's name is Carol.
We have been married for 20 years.
We have two children.
Tia is 13 and Robin is 10.
We also have a parrot named Flutter.
I have lived all over the world.
My wife and I especially love Holland.
I also love bike riding, astronomy,
and driving my green sports car.
I love anything and everything that is Italian.

Later in the day, after the family had left and the bandage change was over (David had assisted), I sat with Eric. Suddenly, a buzzer sounded on one of the machines. His blood pressure shot up, and numbers that had been constant changed. I didn't know what they meant, but I knew it was different. I ran out to get the nurse. She said Eric was agitated, but I heard her call Dr. Russell. I had them call David from the medical library, and by the time he arrived, I was sure Eric was dying.

It took some time for everyone to calm me down. David put his hands firmly on my shoulders and said, "Stop interfering."

Hanging my head, I sat out in the hallway. How could I hurt so badly and still be alive? I wished I could die. I was trying to be Eric's champion, but I was getting in the way.

I had my arms and legs tightly folded when Dr. Russell came out and squatted down beside me. "Carol, he's all right. He got a bit agitated. You may have noticed that happens sometimes after the bandage change. Will you do something for me?"

I nodded uncertainly.

"Will you come with me to speak with Jennifer?"

I shook my head no. I didn't want to see the social worker. She had been hanging around looking at me sympathetically. She was a short, attractive woman, curvy, with kind eyes, but I didn't want therapy. Everyone thought I was having a breakdown, and I was being sent to the shrink.

"Please," said Dr. Russell calmly. "Eric would want you to, don't you think?"

No. He wouldn't.

"Fine," I blurted out. "It won't do any good."

Russell stared at me a bit too long.

I followed her into Jennifer's office and dropped in a chair. The social worker asked me all the usual questions, starting with "How do you feel about what has happened?"

What did she want me to say? I stared at the ceiling.

"I was told you work at the zoo."

Silence from me.

"I also understand you got your master's degree recently."

More silence.

"Did you do a thesis?"

I nodded.

"What was it about?"

I didn't want to explain it to her. "I was studying cats and birds. Eric helped me." I mumbled it quickly.

I'd put years of work into my thesis. According to people at Bombardier, Eric talked constantly about my graduate research project. I got a reputation as "the cat lady" or "the bird lady," depending on one's perspective. I was investigating the impact domestic cats had on birds in the city of Wichita. The research was new. There had been only a handful of studies like it, and until recently, not many people had expressed interest or concern over what cats—introduced exotics that weren't supposed to be here—were doing to our native wildlife.

My suggestion that owners be held accountable for their cats' behavior infuriated many. I was the recipient of hate mail, nasty phone calls, and public name-calling. Some coined me "the cat killer." I was a long-time vegetarian, zoo educator, and animal rights activist, so it hurt me deeply that people would think I'd ever consider injuring an animal, let alone killing it. It was cat owners, not cats, who were to blame for the appallingly high bird mortality my research attributed to dear Fluffy.

Eric was the great defender of my research. He consoled me when I cried because the neighbor down the street accused me of killing her cat. He proofread my thesis and asked questions that made me rethink my strategies. He didn't hesitate to buy me books about cats, purchase supplies for my research the university wouldn't budget for, and even help to pay for federal and state permits. When Sandy couldn't watch the girls while I tracked cats and worked in the lab, he did. He even helped me collect dead birds.

Sometimes I couldn't get to the university lab to store the bird remains, so I deposited them in our freezer at home for a day or two. My research also involved collecting and analyzing hundreds of samples of scat—a fancy biologist word for poop.

Eric described the situation in his typical humorous fashion, and it was a constant source of jokes: "Carol. How long is my freezer going to have cat poop in it?" "I know you're a vegetarian. I respect that, and you know I don't complain. But every time I look in the freezer, there are dead birds but no dead cows. Could a man get a steak around here?" "I'm afraid to look in this freezer anymore. What if I'm tired one day and I accidentally heat up some cat shit?" "Carol, can I eat one of these dead birds? It's the only meat in the house."

When I defended my thesis, he was there, in a suit and tie.

"I don't want someone to think the husband of the big important researcher is a bum," he laughed.

I concluded my thesis defense with a tribute to him. "And lastly, I'd like to thank my wonderful husband, Eric, for supporting me, defending my research, and putting up with dead birds and cat poop for over two years."

He stood up and bowed.

Day 7
Monday, October 16, 2000

*"Doctors will find any excuse to take
away a pilot's medical certificate."*
- Eric

———————————————

I knew something was wrong before Russell sat down in the conference room with me. "Eric is in high-output renal failure, and Dr. Pierce has been called in to consult," she said evenly.

"Does that mean his kidneys are going out? Patty's been reading me the creatinine values. That's a sign of kidney function, right? They've been OK."

"That's correct, but the creatinine is continuing to rise, and now it's 1.4. Dr. Pierce is the dialysis specialist."

"Dialysis…Oh my God…"

Russell held a hand up. "It often happens in cases like this that patients go on dialysis temporarily. While 1.4 isn't that high, we want to be on top of it. Let's get Pierce in here and see what he says." She was calm, her voice steady. She sounded as if dialysis were as common as filling a tooth.

"I know today is going to be difficult for you because your sister is gone and the surgery is tomorrow," she continued. "You probably noticed we have patches over Eric's eyes, and the nurses have instructions to put ointment in them."

"I love him so much. I would be nothing without Eric."

"Can I call Jennifer to come sit with you?" Russell asked gently.

Here we go again. Get the social worker for the distraught, crazy wife.

"No."

Russell continued to look at me intently as we sat in silence. She was too close. I wanted to move away.

"I'm sorry I'm being a pain," I sputtered.

"You're not a pain."

"I'm glad you're here instead of Dr. Knight."

"Dr. Knight is an excellent surgeon," said Russell, moving back, her face showing her sincerity. "He has many years of burn treatment experience. Eric is in good hands."

"He makes me cry."

"He tries not to give families false hope, and sometimes that is perceived as being cruel. Believe me, he doesn't mean to be."

David appeared in the doorway with Lisa and motioned to Russell. "May I speak to you?" His tone was urgent in an I'm-not-being-urgent way.

Lisa sat beside me. Her voice was unfaltering as she spoke. "David and I were at the fire station. I don't think there's anything you don't already know. I got the feeling they were understaffed and without some of the equipment they were supposed to have. They probably should have practiced for something like this." She paused. "I guess they did the best they could."

Right now, I couldn't dwell on something that had already happened. It couldn't be undone. We'd learn the truth when the NTSB report came out.

"Eric might have to be on dialysis." That was what I needed to worry about right now.

"I know," said Lisa. "David told me. That's why he wants to talk to Russell. I'm going back to the house in another hour or so to get Dad. He and David are going to Bryan's service today." She patted me on the leg as she reached for a magazine.

A nurse stuck her head in the door. "Someone named Dr. Sanders is here. He says he's Eric's family doctor."

I followed the nurse down the hall. Dr. Sanders was the only doctor Eric had ever liked, and one of the few doctors he'd ever thought was competent. Sanders had Eric's chart in his hands as I told him about the dialysis and about what Eric had been going through.

"If anyone can pull through this, Eric can," Dr. Sanders said. He cut a distinguished figure: upper fifties, graying, handsome, dignified. "There isn't much I can do. Burn medicine is specialized, but I believe he's in excellent hands with Dr. Knight. However, my entire office is available, should you need anything."

"Thank you, Dr. Sanders. You know, Eric likes you. And he doesn't like many doctors."

Dr. Sanders grinned. "He told me. We had quite a conversation when he was in my office in January."

"That's when he caught pneumonia on a business trip to Paris. I was in Costa Rica. He told me he was pretty sick when I was gone."

"Why were you in Costa Rica?" he asked.

"I was studying tropical field biology. Eric was great about letting me go, but he had no desire to go to Costa Rica. I think he was afraid there'd be camping."

*   *   *

Eric hated camping. He despised it. He felt it had absolutely no redeeming qualities and involved sleeping on the ground, living without flush toilets and running water, and getting stung by nasty bugs. There were no electric outlets for shaving, and one got dirty. Camping was a miserable experience. His comments would have been funny except I adored camping.

Camping was one of the few happy experiences of my childhood. My mother didn't like animals, so it was the only time I was able to surround myself with them; reptiles particularly fascinated me. I was able to be alone and away from my parents, exploring and wandering, watching birds, chasing after small mammals, picking up amphibians, collecting rocks. I felt most alive in the woods. I even liked sleeping in tents. Occasionally with my Girl Scout troop, I slept without one, under the stars, surrounded by my animal friends.

Eric spent his summers on Cape Cod, in a modern cottage, eating at restaurants with loving parents and grandparents, and playing in the ocean with David and Lisa. He collected seashells and watched hermit crabs. He'd never slept in a tent. He didn't want to sleep in a tent. He certainly couldn't think about life's big questions in a tent.

Eric and I reached a camping impasse after three failed trips—all of them in a tent. The way I saw it, Eric wouldn't let me be happy out in the woods; the way he saw it, I was forcing him to do something I knew he hated. I refused to believe he didn't like it, so I kept trying. But as the years went by, I realized it was hopeless and decided to take the girls and go without him.

He appreciated that I enjoyed camping. He didn't understand it, but he was supportive. He was delighted that we'd come to a compromise about the whole thing, and he did agree the girls needed to be exposed to nature.

In March 1999, I took a geology class in Belize as part of my second master's degree. I love field study classes (sometimes they involve camping), and this seemed the perfect opportunity to earn three credits. Eric was mortified when I asked to go.

"Where are you staying? In a quality hotel, or are you (gasp) camping?"

When I returned from the trip, I stripped in the garage. "Sand fleas," I said, trying to sound casual as I ran up to the shower.

"WHAT?"

He was appalled, but it quickly turned into a joke. He took the catchy jingle about a dog having fleas and changed the words to "my wife has fleas."

The following year, I went to study in Costa Rica for over three weeks. This time it was a biology field study class, much more interesting than geology. Eric kissed me good-bye and yelled after me, "Go save the rainforest."

Upon my return, he met me at the door. "Leave all creepy crawly things outside."

"I didn't bring fleas this time, but there might be some army ants in my bag."

He started to protest before he realized I was joking. "All the same, leave your stuff outside."

He looked at all my photos and asked many questions about the plant and animal life. "Do you want to come with me sometime?" I asked.

"No thanks. There are no Hiltons in the rainforest."

People at Bombardier were well aware of how fussy Eric was about hotels, and it became quite a joke with the staff in charge of travel arrangements. Sometimes Eric would switch hotels not just once but several times while on a trip.

* * *

Dr. Sanders interrupted my thoughts. "He was in my office briefly a few weeks ago for a sinus infection. He said he'd had some nasty headaches."

I frowned. "He's had headaches for years."

"He never told me that."

Of course he hadn't, and I knew why. Eric was convinced, like many other pilots I'd known, that doctors would find any excuse to take away their flight medicals. Without a medical, you couldn't fly. Being grounded was every pilot's worst nightmare.

Eric spent a good part of his adult life in pain. I'm not sure when the headaches started, but as long as I can remember, Eric suffered from them. They were much worse after his three-year assignment in the F-15 at Camp New Amsterdam. I always suspected he'd pinched a nerve or compressed a vertebra from pulling all those Gs. I didn't have a shred of medical evidence to base that on, but it sounded reasonable. Eric adamantly refused to see a doctor for fear of losing his medical. I told him he was paranoid. I begged and pleaded, but he refused. He would not go to a doctor, and there was no reasoning with him.

He lived with the headaches. Sometimes they were excruciating, but he learned to carry on. After years of popping aspirin, which he bought in large quantities, he started to develop stomach pains. His solution? Pop antacids.

I pleaded. "Eric, why won't you go to the doctor? I know your headaches are bad, but you're going to ruin your stomach. Please go to the doctor."

"I'm not going to the doctor. Stop bugging me about it. You know they'll try to take my medical away."

I tried another approach. I begged him to keep a log of what he ate, what he drank, how he slept, and how much he exercised. I speculated there might be a pattern to the pain, but he didn't believe it. "It's a total waste, and I don't have time to keep a log. Besides, it's nothing I eat or drink."

He was unbelievably stubborn. I felt bad for him, but sometimes I lost my patience. Invariably a killer headache would occur as we were about to do something important to me. I knew he didn't do it on purpose, but…if only he would go to the doctor.

Besides using aspirin and ibuprofen, Eric had several methods for alleviating the pain. His favorite was to put a bag of frozen peas on his forehead. He said peas worked better than other vegetables. Whenever I tried to cook and serve peas for dinner, there would be protests from Tia and Robin. "We can't eat those. They're Daddy's headache peas."

Eric usually had a comment too. "Great…now you've cooked my headache peas."

He didn't have frozen peas at work, so he held a cold can of soda to his forehead. I don't believe he was trying to advertise his pain. Few people knew of his headaches, but the cold soda was going to help, so he was going to put it on his forehead. I doubt it ever occurred to him that people might wonder about it, but if it had, I'm sure he wouldn't have cared. It was one more thing that made Eric seem a bit quirky, a bit more memorable.

Several of the Bombardier visitors had mentioned their fond images of Eric walking the halls, making jokes, and socializing—all with a can of Coke held to his forehead.

What would he do now? When he came off the heavy-duty medicine, the pain was going to be excruciating. The headaches would be unbearable. He was going to lose his medical. He would never fly again.

Never.

Dr. Sanders told me he'd be back and questioned me about my eating and exercising. "It might do you good to get out for a run," he added as he left.

Right now, I didn't care at all about running, once the most important thing in my life aside from the family.

* * *

For people who don't run, watching a road race can be dull. Held early in the morning under all sorts of weather conditions, the activity starts out with the wait at the registration table to pick up the race packet. The observer is required to arrive early so the runner can scope out the competition, gab with old friends, check out the course, and do an inordinate amount of stretching. By the time the race starts, a few hours have usually elapsed. There's the cheering at the start line, then more waiting until the runner approaches the finish. In my favorite races, like the half-marathon and fifteen-mile, there's well over an hour and a half of waiting. Then, more waiting is required to find out official times and places and perhaps to pick up an award. Organizers don't cancel races due to weather, so I ran not only in the heat and cold but also in windstorms, rain, and even snow.

When Eric was in town, he came to all my races. He never once complained. He gave me last-minute advice, kissed me for good luck, and cheered loudly. If I won a trophy or ribbon, he would parade around with it as though he had won. When I ran my first and only marathon, in Rotterdam, he took the subway and appeared at various places on the route to cheer me.

We planned vacations around races and scheduled dinners around training runs. Conversations often centered on upcoming events, complete with lengthy and fascinating discussions about running shoes. I wonder how he suffered through it.

When Robin was two years old, I developed a hepatic thrombosed hemangioma—a benign liver tumor with a blood clot. At the height of my running career, a specialist told me I would never run again. I was devastated.

As time passed I began to run again, though slowly, but Eric made me promise I would never race again. It was a hard promise to make. He knew if I couldn't race, I wouldn't push myself in practice runs, and that meant my liver wouldn't bleed. He wrote his one and only poem for me during this difficult time in my life.

I am a Runner
By Eric Fiore for my little redheaded girl

Some drive fast cars or fly fast planes
Some read novels or watch movies
I run to feel the speed locked in my legs
I run to feel the power hidden in my body

Running is a sport to some
Running is a form of exercise to others
I achieve goals that once were beyond my reach
I overcome adversity with hard work

Running lets me escape from the daily hassles
Running lets me enjoy the simple things
I can hear the birds sing
I can see the cows graze

Running is my method of introspection
Running is my form of expression
Why does an artist paint
Why does a pianist play

Running gives me friends to share my interests
Running gives me solitude to be a friend to myself
Running has been good to me
I will not forsake it

I am a runner

* * *

How silly it all seemed now: the years of fussing about the running and feeling sorry for myself, as though some great tragedy had befallen me. Now something truly awful had happened, and the running was nothing in comparison.

David walked up to me, trailed by Knight, and said, "Dr. Knight needs to speak with you."

I might as well start crying now because anything out of Knight's mouth was sure to make me sob. I asked the important question, quickly, before I was unable to speak. "What about Eric's eyes?"

Emotionless, Knight said, "They've been covered, and we're putting ointment in them. There's nothing else we can do right now."

"But...but...what if..."

Knight looked at me impatiently. "They are what they are. The damage has been done."

There was a long, uncomfortable pause. David shifted from foot to foot.

Knight cleared his throat. "First of all, reporters are calling constantly about his injuries. There are rumors circulating. It might be best if you gave the press a statement."

"It's nobody's business about Eric's injuries. I want the hospital to say 'critical' or whatever word you use. Nothing else." I said it in a strong voice. Eric would be proud of me.

I had been convincing myself for six days that Eric would come home eventually. I knew he wouldn't want people to know about his injuries. He wouldn't want any deformities he might be left with to be the topic of conversation.

Knight shrugged and continued. "Secondly, in order for the lungs to recover, we are going to have to put him on a circle bed."

A round bed. OK. Fine. But why did Knight always refer to Eric as "him" or "the patient" instead of by his name?

Knight looked at me and said, "Because of the vertebra burst, there is a possibility the circle bed could make it worse. There's a chance it could reduce his ability to walk."

"What?" I felt myself gasping. I obviously did not understand what this bed-thing was. "Then you can't put him on it. I won't give you permission if it means he'll be paralyzed."

David exhaled loudly and stared up at the ceiling.

Knight spoke curtly and abruptly. "I'm not asking. I'm his doctor, and I will do what I have to in order to save his life. His lungs will not recover without the use of a circle bed."

"So you're going to do it anyway, even if I say no?" I barely managed to get the words out.

"That's right."

I began to cry.

David shook his head, clearly embarrassed by my behavior. I didn't care. I knew what Eric would say. "David…tell him…tell Dr. Knight he can't—"

"Carol," David interrupted. "He needs to be on the circle bed."

I ran into Eric's room. I stood by his bed for a long time. I was crying so hard I couldn't talk. Brenna and Jan, Eric's day nurses, tried to explain about the circle bed. It wasn't a round bed at all. It was exactly like other beds but held inside a big metal circle that turned the bed 360 degrees. Eric could be strapped in and turned upside down, facing the floor. It sounded uncomfortable, but I didn't understand how it could paralyze him. Still, if it could, then I didn't want Eric on it.

At exactly 11:50 a.m., a thirtysomething doctor walked into Eric's room. He was of average height and weight with russet-colored short hair parted on the side, ordinary and unremarkable looking. His name tag said Pierce. He held out his hand. His handshake was friendly, his mannerisms kind, and his smile sincere. I liked this Dr. Pierce.

"Are you the kidney guy?" I asked.

He chuckled warmly. "Is that what I am? The kidney guy?"

I forced a smile. "Yeah. And Russell is the Burn Lady."

"Are you going to tell me what you call Dr. Knight?"

I hesitated.

Grinning, Dr. Pierce said, "I won't tell him. I promise."

"Dr. Doom and Gloom." I said it quietly so no one would overhear.

"I don't think you're the first to call him that. You realize he's got a tough job, though."

"I know, I know. He's the best burn surgeon *ever.*" I was as sarcastic as I could be. Pierce smiled and gave me a look that said, "He is." We discussed dialysis and what it meant and how it did not mean Eric would be on it for the rest of his life. Pierce was watching all the vitals and lab results and felt it would be wise to consider dialysis, but not today. He even asked about Eric. He seemed to have lots of time to chat.

"What made him want to be a test pilot?" he asked.

"He's wanted to fly since he was a toddler. Being a test pilot was almost the top of the aviation heap for him."

"What was the top?"

"Being an astronaut," I answered sadly. "I think he would have been one if he'd had his master's degree."

"What's his undergraduate degree in?"

"He has a BS in aerospace engineering."

"Was he in the military?"

I nodded. "He was a fighter pilot during the Cold War. He was part of the prestigious Thirty-Second Tactical Fighter Squadron, the Camp New Amsterdam Wolfhounds. We lived in Holland for three years. Our oldest daughter, Tia, was born there."

"That must have been fun," replied Pierce.

"It was great, but the weather was awful."

"Lots of rain?"

I felt myself smile slightly. "There was this one day, back in 1985, when the sun was shining…"

*　*　*

The Netherlands is an exquisitely scenic country with absolutely the worst weather imaginable. Eric and I used to joke that there was only one season—a cold, rainy one. I can remember every sunny day in the three years we lived there. There weren't many, but when they occurred, it was a celebration. The Dutch closed shops, took off work, and went to the beach. The North Sea coast was usually chilly, even on the few rain-free days, but there were a few lakes worthy of picnics and family outings. We were fortunate to live less than three miles from one of the prettiest, Lake Woudenberg. Eric heard about this lake shortly after he started flying at the base. It was a famous flyover area.

"I've flown over Lake Woudenberg. It's great. I can't wait till summer." Eric was grinning from ear to ear. I looked at him with curiosity. Something else was up. He was way too excited about a lake.

"Do people wear their bathing suits and swim in the lake?" I asked.

"Sort of."

"What do you mean 'sort of'?"

"Well," he said sheepishly, "bathing suits are optional."

I looked at him with amusement. We lived in a conservative, ultra-religious Dutch town. "You're kidding. We live by a nude beach?"

"The guys tell me most of the beaches in Holland are topless. It ought to be fun flying over the beach this summer." He was grinning again.

I looked at him and casually tossed out a remark. "I can't wait to go. Maybe I'll go topless too."

"What?"

"If the Dutch can do it, I can too." I pretended to examine my nails.

"No you're not. I mean, what if someone sees you?"

I looked at him. "Why? Would you be embarrassed of me?"

"Of course not. I mean you look great, and...I don't think it would be appropriate...I mean, my commander..."

I enjoyed his squirming. He hadn't expected my response. All of a sudden, his face lit up with triumph. "Fine. What if one of your students sees you? Huh?"

I had started teaching at the University of Maryland's European campus on the base. I took the job seriously. We both started to laugh. He knew I was too modest to do it.

On the first sunny day of the summer, we packed up the towels and beach blanket and headed for Lake Woudenberg. The traffic jam was expected, and the beach was crowded and full of families. Most of the women were topless: grandmas, young girls, teenagers, and moms. Some of the sights were not pretty, and Eric made a face as we passed one family. "Some things should definitely remain covered."

There were the attractive sights as well, and Eric was doing his best to act casual. I poked him in the side and whispered in his ear, "Get your tongue out of the sand."

"What? I wasn't…I was only…"

"Sure you were. Keep it up, and my top comes right off."

Eric pretended to look off in the distance. "Isn't that one of your students over there?"

We had a perfectly glorious day. We lounged around talking and laughing, and when Eric got bored, he stood up, brushed the sand off, and casually remarked, "I think I'll get frites."

"You hate French fries."

"I feel like some today," he said, unconvincingly.

I anticipated what would happen when he took off on his search for frites. I looked at my watch. The countdown had started. Over half an hour later he returned, empty-handed, and said, "Couldn't find the frites."

"That's because they're right there." I pointed to the wagon.

"Was that there when I left?"

"Eric, please. I'm not falling for that one. Now you have to buy me frites."

"Do you really want them? They're so greasy," he whined.

I gave him a hard stare. He went to stand in the long line. It wasn't actually a line, but a cluster of shoving people. The Dutch don't queue for anything and generally push and shove. It was always a mystery to me how such charming people could resort to pushing once they got in lines. Eric and I supposed the whole queue thing was something only the Brits and Americans did. We were no match for the pushing Dutch, who towered over us.

Then I remembered I'd forgotten to remind Eric to get me "frites met," which meant with frites sauce—a condiment resembling mayonnaise. Eric detested frites sauce, but I'd taken an instant liking to it, preferring it to catsup. I yelled over to Eric.

He turned around quickly to answer me, and his face slammed into the large, naked breasts of a six-foot-tall, twentysomething, attractive Dutch gal. He tried to move away, but the pushing mass of people forced him in closer. She looked down at him, hands on her hips, but didn't appear to think it was anything unusual. When he was able to extricate himself, he looked over at me. The grin on his slightly flushed face was mischievous. "Whoops," he giggled.

It was one of the funniest things I'd ever seen. All thoughts of frites vanished. By midmorning Monday, the entire squadron had heard the story, and by midweek, the entire base knew. One of Eric's fellow pilots accurately expressed the feelings of most of the guys. "Damn that Fiore. Why does he always get the luck?"

* * *

David informed me that we had to leave the conference room.

"But why?" I asked.

"They do have a waiting room. It is a conference room, and there are other patients."

That meant I would have to go out, past the steel doors to a world beyond Eric and the nurses I had come to like. I hadn't been out of the steel doors, not once in seven days, and I didn't want to go. I walked slowly back to the conference room. I suspected I'd lose my sleeping room next.

The family was packing up the food, flowers, and cards. Tia was attempting to remove a banner given to her by classmates. When she saw me, she said, "Hey, Mommy, the security guy in front of our house is sort of hot."

Dad spoke up. "One of the visitors told me he ate lunch with Eric the day of the accident. He said Eric was complaining about the sauce." His voice dropped to almost a whisper. "An hour later he saw the smoke."

Silence.

Before long, everything was packed, and Lisa left with her parents and the kids. The remaining visitors went out to the main waiting room, but I wasn't ready to go out there yet.

As I was sitting outside Eric's door writing in my journal, I sensed someone standing near me.

Knight.

"I need to speak with you for a moment," he said gruffly.

I felt my insides contract painfully. I looked up and down the hall. No David. Then I remembered he was in the room helping with the bandage change. I was going to be alone with Dr. Doom and Gloom.

"I don't want to hear what you're going to say." Did those words come out of my mouth? I almost put my hands over my ears.

Knight grunted and folded his arms across his chest. "You're his wife. You have to sign the consent slips. It's the law. So that means you have to listen to what I have to say."

I might as well start crying now.

"You will have to sign a consent slip for several procedures we're doing tomorrow. I believe you already know about the tracheotomy. Dr. Russell spoke with your sister earlier. The vent is only used temporarily."

I nodded. Yes, I understood about the trach thing. Patty had explained it. She said they had to do it. They would cut a hole in his neck. I had seen people before with trach scars.

"Dr. Pierce will let you know if you have to sign a consent for dialysis. He said he spoke with you this morning and you understand the situation."

I nodded again.

"And we'll need a consent for tomorrow's surgery. We'll be doing a debridement of the face, neck, and upper shoulders. It's likely he will lose his left ear and some or all of his nose."

He paused and looked at me as I wiped at my wet face. I knew about the ear. There was nothing left to save. I'd seen it the first day. I knew, even if I didn't want to admit it, but I would try to be hopeful about his Roman nose. Eric had a lot of nose there. From the way Knight was staring at me, I knew there was something else.

"And Dr. Evans will be coming in during the surgery to look at the eyes."

My journal fell to the floor. "Thank you, Dr. Knight. Thank you so much."

Knight's expression seemed to soften. "Do you have any questions?"

"No. Thank you, thank you…"

Day 8
Tuesday, October 17, 2000

"I can't wait to see Greece. Let's buy more books on Sparta."
- Eric

Eric remained paralyzed on a drug called Norcuron, a neuromuscular blocking agent that prevented patients from fighting the vent. I knew there would be no movement of his arms or legs, no nodding of his head, no sign he knew I was there, but I still spoke to him as though he could comprehend everything happening around him. I ached for a sign, any sign, that he could hear me.

My days of living on coffee, hardly any food, and little sleep were catching up with me. I felt weak and shaky, not at all my normal high-energy self. It was more than being tired, more than being sad and scared. I was losing myself. I looked in the mirror, and the face staring back was not mine. As my footsteps reverberated through the halls, I wondered: whose are they?

People's voices were beginning to sound odd, their faces blurry, their words unintelligible. I wondered if this was what it felt like to slide into a breakdown.

I sat with Eric for a while and then grabbed some paper and a pen from the nurse's station and began to write the article for the newspaper, as I'd promised Tim. The one I'd written to the company had been personal. This one needed to be more about what it meant to be a test pilot and the responsibility it carried, not only for the pilot but also for the pilot's family. It was my chance to show the world, or at least Wichita, who Eric was.

I looked at my watch. I had never written such an important paper at 5:30 a.m. on nothing but a week's worth of coffee. Without a thesaurus, a dictionary, or my computer, I wrote the best piece I could. I read it to Eric when I finished, and somehow I knew he could hear me. I tucked the folded papers into the pocket of my jeans as the shift change started.

Dr. Russell squatted down beside me. "Things are about the same. Are you going to be able to handle the news about Eric's eyes today?"

"I want him to see the Parthenon."

Russell looked at me sadly. "Were you going to Greece?"

"Yes. And Eric loves to read. He needs his eyes."

Eric was always reading. He loved bookstores, and it was the first thing he searched for in every new town we lived in. If the bookstore had a café that served cappuccino, he was delighted.

He was interested in all kinds of books: art, history, fixing cars, astronomy, bicycling, car racing, and of course aviation. He particularly liked guides on how to succeed in business, the workplace, and life. He was talented at teaching himself all sorts of things, and he often said there was nothing he couldn't learn to do if he had the right book: prepare taxes, mend plumbing, install ceiling fans, repair a car. I used to joke with him that I was going to hire him out in a rent-a-handy-husband program. He beamed when I repeated this to others.

Eric usually had his head in a book from 8:00 p.m. onward, and I would invariably bother him. I tried to get my homework done during the day, so I wanted to talk when he wanted to read. He was normally patient with my incessant chattering, but occasionally he'd get cranky: "Can't you see I'm reading?" "I can't finish if you keep interrupting." "What is it now?" Occasionally he would close his book roughly.

His latest reading passion had been Greek history, treatises on Sparta, accountings of Greek battles, and long descriptions of Greek armor and military leaders. I was sure his book on Sparta was still sitting on his bed stand. We had paid for the airfare to Athens a few weeks ago. Eric couldn't wait to go to Sparta, and I had been eagerly reading about Greece myself. We took our traveling seriously.

There would be no Greece trip now, and I didn't know whether Eric would ever be able to read again.

What would the eye doctor say today? What if Eric were blind? I wanted him to look up at the Parthenon, gaze around the Agora, marvel at the pass of Thermopylae, and see the Spartan battlefields.

The left eye didn't look viable. But what about the right eye? What if Eric thought David and I hadn't done enough? Would he hate us? Was there something else I should be doing?

While I waited for the surgery, Jennifer, the social worker, came by and asked me to talk with her. It was my morning psychoanalysis, and I was only doing it to make David happy.

Jennifer told me burns were the worst; people needed lots of therapy to deal with their disfigurements; the family needed lots of counseling. I sat in her office for almost an hour. I didn't want to talk about the burns. I didn't want to talk about how I would deal with them. I wanted to tell her how wonderful Eric was. I told story after story about him, all good, though Eric had been difficult to live with at times. He'd done some things that weren't nice, and I'd done some things I wasn't proud of. We'd had problems, but I loved him. I didn't realize until the last few days how much.

I knew Eric loved me. Why else would he be fighting so hard? I wouldn't tell Jennifer the bad things; I wouldn't tell anyone. Eric was a hero, and I didn't want anything even remotely unflattering said about him.

Still, some people knew we'd been having trouble lately: his parents, Patty, a few friends at work. This past summer had not been a good one for us. The four years of intensity I'd put into school had ended in May when I got my second graduate degree. Eric was too busy to come to my graduation. I had so many degrees he didn't see it as a big deal. I went to the registrar's office and picked up the diploma I'd worked hard for. Eric wasn't going, so I wouldn't bother to go either.

I was shocked that employers weren't scrambling to hire me. It seemed ecologists were in great supply and the jobs were not. I was stuck in Wichita because of Eric's job.

For twenty years, I had followed Eric. I wanted a career. I wanted to be the important one, but I could never earn as much money as Eric, and I knew his job would always come first. Since he'd started with Bombardier, I felt I couldn't count on him to watch the kids or fix anything around the house because he was gone so much; often he had no definite idea when he'd be back. If the kids were sick, I had to deal with it. If the kids needed something, I had to get it.

I wanted to be as respected as Eric, as smart as Eric. He was an important test pilot; I wanted to be an important ecologist. For once, I wanted to be first instead of him.

Often he would come home from a trip and criticize how I had handled things while he was gone. The constant yelling was hard to take. He said it was his personality; he wasn't yelling at me, he'd say, he was venting. He told me I took it too personally. Eric was the classic type A personality, and he liked things done the way he wanted. I told him he was controlling; he insisted he was not.

He felt I didn't appreciate him. He said he always listened to me talk about school, but I didn't pay enough attention to him. He said he loved me and I needed to solve my issues. I told him he had to stop yelling and telling me what to do. I threatened to live with my sister in Colorado. He quietly took my name off the savings account.

At the end of July, when he returned from Argentina, he was a different person. Things were much better. He called the bank and put my name back on the account, and he tried hard not to yell. I told him I was sorry for threatening to leave. He even scheduled an appointment with a marriage counselor for this week, but I couldn't cancel the appointment because I didn't know who the counselor was.

I wanted to tell the social worker about the appointment, but I couldn't. It might seem Eric and I didn't love each other. Patty said because we were willing to work it out, that showed we loved each other. "Lots of people go to marriage counselors," she said. "That's a good thing, not a bad thing."

The guilt was crushing me.

At 11:00 a.m. precisely, the surgical team arrived. Knight nodded at me as he and Russell gave orders. It was a repeat of the last time. As before, I got a horrible feeling I would never see Eric again. I shouldn't have watched all those doctor television shows when I was growing up. People went in to surgery and they…I couldn't think the word.

"Where's the eye doctor?"

Russell pointed. "Dr. Evans is right there, talking with David."

I barely got a glimpse of Evans as the whole team bustled down the hallway. I tried to follow again, but David grabbed my arm and practically dragged me to the waiting room. Mom, Dad, Sandy, and Lisa were already waiting.

Tia and Robin weren't there. Mom told me she thought it best if they didn't come to the hospital because they were going back to school tomorrow.

"The little loves need a normal day," Sandy added. "They're playing with their school chums." She told me the friends' names. I'd known their mother for years, and the girls enjoyed playing at her house.

I told Dad I'd written the article for the paper, and he asked if he could proofread it. I hesitated before pulling the crumpled papers from my pocket and handing them to him.

He sat down and began to read. A pen soon emerged from his pocket. David whispered to me that it would be good for Dad to proofread my piece; it would make him feel useful and give him something to do. Besides, David insisted, who better to edit an article than a retired English teacher? I agreed, but with some trepidation. Dad had looked at some stories I'd written in the past. I was no Hemingway, and he'd let me know it.

"Carol?"

I looked up to see Linda standing in the doorway. Soon she had her arms wrapped around me. We didn't speak, just hugged. Linda took her glasses off and wiped at her eyes—one an aquamarine blue, the other a Caribbean blue-green. She joked about her eyes, but it wasn't the most remarkable thing about my fellow graduate student.

Linda was brainy. She'd been my lab partner in our environmental science core classes, and her laboratory skills were superb. Mine were sad. Linda had saved my ass more than once, and her knowledge and understanding of chemistry approached Eric's. I excelled in my classes partially due to her help.

About six years younger than I, several inches shorter, curly brunette hair, big glasses, Linda had an easy smile. But not today.

She sat down on the couch next to me as RB walked in. He'd flown back to Wichita from Atlanta. Again. He quietly took a chair in the corner.

I introduced Linda to everyone. She was one of only three girlfriends I had. The other two were mothers with children who were friends with Tia and Robin, so our relationships often revolved around the kids and their activities. They had been calling, as had Linda, even sending food to the house and the hospital. Patty had been speaking with the three of them and then giving me messages. After my sister left, the nurses relayed the messages.

My relationship with Linda wasn't about the kids. It was about science and the environment and wildlife. I could be geeky and academic with her, even laughing over biology jokes that would cause anyone else to think we were odd. Linda and her husband had been to our house for dinner recently, and for the first time, Eric took a liking to the husband of one of my friends. I was thrilled at the thought of having some couples nights out, the four of us having drinks, dinner, and great conversation.

"Carol," Linda said softly, "I hope it's OK. I set up a website so people can send stories about Eric."

Linda knew me well. Of course I wanted stories about Eric—lots of them. "Thank you, Linda. How did you know?"

She didn't say a word as she stared at me with tear-filled eyes.

At about 2:30 p.m., Dr. Russell came into the waiting room. Knight wasn't with her, and neither was the eye doctor. "Eric came through the surgery with no complications. He'll be back in his room shortly."

I stood up. "Where's the eye doctor? What about Eric's eyes?"

Russell looked confused. "Didn't he come in to speak with you?"

The Fiore side of the waiting room spoke in unison. "No."

Russell quickly left, with David behind her. Mom was fuming as she repeated several times, "What's going on?"

Ten minutes later, Russell and David were back. David was noticeably angry as Russell addressed us. "Dr. Evans had to leave. He had another appointment."

Mom was furious and let everyone know it. "That is inexcusable. He knows we are all here waiting. He knows how important this is to my daughter-in-law, to all of us."

Dr. Russell mumbled some apologies and told us what she knew. "Both corneas are badly burned, but he didn't say Eric can't see. I will have him speak with you tomorrow." She squatted down beside me. "I'm sorry I don't have more information for you about the eyes. But, about the surgery we performed…"

She paused. The room was absolutely still. "We did do the tracheotomy. There were no problems. As far as the debridement…we used about two square feet of cadaver skin. The right side was less burned than the left, as I think you know. As I told you, with severe burns, the dead skin has to be removed, or you open up to all sorts of serious infections. We were unable to save the left ear. We were likewise unable to save Eric's nose."

There was stunned silence in the room. RB dropped his metal notebook with a resulting loud crack. Lisa spoke first. "His whole nose?"

"I'm afraid so," said Dr. Russell.

I buried my head in my hands. My chest began to hurt from the sobs. I couldn't stop. Eric without his Roman nose?

Russell stood up. "I'm so sorry. There are amazing advances in reconstructive surgery. I'll ask Jennifer to give you one of the books we have."

Dad continued to work on my article. I looked at the book the social worker brought by, and everyone tried to console me that it would be all right. Eric would get a new ear and a new nose. Lisa even tried to make a joke. "Let's make him pick one that isn't quite as big as the other one."

Before leaving, Linda made me promise to do my knee exercises; Patty had apparently tattled on me. Stupid roller blades. I always fell, and a couple weeks ago when Eric was in Amsterdam, I'd wiped out and had to go to the doctor. I didn't have time for physical therapy while Eric was suffering. What was a banged-up knee compared to that? Patty didn't argue. She consulted with someone and then showed me how to do some exercises before she left.

RB came over and sat beside me. "Do you need me to get those airline tickets refunded for you, Carol? Weren't you and Eric going to England?" He was obviously trying to distract me, his slight drawl peeking through. Patty had taken a particular liking to him and seemed surprised that such a polite Southern gentleman could be Eric's best friend. "He's so quiet," she'd remarked. "And Eric is so loud."

They shared a mutual love of airplanes. They'd been flight instructors together, and they'd both flown the F-15. Leaving the Air Force at almost the same time, they still managed to see each other even though Eric became a test pilot and RB became an airline pilot.

"I think it's too late to get the money, but you could try," I answered RB. "Anyway, we were going to Greece. We've been to England many times."

RB left to catch a return flight to Atlanta. Everyone else slowly started to leave. As Dad headed for the door, he handed me the article. "I made a few changes."

When Russell allowed me to see Eric, I could tell from the shape of the bandages that his nose was gone. I stood over him and I cried—for his lost ear, for his nose, for his eyes we had no answer about; for all he had lost.

I had visitors, so once again I trudged back out to the waiting room. Three official-looking people introduced themselves, all from Bombardier. They seemed to think I would be worried about financial things and assured me they would take care of everything. Truthfully, I didn't care. Nothing mattered but Eric. Nothing.

Candice showed up in all her perky glory before I could escape back to Eric's room. She knew about the surgery, as did almost everyone at Bombardier. I was not going to tell her Eric lost his ear and nose, so I mumbled something about removing dead tissue.

"Things could be worse, Carol," she exclaimed.

How many more times was she going to say that? I clenched my teeth so hard my jaw began to ache.

"We're having a wives meeting tonight, and we'd love it if you could come."

Was she serious?

"Most of us are upset about the way this whole thing has been handled. I mean, nobody called us, and we couldn't reach our husbands. We were left completely in the dark."

I wondered if anyone would notice if I slapped her.

"But of course we'll understand if you can't come. I was wondering if you'd like to send a message."

I thought of a message I'd like to give her right now. Instead, I said, "Please thank everyone for all the flowers and food."

She jabbered away, and when I couldn't take any more, I told her I was going to see Eric.

"Good-bye, Carol," she said loudly. "You take care of yourself. We'll be praying for you, and I'll keep those meals coming. You call if there's anything you need. Anything at all."

I knew she was trying to be kind, so why did she irritate me so much? I barely knew her, so why was she here all the time, doing all this work, trying to be in the center of things? Mom told me earlier that Candice had been calling the house several times a day. Mom found her grating too; she'd stopped answering the phone when the caller ID displayed Candice's number.

One of the nurses handed me a newsletter from the Phoenix Society, an organization for burn survivors and their families. I thumbed through it. There were conventions, workshops, and support numbers. I became more excited as I read, determined to take Eric to a convention. I knew he would be an inspiration to others, and I told Tim that when he showed up a short time later.

"I agree, Carol. Eric is a wonderful speaker. I think it's a great idea."

I gave Tim the crumbled paper with the article I'd written. "Eric's dad edited it."

"Thank you for doing that. I'll have our secretary type it up, and we'll send it to the newspaper." He paused. "You're making us all proud."

I forced a smile. I didn't care about the company being proud; I wanted Eric to be proud. I knew how he'd always tried to impress Tim because his was one of the few opinions that mattered.

Dr. Knight asked whether I had questions about the day's surgery. I mumbled that I would have liked to speak with the eye doctor. Knight seemed to share in my frustration, shifting from foot to foot and shuffling the papers in his hands as he said, "If this were the 1800s, he'd be blind, but nowadays he can get cornea replacement surgery. He won't see as well as before, though."

Was that concern I saw in his face? He didn't say Eric would be blind either. He said "won't see as well as before." He still didn't call Eric by his name, but perhaps this was a start.

Dr. Pierce, the kidney doctor, showed up and spoke briefly to Knight. I followed Pierce into Eric's room.

"Did you sign the authorization for dialysis?" he asked me.

"Yes."

"Hang in there. From the stories you've told me, I think your husband is a fighter." He frowned. "But this Major Tom stuff is pretty serious."

He read the sign over Eric's bed, the one the nurses had written. "So Eric is of Italian descent. I thought the name sounded Italian. Fiore means flower, doesn't it?"

I nodded. "I love my last name."

"Did Eric ever go to Italy?" Pierce asked.

"Yes. He loved it there. He called the Italians 'his people.'"

*　*　*

The first time Eric was able to take leave from his F-15 at Camp New Amsterdam in Soesterberg, the Netherlands, we planned a trip to Italy. The long, winding drive took us from Holland through Belgium, France, Germany, Switzerland, and down into Italy. That was where Eric started to get in trouble—with me. Those Italian genes must have come out because he started to scream along with the natives, even more than usual. Everything became a major crisis.

Traffic jams in Germany and Holland were civilized affairs as people sat quietly in their cars and waited it out. Once, we'd seen people spread out a picnic lunch in the midst of a severe traffic snarl. Not in Italy. A traffic jam outside Florence prompted several dozen Italians to get out of their vehicles, screaming, hands in the air, and fists pounding on the hoods.

Eric flew out of our car into the warm, noisy air and started screaming along with them. His fists pounded madly on the hood of my rusty old BMW. After about three or four minutes, he calmly got back in the car and looked at me, a grin widening on his face. Triumphantly he announced, "Now that's the way to deal with a traffic jam." I couldn't help but laugh. He'd found his beloved ancestors.

"I can finally look people in the eyes," he added. "I was getting a kink in my neck from always looking up at the Dutch."

Later Eric would remark that traffic lights were just pretty colors to the Italians. It was one of many observations about "his people." He thought Italians had their priorities straight: family and good food. He loved what he perceived to be a certain craziness about them, how they argued and said exactly what they thought. They were opinionated and loud, like him, and often they didn't follow the rules, such as the time we'd taken the train down to Rome. Despite signs that read "Don't hang out the window," every Italian on the train was doing precisely that, and screaming while doing it. Eric felt he had to do it too, all the while laughing and saying how much he loved his people.

Eric frequently said when he retired, he was going to move to Italy, buy a villa, and grow grapes. I could never visualize him doing that, and I told him we could never retire there because we'd kill each other with all the screaming. He used to tell me I needed to eat more—the Italians would be mortified at how skinny I was. I would tell him he was crazy, and he would laugh and say when we moved to Italy, he would get a whole lot crazier.

The parents of Eric's father were both from a town called Controne, outside Naples. Eric was extremely proud of his Italian heritage. He talked about going there to trace his ancestors, and he used to imagine a huge homecoming party for the triumphant fighter pilot. They would be immensely impressed with his jet, the F-15. Italians, he said, loved machines, building the best bicycles and cars. After all, wasn't da Vinci an Italian?

Everywhere we went in Italy, people spoke to him in Italian, perhaps because he looked so much like them. When he'd tell them he was from New York, they'd invariably ask, quite seriously, if he knew a certain Vinnie or Angelo.

* * *

Dr. Pierce told me to call if I had a question. Then Knight was back with Russell and the bronch equipment. Twenty minutes later, he said the lungs were worse, lots of mucus, and they were putting him on the circle bed tomorrow. I started to argue with Knight, but he held his hand up in a stop gesture and said, "Your husband could die if we don't use the circle bed."

The surgery, the eyes, the dialysis, the circle bed…

A few minutes later when Patty called, I was out of control. The nurses were staring as I sobbed uncontrollably, blubbering to Patty about how I hated the circle bed, about the eyes, everything.

She tried to cheer me up, but it didn't work.

I ran back to my room in the pediatric ward and threw myself on the bed. Clutching the hugging monkeys, I cried for my once-happy life, now over.

I was not being strong.

What a failure I was.

There was a knock on the door. Eric's immediate supervisor, Alec, was in the waiting room. Wiping my eyes, I went out to see him; this would be the last visitor. I'd had enough.

Alec and I talked. "Eric has a great sense of humor," he said. "That's one of the things people love about him. I could always tell when he was coming down the hall. He has a hop, skip, and a jump to his walk. It's a happy, cheerful walk."

It was true, about the happy fast walk and the sense of humor. Eric's was truly wicked. Like Mark Twain, he liked to challenge taboo topics and get people to think. He loved to play the devil's advocate. He would argue, loudly, with such passion that it was quite a surprise to discover he didn't believe what he was saying. He had friends who were loyal to the point of worshipping him. Eric was like an exotic dish—you either loved him or you hated him.

The list of Eric-haters was not long, but it included a former superior officer in the Air Force, a Parks College English professor, and the odd coworker or classmate. They claimed he was overbearing, pushy, loud, and self-centered; a know-it-all. A few saw Eric as a threat, perhaps because he challenged basic beliefs. His genius was intimidating to some, and others found his personality abrasive. A bitter Air Force supervisor had told Eric he wouldn't become a test pilot and was furious when Eric laughed in his face.

Eric filed his papers to get out of the Air Force after serving slightly less than ten years because the possibility of attending the US Air Force Test Pilot School looked remote due to the politics. In addition to applying to the airlines, he sent off a resume for a civilian test pilot job to Fairchild Aircraft in San Antonio.

After an interview and several correspondences, the letter of a job offer as a test pilot came in the mail. Eric yelped for joy, twirled me around, and paraded around with the letter held high above his head. His whole being celebrated. He was going to be a test pilot, just as he said he would when he was a young boy. It was as though everything in his life had led him to this point.

He continued to ride the wave of success for several days, and it was wonderful to see him so happy. Then one afternoon he yelled, "Hey, Carol, come here for a minute."

I walked down the hall toward his voice. He sounded silly and full of himself. He was down on all fours, laughing, and pushing something white along the hardwood parquet floor with his nose.

"What are you doing?" I asked.

"Don't you know?" he giggled.

I hesitated. "Being silly?"

"I'm pushing the envelope. I'm gonna be a test pilot!"

Day 9
Wednesday, October 18, 2000

*"I've flown over two hundred
different types of aircraft, but the F-15
is the lady who stole my heart."*
– Eric

The man writhed in agony, the screams becoming shrieks. Someone had tied him to a rock, and a terrible dragon-like creature was lunging at him, burning his flesh with its fiery breath, ripping at his face with dagger-like claws. The man could not escape, but despite his cries, there was something courageous about him. I hid behind a rock and watched. What a coward I was. I was afraid of the dragon-thing, afraid of the fire. After the horrifying creature left, I inched closer.

I smelled the burned flesh, and as I looked, a strange thing happened. The man's torn and blackened fingers seemed to be growing back, his face became more recognizable, and the bloody eyes seemed to heal. How could this be happening?

The dragon-thing was back, racing toward the bound man. He screeched as the creature rammed a claw into his left eye. I cried out in horror, and the man turned toward me. I gasped. "Eric!"

The dragon-thing looked at me with eyes that sent fear through my body. The face was Dr. Knight's.

I woke, sweat pouring down my face. I jumped out of bed and stood, breathing heavily, in the stark white room. A dream, I told myself, a stupid dream, nothing more.

A short time later, I was on the phone telling Patty about it.

"Makes sense to me," she said. "Sounds like the Prometheus story. You and Eric were going to Greece, and you told me you've been reading a lot of mythology. I think it's obvious to anyone why your subconscious made the bad guy out to be Knight, but you know he's a good surgeon."

"I know."

"I think the original story had a bird, like an eagle or something. I think it's interesting that even in your dreams, you couldn't make a bird into something evil."

"I love birds." As soon as the words fell from my mouth, I felt a longing to see the animals I adored.

"I know you do," Patty continued. "I think those birds at your zoo are lucky to have you taking care of them."

Those exquisite birds. Until now, I hadn't thought about them once in eight days. I missed them. Of all the many wonderful and fascinating creatures on the planet, I am most enamored of birds.

Eric was always a bit confused about my love of birds, so I tried to explain it to him. "As a group they've accomplished the most remarkable feats. A hummingbird weighing no more than a nickel can fly all the way across the Gulf of Mexico on its migration, and the arctic tern migrates from one pole to the other. Birds have been known to use tools, and the corvid family, which includes the crows and jays, is incredibly bright and..."

Grinning, Eric held up his hand in an attempt to interrupt my ramblings. "I think you like them because they fly. Maybe that's why you like me."

"Oh," I said, attempting to be cute, "I like you for other reasons too. But I have to admit, I liked you first because you were a pilot."

I would go on and on about birds, and Eric listened to everything I said.

Tia was always jealous that her sister had the same name as a bird. "I want to be named after a bird too," she'd shouted at us years ago. Eric came up with the name Tia-wee, a spin on the name of a bird called an eastern wood-pewee, and he used it as his special pet name for her.

I hung up the phone and sat at the nurse's station. I missed hearing Eric's voice and the way he teased me about my love of birds and my job at the zoo. I had worked hard for almost five years to get the job I now held as a zoo education specialist. It had meant going back to school, and that meant taking chemistry—I couldn't graduate without it.

Chemistry had always scared me. I'd developed a deep lack of self-confidence in high school. I'd entered chemistry class as a freshman at Parks Air College with trepidation and that all-too-familiar pain in my gut. I couldn't do it. I'd convinced myself I was too stupid to learn the subject.

I muddled through the lab. It was difficult, and I had never learned proper laboratory techniques, but I was doing well in the classroom part of the course. This was my chemistry situation, about halfway through the first semester of my freshman year in 1977, when I started dating Eric. It didn't take him long to realize I was having trouble.

What started out as help from Eric turned into me gazing dreamily at him as he wrote my lab reports. I was enamored of his brilliance.

"It's easy," he casually remarked. "It doesn't take a rocket scientist. I did this stuff when I was in grade school."

I was too busy being impressed to feel inferior. That came years later when I actively started to compete with him. Knowing I would never be as smart as he was, I consoled myself that I had other abilities. At times, it was tough because I knew I would never approach his genius. He never tried to make me feel dumb; I just did.

Almost eighteen years later, I went back to school to get my second master's degree. To my dismay, I realized I had to take graduate-level organic chemistry. I thought that old chemistry fear was gone, but I was seriously mistaken. After two weeks of class, Eric came home to find me with my head buried in my hands and crying, "I can't do it."

"Yes, you can," he calmly told me. "I'll help you, like at Parks. You did it then, and you can do it now. We're Parks graduates. That means we can do anything."

Sometimes he yelled, sometimes he threw his hands up in exasperation, but he never quit helping me. He never stopped insisting I could learn it. I wanted to prove something to myself, to him, and to the instructor who had told me at the beginning of the semester, "It's my experience that students like you don't do well in my class."

I lived, ate, and breathed chemistry for the entire semester. At the end of it, not only did I get an A, I had the highest average in the class. The professor was speechless. Ha! Take that, I wanted to tell him. Had I slain the chemistry demon at last?

The next year I applied to be a graduate teaching assistant in the biology department. The chemistry department offered me a position instead. I planned to tell them no. How could I teach chemistry? It was absurd.

I told Eric about it that evening. I'd make a great chemistry instructor, he repeated. He promised to take time off from work to help me with the labs. He made me believe I could do it.

After much deliberation, I accepted the position. After a few weeks of teaching, I found I could do it without Eric's help. At the end of my two-year stint in May 2000, as I was ready to graduate, I realized I'd conquered my phobia. I even liked chemistry.

Eric had helped me beat my chemistry fear, and now it was my turn to help him. What he faced was harder than anything I'd ever done. No matter what it took, I would not fail him.

I would do better today, I promised myself. I would be stronger. I would make Eric proud of me, and I wouldn't melt into tears every time Knight looked at me.

Walking into Eric's room, I immediately put my hand over my nose and mouth. The smell was awful, reminding me of decaying fruit and veggies in the bottom drawer of the refrigerator. A dark-haired nurse, writing on her clipboard, seemed not to notice the smell. Eric's arm and face bandages were wet, with ugly brown stains. The fist splints held dirty blotches.

I felt my face flushing with anger as I tried to remain calm. "Don't you think the bandages should be changed?"

The nurse looked up from her clipboard. I detected impatience as she quickly clicked her pen. "I believe there's some drainage due to yesterday's surgery. I'll tell the day nurses as soon as they arrive." The pen clicked again before she went back to her clipboard.

I spoke to Eric in the strongest voice I'd used in a week. "You're not giving up, Eric. I won't let you. We're a team. Remember when I was pregnant with Robin? You didn't let me give up, and I won't let you give up either."

* * *

"Get out of bed. We'll try again later." Eric exhaled loudly.

I was furious. "So what are you saying, Eric? Are you saying I can't do it? Are you saying I'm not tough enough?"

"I'm saying it's too much for you."

"Oh, really," I shouted. "You'll see. I'll show you. I can do it. And you know what? I'm going to do it."

How dare that man say I wasn't strong enough? I could do it. I'd stayed in bed for three weeks already, and I could damn well stay in bed for another six months. I'd show him. I crossed my arms in front of my chest and refused to look at him.

Eric didn't say a word as he sat down on the bed. When he spoke, he was almost whispering. "You know I love you, Carol. I wouldn't want to do this, so I couldn't ask you to do it."

Two-year-old Tia skipped into the room. "Mommy. Read me," she squealed, climbing up on the bed next to me.

I put my arm around her and said, "What book do you want me to read to you, pumpkin?"

Eric lifted Tia up off the bed and gave her a big kiss. "How's my silly girl today? How about if Tia and Daddy go in the kitchen and make Mommy some breakfast? And then I'll read my sweet Tia a book."

"Daddy, yes," came the tiny voice.

They both scampered out the bedroom door. I knew Eric loved me and wanted the best for me, but I hadn't anticipated this whole pregnancy thing. We wanted this baby, but the thought of staying in bed for the rest of the pregnancy, quitting my teaching job, not being able to run, and having my mother live with us wasn't what I'd planned. I was barely three months pregnant when I started bleeding and cramping. I called my doctor, a fellow runner, and explained the situation.

"It'll be fine. Don't run for a few days," he said in a confident voice.

I didn't, but it got worse. By the time Eric took me to Sheppard Air Force Base's regional hospital, the medical people told me I was having a miscarriage. Eric was furious at my doctor. Being a pilot, he was able to get the flight surgeon and other key hospital personnel on his side; the head of the obstetrics department became my doctor.

The diagnosis was not good: a partial abrupture and a placenta previa. At a critical stage during brain development of the fetus, part of the placenta had died. The likely result was retardation, but there was no way to tell until the baby was born. The doctor's advice was to stay in bed to avoid losing the baby, or get up and lose the baby. Carrying the baby to term looked doubtful in the first weeks, and giving birth naturally looked impossible. A C-section loomed, and the chance of a damaged baby seemed likely. I didn't think I could deal with a handicapped child, and we discussed ending the pregnancy. Eric continued to repeat that it was my decision and he would support it—whatever the outcome. He adamantly refused to make the decision for me. It was infuriating. I wanted him to tell me what I should do, but I was completely on my own.

Then there were the pictures.

I rode in a wheelchair almost every day to have an ultrasound image of the baby taken. From the start, I could see this wonderful life inside me: sucking on its hands, fighting so hard to stay alive. How could I terminate its life? In the end, I couldn't, so I stayed in bed. It was mind-numbingly boring. I wanted to go to work, play with my two-year-old, go for walks with my husband, and most of all, run. I couldn't do anything but lie in bed, watch boring shows, cross-stitch, read, then repeat. It was a nightmare, and all the while, there loomed the possibility of having a baby with physical or mental difficulties, or both.

Eric brought me flowers, presents, and meals. In the weeks before my mother arrived to help, Eric decided the best lunch for me was tuna. He brought me tuna every single day for weeks, pleased he'd found something so healthy. He expounded on the virtues of tuna at every opportunity.

What could I say? He was sweet. He was caring. He was excited about that smelly tuna. I considered hiding the sandwiches, but I knew he'd smell them rotting under the bed. I tried to get Tia to eat them, but she wrinkled her nose and shook her head vigorously. I tried telling Eric I wasn't hungry and please don't bring me lunch.

"But Carol," he'd say, "you have to eat. I brought you half a tuna sandwich with a pickle. You can eat half, can't you? I made it just for you."

He'd make a sad face, and I'd choke it down. I was relieved when my mother came and gave me peanut butter instead. I overheard Eric's conversation with her one afternoon. "But I think tuna might be a healthier choice."

My mother claimed we were out of tuna, but it never worked for long. Eric stopped by the commissary on his way home and picked up several tins. After it was all over, we both had a good laugh about the tuna, and I explained to Eric that it was a good thing because it helped me to become completely vegetarian.

I finally gave birth to a baby girl. There were some problems, but the day I took my Robin home was a happy one. We lived in fear that some sort of learning disability would pop up, but she appeared to be bright and curious, progressing exactly on schedule. We gradually started to let go of our fears.

One day, when Robin was about three years old, Eric and I were having coffee in the kitchen. Robin was happily singing to her dolls in the adjoining room, and I thought of that difficult pregnancy and my belief that the tiny life inside me deserved to live. Such a strong-willed being would grow up to make the world a better place.

I smiled at Eric. "Thanks for not letting me give up."

"I knew you wouldn't. Don't let the dolls fool you; that little girl in there is a fighter."

* * *

Russell showed up precisely at eight o'clock to check on Eric. I was determined to keep it together as she spoke. "We're going to be putting Eric on the circle bed later today."

The damn circle bed. I felt the tears start. My attempt to be better had lasted less than two hours. I'd hoped Knight would change his mind.

"I know this is difficult. You're doing great."

No. I wasn't.

Russell pulled a chair over and sat beside me. We talked about Eric and his hobbies. She asked whether he'd ever had problems in an airplane before.

There was that time he lost an engine.

* * *

During the time Eric flew the F-15, I longed to go for a ride in the jet, and this desire became quite a joke with our friends. The Air Force wouldn't allow wives to go up: a taxi ride yes, a leave-the-ground-and-streak-through-the-sky-at-Mach-speeds? Absolutely not. Oh, and make that a taxi ride with another pilot, not your husband. I had heard there was an accident once, and that was enough to cause the Air Force to change their policy. The reasoning was that they didn't want children to be orphans.

I eventually got a taxi ride in the F-15 with one of the other pilots, but none of my pleading and begging would persuade him to leave the ground. Eric had warned him I'd try. Everyone got a good laugh, and I pretended to pout.

I enjoyed watching the F-15s, as did the Dutch, who would line up at the end of the runway and wave American flags. I was proud of Eric. His plane was hot. He was hot.

Once I went out to the end of the runway in the official Air Force van to watch the jets. Shortly after Eric's takeoff, I noticed the light in the back of one of the engine cones had gone out. *Gone. Out.* No fire. It felt as though someone had punched me in the gut. An engine failure!

"Wasn't that...wasn't that..." I stammered breathlessly to the people in the van.

They assured me it would be OK and turned up the radio so I could hear Eric. Cool as Chuck Yeager in a crisis, he turned the plane around, perfect control in his voice, and announced his landing plans. He got down fine, but I was terrified. My hands tingled from gripping the sides of the van seat. When I saw Eric an hour later, he seemed amused. "I have two engines, Carol. You're a pilot. You know we practice this stuff."

That was probably the time when doubts about Eric's safety started to creep into my thoughts. Maybe something could happen. It wouldn't, of course, but maybe…

Years later when Eric was a test pilot, I told him, "I don't worry as much about you now that you're not a fighter pilot."

He'd gazed at me with a strange look on his face. "You're wrong. It was much safer in the Air Force. In a production environment, you have to take chances. It isn't nearly as safe. There have been accidents, and there'll be more. When the bottom line is making money, it's dangerous."

A few months ago, he had casually thrown out a remark at dinnertime. "Bombardier is due for another accident. It's been ten years since the last one."

*   *   *

David arrived and handed me a folder with my mail and my checkbook. He also gave me a blue-flowered tote bag Tia had packed. Now I had something constructive to do during the times I couldn't go in Eric's room. I didn't want even one bill to be late.

"The blood drive is set for tomorrow at Eric's company," said David. "The Red Cross sent the press release. I have some friends looking for an eye surgeon. My plane leaves around noon, so I'll have to go soon. Lisa is probably flying back tomorrow. I'm not sure when Dad is leaving, but Mom will stay to help." Pausing, he added, "And another thing. You need to go home. You need to be a mother to those kids. They should be your first priority. You don't need to be here all the time."

"But…" No more words would come out.

Eric needed me. He would never leave me if the situation were reversed. Many people were caring for Tia and Robin, and I called them several times a day. I missed them, but for thirteen years, I put them above Eric. Always above Eric. He'd complained about it, said we needed to work on our marriage too, but I didn't listen. The kids always took precedence over everything Eric needed or wanted. Not now. I loved them deeply, but Eric needed me, and I wasn't leaving.

A nurse walked up to us. "I'm sorry, but you'll have to leave the call room in the pediatrics ward first thing tomorrow morning."

I'd been expecting it; I knew it was going to happen. I would sleep in the waiting room. I was not leaving the hospital.

Before David left to find Russell and Knight, he leaned over me. "It's time to go home."

Sitting in the hall, I looked through the bills, paid a few, read some cards people had sent. I opened up the bag to see what Tia had packed. I couldn't suppress a smile when I saw all the makeup. Not one to wear much at all, I had few containers of the stuff. Tia must have packed every bottle and tube I owned. She'd written a note: "So you can look good for Daddy." I rummaged around in the bag and felt a piece of paper at the bottom. It was an old note from Eric.

Happy Anniversary,
Thank you for being the joy of my life and for
helping me become a test pilot. I couldn't
have done it without your support.

He'd signed it with his signature trademark—a scribbly heart with a face on it.

* * *

Writing notes was an important part of our relationship. The notes were usually silly. If Eric left early for work, there would be a note waiting on the counter for me. If it was my first day of the semester, there would be a note sticking out of my textbook. The girls often received notes in their lunches from both of us. When Eric went on trips, I stuffed his suitcase full of notes. He would unpack to find pieces of paper spilling out of underwear, T-shirts, pants pockets. Eric called me nearly every day when he was on a trip, and the first thing he usually said involved something about the notes: "Thanks for the notes." "Hey. Last time I got more notes." "I missed one of your notes, and when I went to take a pen out of my pocket at the meeting, it fell out. Sort of embarrassing, Carol." "I only got one note this time. I got cheated."

He never forgot to hide a note under my pillow before he left on a trip, and if he was gone for long, he sent postcards with silly sayings. Once I was busy and forgot to write notes, so I quickly dug in his dresser drawer, grabbed some old notes, and stuffed them in his suitcase. He called that night. Despite the silliness, there was a hint of sadness in his voice. "Carol, those were used notes. I can tell. I'm sad because I got cheated out of good notes."

"I'm sorry, Eric. I was busy."

"I guess you were being a busybacksoon and didn't have time for your boy. I miss you."

The term "busybacksoon" was one he'd adopted from a Winnie-the-Pooh story. "Acting too big" was another phrase we frequently used. The use of these terms indicated the person had forgotten the important things in life: writing notes, for instance.

"You are absolutely right, and it won't happen again," I said in my silliest voice.

"I hope not. I would never leave you with used notes."

After that, I would sometimes write at the bottom of the note, "This is not a used note." I usually wrote silly things like "fly big, but not too big" or "I miss you blind, and I can't see a thing."

* * *

In the waiting room, a pretty blonde greeted me. Had I met this woman before? She quietly said, "I'm Bryan Irelan's girlfriend."

I told her how sorry I was. Looking at me, she stammered, "Did Bryan say anything before…uh…before…you know? Did Eric tell you what he said? Would it be all right if I ask Eric what Bryan said?"

"Eric hasn't said a word since he came in. He's on a respirator, and he's on a paralyzing drug so he can't move either. There's no way he can answer your question. I'm sorry."

"I…I didn't know. But—"

"I want to know what Eric said too. I keep trying to find out. Eventually the NTSB will release the transcript from the cockpit voice recorder. We'll know someday."

There was a long pause before she said, "Bryan never flies the Challenger."

"Are you sure? That was definitely not Eric's plane. He flew the RJ; he had less than an hour in the Challenger. He went to simulator training in Montreal last month. Alec Sorrentino told me Bryan flies the Challenger all the time. I think maybe you're mistaken."

She shook her head. "I don't think so."

Something wasn't right, or maybe she was confused. I would ask Alec, if I remembered. I couldn't seem to recall the smallest details lately; I had never been so forgetful.

Lisa called to tell me they weren't coming in today. Her parents needed a break. "My mother is hiring a maid to clean the house. It's too much for her to take care of."

"I wish she wouldn't. I don't like the idea of some stranger going through my things. Please leave it. I don't care if it's messy. The girls can help."

Lisa was insistent. She told me her parents were spending lots of money to maintain the household. My household.

"But aren't people bringing meals over?"

"Yes, but you know what my mom is like, and Dad can't eat much of it."

Dr. Pierce stopped by to check on the dialysis. We chatted for a few moments. "What military jets did Eric fly?" he asked.

"The T-38, T-37, and the F-15."

He gave a low whistle. "The F-15 Eagle...What a plane."

"He loved it. That's what he flew when we were in Holland. He got the best assignment in the Air Force. He even got a medal because he sat alert during the Cold War."

Pierce wanted to hear all about it.

* * *

The alert facility, or Zulu, at Camp New Amsterdam, was in a bunker out on the side of the runway. Twenty-four hours a day, 365 days a year, the US Air Force's Thirty-Second Tactical Fighter Squadron kept two F-15 jets fully loaded and ready to scramble. The two Zulu pilots were NATO's first line of defense in safeguarding North Central Europe. The Cold War was in full gear, and Eric was one of about fifty pilots stationed in Holland ready to take on the communists. A loud alarm would signal it was time to scramble. The guys would run to the jets, and with the help of the support crew, they'd be off.

I always joined Eric for a few hours when he sat alert. We'd watch movies, talk, or play pool. He went on a live scramble only once. I knew when it happened because he came home late from Zulu with a huge grin on his face. I pestered him continuously but he just smiled and repeated the same line. "If I tell you, then I'll have to kill you."

Years after he left the Air Force, I got part of the story out of him. It had been defecting geese from East Germany. He'd grinned and jokingly said now he'd have to kill me. I reminded him that the Cold War was over, his base was deserted, and the Russians were our friends, sort of. He'd smiled. "It was so cool."

When the Cold War ended, the American side of the base was one of the first closed by President Clinton. The Americans pulled out, and the jets flew home. Eric had tried to get on the base when he went to Holland before the accident and was irritated because the Dutch authorities wouldn't let him in. He was shocked that they didn't seem to care that he had flown an F-15 in defense of *their* country. He bitterly pointed out that the kid at the gate was probably too young to know there had been F-15s there.

Eric hiked to a vantage point overlooking the abandoned American side. Calling me from Holland, he said he'd stood in the rain for a long time, gazing down at the runway where he'd flown his F-15. I could hear the sadness in his voice when he described the grass growing up in the cracks of the long-abandoned runway, the deserted bunkers, the boarded buildings. He sighed loudly and said, "My heart will always be with the F-15."

*　*　*

It was midafternoon before Knight showed up with the bronch equipment, followed by Russell. The bandage change was just finishing. Knight's report was short. "He has some mucus and plugs and some tissue debris. The circle bed will be down in a few hours."

Then he left. Couldn't he say Eric's name? Just once?

Squatting next to me, Russell said, "I know you're upset about the circle bed, but the lungs aren't improving. Eric's spine may be at risk, but Dr. Knight feels we don't have a choice. The neurosurgeon is being consulted, of course."

I was crying again. *Damn.*

"We did find some fungus on the dressings, but we're aware of it and are doing everything we can. His bowels seem to be working."

The poop again. Who cares? Fungus? I guessed it wasn't anything serious. I was sure there were ointments and stuff for that. What I cared about was the damn circle bed thing. They were going to do it. They really were.

Leaving, she said, "You can go in now."

I noticed right away that the putrid smell was gone. The room smelled disinfectant clean. The bandages were white and dry, and there were new fresh patches over Eric's eyes.

Several people wheeled a huge contraption toward me. The circle bed. I watched them set it up. It took quite some time and six people to transfer Eric. When he was in place on his back, the entire bed rotated upside down so he was lying with his stomach pointing toward the floor. The whole thing looked uncomfortable. Almost immediately Eric's blood pressure rose.

I started to object and pointed to the instruments. Nurse Brenna assured me it would be all right, the rise was expected, and of course Eric didn't like being in that position. Who would? But it was for the best because his lungs were in bad shape. She was on top of it, she said. Try not to worry.

Day 10
Thursday, October 19, 2000

"Pilots are born, not made.
Everyone else has to figure out
what they want to do."
– Eric

"Thank you for letting me stay." I dropped the key into the open hand of the pediatrics nurse.

"It's time to go home," she said with no hesitation.

I didn't reply as I turned toward the burn unit. I was not leaving Eric.

I liked Eric's day nurse Rod almost immediately; his flamboyance was endearing, and he spoke to Eric in an upbeat way, as though Eric could hear everything. Rod asked many questions, and I was grateful for the concern he showed. He was interested in hearing about my job at the zoo and asked if Eric liked animals too.

Eric had a childlike fascination with animals and a sense of wonder and curiosity about them, though he tried to hide it around everyone but the kids and me. His sensitivity toward animals was a magnificent and fundamental part of him, the aspect of his personality I loved the most.

"I never would have guessed a test pilot would be like that," Rod said after I told him how Eric rescued tortoises out of the road before a car could hit them.

Leaning over Eric, I said, "I hope you don't mind my telling Rod about you." Rod looked at me sadly. "He won't remember any of this."

"He won't?"

"No," said Rod, shaking his head. "Patients who are given this much morphine and Ativan never remember anything."

A thought occurred to me, almost too terrible to ask. "If he's being given so many drugs that he won't remember..." I took Rod over in the corner and whispered. "Will he be addicted? You know, to the drugs?"

Rod's azure eyes focused on me. "Yes. But don't worry. We'll bring him off it slowly. Russell and Knight know what they're doing."

Dr. Doom and Gloom walked in. He looked around, flipped some pages on the chart, nodded at Rod, and left. I started to cough and realized I'd been holding my breath. "He makes me cry."

Wiping a strand of straight blond hair back from his forehead, Rod bent close to me. "Sometimes he makes us cry too."

Around noon, the dialysis stopped completely and, despite the efforts of several medical people, couldn't be restarted. Pierce showed up, and I overheard something about a kink in the line. I signed yet another authorization form, and Russell arrived to perform a procedure that would get the dialysis back up and running. She explained it to me, but I didn't understand, and I was too tired to concentrate on the workings of a machine I had no control over. I wanted the damn thing to work. Now.

Lisa came to say good-bye. "See ya, Carol" was all she said as she hugged me firmly, turning quickly to go. Mom and Sandy arrived soon after.

I was amazed at the strength of my mother-in-law. I had always pictured her as a person who would fall apart if anything bad happened to one of her kids. She confused me, and I supposed that after twenty-three years, I didn't know her as well as I thought. Eric often said he owed much of what he'd become to her. He loved both his parents deeply, but it was often difficult for him to express those feelings. He frequently told me, and sincerely meant it, no one had ever had parents as wonderful as his. Not only did I believe him, I was sometimes jealous. Why couldn't I have parents like that? Eric said I could share his, and I even called them Mom and Dad.

Countless times over the years, my mother-in-law would grab Eric in a tight hug, gaze at me, and say, "Look at this handsome man I gave you." She told stories about his high intellect, and her favorite was the "flat and straight story."

"Carol, I believe all parents think their children are bright, but when Eric was about four years old, that's when I first realized he was not only bright but a creative thinker as well. He'd been playing outdoors with his friends, and I was working in the kitchen when he came in the door. With no introduction about why he was asking, he said, 'Mommy, what's the difference between flat and straight?' As I mumbled an answer, he said, 'Oh, I know the difference. Flat has no bumps and straight has no curves.' I knew right then; this was an exceptionally bright child."

I told her and Sandy one of my own stories.

"He has this amazing ability with math. I can work the problems and I even got a math scholarship, but when it comes to taking the math and applying it to real life, like using equations to describe airflow around a wing, I can't do it. I can't make the leap from math as a tool to math as an explanation. I've tried. Eric is different. He sees equations, and they speak to him. They explain movement, dynamics, and the way the world works. Equations sing to Eric. They don't sing to me."

"But Eric isn't just bright," my mother-in-law interjected, "he's creative too. When he was in kindergarten, his teacher was doing a reading readiness exercise with the children. She gave them a picture of a turkey, and the instructions below the picture said 'Color this turkey brown.' Eric, true to his own creative sense, colored the turkey many bright colors. His teacher, knowing he could read the instructions, said to him, 'Eric, you know it says to color the turkey brown.' Eric responded, 'Yes, I know, but look how much prettier mine is.' Eric's teacher recognized his creativity and told me this story."

I had heard the story many times. Once, I'd asked Eric what happened to his famous turkey masterpiece. "Why, didn't you know," he'd exclaimed in a dramatic voice. "It's at the Louvre."

My mother-in-law got up from her chair. "I think I'll see my boy now."

Sandy watched her leave. "That poor woman." She paused. "Is there anything I can do for you?"

"You've been wonderful. Really. I appreciate everything you're doing to help with Tia and Robin."

"They're dears. They worry about you."

In less than five minutes, Mom came back out to the waiting room. "I can't stay any longer. I'm going back to the house." There were no tears, but there was anger. She roughly and loudly gathered up her things and Sandy followed her out.

One of the nurses stopped to ask me if I needed a place to stay for the night.

"No. I'm not leaving the hospital," I said firmly.

"Of course not, sweetie. How about the Wichita Inn?" She pointed as she spoke. "You go out the back door, cross the parking lot, and it's right there. A lot of patients' families stay there. It's a decent hotel, not too expensive, and I know they give special rates if a relative is in the hospital."

I started to protest. Rod overheard and said, "It's right next door. Here, come look out the window in your husband's room." Guiding me to the window, he pointed. "See, that's it right there."

I walked across the hospital parking lot to the hotel. I'd given Rod my cell phone number. I clutched my phone firmly in my right hand, my bag in my left, and the hugging monkeys tightly under my arm.

About twenty minutes later, I was back in Eric's room. Rod smiled and said, "So? How's the hotel? I know it's not a Hyatt Regency, but the décor has to be better than the waiting room." He winked.

The damn dialysis machine went down. Again. I accosted Dr. Pierce when he came to check on things. "This dialysis is ridiculous," I snapped. "They can't keep it up and running."

Trying to distract me, Rod pointed down the hall to a man in a wheelchair who was speaking with several nurses. He seemed to have quite a fan club around him. I had a fair view of him—a regular guy, nothing remarkable. Rod leaned over to me and whispered, "He had forty percent burns. He was a patient here."

I gasped. "Really? He looks fine to me. I don't see any burns."

"He does look good. It's been a tough road, though. Trapped under a burning truck, I believe. Almost died.

His family owns a big construction business. That's his mom with him—salt of the earth, a great lady."

That afternoon, Knight and Russell were back to observe the bandage change, and I sensed something wasn't right. I stared nervously at the closed door.

About ten minutes later, they both came out. Knight paused and nodded at me. Apparently, Russell had been elected to tell me what they found. Knight was probably tired of my crying.

"Eric has a *Pseudomonas* infection in his leg burn," said Russell. "We're giving him antibiotics for it."

Pseudomonas. I searched my brain through clouds of exhaustion and emotional pain. I knew I'd heard that word before. At Wichita State University? Yes, that was it. In one of my classes. Which one? It must have been one of the biology classes, maybe a lab. Then I remembered. I mumbled what I knew, to myself more than to Knight and Russell. "*Pseudomonas*...prokaryotic, no nucleus. It's a member of Eubacteria. I think there are several different species in the genus *Pseudomonas*. Some are involved in denitrification. I know there's one, I don't remember the species, that can protect plants from freezing because ice can't adhere to its surface."

Knight raised an eyebrow but said nothing.

"It's not an especially bad bacterium, is it?" I asked.

"We're watching it. We have antibiotics that can control it."

They left. I'd been on the verge of tears, but I didn't cry. Points for me.

Brandon, the young blond orderly who usually helped with the bandage changes, came out to speak with Rod. Brandon had already complained to me that he did more work than the nurses did but made much less money. I told him he should go to school, but he'd frowned and said, "I'm married, no time." He seemed to work hard, and I often caught sight of his short, chubby form walking quickly through the halls, shirt untucked, retrieving some thing or another for one of the nurses or doctors. As he was going back in, I cornered him. "Brandon, what's up?"

"Knight and Russell were looking at the wounds, making sure everything is OK."

"Is it?" I asked cautiously.

Brandon shrugged. "I think he's got an infection in his leg."

"Russell told me. *Pseudomonas.*"

"They were checking that the cadaver skin and the porcine were intact. There are some areas of green and some smaller areas of black tissue..."

Black tissue.

I sat in the burn unit waiting room. Sometimes I had to get out, away from the smell and the medical talk I didn't understand. Sometimes I felt I couldn't breathe.

It was a big waiting room with several televisions and a small kitchenette. I always hid in the same corner, in the same chair. I didn't like it when other people were in there. I didn't want to share my story, but I supposed they all knew who I was anyway.

Then she came in, bursting through the waiting room door, all smiles as usual, her arms full of packages of food. I felt myself tensing. Candice was the one person who offered no comfort. It wasn't that she didn't try. She was all perky, smiley, and brimming with cheerful advice like "things could be worse" or "everything will be fine" or "God has a plan." The last one was the worst. What plan? Perhaps people should think before they start yakking about God's plan. I was the one who kept trying not to hurt everyone's feelings when what I wanted to say was stop telling me about the damn plan. Stop bringing me religious books. I wondered how much longer I could hide in the atheist closet.

I first met Candice two months ago at the zoo. She'd recently become a volunteer in the education department where I worked. Her husband worked at Bombardier, but when I mentioned him to Eric a few weeks before the accident, he insisted he didn't know him.

For almost five years, I'd worked hard to break into the zoo world. I'd returned to school, volunteered long hours, and held a temporary half-year job as a paid bird zookeeper. I would do anything to help the animals.

I cleaned, prepared animal diets, and washed dishes and dishes and more dishes. I scrubbed until I got blisters. I bleached stalls, inhaling fumes that left me gagging and coughing. I cut open rats and put vitamins inside. I dipped my hands in bowls of live wiggling worms and cleaned up after hissing cockroaches. I went without breaks and returned after signing out to finish chores. I did it all cheerfully, gladly, and with a profound thankfulness that I was there.

As Candice flounced into the room, I was somewhat prepared for the onslaught of advice and holy thoughts. Don't be rude, I kept telling myself. Say thank you, and then she'll go away.

"Hello, Carol. Why the long face?"

Oh no, here we go again.

"Hmmm," I replied. "Let me see. Could it be my husband is in a hospital bed?" My sarcasm was obviously lost on Candice. I never went into detail about Eric's injuries. That would have been the same as giving a press release to the entire city.

"Things could be worse, Carol. Always remember that."

She went on for several minutes, but I was unprepared for what she said after the usual "how is Eric" and "try to remember God has a plan."

"I need to get your zoo key from you. You know how the assistant director is about those keys." She laughed unconvincingly. "Do you have it with you?"

I could feel my mouth fall open. My body parts seemed to be frozen. "My what?"

"Your zoo key. The assistant director wants it back." She smiled weakly.

"But why?" I stammered.

She looked off to the side. "Because you're not going back to work, so...uh...we need your key back."

Even I could hear the pleading in my voice. "But I want to, when Eric gets better. Go back to work, I mean. I love my job. I'm not going to let the lions out or anything. I keep the key in a safe place. It isn't going anywhere, and—"

"He sent me to get the key, Carol. They have to fill your position, so I need the key."

I was being fired, and the assistant director was too cowardly to do it himself.

I felt cold. Sydney the cockatoo, and Bonzer the bearded dragon, and Yip and Yap, those darling prairie dogs...

I was supposed to do a presentation next week. I needed to get those slides put together. Chilly, the chinchilla...Would anyone remember to give her a raisin every morning? My hands were so cold. Yip and Yap loved to play in their digging bucket. They made me laugh. Eric liked the stories I told about them.

Slowly I said, "I don't have it with me. It's at my house."

"If you tell me where it is, we'll send someone to your house to get it."

Silence. Candice shifted in her chair. She coughed. More silence.

"I can't believe you're doing this to me." I wasn't cold anymore as I continued, "I think this is a really mean thing to do. The assistant director knows how much the zoo means to me. He knows Eric. I'm in Audubon with him. How can he do this? He has a cabinet full of keys. He knows I'm responsible."

Candice stared at her painted nails. "I'm sorry."

"Sure you are, Candice. The key is on the top of the vanity in my bedroom. It's on a blue key chain. Don't you dare take the key ring, because Eric bought it for me when I got the job."

I shuffled though the metal doors to Eric's room. The walls were blurry; the floor was blurry. I sat down at an empty nurse's station, put my head in my hands, and sobbed. I cried for all that would never be. I cried for Eric and the pain he was suffering. I cried for his eyes and because he would never fly again. I cried for the trip to Greece, which we'd already paid for but would never take. I cried because he might die, because I needed him, because I couldn't live without him. I cried because he was my best friend, my supporter, the one person I could always depend on. I cried because his children needed him. His parrot needed him. I needed him. I cried because I loved him with everything I had and he wasn't here to tell the assistant zoo director not to be mean to me and take away the only thing I had left: the job I loved. Everything I loved was in ruins. It was never going to be the same.

Did they know, at the zoo administration, what they'd done that day?

Jennifer, the social worker, put her hand on my shoulder and guided me into her office. I fell down on the bright-blue sofa.

"What's wrong, Carol? I thought things were fairly stable with your husband."

Between sobs and angry fits, I managed to get the story out.

"That's awful," Jennifer replied. "It shows a great insensitivity on the part of the zoo."

"And...I...I even jumped in the moat."

"Excuse me?"

I felt my voice cracking as I told her about the one time in my life I'd been a hero.

* * *

Years ago, before the zoo hired me as a bird keeper and before my current job as a zoo educator, I'd been a regular volunteer. I was thrilled to be at such an excellent zoo and wanted to learn everything at once.

One particular day, my boss, the head bird keeper, tired of my endless questions, sent me with a pair of binoculars and a clipboard to the Africa exhibit. The large open enclosure housed a pair of bontebok, African antelope with long curling horns. The male was particularly nasty, and few keepers wanted to mess with him. The enclosure also held a stunning pair of East African gray-crowned cranes. With a crown of stiff gold feathers; red cheeks; and multicolored feathers of yellow, white, gray, black, and russet, this crane was easily one of the world's most elegant animals. Three days before, the cranes had become the proud parents of two babies, or "colts." One of the babies had mysteriously disappeared without a trace.

My boss asked me to watch the exhibit and write down anything unusual. I was delighted at the chance to play wildlife biologist, even though I suspected why she'd sent me on this important mission.

I climbed over a short fence and leaned lazily against a tree overlooking the moat that separated the enclosure from the public. Under the sunny spring sky, I heard a male house finch sing his warbled, drawn-out song, while a robin loudly called "cheer up cheerily." The smell of flowers in bloom permeated the air. I felt happy to be here, at my zoo, with an important task. It was a good day—no, a *great* day.

The male crane was picking through some vegetation as the female lazily walked around. The fuzzy yellow baby ventured farther and farther away from Mom. I watched as the darling thing walked within a few feet of the moat. A huge frog leaped from the water, grabbing the chick by its head. I dropped the clipboard. Before I could utter a word, the frog jumped back in the water, the squirming legs of the chick sticking straight out of its mouth.

Cries erupted around me. Several zoo guests had witnessed the episode. All eyes fell on me to do something. *Save the baby*, their eyes said.

I gaped at the visitors. I gaped at the moat. I had seconds to act.

Those birds were endangered, weren't they? Or probably threatened at least. I loved birds, didn't I? Wasn't I in charge? Wasn't I responsible? No one else was around. I had to take action immediately. I was not going to tell my boss a chick had died on my watch. I was not going to go home and tell Eric I did nothing while an exquisitely beautiful and quite possibly endangered bird died. I did what any bird lover in my position would do.

I took my boots off and jumped in the moat.

I can't swim at all. I learned later the moat was about ten feet deep. Somehow, I grabbed the frog, and it let go of the chick. I clutched the baby and hauled myself out of the water. It all happened quickly. The baby lay limp in my arms as I stared down at it. All that, and the baby was dead. Those were my thoughts as I stood on the bank, soaking wet, holding a baby crane in my arms. As the reality of what I'd done hit, I quickly crouched behind a large bush. Amazingly, the mom and dad crane hadn't seen it. Cranes are big birds with big, pointed beaks. I was well aware of the aggression of parents with young.

It wasn't long before a keeper climbed over to the opposite side of the enclosure. He couldn't get in from his point, but he called over to me. "Hey. Did you fall in?"

"No. I jumped in. A frog swallowed the baby." I motioned with my head toward the baby in my arms.

"Hang on and we'll get you out. Don't move till we get the bontebok out of the yard." After a slight pause, he repeated, louder this time, "Do not move."

Soon my boss arrived, followed by the bird curator. Two mammal keepers were with them. By the time keepers coaxed the male bontebok out of the yard, the baby had sprung back to life. It was squirming when I handed it to my boss.

The two mammal keepers were furious; they wanted to have me thrown off zoo grounds. No way, said the bird curator. He declared me a hero while my boss smiled and nodded in agreement. People in the bird barn congratulated me, and there was even talk of writing an article for the paper.

Even though everyone at the zoo knew the story, it was eventually hushed up because the administration didn't want it to seem as though it approved of a mere volunteer doing something so dangerous. According to the mammal keepers, what I had done was very dangerous. Think of the liability, the administration declared.

Eric was home when I returned, wet and grimy, my long hair matted. I told him what happened. I left off the part about the dangers of the bontebok.

"You can't swim! You could have drowned," he yelled, dropping his book.

I stared at him and smiled. I held my hand up to the window, pretending to inspect my nails. "Admit it, Eric," I said as sweetly as I could, "I'm a hero. You know you think so."

He tried to suppress a smile as he hugged me. "Promise you won't do anything stupid again. People get killed at zoos, you know." He hesitated before whispering in my ear, "You're a hero."

Eric called me the "birdie saver" after that. Later at the zoo, I pointed out *my* crane to him. It grew into a magnificent bird, which was, according to Eric, the prettiest crane in the whole world.

A year later, the bird department hired me as a temporary keeper. Eric said it was because I was a hard worker, dependable, and knew the routine so well.

"You're wrong," I said. "It's because of the moat incident. The curator said I was a hero."

* * *

Jennifer leaned back in her chair. "That's an amazing story. I want to say again how terrible I feel for you. When Eric is well, I'm sure you can work there again. We all admire your dedication to your husband. I think you're where you want to be, where you need to be. Am I right?"

"Yes." No job was more important than taking care of Eric. I wiped my eyes and stood up. "I'll never work at that zoo again." I knew it, I felt it.

I would always look back on this day as the time when my aspirations for a zoo career ended.

"I know of a good psychotherapist at Catholic Community Counseling. Your brother-in-law thinks you should see someone. Can I give you her name? She's right down the street. We'd call if there are changes with Eric."

"No."

"Will you think about it?"

I left.

I wanted to tell Eric what had happened, but as I stood over him, I knew it wouldn't be fair to cry over my seven-dollar-an-hour job. "I heard what happened," Rod said, walking into the room. "That's rotten. Maybe we should boycott the zoo."

"No, it wouldn't be fair to the animals," I said. "It's the nasty administration. Maybe it's actually only one person. I have many friends who are keepers, and the people in the education department are wonderful. They work hard for low pay. They're good people. I love my zoo—just not the administrator."

"I'll bet your husband will give them a piece of his mind when he gets out of here. From what you've told me, he's quite the animal lover."

Yes, Eric had always loved animals. If there had ever been doubts about how much, they dissolved after the rabbit murders.

* * *

Eric was a lowly second lieutenant in the USAF Euro-NATO Joint Jet Pilot Training Program when his flight commander, Kevin, told me about survival camp. It was the summer of 1984, at the Sheppard Air Force Base Officer's Club. I was waiting for Eric when Kevin and I started talking. I'd been worried about survival training and was pressing Kevin for information he didn't want to give.

"We all have to go," he said matter-of-factly, running a hand over his short, light-brown hair. "Eric will be fine. It's not fun, just something you have to get through."

"Is it true they stick you in a box and beat on it in POW training? Do they actually dump you off in the middle of the woods? Do they make you eat bugs? Do they—"

"You know we're not supposed to talk about it," Kevin interrupted. "It's important to have this training in case you get shot down and have to evade the enemy."

"So there's nothing to worry about?"

"Eric will be fine. But there's…" Kevin took a big drink of his beer and quickly changed the subject. "So what time was that bike race over at—"

"Kevin, what were you about to say?"

"Nothing." He took another gulp of beer and shifted on his barstool.

"Tell me."

He could see he'd blown it and there was no shutting me up. He lowered his voice. "It wouldn't matter to anyone but you. Seriously, no one else would think twice about it."

Kevin took another sip. He was squirming noticeably on the barstool. "Uh…they give you a rabbit after the week of evasion."

"They do what?"

"They give you a rabbit. You have to kill it and eat it."

"You have to do *what*?"

"It's just a rabbit. People eat them all the time."

"Eric better not kill an innocent fuzzy bunny." People were staring. I must have been shouting.

"He better do it," cautioned Kevin, giving me the full gaze of his hazel eyes. "He won't pass the training. He won't get his jet if he doesn't finish survival school. I know you don't believe in hunting, but think of his career."

How could the Air Force make you do something like that? It was outrageous. I thought of the poor rabbits, butchered. Then I thought of the many evenings we'd spent petting the rabbits at the pet store. I wondered how Eric would be able to do it. I wondered if he knew about the rabbit murders.

I sat in silence at the bar. What could I say? I couldn't jeopardize Eric's career. Before long, Eric walked in, waving at us. "Hey, Carol. Hello, sir."

"Kevin was telling me about survival training," I said.

"I told her about the rabbit," Kevin admitted.

Eric thumped his hand to his forehead. "I wish you hadn't told her."

My voice was shrill. "You mean you knew?"

"Yes, but let's talk about this later."

I had sense enough to shut my mouth—for now. When we got home, I cornered him. "Eric, you wouldn't really kill a sweet fuzzy bunny, would you?"

"What am I supposed to do?" He hung his head. Eric the problem solver, Eric the man who could finesse his way out of or into everything, looked dejected.

"I see your point," I said. "I don't want you to jeopardize your career, but you love rabbits. Remember the rabbits at the pet store? We always played with them."

"Please don't remind me." The corners of his mouth drooped.

About a month later, as he was getting ready to leave for survival training, I kissed him and said, "Don't come back if you kill that bunny." I shouldn't have said it.

"I'm not going to kill the bunny," he replied.

When he returned from training, I resisted the urge to ask him straightaway about the rabbit. We talked about other things. He said he couldn't tell me about the POW training or he'd have to kill me. "You didn't ask me about the bunny."

I could tell right away from his expression that he hadn't killed it.

"You didn't kill it, did you?"

"Nope. I told you I wouldn't, and I didn't."

"How did you get out of it? Or did the Air Force wise up and stop conducting mass bunny murders?"

"No, they had the rabbits. They were all in cages, and there was one rabbit to four guys. We were supposed to kill and eat it. They looked like the bunnies at the pet store."

"But you said you didn't do it," I shouted.

"I didn't. I told the other guys if I killed it my wife wouldn't let me come home. So I told them I'd buy them all pizza if they'd do it."

"So...the bunny was murdered."

"Yes. I didn't like it, but one of the guys in our group did it quickly so the little thing didn't suffer." His voice was almost a whisper.

I couldn't think of anything appropriate to say.

"He was a gentle bunny," he said as he walked into the bathroom and shut the door. I could hear water running, but it didn't completely cover up a different sound.

Day 11
Friday, October 20, 2000

"You don't get to fly fighters unless you're tough. And cool."
- Eric

I flew out of the hotel, across the parking lot, through the back door of Saint Cornelius Medical Center, and up several flights of stairs to the burn unit. I had one thought: today it will be ten days.

Ten days.

I looked down at my cell phone. No messages. Good, good. I picked up the pace, around the corner, down the corridor, quick, quick.

Ten days.

I looked at my watch. I could talk with Amanda before the shift change.

Ten days.

Racing down the hall to room 29, I almost ran into Amanda's sizeable body. I was out of breath as I asked, "How's Eric? Did anything happen?"

"Things are stable. It was a quiet night. Dialysis problems, but it's fine now."

I glanced at the instruments. Things seemed to be as they should be.

"Ten days," I insisted, perhaps a bit too loudly.

"Excuse me?"

"It's been ten days. Today. My sister says that's a major milestone." I tried to smile.

"I suppose it is." Her face revealed doubt, a definite pessimism about Eric's chances.

I congratulated Eric for being so strong. Ten whole days, I repeated to him.

An hour later, a muscular, tanned man in his late thirties shook my hand, introducing himself as Dr. Evans. Finally, the eye doc had come to speak with me. I was still angry that he'd disappeared after the surgery.

"Eric is going to need his eyelids reconstructed," he said. "I'll speak with your brother-in-law at length about this. We'll be involving a plastic surgeon."

"Eric's eyes. Can you fix them?" I felt the words pour out in a breathless rush.

"It's difficult to assess the damage, but our first step is reconstruction of the eyelids. Without those, the eyes can't be viable."

He said eyes. Plural.

"Is his left eye still functioning?" I asked.

"It could be. We don't know yet. I will keep you informed as we progress."

I thanked him profusely.

Ten days.

The news about the eyes was as good as I dared hope.

Caitlin and Brenna were Eric's nurses today. The tall, thin build of Caitlin contrasted with Brenna's short, athletic shape. They were both supremely competent and made a good team, working together efficiently. I told them several tales about Eric, but they seemed most interested in the stories about his former position as a fighter pilot. They wanted to hear about one of the craziest things he'd done.

* * *

Eric went through F-15 training at Luke Air Force Base in Phoenix. That's where I first saw him eat a raw egg. What could be zanier than that?

Fighter pilots eating raw eggs? I never understood it. Were they trying to be cool? Perhaps they were trying to impress one another, or maybe it was a competition, a guy thing. Eric claimed it was a tradition. An important one.

Eric, with much fanfare at the squadron bar, slipped the entire raw egg in his mouth. I could hear the sickening sound of crunching eggshell as his fellow pilots cheered. I felt my stomach lurch as I watched him chew. It was definitely not cool to let the slimy yolk slip out of the sides of the mouth, and you couldn't let the white part make an appearance either. Using hands or gagging was taboo. It was the ultimate sign of weakness, the supreme proof you were unfit and unworthy to fly a jet as cool as the F-15 if you—the word was too horrible to comprehend—puked. Perhaps there was some association with barfing up that egg and tossing your cookies in the jet.

Eric ate his raw egg. The cheers echoed loudly through the bar as he downed it with dignity and super cool fighter pilot finesse. Not a smidgen of egg or shell left his mouth. No gagging. No hands. Elegant. Sophisticated. A latecomer would have thought he was finishing the last bits of a delightful meal. The ordeal was followed by beers, toasts, more beers, more toasts, and, just to make sure, more beers.

I told Eric it probably wasn't that bad for someone like him who enjoyed eating raw oysters and anchovies. I pointed to the polite single pilot who'd had some trouble with his egg. He was a Texas boy used to steak and potatoes.

Eric was unsympathetic. "But weren't you impressed with me?" It was more a statement than a question. "There was a guy last weekend who puked. Not cool." He continued to shake his head in amazement. "Definitely not cool."

Boys. Who could understand them? Over the years, I'd never managed to make sense of the egg-eating incident, but to Eric it was perfectly logical. "You have to be tough if you want to fly the hottest jet in the sky," he'd declared. "What isn't there to understand?"

* * *

Brenna and Caitlin were laughing about my egg story as Knight emerged from Eric's room. "The lungs look better."

I stared after him as he walked down the hallway.

"Did I hear what I think I heard?" I said. "Did Knight say Eric's lungs look better? Did he actually say something good?"

The nurses smiled as Russell confirmed Knight's report. "Yes, they do look better. The circle bed is helping."

"Does that mean you can take him off it now?" I asked.

"No. Not yet. But sometime, hopefully."

Pierce gave me an encouraging dialysis report. It was a much better day today. I could feel it—things were turning around.

As always, Pierce seemed in no hurry as he asked, "Don't fighter pilots have nicknames like Iceman or Maverick? What was your husband's?"

"They only have cool nicknames in movies like *Top Gun*. In real life most of them are dumb."

Eric's definitely was.

* * *

The biggest insult anyone could pay Eric was to compare him to someone else or to imply he was like someone else. Eric saw himself as unique—completely and totally different. He had a healthy ego, especially about his intelligence and talent for fixing and building.

"Thank God he doesn't realize he's good-looking," my sister Patty had remarked, "or he'd be insufferable."

When we arrived at Camp New Amsterdam in the Netherlands, people at the base told us, almost immediately, Eric looked like one of the other F-15 pilots. He was appalled. He did look like Vinny, though. Once at the bar, I went up behind a guy I thought was Eric. I bear-hugged him from behind and kissed the back of his neck. Then I caught sight of Eric waving to me from the other side of the room. Ever so slowly, Vinny turned around, a big grin on his face. I was mortified, probably turning several shades of pink and red, but everyone in the bar, including Eric, was laughing.

Fighter pilots usually get a nickname while at their first squadron assignment. Eric had been pushing for the name "Ragu," but fighter pilots will tell you that you rarely get to pick your own name. There were names like Booger, Bones, Nitty, Wheatie, and Snot. Eric didn't escape getting a dumb name. He tried to get rid of it, he complained, he protested, but the more he fussed, the harder the name stuck. The name, eventually finding its way onto the side of his F-15 and all his Air Force correspondences, was Clone.

* * *

There were always people coming in and out of Eric's room: nurses, dialysis people, respiratory therapists (RTs), occupational therapists (OTs), doctors, Brandon and his bandage helpers. Then there was the RT lady—frizzy, shoulder-length, tawny hair; pale, small rectangular glasses. She wasn't like the others. I felt nervous and unsettled when she was around. She rarely spoke, so I was surprised when she stopped what she was doing, turned to me, and said, "Your husband won't get better unless you put his life in God's hands. You must pray for your husband. If you don't pray, he isn't going to get better. His injuries are worse than you think."

The audacity of this woman stunned me. I'd been trying not to hurt people's feelings about the whole God thing, but this was too much. Was there anybody who cared about Eric's wishes? Was it such a difficult thing for them to respect what he wanted? I knew this was a Catholic hospital, but what about patients' wishes? I glowered at the RT woman, who had gone back to fiddling with Eric's ventilator.

She didn't even turn around as she added, "I'm not the only one who feels this way."

A moment passed as I tried to recover. "The only person who matters in all this is Eric. I've been married to him for twenty years. I know what he wants, and he doesn't want people praying for him." I refrained from using the word atheist because some people acted as though they were gasping for air at the mention of the word.

She spun around. "Maybe you're wrong. Sometimes when people are injured this badly, they change their minds."

I had no doubts about Eric's wishes. None at all.

She finished with the ventilator and wrote on a clipboard. Gathering up her supplies, she said, "I've seen many ill people. When the families don't pray, they die. I've seen it a lot, so I'm telling you, pray."

Before I could say anything else, she was gone.

How dare she say that to me? She had no right. The day had been going better than usual too. Until now.

When Caitlin came in, I told her what had happened. Quietly, in her melodic voice, she said, "Some of us are upset because you don't want the priest to come in. Are you sure it's what Eric wants?"

I started to open my mouth, but she'd said it with so much gentleness; I stopped what I was about to say. I liked Caitlin; she was good to Eric. "I'm sure," was all I said.

When I told Sandy later, she became angry too. "Bloody witch," she exclaimed loudly. "Shall I go in there and have that devil sacked?"

Aside from family members, Sandy was the first atheist I'd met who was over fifty. She made me laugh when we talked about religion. She made me feel I wasn't alone.

Eric's parents waved the incident off as being of "no importance." Dad said, "We all know what Eric wants."

Tim said Eric would show them all. Was Eric's boss a nonbeliever? I wondered what the devout Kansas Christians would think if they knew there were so many of us "evil" atheists: kind, hardworking, and ethical. Regular folks, like them. Maybe that was exactly what made us scary.

My university friend Linda stopped by to tell me the website was up. "People can start sending stories," she announced, obviously pleased with her work.

"I took a web design class last month," I told her. "Eric thought it was a great idea."

"Maybe someday you'll set up a really good website, when Eric gets better, of course. Maybe there was a reason you took that class."

"I thought I took it so I could help with the zoo's web page. But I don't have a job there anymore since they sent Candice to get the damn key."

There was an uncomfortable silence before Linda said, "I heard. They probably didn't know how much it would hurt you."

"They should have. I worked hard for almost five years, and for what? So they could kick me when I was down?"

"They probably didn't mean it like that." She patted me on the arm as though I were a small child.

"That administrator should have known."

"Candice shouldn't have done it," Linda replied. "She needs to be somewhere else other than here at the hospital."

Dr. Pierce showed up while the bronch was in progress to tell me he was increasing the heparin. Maybe that would stop the clotting problem with the dialysis machine—the Prisma, as the nurses referred to it.

"Do you understand all this burn stuff?" I asked Pierce.

"Of course not," he replied casually. "Medicine has become extremely specialized these days, especially with regard to burns."

I glanced at the closed door and frowned. "Knight and Russell are taking a long time with the bronch today."

"Are you going to tell me another story about Eric?" asked Pierce.

"We lived in Holland for three years. Do you want to hear about that?"

"Do tell."

I couldn't help the slight smile. Now it was funny, but when it happened...

* * *

Eric and I first arrived, exhausted, into Amsterdam's Schiphol Airport in late March 1985. I noticed the flowers immediately; big yellow daffodils paraded their petals atop long green stems as purple crocuses gathered beneath them. The tulips, I was told, would be arriving soon, spreading in a riot of color around the country. The multitude of bicycles, the strange road signs, the canals everywhere caused a growing excitement in me. I wanted to see everything at once.

A representative from the base immediately whisked us off to meet loads of new people, sign paperwork, and do some general sightseeing around Camp New Amsterdam/Soesterberg Air Base. We knew, of course, housing was difficult to come by. We'd done our homework and were ready to pounce on the first remotely acceptable dwelling that became available. We weren't fussy; we'd lived in small apartments, temporary quarters, base housing, and even a few hotels.

Late that afternoon when the exhaustion of meeting so many folks and a bad case of jet lag hit us, so did the opportunity to jump on a place to live. One of the pilots was going on to a new assignment, and his landlord was looking for another American to rent his house. We were unable to locate the pilot or his wife, so the landlord couldn't let us into the house, but a gentleman from the base housing office drove us out to the tiny town of Woudenberg. He had the paperwork with him and told us the landlord would approve anyone stationed at the base.

It was a white brick house with a detached one-car garage on a charming flower-lined street behind the city hall. Across the street was a small pond with a pair of mute swans floating on it. It was a picture postcard. No matter that we couldn't get in; the enormous front window afforded us a view of a spacious living room. There was even a redbrick patio around back and a big barn. It couldn't have been better. The helpful person from the base assured us if we didn't jump on this beauty, someone else would snap it up within the hour. We beamed at each other and our good fortune at having found it first. We signed the lease immediately.

We chatted excitedly during the fifteen-minute drive back to Woudenberg three days later. Eric told me about the extremely cool F-15 he would be flying, and I told him all about the town of Zeist, the cute shops, the pastries, the deer park, the location of the train station, and my afternoon run—in the rain, of course. The explorer in me was not about to waste a minute of this wonderful experience. I only had three years here. Only three. So much to see, so much to do. Eric told me he'd talked to a woman in the base's education department who was looking for a computer science instructor, so it appeared I might have a job too.

Pulling up in front of the house, we saw an elderly white-haired man waiting. After some pleasantries, the landlord let us in, making a half-hearted attempt at a tour. From the minute we walked in the door, we knew we were in trouble. Smelly worn carpet covered the entry hall floor. There was a half-bath under the stairs with a discolored toilet and a miniscule sink with only a cold-water faucet. I estimated the diameter of the sink to be less than eight inches. The kitchen was shabby and drafty, and most of the windows appeared to be ancient and leaky. I was sure I could hear the sounds of mice scurrying about; we later discovered they had infested the house. There was a dark cellar I was sure I would never enter.

Going upstairs, we grimaced as a musty mildew scent greeted us. There were three bedrooms, one so small the pilot living there had used it as a closet. The walls were not symmetrical, typical of buildings of past centuries, and it might have been charming except for the smell and the torn, garish wallpaper throughout. There was a long, vertical tear through the walls in two of the bedrooms. Was the house falling down on one side? The master bedroom had a small balcony with a door, and although there was no closet, at least the wall wasn't cracked like the other rooms. At the end of the hallway was a sink.

I looked at Eric as he stared back at me. We were mortified. "Where's the bathroom?" Eric asked. "I saw the toilet under the stairs, and there's a sink at the end of the hallway, but where's the real bathroom?"

The landlord looked confused. "*Badkamer*? It is old house. The other pilot did not mind."

"How are we supposed to take a shower? Outside in the rain?" I retorted.

Eric shot me a glance. I hadn't meant to be rude, but honestly.

The landlord smiled. "*Ja ja*. This house has shower. I do myself." He walked us back into the master bedroom and shut the door. We hadn't noticed the door behind it. I heard Eric sigh in relief. The landlord opened the door to reveal a shower nestled into the tiniest closet I'd ever seen. I couldn't believe it; I'd never seen anything like it before. There was no possible way to shut the door while in the shower. There was no light, no room for a towel bar, no shelf for toiletries.

"*Heel goed*? I do myself," the landlord announced.

Eric fumed, I felt sick, and the landlord beamed. "You move in after pilot leaves, in three weeks, I think. Ask at base. They give you key. *Dank je*."

With that, he walked down the stairs and out the front door. Eric and I stared at each other. After a long pause, Eric shook his head. "I can go to the base and complain. Perhaps we can get out of the lease we signed, but it's not going to make a good impression. I'm only a first lieutenant, and this is my first assignment. The base is small. It'll get around."

"I don't think you should do anything to hurt your career."

"Carol, your happiness is more important. There's no way I'm going to let you live in this dump. It doesn't even have a bathtub, for God's sake, and I know how much you enjoy taking a bath."

I hesitated. It could take months to find another place. I'd met a wife yesterday who was still living in a small hotel after three months. Could I live with this? The town was cute, the grocery store was within walking distance, and the bus stop was at the end of the street. Those swans. That pond. I'd noticed an incredible running course on the drive here; I could go right out the front door and run through breathtaking countryside.

"Eric, there isn't anything you can't fix," I said. "What if we ask the landlord for paint and new carpet? Maybe there's a wood floor under that gross carpet in the entryway. One of the wives said the base would give us a real refrigerator to use. I'll bet we can even put up some new wallpaper."

"I'm not spending my money on this dump," Eric shouted, moving into the hallway, glaring at the sink, and then stomping into the second bedroom, running his hands along the crack in the wall.

"If the landlord buys the stuff, will you help me fix it?" I asked cautiously.

"I'm supposed to be studying and flying my jet, not fixing up some stupid rental."

Eric walked slowly back to the master bedroom. He looked in the shower closet. "How are we going to live with this? I can't install a bathtub."

"I can live without a bathtub. The living room is great. Those windows are huge."

We stood in silence for quite some time. Eric groaned loudly. "If you're sure, let's go talk to the landlord."

After trudging down the stairs, we found the landlord standing in the front yard chatting with the neighbor. We took him aside, politely expressed our hesitation with the house, and offered our proposition for fixing it up. Eric made it clear, if he didn't agree, we would go to the base and insist on breaking the lease. I smiled as sweetly as I could and said, "You should take advantage of my husband's offer. He can fix anything, and your house will look great when he's done."

"Please show me."

We walked through the house and Eric pointed out to him, room by room, the repairs he would make, the supplies he would need. After an hour of negotiating, the landlord agreed. I was happy because I would get all new carpeting upstairs, and we had permission to rip up the entryway carpet and lay down linoleum. The landlord agreed to pay for everything as long as we did not go over a certain set amount.

We were almost to Zeist before Eric spoke. "You're a good sport. That must be why I married you. I guess it's a cute town, but that bathroom thing is shit."

"Think of it this way, Eric. It'll make for a great story. We can always blame it on jet lag."

We lived in that house for over a year and a half, but when base housing became available in the neighboring town of Soesterberg, Eric took it immediately. He'd had enough of the mice, the drafty winters, the shower in the closet, and the barn filled with horse shit. We could only run one appliance at a time in that house or the fuses would blow, and the dryer emptied into the kitchen, adding to the heat and steam. Still, I enjoyed my stay in Woudenberg tremendously, and I missed it when we moved to Soesterberg. I felt a deep ache for the swans, the market, and my running courses. The inconveniences of that old house seemed a small price to pay for the immense experiences I reaped from having lived there.

* * *

I finished the story as Knight emerged from Eric's room. "Looks better."

I called Patty and David and gave them the good news. David was working on locating an eye doctor. He'd heard about some revolutionary new treatments for cases like Eric's. He sounded hopeful, but before he hung up, he said it again. Why did he have to keep saying it? "Go home, Carol. It's time to go home."

Deflated once again, I sat at the nurse's station, my head in my hands. Damn, he had to say it.

Day 12
Saturday, October 21, 2000

"I've never read Harry Potter, but if Robin likes it, then it must be a great book."
- Eric

The shift change hadn't yet occurred, and already I was crying. Yellow mucus was spilling out of the holes in the smelly, wet bandages and onto the towel under Eric's head. I wanted him cleaned up. He deserved as much dignity as possible.

Amanda suctioned the mucus and replaced the towel. A few minutes later, it was dripping again. How was I going to get through another day?

Then I noticed it. "Amanda, there's blood in Eric's trach tube."

"I'll tell Dr. Russell as soon as she gets here."

Brenna peered in the room on her way to the morning meeting and introduced the other nurse, Rochelle. She was the one who'd been so nasty to me when Eric had gone to surgery in those first days.

I pointed. "Brenna, there's blood in Eric's trach tube."

Amanda whispered something to Brenna, who nodded. Normally I would have gone out to the waiting room during the shift change, but not today. I sat in the chair across from Eric's room and waited.

"How are you holding up this morning?" Russell asked when she arrived.

"There's blood in Eric's trach tube," I repeated dully.

"It's probably from the heparin, but I'll discuss it with Dr. Lewis. He's filling in for Dr. Knight today." She seemed calm, and nothing in her demeanor betrayed worry.

Another new doctor. It was hard keeping track of all the medical people. I got faces, names, and specialties confused. There were so many.

I called Patty while I waited for the bronch. "What does Russell say?" she asked after I told her about the bleeding.

"That it might be the heparin."

"I'll call her in about an hour or so and get back to you. I spoke with David late last night. He says he's coming back on Friday. He's excited about some eye guy he's located. He says he wants to take his mom home with him to Nevada next Monday."

"Who will watch the girls?" I asked. "Eric needs me. I have to be here."

"I'll be coming back when David leaves. What if you go home at night? I'm sure Sandy can get the girls

from school, and I know there are lots of helpers willing to drive them to lessons and school functions."

"But I don't think I can drive back and forth. I don't
feel—"

"Carol," Patty interrupted. "I know you're not eating. That's probably why you're dizzy and feel sick all
the time."

"I'm not hungry."

"Eric would want you to eat," Patty insisted. "I'll
call later. Hang in there."

I rushed over in time to hear Russell's report. "The
lungs look better."

Dr. Lewis introduced himself and shook my hand.
Amber-brown eyes, around six feet tall, fortyish, the
new doc explained that the blood in the trach tube was
"most likely due to the heparin." He didn't think we
should be overly concerned.

Visitors and the bandage change filled the morning. Brandon was in a crabby mood, and I cautioned
him to be gentle with Eric. I wasn't sure whether he
heard me over his grumbling.

I was comforted to see my girls. Tia had brought
all kinds of materials, such as feathers and fuzzy
pipe cleaners, to decorate pens. She explained that
she was setting up a shop to sell them right there in
the waiting room. When I started to protest, Sandy
whispered, "Let her." Throughout the morning, several people, including some of the nurses, bought her
pens.

Robin spent part of the morning on my lap with her two Harry Potter books. I'd given her a Harry Potter-themed slumber party for her tenth birthday a few weeks ago. Since there were no party favors available, I'd had to invent my own. In order to do it, I'd read the first book. Eric was quite impressed with my hard work, even dressing up as a dementor—a scary character from the book.

Several people in the waiting room listened as Robin told them about her party and how I'd decorated the whole downstairs to look like Hogwarts. I told her she should read Harry Potter to her daddy, but I could tell she was afraid to go in the room. She still called out to him from the doorway, refusing to enter.

"I could set a chair in the doorway for you so you could read to Daddy," I said.

"Will you read Harry Potter to Daddy?"

"Of course I will."

From across the room, Tia carried on an animated conversation with two of Eric's pilot friends who'd come to visit. The friend from Cessna was busy buying several pens.

"Is there anything at all I can do for you, Carol?" the pilot from Raytheon asked.

There was something. I had my purse with me, and I opened it and took out a baggie. *The baggie.* The one with Eric's things in it. I opened it and handed him Eric's watch. "Can you get Eric's wedding ring off the watchband?"

About ten minutes later, I was wearing the ring on a black cord, compliments of Tia. She put her arms around me. "I love you, Mommy. Daddy will get better."

Tia and Robin were going to spend the night with me at the hotel. After a final check on Eric, the three of us trooped over to the hotel to deposit their overnight bags.

We walked back to the hospital in silence.

Linda brought two large shoeboxes full of supplies: colored paper, markers, tape, fancy scissors, and stickers. Tia was happiest when she had an art project; she loved to create things. Linda, who wasn't just book smart, had figured it out.

Linda was amazing with the girls, especially considering she had no children of her own. Tia liked the way Linda treated her as an adult, and Robin thought my university friend told funny stories.

"Sit with Eric," Linda told me. "The three of us are going to be busy."

"I didn't know you were such an artist. Is that why you were so good in chem lab?"

"Can we do chemistry experiments?" Robin asked excitedly.

I shook my head. "You have lots of thank-you cards to write."

"Art's better anyway," Tia said, bending over a piece of pink construction paper, the marker in her hand flying furiously.

I started reading Harry Potter, much to Robin's delight. Brenna was impressed with the girls and asked many questions: where they went to school, what they liked to do. "Were they born in Kansas?" she asked.

"No. Tia wasn't even born in this country."

* * *

Eric was with me for Tia's birth in the Netherlands, and he liked to remind me of it. As proof, he would point to a copy of the medical record from my Dutch doctor. She'd written "And Mrs. Fiore gave birth with the tremendous help of her husband." Eric was quite proud of that and loved to explain his revolutionary approach concerning childbirth to anyone who would listen. It involved a bag of presents, one to be given after each contraction.

I remember one nasty contraction after which Eric whipped out a book from the present bag. It was an aviation book detailing appropriate speeds for the aircraft; I'd been gazing at it fondly in a catalogue. Eric proceeded to explain, in much detail, about a particular point in the book. After twelve hours of labor, I wasn't in the mood to discuss aircraft speeds, but I said nothing. After Eric rambled on for quite some time, during which he failed to notice two more contractions, he stared at me and commented, matter-of-factly, "I don't think you're paying attention at all."

That may have been my chance to smack him, but I didn't. My glare said it all. He shut up and went back to encouraging me—about the contractions, not my flying knowledge.

My Dutch doctor had warned me beforehand, "Women have been having babies for thousands of years, and you can too." That was Dutch for "you're not getting drugs, honey." Other than being tired from the all-night labor, I was fully awake and not drugged: no epidural, no medicine, and I walked back to my room and took a shower.

When Eric heard women whining about their labor and delivery, he would remark, "I didn't think it was that painful, but it was boring." I knew he was teasing, but more than one woman looked as though she wanted to kill him.

Eric's face was rapturous when he held Tia. He cut the umbilical cord and wrapped her in a soft pink blanket. My doctor proceeded to tell me again how she'd never seen a husband quite so incredible. He'd been amazing all night and into the morning, encouraging me, walking with me, getting me ice. During all of it, I never yelled at him or called him names, but at one point, I did tell him to be quiet and let the doctor talk.

There was silence as my Dutch doctor turned to me and said, "Listen to your husband, Mrs. Fiore. He is doing a wonderful job."

Eric was unbearable after that.

*　*　*

Brenna was delighted with my story. "You should write that down. It says a lot about Eric."

For the rest of the afternoon, I alternated between Eric's room and the waiting room. Tia told me in detail about the cheerleading tryouts on Tuesday.

"Are you sure you still want to try out?" I asked.

"Yes. Daddy said I could. Daddy said I'd be a good cheerleader."

He had. We'd discussed it several times. I wanted to discourage the whole thing, but Eric insisted Tia should be free to explore what she wanted. I reluctantly agreed.

"But Tia," I said, "you wouldn't want them to pick you because of the accident."

She'd tried out before and hadn't made the squad. I had no doubts if she tried out now, the judges would pick her. I didn't want my kids to get things because of a tragedy. It felt wrong.

"I'm a good cheerleader. I deserve to be picked."

I could see there was no discouraging it. I watched as she reached for another cookie. Robin whispered to me that Tia was hiding food in her dresser drawers.

"Tia, why don't you have some of the fruit Daddy's friend brought instead of all those sweets?" I asked in my happiest, most upbeat voice.

Tia's response was to grab a handful of cookies and cram them in her mouth. As I looked away, I caught a glimpse of her shoving another handful into her backpack. I pretended not to notice, but I knew one day I would have to notice.

I gazed sadly at my two beautiful girls and wondered if, years from now, they would look back on this time and concede that this was when their childhood ended.

Day 13
Sunday, October 22, 2000

*"Encourage kids to debate and question,
even if it means they'll argue with you.
And you better believe Tia will."*
– Eric

I rolled over and stared into the face of an angel, cascading honey-blond hair, eyes shut tightly, mouth slightly open. She was barely ten years old, still my baby, but trying to be a big girl. When Robin fell asleep, she was in the other double bed with Tia. I had slept all night, the first time since the accident. Perhaps having my girls with me and being away from the hospital brought some sense of normalcy. I didn't want to go back to the hospital, feeling an almost desperate need to stay here.

The tears welled up as I watched my sweet Robin sleeping. Why did she have to go through this? I felt a hard lump under my leg and reached around for the source: my cell phone. I must have fallen asleep with it in my hand. I quickly looked down at it, noting, thankfully, there were no calls, but I panicked when I noticed the time. It was 6:30 a.m., and I needed to get going before the shift change.

I leaned over and kissed Robin's forehead. Slowly opening her eyes, clutching the hugging monkeys, she said, "Mommy, are you ever coming home?"

As I struggled with a reply, Tia's strong voice sailed through the room. Clearly, she'd been awake for some time. "Don't make Mommy feel bad, Robin. You know she has to stay with Daddy."

I looked over at Tia. She was lying on her back fiddling with her waist-length blond hair. "I love you, Tia-wee," I called to her.

She rolled over and faced the opposite wall. "Daddy's the only one allowed to call me that."

I crawled in bed with her. She moved away at first, but then reluctantly gave me a hug. "I guess we have to go back over *there*."

I nodded.

"I want to go home." She said it slowly, enunciating each word.

"Mimi and Ba will be coming to get you later this morning," I assured her. "What if I go down to the lobby and bring up some juice and donuts for you? I was thinking maybe I'd come home tomorrow, for a few hours. Maybe I could meet you when you get off the school bus. How about that?"

Robin clapped while Tia inquired about the donut variety.

A half hour later, we walked back to the hospital. Tia had eaten her own donuts, plus Robin's.

Eric was on his back, upright on the damn circle bed. The report from the night nurse was that he had been "boring." I always liked that report because it meant nothing bad had happened, except, of course, the dialysis machine. The stupid Prisma was down again. If Eric was supposed to be on it, then he should be on it. There wasn't blood in his trach tube, so I reasoned that must mean there was less heparin in his IV bag, which meant his blood was too thick, which meant the dialysis filter had clogged. I had no idea if that reasoning was valid, and I was too tired to ask.

Brenna introduced me to Lydia. The new nurse looked older than the other mostly young nurses and wore a yellow-dotted hairband in her curly brunette hair.

Robin decided to read Harry Potter to her daddy, and Brenna set up a chair for her in the doorway. There was still plenty of room for people to get around her as she read. I promised I would read to her daddy all week while she was in school.

Robin was reading when Tia pushed past her and started a loud explanation of why she was trying out for cheerleading. Robin's voice became louder as she tried to read over Tia's talking. Shutting her book with a huff, Robin yelled at her sister, "You are so rude, Tia. I'm reading Harry Potter to Daddy."

As I started to intervene, Tia turned to Robin and said, "We shouldn't be fighting. Daddy wouldn't like it."

Lydia and Brenna suppressed a smile as Tia left for the waiting room. Robin opened her book and continued. "OK, Daddy. Back to Harry Potter…"

Out in the hall, I whispered to Brenna and Lydia, "It's a good thing Eric is covered in bandages. I don't think they could handle it."

"Have you seen his face without the bandages?" Lydia asked.

"Only when he first came in. I haven't…uh…not since the surgery."

Brenna and Lydia looked at each other.

"I'm going to look one day. I will," I said.

Brenna whispered softly, "You don't have to."

Lydia went back in to check instruments and change IV bags, and I heard her speak to Eric, softly so as not to disturb Robin's reading. "You've got great kids there, Eric. Your wife is pretty great too."

In the waiting room, I took money out of my bag and handed it to Tia. "Robin, your sister is going to help you get something to eat."

"No, Mommy. I want you to come with me," said Robin.

"Tia knows where the cafeteria is. Don't you, Tia?"

Tia nodded furiously and yelled at Robin to hurry up. Robin folded her arms tightly across her chest. "I'm not going without Mommy," she said.

"All right. Let me tell the nurses. But we have to get it to go. OK?"

Ten minutes later, we were in the coffee shop. They were still serving breakfast food. I obsessively checked my watch as Tia reached for several donuts. "Tia. Honey. Please get something healthy."

A few angry words flew from her mouth, but she decided on bacon, a waffle, and only two donuts. Great. Grease, carbs, and sugar. As we neared the cashier, Tia reached for a can of Coke.

"Please, Tia. No soda. Get juice or milk," I said in my sweetest voice.

She plunked the soda can down loudly. "Fine. I'll have water."

Robin pointed down at her tray. "Mommy, I'm having scramblers, but I'll bet they're not as good as Daddy's."

Tia shoved herself between us. "Stop making Mommy cry."

Robin whispered to me that she was having sausage too.

Eric and I laughed about Robin and her sausage. She'd tasted summer sausage when she was two and since then had carried on a love affair with almost every variety of sausage. It was absolutely her favorite food. As a toddler, she would do a squirmy happy wiggle when I served it for a meal. Eric called it the sausage dance. He was always careful to put a small summer sausage in Robin's Christmas stocking every year.

The girls ate in the waiting room while I went in to check on Eric. Brenna had paged Russell. "She wanted to be present during part of the bandage change," she told me, trying to sound casual as she adjusted her light-blue standard-issue scrub top. Brenna didn't experiment with scrub top colors and patterns as some of the other nurses did. It was always the same professional blue color.

I watched Russell go in, shutting the door behind her. I knew what she was going to say. I had tried all morning not to think about Eric's fingers.

About ten minutes later Russell squatted down beside me. "Several grafts are yellow. Eric has some necrotic fat on his face, and there are signs of infection on the left side. His fingertips don't look good. We're going to have to get him back into surgery. Dr. Knight will be here tomorrow, and we can discuss it then."

I was ready, yet I wasn't. "Please save his fingers."

"We'll do our best."

I sat outside Eric's room while the bandage change continued. I was a mess, and I didn't want the kids to see me like this. Russell had used that word again: necrotic.

Dead.

I wiped my face, blew my nose, and slowly walked through the big double doors that led to the waiting room.

Tia was busy complaining about the music coming softly over the speakers. "Daddy wouldn't like this dumb music. Can't you make them turn the channel?"

"Daddy wouldn't care," I said. "Music wasn't all that big of a deal to him."

"It's dumb."

Actually, she was right. Eric would have hated it.

* * *

Music is an essential part of my life. Listening to music, keeping up with current trends, discussing artists and music trivia were important to me and had been since I was in high school and regularly read music magazines. Eric found it all a waste of time.

Eric enjoyed the sound of silence. I liked background music, but Eric did not, referring to it as noise. He absolutely detested my favorite artist, Prince, and it was a source of friction between us. If Prince was on, Eric would turn it off. He didn't think I should subject him to what he called Prince's high-pitched, unmusical screams. I was furious I couldn't listen to my favorite music.

Eric's all-time favorite group was the Rolling Stones, and he owned most of their albums. When we were first dating, he often played their music. Our song was "Wild Horses."

* * *

"Are you done, Robin?" I pointed down at her plate. She'd left most of her sausage. "Don't you like your sausage?"

"I'm not hungry."

Tia was still complaining about the music when Eric's parents arrived. Dad said my article still wasn't in the paper, but there had been an apology. The paper was sorry for any pain they may have caused the families.

Robin went over to her grandfather. "What did they do, Ba?"

Tia spoke right up. "I know what they did. They said the firemen heard screaming. Some kids at school said Daddy was screaming, and I said that wasn't Daddy screaming 'cause my daddy—"

Mimi made a loud "hush" sound to Tia.

"What?" I'd heard whispers, but I'd tried to ignore them. There was a reason I refused to read the papers. Now it seemed what I'd heard was true. Men screaming for their lives...

I ran into the bathroom, slamming the door behind me. I sat on the floor, in the corner of the enormous room, under a coatrack, my head in my hands.

After a few minutes, there was a knock at the door. "Carol, it's Mom. Are you all right?"

I mumbled out a weak yes, but I wasn't fine. Images of the fire and flames had haunted me for over twelve days. I'd been having terrible nightmares, and now this. The sounds of men screaming for their lives had been added to the horrible vision I'd formed in my head. Sounds of Eric screaming. Visions of Bryan and Dave burning to death.

When I returned to the waiting room, Eric's parents were speaking with the head of Bombardier, Colin White. Maybe I should have him look at Eric's face without the bandages. I hid my anger once again, shaking his hand. Was the concern he showed sincere? I wanted to yell at him, to throw things at him, but I couldn't because Eric wouldn't like it.

Mr. White handed me a check to help cover expenses while Eric was in the hospital, saying it was for family members' airfare; he knew many people had been flying out to help. He'd also heard what the zoo did. He was furious and said someone would be calling the zoo about it. I shrugged because it was too late now. I took the check and thanked him. I knew Eric's parents had already spent several thousand dollars on airfare for themselves and Lisa.

I looked down at the check. It could have been a million dollars and I would have felt the same: I was grateful; it was generous, but Eric was still lying in there. No amount of money could make it right.

Mom and the girls left for the house. Dad was flying back to New York; he'd had enough. I kissed him good-bye. What could I say? That it was going to be OK? We all knew it wasn't. I said the only thing I could. "I'll never leave your son. I'll be here every day and make sure things are done right."

He nodded and wiped at his bloodshot eyes. His shoulders slumped as he gave me a weak hug.

The nurses had the television on in Eric's room, and there was coverage of a NASA shuttle launch. I told Lydia and Brenna how Eric had always wanted to be an astronaut and how he applied to NASA every year. He had applied this year; we hadn't received the letter yet—the "they don't want me" letter, as Eric called it.

"Don't you have to be in the military?" Lydia asked.

"No," I said. "It helps, but NASA hires civilians, especially mission specialists."

"But your husband was in the military, wasn't he?"

"Yes, for over nine years."

"I've heard they do some intense training," Brenna said.

"They do." I paused. "But they do some intense partying too."

Lydia smiled. "You know you can't leave us without details. Spill."

"When he graduated from Air Force pilot training back in the early summer of 1984…well, that was a party."

* * *

I leaned back on the picnic table bench. Graduation was over, and I was glad to be out of that formal dress and back in my shorts and T-shirt. The sounds of a party in full swing echoed through the warm Texas night. The lights from the base exchange parking lot flickered down the street, and I could hear laughter coming from inside the foreign pilots' duplex.

A firecracker shot by my head. Startled, I rose from the bench. That was a bit much. You'd think pilots would have more sense. I sat back down and kicked off my sandals.

Eric had graduated first in his pilot training class. Thirteen months of hard work had ended, and soon we'd be leaving Sheppard AFB, but not until I finished my research project. That was a smart move on my part, working on my computer science master's degree. Some of the other wives had spent the time bothering their husbands, but not me. I stayed out of Eric's way so he could concentrate on studying. I congratulated myself.

Soon we'd be off to Holland. Everybody said an F-15 to Camp New Amsterdam was the best assignment in the Air Force. Eric got his dream plane, and I would get to live in Europe. Yep, life was good. I peered down at the empty glass on the table. Maybe I'd get another rum and Coke. In a minute… It was relaxing to sit here, look at the stars, and listen to the sounds of half a dozen languages.

I spotted two of the American wives strolling toward me, and I sank down a bit and shifted position. I didn't want them to interrupt my thoughts, and truthfully, I preferred the foreign wives. If a woman was going to gossip, it sounded better with an accent.

"Carol," exclaimed one of them breathlessly as she sat down next to me, "did you see her? She's walking around the kitchen with no top on."

The other wife stood in front of us, nodding furiously.

"Yes, I saw her. Is that what our party dues paid for? The stripper?"

"I told my husband he'd better stay away from her," exclaimed the standing wife, arms folded across her chest.

The other laughed. "Oh please, she's not even good-looking. What do you think, Carol?"

I smiled. "I saw her, and let me say, I'm not worried."

We giggled like naughty schoolchildren. After a few moments, the two wandered off. When the music started up, I suspected the stripper was dancing again. Only a bunch of fighter pilots would hire a stripper to dance on a picnic table in full presence of the security police. When assignments were handed out last week, the whole class got fighters—no transports or tankers for this bunch of hotshots. Eric got the best plane in the whole class. I was glad he got an F-15 instead of an F-16 because two engines were definitely better than one.

The American girlfriend of one of the young Norwegian pilots came hurrying up to me. "Oh my God," she squealed, "look at your husband."

I wheeled around to where she was pointing. Rising, I followed her toward the noise. Eric was on top of a picnic table with the stripper, swinging his hips and waving his arms like some silly fool, and as if that wasn't enough, the stripper was trying to remove his pants. I watched, mortified, as a couple of the wives helped rid him of his jeans. I covered my face with my hands and peeked out. No question now about his choice of underwear. Everyone was looking at the purple briefs I'd bought him for Christmas last year. He was still wearing his Nocona cowboy boots—his first purchase when we arrived in Texas because he "wanted to blend."

Sure. OK. He was blending now.

Amid the cheers, a couple of the German wives started to stuff dollar bills in his purple briefs. I retreated to a picnic table, sat down huffily, and turned my back to the action.

As I pouted, Eric's flight commander, Kevin, the one who'd told me about the bunny murders at survival camp, whispered, "He's worked hard. Let him have his fun."

It only made me pout harder. Maybe Marcos, the loser I'd dated at Parks before Eric, had been right in pegging me as a prude all those years ago.

"Don't be mad," Kevin cautioned. "Be the supportive wife you've been for the past thirteen months. This is a big night for him. He got his jet, and now he's letting loose." He patted me on the shoulder as he walked away. "Be a good sport."

The two American wives who'd spoken to me earlier waved in my direction. Oh, the gossip that would start over this. In an attempt to be a good sport, I called over to them, "Stop looking. He's taken." He'd danced in those tiny purple briefs for me. The other wives shouldn't get to ogle him.

One of the German wives stumbled toward me. She'd obviously had several drinks. "You're lucky," she said, slurring her words as she motioned to Eric. "He has the cutest butt, and…" Her words trailed off, unspoken but implied. He filled out those briefs nicely.

I smiled weakly.

When I couldn't stand it anymore, I moved to where I could see the show. Eric struggled to get his pants back on amid the laughter. Guys patted him on the back. He started toward me, surrounded by several of the pilots and accompanied by Kevin.

"Carol, look. I made seventeen bucks." He planted a wet kiss on my cheek. "You're not mad, are you?"

Kevin, the ever-present flight instructor, eyed me intently. "No," I said.

Eric laughed that young boy laugh of his, that charming sweet laugh that said he was being silly, having fun, and getting all the attention because he was Eric. "I'm going to get another beer. Want something?"

"Sure. A rum and Coke. We're walking home, right?" I tried to sound casual, as if near-naked tabletop dancing with strippers was an everyday occurrence.

"Of course we're walking. This party's just getting good."

I didn't need anyone to point it out. I'd always known he had a cute butt, especially in those tiny purple briefs. Maybe I wasn't such a prude after all.

*　*　*

Brenna grinned as I finished my story. Chuckling, Lydia said, "You're in trouble now, Eric. Carol told us the whole thing."

"It sounds like he has quite a sense of humor," Brenna added.

"And he must be smart to be a test pilot," Lydia said. "What a great combination."

"He's sophisticated too," I replied. "But he's careful not to let people see it."

Eric didn't want people to think he was too cultured, especially not his pilot and mechanic buddies. Perhaps it seemed a bit unmanly to him. Parents with advanced English degrees had raised him. Their home had a large bust of Shakespeare in the entryway, and books overflowed shelves onto piles on the floors, in the attic, even in the basement. The family discussed art and literature, and since Eric's mom had studied ballet, dance was a frequent topic. They argued nuances of books over the dinner table, with grammar promptly corrected. Visitors to the Fiore household could expect passionate discussions and debates. It was an unusual atmosphere for a scientifically minded kid like Eric to grow up in, but it helped to mold him into the Renaissance man he became.

As a teacher, Eric's father had helped to introduce an underprivileged group of youths from New York City to culture through a group called the Cultural Horizons. Eric thought the whole concept was ludicrous. Teaching at-risk kids about art and literature was ridiculous, he flatly stated. Train them in a craft, help them get a job, teach them basic math skills, but why bother trying to explain to them what a poet intended when he wrote a piece? Eric started referring to his father's group as the "cultur-izing" club. Later, the word "culturizing" came to stand for an attempt by his parents to expose anyone, including himself, to culture.

Eric's parents retired to a charming upstate New York town. If we happened to be visiting in July, they took us to see a performance of the New York City Ballet. Eric referred to it as being dragged to the ballet because he wanted to make it clear he was not going of his own free will. It was, he insisted, all part of his parents' plot to culturize him. He would never have admitted that he could have discussed the performance with the insight of a critic or that he was quite familiar with the pieces and had even met some of the dancers. He loved to tease his parents with phrases like, "When is the singing going to start?" or "Why are those people leaping? Do they have a disease?" There were also comments about men in tights. He said it only when his parents could hear. They knew he was culturized, and he knew he was culturized, but he liked to keep up the act anyway. When the kids got older, Eric told his parents, "Stop culturizing me and go culturize your grandkids."

Forced to attend an opera with her school class, Tia had complained about the woman who sang on and on about her shoes being too tight. Eric had gleefully exclaimed, "Getting culturized is good for you."

Eric wasn't that fond of the ballet or the opera, but he adored trips to a decent art museum. I felt as though I had my own personal art expert. He knew hundreds of stories and had a deep appreciation for art. His sense of humor would frequently leak out.

Once in the Metropolitan Museum of Art in New York City, as we viewed a huge white canvas with a big black blob in the middle, Eric leaned toward me and said in a stage whisper, "You know, I am quite well versed in this artist's style. I'm shocked the Met would hang a masterpiece like this upside down."

I played along. "You're right. It's shocking. Do you think we should call him?"

"Maybe we should consider not mailing our yearly check to this museum. I realize half a mil isn't that much money, but it could be a lesson for the future."

Eric pointed out to me later that it was important to have fun while being culturized.

Day 14
Monday, October 23, 2000

*"You know I love you, Carol.
I made you a tool bit."*
- Eric

I pulled at my hair, jumped at every sound. Knight was going to come out of Eric's room. He was looking at more than Eric's lungs. He was looking at his fingers.

The dialysis had been down during the night, but now it was back up. I couldn't think about the stupid Prisma this morning. I could only think about Eric's fingers.

The door finally opened. I held my breath. If I ran to the bathroom or to the waiting room, Knight couldn't find me. He couldn't tell me. Before he opened his mouth, I looked at Russell. She was looking at her shoes. I knew what Knight was going to say.

"Lungs look a bit better."

I had already decided I wasn't going to ask. I shifted nervously, and as I was about to exhale, Knight spoke again. "He'll be going to surgery tomorrow, so I'm going to need an authorization signed. We'll be debriding the face and extremities, and possible amputation of the digits on both hands."

They were going to cut off Eric's fingers.

How was I going to tell Eric? What words could I possibly use? His hands were his life. How could they be functional without fingers? They would be stubs. He couldn't fly or grip his bicycle handlebars or shift his sports car. He couldn't paint, tinker with power tools, build amazing things. Could he hold ski poles? Would we be able to go cross-country skiing together?

Mom arrived. For the first time in thirteen days, I was going home for a visit. With my cell phone clutched in one hand, I followed her out to the parking garage. It felt strange to be leaving the hospital. Always a nervous driver, Mom was an absolute wreck.

"Whose car is this?" I asked her. "Why aren't you driving our Jeep?"

"This is a rental. I didn't feel comfortable driving your car," she said.

"But you know I don't care if you drive the Jeep."

"I didn't want to." Her eyes were fixated on the road ahead, her hands tightly gripping the steering wheel.

Why wasn't she going down the main highway to get home? She was driving through the middle of town and hitting every stoplight. I wondered if I should say something. I didn't want to pick on her; we were all wrecks, but I seriously wondered if she should be driving. I knew I shouldn't be.

"Why don't you use the highway? It's faster." It didn't come out as delicately as I'd hoped.

"It scares me to merge with all those lanes."

She was doing her best. Far better than me. "Eric would be proud of you for driving. Wichita is a big city."

"Thank you for saying that, Carol."

I felt as though I hadn't seen my house in years. I noticed the unmarked police car, the one Tia had described, sitting in front of the house. The officer appeared bored as he glanced out the window, nodding to us. I looked at my watch. The girls would be getting off the bus in ten minutes, and I'd planned to walk down to the end of the street to meet them. I had about an hour to spend with them before Linda picked me up.

I walked up the sidewalk to the front door. Someone had mowed the grass. Entering, I smelled a dozen different scents. A huge basket filled the entryway, the dining room table held vases and pots of greenery, and there were flower arrangements in all corners of the living room. Food covered the kitchen counters. The place was a mess. I didn't recognize my house anymore. Eric, my zoo job, my home…All gone.

My yellow-and-gray cockatiel peeped loudly as I approached her cage. She hissed and refused to come out. "Flutter, I'm so sorry. He's not coming home for a long time. But he loves you." She continued to hiss and wiggle her wings in a threatening pose. I considered getting the glove and pulling her out but decided against it.

I took Dusty, a rescue rabbit from the city shelter, out of her cage. "Dusty, my gentle bunny, I missed you." I buried my face in her black-and-white fur. I knew no one had let her run around the house even though she was litter box trained.

My sweet pets...

Then I remembered.

I walked quickly up the stairs, down the hall, into my bedroom. I looked on my vanity table, but I knew what I'd find. My blue key ring was sitting off to one side, and the key that had been on it was gone. They'd come. The assistant director of the zoo had sent someone to get it.

"Carol," Mom called. "You'd better get Robin."

Too late. I heard Robin coming through the front door; I'd missed my opportunity to meet the bus.

"Robin, guess who's here?" My mother-in-law's voice rang out.

I hurried down the stairs.

"Mommy!" Robin leaped into my arms. "You came home."

"Of course I did, pumpkin," I said, hugging her tightly.

"Is Daddy all right?"

I struggled against the tears. "Yes, honey. I read Harry Potter to him today. Tell me what's going on at school. Wait a minute. Where's Tia? Did she miss the bus?"

"She has a stupid meeting for cheerleading tryouts. Remember?"

"That's right." I'd forgotten. *Damn.* I wasn't going to be able to see Tia today.

Robin and I sorted the mail. There were piles of get-well cards, but I left them for later. I didn't want to waste what little time I had; Robin needed me. She pointed to a big box by the front door and insisted I open it.

"It's Flopsy's marker," I said.

Eric and I had ordered a small gravestone for Tia's old bunny. Dusty had been with us only two years, but Flopsy had been a part of the family for over eight. A few weeks ago, Eric buried her. I still had the note he'd written and left on her empty cage.

> *Thank you for taking care of me my whole life. I am a very lucky bunny to have had such a good life.*
> *I left this world peacefully and now I'm playing outside with the wild rabbits.*
> *I'll always be your bunny.*
> *Love, Flopsy*

Robin interrupted my thoughts. "Can we put it on Flopsy's grave?"

After laying the small marker on the grave, Robin and I walked around the yard, and she showed me a tree house she'd built in our woods. "Daddy would be proud of me 'cause I built it by myself." She beamed.

"Yes, he would. Do you have homework I can help you with?"

"No. The teacher said I don't have to do it, but I am anyway. It's easy."

"Do the teachers tell Tia that too?"

"Yes, so she doesn't do her work," she said, giving me an isn't-it-obvious look.

Looming problems.

"Tia says she'll be a cheerleader," continued Robin.

A short while later, Linda knocked on the door.

"Do you have to go, Mommy?" Robin asked.

Mimi took her by the hand. "Let your mommy go, Robin."

I watched Robin wave from the window as we drove off. I wanted to be with my girls, but I had to be with Eric. I felt sure that in time they would be proud of how I'd stayed by their father's side. Sometimes the right thing isn't the easy thing. Hadn't Eric said those words to me many times? It would be easier to leave the hospital, to come home, but I couldn't abandon Eric.

"What's going on?" Linda asked.

"Eric might lose his fingers."

Linda gasped and gripped the steering wheel with both hands. "I'm so sorry."

"He made the first Christmas present he ever gave me," I blurted. "In 1977. I was eighteen, and he was twenty."

* * *

Every time I saw Eric running around campus in his overalls, tools hanging from his back pockets, I sighed. He was adorable. He rarely walked. He was always running, and when he did walk, it was the fastest gait I'd ever seen. He admired me more than once for being the only girl who could keep up with him. He was fast, he was loud, and you always knew when he was coming.

I was fascinated with the things he did in his airframe and power plant (A&P) classes. He was so educated and cultured, discussing art and history, that it was a bit of a mystery to me why he was learning to be an aircraft mechanic. He delighted in riveting, pounding, welding, building. He wanted to know everything there was to know about airplanes. He'd started out as an aerospace engineer at Parks but had switched to the A&P program, which resulted in his airplane mechanic's license and an associate degree. A few years later, after working as a flight instructor, then a corporate pilot, he'd returned to Parks. After two and a half additional years, during which time I supported us, he received his BS in aerospace engineering. He was proud of the degree and all the pilot ratings, but the

A&P license set him apart. There were engineer pilots, but the engineer pilot who was a licensed mechanic was rare.

When we first met, he was a mechanic student. To me he was always a brilliant pilot playing at being a mechanic, but I enjoyed going to his A&P classes to meet people or to see what he'd been building. I never understood his fascination with welding. He'd put on a hood and goggles, a big grin on his face as he held a glowing torch.

Before Christmas, he'd talked endlessly about a tool bit he was making. I didn't know what a tool bit was, so he showed me. The two-and-a-half-inch-long piece of pointed metal didn't look that impressive, but he was so enthralled with his creation I couldn't help but laugh. We'd been dating steady for about a month, and the subject of tool bits became a "bit" of a joke with us. Right before the end of the semester when he asked me what I wanted for Christmas, I replied immediately, "I want a tool bit."

He was elated. What guy wouldn't want to hear that his girlfriend thought he could make cool stuff? He laughed and asked what else I wanted. I don't remember what I told him, but he did buy me something. I only remember my tool bit, all wrapped up with a bow, which he presented to me before we left school for Christmas break.

He told me later he'd received special permission from the old crusty instructor to stay after class and use the lathe to grind a special bit for me. According to Eric, the instructor thought he was crazy. He would mutter and shake his head. "You're nuts, Fiore. Your girlfriend is probably nuts too. Making a tool bit for a Christmas present…"

After the holiday break, I met the instructor. "So," he said, looking at me intently, "you're Fiore's girlfriend. Did you like your Christmas present?"

"Yes, sir," I exclaimed. "I love tool bits."

Eric grinned as the mystified instructor walked away mumbling something about the two of us being "odd."

Of all the presents Eric ever gave me, the tool bit was the best. As the years went by, he brought it up frequently. If things were tough or if I ever said I doubted his love, his response was always the same.

"You know I love you. How many guys make their girls a tool bit?"

Day 15
Tuesday, October 24, 2000

"Life isn't fair. Fare is something you buy to ride a bus, a train, or a plane."
- Eric

Eric was stable overnight, despite grotesquely swollen feet and yellow facial mucus, and he was off the paralyzing drug. The dialysis was down. I shouldn't have been so upset about the mucus, so obsessed with it, but I was. When Rochelle—the only nurse I didn't like—announced she was in charge of Eric, I was certain it was going to be a bad day.

I called Patty again. "Why wasn't Eric wearing his helmet and gloves?" I knew I was wailing. "The Air Force always made him wear them. He got in trouble if he rolled up the sleeves of his flight suit. If he'd had his gloves on, this wouldn't be happening, and Eric wouldn't…why wasn't he wearing them…and…"

Patty did her best to say what I wanted to hear.

As I sat outside Eric's door, waiting for the bronch to finish, a young priest walked over and squatted down beside me. "Mrs. Fiore? My name is Father Luke. I won't bother you, but if there is anything at all I can do, please let me know."

I moved back slightly. "OK."

Father Luke was young, pale, dark-haired, and good-looking. He didn't appear to be pushy like that other priest, the one I'd thrown out of Eric's room. Still, he was a priest. I had bad memories of many of the priests my religious parents had invited over for dinner when I was growing up. My mother had wanted me to be a nun, but the more my parents shoved Catholicism down my throat, the more I rebelled. I did not like being told what to think, and I didn't like the harsh responses to my many questions. I had a low opinion of priests in general.

"Please ask if I can do anything for you," he repeated as he turned to leave.

What makes a man become a priest? I would never understand it. But maybe there was something that priest could do for me. I should have asked him to demand his God fix Eric's hands. Could he make Eric's fingers whole, so he could once again build a gift as exquisite as the one he'd given me for Christmas seven years ago?

* * *

"Do not look under the towel on my workbench," Eric shouted playfully.

I looked at him with curiosity. "Why? What are you hiding under there?"

"Never mind. You're such a peeker. Don't ruin your Christmas present."

"But Christmas is months away. What could you possibly be doing out there?"

Eric smiled mischievously. "It's the best gift I've ever made, even better than the tool bit."

Over the next few months, I heard him pounding in the garage, looking for tools, humming to himself, giggling like a child with a secret. Sometimes he would say he had to go to the hardware store and remind me not to look on his workbench. Occasionally he'd appoint Tia to be in charge of making sure I didn't go out in the garage. She took her job seriously, and I knew she'd tell, so I never peeked. I wanted to, but I didn't.

As Christmas approached, I could see he was excited as he dropped lines like "just wait…" or "you're going to be so impressed with your boy…"

On Christmas morning, Eric made a big production of presenting the gift. The girls cheered as he carried the large wrapped box into the living room.

"Be careful when you open it," he warned.

The children danced in place and squealed for me to hurry. I cautiously opened it and lifted out the most exquisite carousel I'd ever seen.

"I made the whole thing myself, except for the porcelain figures. I put a music box in it too."

Eric knew I loved carousel horses. I had a small collection. His creation was a foot and a half tall with a base diameter of about a foot. There were five ceramic figures arranged around it: three horses, a zebra, and, of course, an elephant. The base, which held up the peaked roof, had miniature metal pipes made to resemble an organ, and there were three tiny bells attached to the center posts that also contained cutouts of various animals. The roof was in eight sections, each one painted a different bright color: green, yellow, red, and blue. He'd painted gold posts where the metal braces attached the platform to the roof, carefully attending to the smallest details. The roof and base were lacquered; the entire object gleamed, with glass jewels sparkling on the roof.

It was magnificent.

"I'm sorry," he added. "I didn't have enough time to make the base revolve when the music box plays."

"I love it, Eric. It's the most incredible present you've ever given me, right up there with the tool bit."

"This is better than the tool bit. Turn it over. I wrote something on the bottom."

On the underside of the base, he had written the following:

Christmas 1993
To my little redheaded girl.
Love, Eric

I threw my arms around him. "Thank you so much."

"Daddy let me help," six-year-old Tia exclaimed. "I like the zebra the best. Daddy said it had to have an elephant, but I said Mommy likes the horses best."

Robin, only three, turned to Tia and wrinkled her nose. "Mommy's gonna kiss Daddy."

Tia covered her sister's eyes and giggled.

*　*　*

The surgery inched closer.

David called. He was excited about a procedure that used amniotic tissue to protect the integrity of the eyes. Only a few doctors in the country were doing it, and one of them was right here in Wichita.

"Hello, love," Sandy said as she walked into the waiting room. "I've come to sit with you during the surgery." She told me Mom was not emotionally able to come and was waiting for her sister Marjorie, who was arriving today from Boston. "A maid's been to the house," Sandy added.

I felt a rush of anger. Nobody respected anything I said. I told Knight I didn't want Eric on the circle bed, and he did it anyway. I asked Mom not to get a maid, and she did it anyway. I wouldn't leave Eric to go to my job at the zoo, so they sent someone to take my key. I had no control over anything in my life.

The operating room transport team arrived. Panic welled up inside me as I gently held Eric's bandaged right hand. I knew underneath the dressings, it was horrific.

I released my hold on Eric's hand as half a dozen people started removing devices, preparing to transfer him to another bed. It was that same nightmare again: loud voices, orders to perform certain procedures, calls to clear the hallway. I started to follow the team down the hall, but Rochelle stopped me.

Rochelle, the nurse from hell.

Why today, of all days, did it have to be her on duty?

"You cannot follow them. Please go to the waiting room," she commanded.

"I always follow him to the doors. I've always…"

Dr. Russell overheard. "Mrs. Fiore may follow us down to the OR doors."

Tears fell. "I love you, Eric," I continued to call, following the team.

I stood in the hallway for quite some time. When I turned, Rochelle was there. "Please take a seat in the waiting room."

Jennifer came down the hall and guided me to her office.

"Make her go away." I could hear myself shrieking, my voice getting higher and louder. "I hate her. She's such a witch. I don't want her to be Eric's nurse anymore."

I knew I was acting like a child, but I couldn't seem to stop.

Sandy was still in the waiting room, but I barely acknowledged her as I sat in my chair in the corner, arms and legs folded.

Before long I was up, then down, then up. Back and forth, back and forth. Through the steel doors and into Eric's empty room, and then back again to the waiting room. Over and over.

"Carol," Sandy said. "Talk to me."

"The nurse is a witch." I told her about Rochelle.

"Shall I go in and tell her to clear off?"

In the midst of this horrible surgery, I felt myself smile. Sandy was serious. She would really march in there and do it.

At 3:11 p.m., Knight and Russell came out to the waiting room. Knight gave his report, emotionless as always. It was short. He'd rescheduled the surgery for Saturday because fresh cadaver skin was arriving in the next day or two. Techs were performing a dressing change in the operating room.

I spoke quickly. "So Eric still has his fingers?"

Knight stared at me with no emotion. "The hands are quite bad, and he will most likely lose his fingers. The burns are extremely deep, and the tendons are beyond repair. The hands will probably be nonfunctional."

I gasped for air as Knight continued. "A plastic surgeon will be joining us in surgery on Saturday. Are there any questions?"

Questions? I couldn't even talk. Russell left with him. She'd probably had enough of me. I was sure everyone had.

Sandy said two words before leaving. "Bloody awful."

Early that evening, orderlies wheeled a patient into the room next to Eric's room. It was a woman, from the sound of the screaming. The shrieks continued for some time. Even with the door shut, I could hear her.

I overheard a nurse mumble, "What did she expect? Lighting herself on fire…"

Patty called a few minutes later. "Patty…Knight said…Knight said…"

"I know," she replied. "Russell told me the burns are deep and Eric will probably lose all his fingers. They can't repair the tendons. He might not have the use of his hands. Carol, listen to me. They make incredible prosthetics nowadays. Let's see what happens on Saturday. You know what Knight is like; he gives the worst-case scenario."

"Can't he be nicer?"

"He's a good doctor. You know I had some of my colleagues check him out. So did David. He's considered to be one of the best burn doctors in the Midwest."

"Eric loves to ride his bike. How is he going to hold the handlebars?"

"People do it. They make the most amazing devices to help athletes who've had amputations. I'll try to find some information on it, OK?" She passed on messages from family members before asking about our parents.

"I don't want them to come," I said. "They never liked Eric."

"I won't let them come, but I keep them updated on his condition."

I didn't want to talk about them. "This young girl came in. She tried to commit suicide by pouring gasoline on herself and lighting it. She's in the room next to Eric."

"That's ghastly," Patty exclaimed. "Say, is Marjorie there?"

"She got here a few hours ago. She's over at the hotel lying down. She's going to spend the night."

"Get some sleep. Take one of those sleeping pills I gave you."

Mom's sister Marjorie, about ten years younger than she, returned to the hospital just as Amanda came on duty.

"She doesn't talk to Eric at all," I told Marjorie, indicating the departing Rochelle.

There was silence from Marjorie, a soft-spoken woman who never raised her voice. Her full, round figure and blond-red hair gave her a warm, caring air, and she had a way of soothing people with her hypnotic voice.

It was almost 11:00 p.m. when we walked to the hotel. Despite the lateness—Marjorie was still on Boston time—we talked for over an hour in the hotel room. She told me stories about Eric as a boy, and I told her stories about Eric as a man. I cried to Marjorie about how I hadn't been a good wife; I wasn't supportive enough, he deserved better. It should be me lying in that hospital bed, not Eric.

Marjorie, who had a degree in social work, looked at me sadly. "Stop it, Carol. I love my nephew, but he's not a saint. I know he's difficult to live with. He's controlling; you wanted your freedom. We all saw it."

* * *

It was probably inevitable that my relationship with Eric would turn into a power struggle. An old college friend had been correct when he compared me to Eliza Doolittle and Eric to Henry Higgins. I had been a bit of a bumpkin when I met the sophisticated and worldly Eric, and as in Shaw's *Pygmalion*, Eric tried to mold me. At first, I loved it. He enjoyed being the teacher with me as the student, but as time went by, I started to resent his attempts to sculpt me into a certain form. I wanted to eat what I wanted to eat, watch what I wanted, read what I wanted, and go where I wanted. I saw it as control. He saw it as love. The result was a power struggle.

For years, I acquiesced. Then I started to fight him, just a bit. As time went by, I became louder, more vocal in my complaints. I screamed, I yelled, I wanted my way. It only made things worse. Eventually I learned I could do what I wanted if I was sneaky, but I shouldn't have had to lie or pretend. Once I was supposed to be at the library, but I went to see a movie he forbade me to see. He didn't understand that I couldn't fight all the time about every freedom I needed. I was a big girl;

I could take care of myself, make my own decisions. Whenever I was starting to convince Eric I could handle everything, something invariably happened that would drive me to tears, and I'd beg him to take control of the situation.

Occasionally I would insist on doing something out of character to show him I was the one in control: the tattoo, for instance. I told Eric I was going to get one. Yep, they were in style and I was getting one. After pointing out to me all the bad diseases I could catch and commenting I would look trashy, he agreed that a tattoo might be OK, but only if I had his name etched on my butt. We laughed and discussed the whole control/power struggle issue.

Over the years, we talked about it many times. Eric knew he was doing it, but he couldn't seem to help himself. In his defense, he always pointed out that he had a type A personality and couldn't curb his instincts. Anyway, he claimed, it was vital to his success in the cockpit—he had to be in control of every situation. I would tell him I was not a plane and he needed to get over it. He would always apologize, promising to do better. He did try, but it was only after he returned from Argentina, just before the accident, that he was able to do it.

He insisted nothing had happened down there, other than testing the plane.

Day 16
Wednesday, October 25, 2000

"The way in which we deal with obstacles in our lives defines us. That's what character is."

- Eric

It was early, and I was lying on a couch in the waiting room when Candice stuck her head around the corner and meekly called out, "Can I come in, Carol? I don't want to upset you, but I have goodies."

I took the bags of food. There'd been so much. I would put it at the main nurses' station as I'd been doing with most of the items people dropped off. I apologized to Candice for yelling at her when she came to ask for the zoo key. She apologized for agreeing to do it. Thankfully, she toned down the perkiness.

As she was leaving, she ran into Linda. "Sorry," Candice mumbled, heading for the elevator.

Linda's mismatched eyes blazed with irritation.

"I don't think she meant to run into you," I said.

"No, it's not that. We've all bumped into people without meaning to," Linda replied as she sat beside me. "Who is she? Really, why is she here all the time? You told me you barely know her, and clearly she's irritating you."

I didn't understand it either. Eric didn't even know her husband.

"It's weird," Linda continued. "I'm your friend, not her." She paused. "Is there anything I can do for you, Carol?"

"Can we talk about environmental issues for a while? Like we used to?"

Linda smiled. "I'd love to."

After Linda left, I walked back to Eric's room; the bandage change was going on. As I was about to go back to the waiting room, I noticed it. One of the blinds near the open cubicle assigned to Eric's room, to the left of the door, wasn't shut all the way. It was up about a foot. I could see the lights from the room and hear voices inside. I walked over to the desk in the cubicle. I could look at Eric with his bandages off. Nobody was around. I would peer in the opening.

I felt myself shaking.

Look.

I inched closer to the window, and soon I was right next to it. I looked down at the desk. I had to turn my head to the right, just a bit, and look up. *One look.* I could do it. I'd always been shooed out of Eric's room during procedures because they didn't want me in there. But David had been there. I could have requested permission, but Patty and David and everyone else told me no. "Do not look," they'd all said. But here I was, next to the window, and I was going to look. I tilted my head up and peered under the blind.

I gasped as I sat down in the desk chair. How long had I looked? Five seconds? A minute? I had no idea. But I knew right away I shouldn't have looked.

Eric was almost completely naked, and it appeared they were bathing him. I had seen the terrible leg burns, his back, his arms. But since the second surgery, I had never seen his face and head free of bandages. His head was positioned close to the window I was peering through. At first, I thought it was the back of his head and that he was lying on his tummy. Then I saw his nipples and knew he was on his back and I was looking at his face—only it wasn't a face. Eric had no face. No ear, no nose, no hair. It was all gone. I couldn't clearly see where his eyes were. Or his mouth. His face was misshapen, red, and hugely swollen.

I was too shocked to cry. Was I still breathing? Never could I have imagined this.

Jan stood over me. "Do you need to use the phone, Carol?"

"I…uh…I…no…I…waiting for…and…"

I was sure my face was the color of the white tile floor, but Jan was busy and didn't notice. "Let me know if I can get you anything." She hurried off, her black, wavy hair secured with a barrette.

I wouldn't tell them I looked; I wouldn't tell anyone. Not Patty. Not David. I shuffled into the big bathroom and sank to the floor under the coatrack. I was afraid. But this time I was afraid not only for Eric. I was afraid for me.

How long had someone been knocking on the restroom door? I opened it, mumbling a "sorry" to the elderly woman standing there impatiently. Out in the waiting room, I sat in my chair in the corner and buried my head in my hands.

Stan, the former astronaut now turned safety officer for Bombardier Flight Test, stopped by the waiting room. He had an all-American hero-next-door look—square jaw, around six feet tall, bright blue eyes, a perfect smile. I felt bad about my refusal to see him the second day. I had been meanspirited and jealous before, and I didn't want to do it again. He was a good man; I knew he cared about Eric.

The image of Eric's face wouldn't go away. I felt distracted, distant, and Stan kept asking if I felt well. I nodded and tried to listen to him. I wanted to know where Stan was when that Challenger took off on October 10, but was afraid to ask, afraid of what would come out of my mouth if I spoke. Maybe safety officers ought to be required to see what happens when people survive crashes: a once-beautiful, vibrant man with no face. I was thankful when Marjorie walked in, picking up the conversation, asking Stan lots of questions about flying the space shuttle. I slipped out quietly, back to Eric's room.

I was reading in a monotone when Russell came in. She smiled when she saw me holding Robin's thick book. "The nurses tell me Eric seems less agitated when you read to him, so keep reading."

Mom and Robin arrived with Sandy, who had driven them both over. Robin and I escaped to a corner of the lounge to watch a show about fruit bats on the overhead television. Candice returned for the second time, but Marjorie was stuck talking to her. I hugged Robin as she watched a show about her favorite animals. She'd been enamored of bats since she'd read the book *Stellaluna* as a precocious five-year-old. She was full of bat trivia and proud to be a card-carrying member of Bat Conservation International, a gift from Marjorie. Robin's great-aunt had even paid for a symbolic bat adoption, and Robin had its picture hanging on her wall. Eric laughingly told people, "Don't bash bats, or you'll have Robin to answer to."

I questioned her about the goings-on at the house.

"We got a maid, Mommy," she exclaimed. Pausing to catch an observation by one of the bat researchers, she gave me a shush signal. At the commercial break, she continued. "Tia made Mimi cry this morning. When Mimi told Tia to pick her clothes up, Tia said,

'I don't have to, that's the maid's job.' It made Mimi mad."

Another reason not to have a maid. "I hear lots of people are bringing food over. I hope you said thanks to them."

"Mimi throws most of it away."

"But why?" I asked her.

"She says it's not the food she likes to eat, but Tia and I like it. Tia hides it in her room. We don't like what Mimi makes. Someone brought fried chicken, and Tia said if Mimi threw it away she'd tell you."

I imagined my mother-in-law was trying to help in her own way, but I didn't understand why she wasn't accepting such gracious charity from people.

"Mimi says you need to leave more money with her," Robin continued. "All the money you gave her is gone."

I'd written a check a few days ago. How could it be gone? I started to feel anger. She throws the food away, she spends my money on a maid, she won't drive my car... *Stop it*, I thought. She's doing her best. Write another check.

David called again. "Carol." He said it forcefully, loudly. There was a long, uncomfortable pause before he continued. "I'm taking Mom back to Nevada with me on Monday. You're going to have to go home and get control of Tia."

"Fine," I said sharply, slamming down the phone.

Knight's afternoon report was brief. "We're seeing some pink. We'll put him back on the Keane bed."

I felt myself straighten up, becoming more aware. Had I heard right? Was Eric going off the circle bed?

After Knight left, I turned to Russell. "Is Eric going off the circle bed? Today?"

She smiled and nodded.

Now it was my turn to smile, and after thanking her, I practically skipped out to the waiting room. "Eric's going off the circle bed." I shouted to no one, to everyone. It was a small victory, and I would take it.

Robin didn't have a clue what I meant, but she could tell it was good news. She jumped up and cheered. "Go, Daddy." She high-fived Sandy.

"Time to make some squidgy chocolate cake to celebrate. Will you help me, Robin?" Sandy asked her.

"Yes," Robin exclaimed, high-fiving her again.

Mom tried once again to justify why she had to hire a maid. She wasn't listening as I implored her, "I don't like the idea of strangers handling Eric's things, especially now. His stuff is important to him, and I want to make sure it's taken care of." He had some obsessive-compulsive tendencies, as did I.

"She won't nick anything, love," Sandy said softly.

"But I—"

"I cannot do it myself," Mom interrupted. "And please don't tell me again that you don't care if it's messy. I care. Anyway, you and Eric have so much stuff I couldn't keep up with the dusting."

It was true about the vast quantity of things. Eric loved to buy me presents. His mother often remarked about it, and I would laugh indignantly and say, "Eric bought me that." Because we traveled a lot, I had knick-knacks from all over the world: tiny Delft windmills, wooden shoes, a mask from Vienna, jewelry, table linens, Christmas ornaments, scores of books. I also had several Gucci purses, all gifts from Eric.

What if the maid took something? Maybe a Gucci handbag?

When Eric was stationed at Camp New Amsterdam, the entire squadron went to Sardinia to practice maneuvers in their F-15s. Sardinia meant Italy, and Italy meant Gucci. What gal didn't drool over the thought of a real Gucci purse? I pretended not to, but secretly I wanted one. Eric was astute; he knew. On one trip before Christmas, he bought me one but tried to keep it a secret. Unfortunately, one of the pilot speakers at a formal function made a joke about Eric's escapade to buy me a Gucci bag.

A squeal escaped me in front of the entire squadron. "You bought me a Gucci?"

While I was sitting outside Eric's door writing in my journal, Dr. Russell walked by. "How are you going to fix Eric's face?" I asked, trying to keep my voice steady.

"He'll have to see a specialist somewhere else. I spoke to David about it today."

"Will they be able to fix it?"

"The damage is fairly extensive. The burns are extremely deep, so it's doubtful he'll have facial movement on the left side."

"Is it going to look like when someone has a stroke? You know, when part of their face looks paralyzed."

"Yes, it will be similar."

That evening, orderlies wheeled the Keane bed down the hall. Seeing it roll into Eric's room was like seeing an old friend. I patted the side of the bed and exclaimed loudly, "Your bed is back, Eric."

After he was safely on the bed, I called Tia to find out about cheerleading tryouts. She sounded ecstatic. "I made it, Mommy. I made the squad. Can you believe it?"

Day 17
Thursday, October 26, 2000

*"Don't be a whiny wife if I'm
ever in an accident.
If you are, that's what people will
remember about me."*
- Eric

"L aurel?"

"Yes, Carol?"

"I didn't think anyone could be this sad and still be alive. Every night when I think I can't go on, I wake up and do it all over again. I didn't realize how much I love Eric. I took him for granted, and I feel incredibly guilty. If I think too much about it, I feel like I'll stop breathing."

I was convinced that all those sad memoirs, touted as being profound, moving, and bravely unsentimental, didn't tell the whole story. Were the writers being completely honest? Had they been that strong when the event was actually happening? Experiencing a tragedy was unbearably painful, and I found it hard to believe anyone could formulate deep philosophical thoughts in the midst of it. Was I the first person to fall apart? Do and say things that were childish and weak? Sure, maybe afterward a person could make up a bunch of quotable and inspirational lines, but that wasn't really what happened. Or was I defective?

Laurel set Eric's records down. "You're a wonderful wife. You have nothing to feel guilty about."

But I did.

I should have been more understanding when he yelled, because it wasn't me he was yelling at; it was who he was—a loud, opinionated Italian New Yorker. Why couldn't I have understood that? It was like the time I wanted to go to the USSR. He didn't want me to go because he was afraid. That was why he yelled, why he initially said no.

He was terrified for my safety.

* * *

"Please come back to me." Eric had tears in his eyes as he kissed me good-bye at the airport in Frankfurt, Germany. It had taken a considerable amount of pleading to get him to agree to let me go to the USSR. The disaster at Chernobyl had recently happened. It was Sunday, October 12, 1986, and the Cold War was in full gear; the Soviet government had detained an American diplomat in what had become a big scandal.

But as I pointed out to Eric, Reagan was meeting with Gorbachev in Iceland, and it was a time of change. He disagreed. There at the airport, as I was leaving, we went through the same conversation we'd been having for months.

"Carol," he said, for about the hundredth time, exasperated that I refused to agree with his position, "I sit alert to protect us from the Russians, and you're going over there to drink vodka with them. You realize if you do anything wrong, our government isn't going to help you."

"I went to the briefing, Eric," I emphasized. "I'm not going to do anything wrong. I'm taking a field study class, learning about art and architecture, for Christ's sake."

"Yeah, yeah. What if they find out your husband is an F-15 pilot in the US Air Force? What do you think they'll say then? Huh? They would love to get their hands on information about my jet."

"Stop being melodramatic. I don't know anything about the F-15."

"You know more than you think." He was shouting again. "Anyway, they're not good people. Read your history. Look at the atrocities they've committed. What about the gulag? The human rights violations? The KGB could *torture* you." His hands were waving, his feet stomping.

"Honestly, Eric," I said. "You're acting like a two-year-old. The Soviet government is bad, not the Russian people. They're people like us, but they're powerless to do much to change things, and they're afraid. I admire the Russians. I think their history is fascinating, and as a people they've suffered tremendously."

"I think you like them too much."

"Anyway, they'd never get any information out of me. If I told them, then I'd have to kill them." I smiled and gave him a playful punch. I was using one of his favorite lines, but he didn't smile back. He grabbed me, hugging me tightly. "Come back. OK?"

"I'll see you in two weeks. I love you. Thanks for letting me go and for driving me to Frankfurt."

As I walked down the Jetway, I looked back to see him waving unenthusiastically. I shouldn't have had to go through such contortions. Save me from pilots and their control issues.

When I returned two weeks later, after one of the most amazing experiences of my life, Eric was waiting for me. He'd driven several hours back to Frankfurt from our home in Holland to pick me up. When I got off the plane, I had Soviet pins and buttons hanging all over my shirt. I looked like the poster child for communism. It was a joke, but maybe it was also my way of showing him I had some control. Eric did not find it humorous.

When we got home, I showed him the stack of books and brochures of Soviet propaganda. He was furious and threw them all out. I was able to save a children's book called *Our Uncle Lenin*, but that was all. I was quite angry with him at the time, but later I tried to understand: he felt his job would be in jeopardy if the government found the materials in our home. I thought he was being overly dramatic, but he thought he was convincing me to see reason. What reason? I liked the Russian people, whom I considered to be intelligent and resourceful, not communism—a repressive, broken system of government. I came to realize later that I'd been somewhat naïve about the whole situation. From that day forward, Eric always referred to the Russians as "your friends, the Russians."

After the Cold War was over, he learned better to accept my fascination and love of all things Russian. I still enjoy reading books about Russian history and art; Tolstoy and Chekhov are two of my favorite writers. I tell Eric how brave my friends the Russians have been throughout their history. He groans but listens anyway. I love to remind him of what I said when I returned from what was then the USSR.

"You're wrong about the Russians, Eric. So is our government. They don't hate us; on the contrary, they want to be like us. You'll see. Communism will disappear in Russia in less than ten years. They're smart people, and they've had enough."

Every so often, I couldn't resist the urge to tell him I was oh so right.

*   *   *

Tim stopped by briefly to tell me my article was on the editorial page, handing me a folded newspaper. The past sixteen days had worn on him. He looked tired and profoundly sad. Already a thin man, Tim seemed to have lost weight and added years, the noticeable bags and bloodshot eyes adding to his haggard appearance. In addition to his grief over three of "his guys," he was answering questions from the NTSB, the FAA, the main Bombardier plant in Montreal, and the press. He was running Flight Test, handling the fallout from the crash, and spending every evening and part of his days at the hospital. Did he feel guilt over the accident? Did he feel responsible? The answer seemed obvious.

I opened the newspaper. I hadn't given the article a name, but the paper had: "Test pilots balance adventure and safety."

> My husband Eric Fiore is a test pilot. He often said most people outside the aviation community had no concept of what a test pilot is or what it means to be one.
>
> The public tends to think test pilots are risk-taking, reckless guys who spend their days trying to see how fast and how high they can fly their planes. The public, Eric would say, had a romanticized Hollywood image of test pilots, which to some extent might be true, but test pilots like Eric, Dave Riggs, and Bryan Irelan spend hours and hours poring over flight manuals, doing preflight checks, attending safety briefings, spending hours

in engineering, and writing volumes of technical reports.

There is something wonderful and different about test pilots that is difficult to put into words. People in the aviation community sometimes say "that's because he is a test pilot," as if that in itself is an explanation.

I believe test pilots possess an inner strength, a desire to push past limits and do things other people have not done. They relish the adventure—they live for it. But at the same time, test pilots are very concerned with safety. My Eric received a prestigious safety award last year. At home, we call him Mr. Safety. But when you are exploring the unknown, there is always a risk! Maybe, in a way, that is also part of the personality of a test pilot. Flying was in Eric's blood, as it must have been with Dave and Bryan.

Eric once said to me it was because of test pilots that people could feel safe flying from place to place. Test pilots like Eric, Dave, and Bryan make the skies safer for all of us.

Eric is a former Air Force F-15 fighter pilot and he is very proud of that. Only a strong guy can be one. The Air Force prepares not only its fighter pilots, but their wives as well. At every new assignment, I attended orientation sessions with other wives where we were told what could happen, what the Air Force would do if anything did happen, and what would be expected of us.

I once told Eric how I would act if he ever crashed. He looked at me and said calmly, "No, you won't, Carol. You'll conduct yourself with dignity, and you'll tell everyone how much I loved to fly and how important the mission was. And you'll make me proud of you."

It will be a long, difficult road for us both, but we are fighters and we'll make it. I now have the most important job of my life—taking care of a hero.

My family feels the quick response of the men on the rescue team made the difference between life and death for Eric. They risked their lives trying to save Eric, Dave, and Bryan.

I am also thankful to the good people at Bombardier Aerospace who truly love Eric and respect his outstanding talents. My family is overwhelmed at the love and support that has poured in from the Wichita community and from our children's school district. We appreciate the incredible expertise and care of the talented professionals at Saint Cornelius Medical Center.[*]

Eric's condition remains critical, but we are hopeful. No further details about the injuries are being released, and the family appreciates the public's respect for our privacy.

"I think it's what I wrote except this one error," I said to Tim. "I have to say, I don't like it, and it's inappropriate. In the fourth paragraph, there's an exclamation mark at the end of the sentence 'But when you are exploring the unknown, there is always a risk.' It makes it sound, I don't know, flippant or something, too matter-of-fact."

---

[*] Not the real name of the hospital

"I didn't think that when I read it."

"I guess it doesn't matter." I frowned at the paper in my hand. I was critical of my writing. Maybe it sucked and no one had the courage to tell me. Maybe I could have done better…

"Thank you for writing that article. It's the sort of thing that helps to pull the community together, and I appreciate it."

"You're welcome. Eric likes you, you know."

There were tears in Tim's eyes as he said quietly, "That means a lot to me."

Speaking to Russell later, I stammered nervously. "You know when you said Eric's face was going to be sort of paralyzed? What exactly did you mean? Uh…I mean…he'll be able to show expression, right? Eric is extremely emotional."

There was a long pause before she spoke. "His facial muscles have been destroyed. There's no way to repair them. I'm afraid he won't be able to smile."

I stared at her in disbelief. "You mean never? He can never smile?"

"Probably not."

"But…"

I sat down, confused. I'd heard the words, but I couldn't seem to understand them.

Russell continued, "His lungs look better today, and I've ordered eight units of blood and two platelet packs for the surgery on Saturday."

I watched her walk down the hall. *Never smile.* I didn't believe it, so I questioned Caitlin and Jan. They looked at each other. No one said anything. I was hoping Caitlin, with her pleasant, clear voice, would reassure me.

She did not.

Jan spoke first. "Eric's face is bad. It does take several muscles to smile."

I walked out to the waiting room in a daze and sat in the corner. *I can't take any more*, I shouted silently to myself. *I can't take it.*

Then, maybe for the first time, I considered Eric's quality of life. I had convinced myself he could overcome anything because I wanted him to live, no matter what. I needed him. Was I being selfish? The horrible possibilities were increasing: blindness, paralysis, missing limbs, severe facial deformities, excruciating pain, drug addiction from the meds, scores of traumatic medical procedures and surgeries… Added to all of it was the thing Eric had always feared.

He would never fly again.

I left the hospital with Mom and Marjorie. They'd seen Eric only briefly. Mom never stayed long; she took a quick peek and ran out, saying, "There's not a lot I can do for Eric." He was unresponsive, so she saw no reason to stay. I disagreed. I believed, as I always had, he could hear and understand. Weren't emotional support and my presence the most important things I could do for him?

I worried about Mom on the drive home. She got lost and seemed distracted. I bit my tongue until I tasted blood. I was not going to criticize her as I had the other day, and I wasn't going to tell her what Russell had said. My Eric, so full of life, so silly. To never see him smile again would be the worst for me. How much more was he going to have to deal with?

Marjorie loudly cleared her throat and said to Mom, "Can I help?"

We finally made it home.

Marjorie whispered to me as we were getting out of the car, "Tia's being horrible to her."

I said nothing.

I knew immediately I shouldn't have gone home. All the doors were unlocked. Eric would not have liked it; he was super fussy about security. The coffeepot was on, the toaster still plugged in. I didn't recognize the piles of stuff everywhere, and there was grease all over the stove, no doubt from the bacon the girls told me Mimi was always frying.

My cockatiel peeped rapidly, her cage only a few feet from the flying bacon grease, possibly cooked at too high a temperature in a Teflon-coated pan (toxic to birds).

The sound of a sweeper echoed through the house. "That's the maid," Mom said casually. That explained the unlocked doors with a total stranger left inside.

I marched up the stairs to meet the maid, who seemed pleasant enough. "I am sorry, but your sweeper has come apart," she said in broken English, holding up the attachment pieces of the expensive Simplicity vacuum Eric had bought me.

I flew back down the stairs, furious, as I handed Marjorie a check I'd written for her airfare. I gave Mom a jar of cash with several hundred dollars. I'd been saving it for our trip to Greece.

I locked myself in the half bathroom Eric had wallpapered in my favorite Laura Ashley striped pattern. There was a matching forest-green flowered border, and he'd put up special molding; even the outlet plug covers matched. We used to joke that it was the prettiest room in the house. Eric had worked on it for weeks.

As I washed my hands, I noticed the once-attractive wallpaper was dark and discolored over about half of one wall. It was noticeable and was going to be extremely difficult to hide. How had it happened? What had caused it? The whole thing was going to have to be redone. By Eric? He was probably going to lose his fingers. By me? I couldn't wallpaper.

When I emerged from the bathroom, I knew on a certain level that I was hysterical. I confronted Mom and Marjorie with all the bad shit in my life. I felt as if I were being stuffed into a small, dark room with hundreds of people. They all smelled like rotting vegetables. I ran out the front door.

I wanted out of there, out of that place that wasn't mine anymore. I wanted to go back to the hospital where I could be with Eric and where the nurses were good to me, and Russell and Pierce listened to my stories. I wanted to be away from all this. Somehow I felt, I knew, it was never going to feel like home again.

I spotted Sandy in her yard. "Will you drive me back to the hospital?"

She had a surprised look on her face as Marjorie quickly rushed over and whispered to her. As I prepared to get in Sandy's car, Marjorie addressed me softly. "I think you need to be on some medication."

"I'm not taking drugs."

As soon as we'd pulled down the street, I tried to explain to Sandy what had happened. I was soon engulfed in a fit of tears and blubbering. "And...Dr. Russell said he'd never smile again, and..."

Was that my voice?

"I can't live without him. I can't. He might die, and I can't live without him."

Sandy pulled the car over and held both my hands. "Yes, you can, Carol. You have two girls who need you, and you must take care of them."

"I can't...I can't...I can't..." My chest hurt with every breath.

Sandy pulled the car back into traffic. Calmly and slowly she said, "Yes. You. Can."

She didn't understand. I couldn't take care of myself. How could I take care of them, especially Tia? I had to protect them from me. I would frighten them. I frightened myself. I put my head in my hands.

I was a terrible mother.

I arrived as the dressing change was starting. Sitting down in the chair across from Eric's room, I stared at the closed curtains. There was no gap today. One look had been enough; I didn't want to see again.

I never wanted to go back to the house. That was exactly what I told Patty barely five minutes later when she called. "And the maid is there, and she broke my sweeper, and…and…the wallpaper is ruined. Eric put it up for me. It's disrespectful to him. I'm not doing my job, taking care of everything. I'm trying…I don't want anything to be wrong with the house when Eric goes home; he has enough to worry about…and the maid… what if she's spraying chemicals around my bird? What if she kills Flutter? Eric loves Flutter. There's grease everywhere, and I've already spent way over half of the money Bombardier gave me because I'm paying everyone for tickets—"

"Carol, calm down. I'll be there on Sunday. Your mother-in-law needs to go home, so let David take her. You have to get some control back in your life. I'll clean the house, so don't worry. As for the money, you need to stop writing checks to people. They can pay for their own airfare. Bombardier gave you the money. You'll need it when Eric gets his reconstruction. There will be hotel expenses and many other things. I'm not going to take money, and David shouldn't either."

"But—"

"Fine. Give me a check. I'll make confetti out of it. It's wrong to take it, and that's all I'm saying."

"Russell said Eric would never smile again." I burst into tears.

Patty told me about innovative surgery as she tried to calm me down. I didn't believe her. There was no surgery that could help Eric smile.

As soon as I hung up the phone, the other line rang. It was David. "What's going on, Carol?"

"Nothing."

"That's not what my mother and Marjorie said."

"I'm sorry, but—"

"Eric wouldn't care about the wallpaper," David interrupted.

Apparently Mom had called him right after I left the house.

"Yes, he would."

"I think you need to apologize to my mother," said David.

I was sorry. I knew she was under a lot of stress, but I hadn't wanted a maid and she got one anyway.

Knight's report that evening was bad, like everything else. "The status of the burns has changed somewhat. He has fourth degree to the forehead, nose, and cheeks and third degree on the lower cheeks, lips, chin, and neck. The grafts are not taking well, especially to the arm."

Mom, Marjorie, and Robin stopped by for a brief visit. Nothing was said about the earlier incident until it was time for them to leave.

"I'm sorry," I said to Mom as she was leaving. I hadn't meant it to sound so flat, so emotionless, but somehow it had come out that way. I really was sorry.

"It's all right. We know you're under a lot of stress."

As Mom took Robin to the elevator, Marjorie lingered behind. "Something happened today, Carol. What was it?"

How could I tell her Eric would never smile again?

Day 18
Friday, October 27, 2000

"Why isn't my jacket in the Cosmosphere's museum?"
- Eric

The dialysis had stopped during the night—no surprise there. The filter had clogged again. Wasn't there someone working the night shift? When the dialysis went down in the night, did the renal care people ignore it? I was betting Dr. Pierce didn't know.

I went in to talk to Eric before the shift change started. I stared at his face, at the bandages. Eric's smile. Of all the terrible things that had happened, it shouldn't have been the worst, but it was. How much more was he going to suffer? How much more would he lose? What sort of life was he going to have? Would he want that life? I had been sure before, that he would want to live, no matter what, but now I didn't know.

I tried not to think about it because I needed him. I couldn't live without him.

Eric looked almost twice his normal size, and it didn't take a medical person to see he was retaining lots of fluid. His shoulder size had nearly doubled, and he had a big, broad chest that took up all the bed. This was not my 140-pound Eric.

When Amanda walked in, I said, "Eric looks like a burly football player, not my wiry cyclist."

"Yes. I know. He weighs 185 pounds."

"What?"

"The swelling is caused by an infection, and it can cause the patient to increase in size."

How much worse? HOW MUCH? I struggled to fight the anger, but there was nothing good right now. Every day something worse happened.

"Carol," Dr. Russell said quietly in the waiting room, "I'm afraid the graft is lost over the hands. The tips of the fingers are black. There is some take of the graft on the upper arms, but it's not good on the left forearm. Tomorrow we'll most likely have to amputate the necrotic fingertips, at least."

"But…but can't you put another graft on?" I felt ice cold. And sick. I hated that word: necrotic. Dead.

"There's nothing to graft on to. I'm very sorry."

After she left, I ran in through the double doors, falling down in my chair across from Eric's room. I felt a hand on my shoulder and looked up at an attractive woman in navy-blue scrubs.

"I'm sorry," Jan said softly. Were those tears I saw in the emerald-green eyes of Eric's day nurse?

We talked, and I asked her questions about Eric's burns. Yes, she'd seen them. Yes, they were bad. Yes, she would look at what Russell had written.

Jan pulled a chair over beside me. "Dr. Russell wrote pretty much what you told me. She also wrote he has a fourth-degree burn to the scalp."

"What exactly is the difference between third- and fourth-degree burns?"

"Fourth means it's burned through the fat and muscle down to bone. There isn't much fat on the head."

"It's amazing he doesn't have brain damage."

"Yes. It's a miracle," Jan replied. "The bandage change is done, if you want to go back in."

I told Eric the Kansas Cosmosphere and Space Center in Hutchinson had accepted Tia to the second level of Space Camp; they liked her essay. I reminisced with him about the fun we'd had there. He'd always been impressed with this first-rate facility associated with the Smithsonian and home to the Mercury spacecraft *Liberty Bell 7*. He was even friends with the director.

"Chuck Yeager's jacket is in the museum," he'd remarked several times. "Why isn't my jacket in the museum? Huh? Why not?" He sounded like a child, and I assured him that his jacket would be in the Cosmosphere's museum someday.

"When I'm a famous astronaut, they'll be begging for my jacket. Maybe I'll even autograph it for them."

Early in the afternoon, Jan started to count and record about forty small glass vials of liquid. I stared at the tiny bottles and asked, "Is that the surfactant for Eric's lungs?"

Jan nodded as I watched her finish counting and writing down information in Eric's record.

"So how much do those cost?"

"About three hundred to four hundred dollars a vial."

"Are you serious? Apiece?"

She nodded while two other nurses threw in their affirmations. I did a rough calculation in my head: forty vials times three hundred each times two days' worth. It would take me over a year to make that much money. Maybe they were wrong. How could it be that expensive? The nurses administered it to Eric a short time later, and I tried to joke with Jan that they shouldn't spill it or drop a vial. She nodded, more seriously than I expected.

David arrived from the airport. I told him about the vials, and he told me Eric's medical bills would be over a million dollars. I hadn't thought about it, and I didn't care. I wanted Eric to live, I wanted him to see, and I didn't care how much it cost.

David came with good news. He'd found an eye surgeon named Dr. Natarajan, who was doing some revolutionary work covering injured eyes with amniotic tissue. I didn't understand it, but I was grateful to David. I told him his mother was scaring me with her driving. I realized I was being critical, but I was worried about her safety as well as my children, who were riding in the car with her.

"That's another reason I'm taking her back to Nevada with me on Monday," he reiterated. His face was expressionless, but his tight body language revealed his firmness. He was taking his mom, and there was no changing his mind.

It was OK. Patty would be here, and it was time. Mom needed a break, especially from me.

The dialysis went down again. The whole thing was almost laughable. Eric would be pissed, and if I were the one lying in there, he'd be ripping into that renal care group.

That evening, after saying goodnight to Eric, I called for an escort and walked slowly back to the hotel, clutching my phone tightly. As I stripped for a quick shower, I caught a glimpse of myself in the full-length mirror. The person who stared back was not me. I looked closer. Strange, I thought. It wasn't so much the dark circles under my eyes, or my hair that could have used a good washing. It was my stomach.

For most of my adult life, I'd chased after flat abs; I was obsessed. Despite my 118-pound frame and constant running, I always had some roundness on the lower part of my stomach. Ugh. I'd done crunches, bought special machines, and read books, but it remained. I'd had it before I'd given birth, and it was the same after. It was never going away. I would stare longingly at the flat abs of models and movie stars and lament. Why couldn't my abs look like that?

Eric had said, more than once, "It's flat. What are you talking about?"

Now, as I looked in the mirror, I saw my stomach was more than flat. I turned sideways. It was caved in, and the skin was all wrinkly.

Weird, I thought as I climbed into the shower.

Day 19
Saturday, October 28, 2000

"I am not a Trekkie."
– Eric

―――――――――――――

"**I** could face almost anything, except being blind." Those words. His words.

Now, after eighteen days, someone was going to do something about Eric's eyes. But what?

As I spoke with Laurel about the surgery, an extremely short man with dark skin and kind eyes moved in front of me and extended his hand. "Hello, Mrs. Fiore. I am Dr. Natarajan. Your brother-in-law has asked me to consult on your husband's case. I will be looking at his eyes to see what can be done."

I clutched his outstretched hand with both of mine. "Dr. Natarajan, thank you so much for coming."

The eye doctor was here. David said he was the best, and at that moment, I felt sure this new doctor would save Eric's right eye.

"I want to check on your husband," he continued. "I have already spoken with Dr. Russell and will be joining the team for surgery today." He spoke formally, properly, without using contractions. He had a slight accent, similar to the professors from India I had encountered at Parks College.

"Thank you...thank you..." I said, pumping his hand.

Dr. Natarajan spent the next fifteen minutes speaking with the nurses, visiting in Eric's room, and looking at the medical chart.

David hurried toward me. "Is Natarajan here?" he asked, sounding out of breath.

Pointing to Eric's room, I nodded furiously. "Thank you for getting him, David. Thank you. Thank you..."

David and Natarajan spoke in hushed tones near Eric's door. I thought it best not to interrupt them, but I caught snippets of their conversation. I strained to listen while pretending to write in the journal on my lap.

"...severe ocular burns...right epithelial desiccation fifty percent tarsorrhaphy...left near one hundred percent no view of cornea...recommend increasing... amniotic membrane transplant vital for long-term visual progress...lids..."

What did it mean? I looked up as they approached me. David's face remained expressionless as Natarajan extended his hand once more. "Mrs. Fiore, I will do everything I can."

David stood completely still as the doctor spoke at length about the procedure. I wasn't sure what all the technical words meant, but I wondered if I'd heard him correctly.

"Is Eric's right eye...is it still there? I mean, can you save it?" I heard myself stammering.

"I am going to do everything I can, Mrs. Fiore. I am hopeful."

I hesitated to ask. "Is the left eye...gone?"

"Not necessarily. I will see what I can do."

I could have hugged the man; maybe there was hope after all. David seemed energized too, but became passive when he saw my smile. Sometimes he acted like Knight. If he saw me being hopeful, he would frown or refuse to talk.

"Let's see what Dr. Natarajan says after the surgery," David cautioned.

I thanked the doctor again as he and David left. I pointed after them and loudly exclaimed to Eric's nurses, Caitlin and Jan, "It's the eye doctor."

At 9:30 a.m., the nurses began prepping Eric for the operating room. I started to feel that familiar panic. When the surgical team showed up, it was the same scenario as before, but this time it was much worse. Eric was going in with fingers, and he was going to come out with at least the tips gone. There were the eyes.

There was so much to lose this time.

I rambled to Eric that I loved him. Again, I had a horrible fear he would die in surgery, and as before, I followed the team down the hall, only this time David took me off into a corner after the team had entered the big doors to the OR. His voice was sharp. "Carol, you need to be on some medication, and for the sake of your children, you are going to see a counselor. I'm going to speak with the social worker about setting it up." He was too close, his face in mine.

I moved back. Inside I was calling David every bad name I could think of, but I couldn't say anything because he'd found an eye doctor.

I forced a reply. "OK."

Mom stayed at home with the girls, but Marjorie waited with me. People called, visitors came and went, and the time dragged by as I thought about all the things Eric wouldn't be able to do if he lost his fingers.

And then, at last, the surgery was over.

Dr. Natarajan was the first to come in the waiting room. He said he would be doing the amniotic tissue transplant and with the help of his associate, they would rebuild the lids. He sounded hopeful and shook my hand before leaving.

Knight and Russell came in together, followed by the plastic surgeon. Knight spoke first. "He tolerated the surgery fairly well and is on his way back to his room."

I looked at Marjorie, who gave me a knowing look. Knight still couldn't say Eric's name.

"I will give some technical details for the medical people in the family," Knight continued. This time he didn't even glance at David, who was sitting on the edge of one of the couches, arms folded in front of him. I didn't understand much of Knight's words. They seemed to run together and sounded like gibberish.

"We performed debridement of the…split thickness grafting to…skin from his lower back, side of his back, and down the buttocks…nine units…showed low blood pressure during the procedure…"

Was Knight even speaking English? I couldn't make sense of his words.

David cleared his throat. "About the fingers…"

The plastic surgeon stepped forward, running a hand through his damp auburn hair. I felt my fingernails dig into my forearms as he began. "The bones of the digits were burned, and the digital vessels were thrombosed. I performed amputation of the right hand with all fingers through the metacarpophalangeal joint. On the left hand, all fingers through the metacarpophalangeal joint except for the ring finger through the proximal interphalangeal joint."

What? Maybe I wasn't listening, or maybe I was trying not to listen.

"His thumbs…did you have to…did you…" I was having trouble talking. My mouth felt as if it were full of concrete.

I looked at the three of them. Knight's face remained expressionless, Russell stared at the far wall, and the plastic surgeon focused gray-green eyes on me. "I'm sorry, Mrs. Fiore. I had to amputate the thumbs. Your husband has severe fourth-degree burns of the hands, and I'm expecting additional surgery on them. The fingers were not salvageable."

Knight and the plastic surgeon slowly walked out of the room as Russell came over and squatted beside me.

"Dr. Russell...I...I...don't understand...how much of Eric's fingers..." I tried to force the words out.

Russell held up her hand as she pointed to the fingers with her other hand. "The plastic surgeon had to remove all the fingers down to the hand except on Eric's ring finger. It was amputated to the knuckle."

"Even his thumbs?"

"Yes, Eric's thumbs are gone. I'm sorry. There was nothing left to save."

I tried to look around the room, but I couldn't see anyone. It was dark and fuzzy. The room seemed strangely silent except for an odd muffled sound. It was me, and I was sure I was dying.

Russell put her hand on my shoulder. She started to come into focus as she handed me a box of tissues. "Dr. Natarajan seemed hopeful," she said.

I wanted to tell her about the things Eric would not be able to do. I tried to talk, but I knew my words didn't make sense.

David interrupted. "Dr. Russell has other patients to see."

"Carol," said Dr. Russell, "will you consider talking with a counselor?"

"I told David—" I stopped abruptly. "Leave me alone about the stupid counselor."

Marjorie whispered, "We love you, Carol. We're worried about you."

That evening David brought Tia and Robin to see me. Tia had heard someone talking and asked me loudly and forcefully about what she'd heard. "Does Daddy have fingers?"

I shook my head and fought the tears. Tia put her arms around me. "It'll be OK, Mommy. Remember that guy in the *Star Wars* movie? He lost his arm, and they gave him a new one. Daddy can get new fingers too."

I sat in the waiting room and hugged my two sweet girls. As we were talking, the small television mounted above us emitted a familiar sound.

Robin pointed up at the television. "Daddy's favorite show is on."

* * *

Star Trek: The Next Generation was Eric's favorite television show. He'd grown up with the original show, knew all the characters, and had seen every episode multiple times, but it was the second series that captivated him. By most standards, he was a Trekkie, but he adamantly denied it. He didn't dress up, attend conventions, or read trivia. So according to him, he wasn't a Trekkie. I disagreed, citing his excitement at discussing the show, plot, characters, and his hurry to get the kids to bed so we could watch it together on the small television in our kitchen. All proof, I'd declared, that he was a Trekkie.

"Hurry up," he'd call almost nightly. "*Star Trek* is on in five minutes."

A few months before the accident, he'd gone to Las Vegas for a flight test convention. I could hear the excitement in his voice when he called me from the hotel. "They have this ride at the Hilton called the Star Trek Experience. It's so cool. There's a bridge like on the *Enterprise*, and you fly a mission. There are people dressed up like Klingons and Ferengi, and there's even a pub modeled after Quark's Bar. I know it sounds hokey, but it's not. I'll bring you here someday. You'll love it. They also have..."

He went on and on, all the while assuring me he wasn't a Trekkie. "It's so cool," he repeated. He brought T-shirts home for the kids and, for me, a tribble. I was thrilled with the fuzzy replica of a harmless but prolific creature from the original series.

Of all the characters on *Star Trek*, Eric's favorites were the Klingons. I was always trying to analyze his fascination with a warlike species that placed the utmost importance on courage, believing death was preferable to dishonor. There was nothing academic, nothing intellectual, about the Klingons. Why didn't he prefer the Vulcans, who were all about science and logic? They were much more like Eric: brilliant, careful, precise. Why was he so fascinated with the Klingons?

Eric told me once it was about honor, but I don't think he would have been willing to die for the sake of honor. Life was too precious to him. When he was in the Air Force, he would have fought against and even shot down enemy fighters to be the ace he secretly wanted to be. Yet, that was a bit different from this whole Klingon business.

Eric's favorite character on *The Next Gen* was Worf, a full-blooded Klingon raised by humans. Despite his upbringing by non-Klingons, Worf constantly strove to be what he called a true warrior. Eric wanted to be a hero. He wanted his life to have meaning, to be important, to have honor.

"Wouldn't it be terrible to die and have everyone forget you?" he'd asked me more than a few times. "Dying in combat is probably the best way to go," he'd added. The Klingons believed that.

I realized what a Klingon might do in his circumstances. I knew a Klingon would never want to live without his hands to hold his weapons. How could Eric cope without his fingers?

Day 20
Sunday, October 29, 2000

"Nothing is more romantic than a warm, clear night, under the stars, on a grass strip."
- Eric

Midnight, 12:45, 1:33, 2:20, 3:50…I paced, wandered to the bathroom, stared at my cell phone, looked out the hotel room window. I did everything but sleep.

"You're here early this morning," Laurel said as I walked into the burn unit. It was 5:00 a.m. and the lights were still dim; the halls were empty.

I stared at the bandages on the stumps that were now all that was left of Eric's hands. Laurel put her arm around my shoulders and gave me a big hug. "I'm sorry. They make amazing devices nowadays, and—"

"I know."

We stood in silence for several minutes. I pulled Harry Potter from my bag and held it up to Laurel. "I'm about halfway. My ten-year-old insists I read it."

Laurel pushed a chair next to Eric's bed for me.

"Eric didn't lose all of his ring finger," I said quietly. "I think that's a sign he loves me and he's not going to leave me."

"I'm sure you're right, Carol."

Her words were kind, but said quickly, without making eye contact.

An hour later, I was tired of reading and went out to the dark, eerily quiet waiting room. Picking through a pile of books, I spotted a farming magazine with a cow on the cover. Its sad brown eyes stared up at me.

* * *

Eric had always been fond of cows. Patty thought his fascination with them was weird. We'd attended high school in central Illinois, where cows were a common sight, so we'd never thought much of them. Patty assumed that Eric, having lived so close to New York City, had never seen fields of cows until he went to Parks. What other explanation could there be?

During the years Eric and I lived together, and then early in our marriage, we shifted from one place to another looking for a special location that felt like home. As soon as we saw the two-story redbrick building about eight miles from Parks College, we knew immediately: this was it.

Located at the back of a well-kept subdivision on the outskirts of Belleville, Illinois, the building held only four one-bedroom apartments. The backyard bordered on a farmer's pasture complete with rolling hills and surrounded by trees.

Eric was so thrilled he was dancing in place. "Are there cows?" he asked excitedly.

The landlord replied that of course there were, and sometimes they came up to the fence. I could see the happiness in Eric's eyes as he exclaimed, "We'll take it."

Frequently the cows came up to the fence. Eric rushed outside whenever he saw them to pet their fuzzy heads. Sometimes he took an apple or a carrot for them. When Patty came to visit, she thought it all a bit odd. "Hasn't he ever seen a cow before?" she questioned as she watched Eric feed the big black creatures. "What's wrong with him?"

We had many encounters with animals at that apartment: the rabbit hiding under my car in the mornings, the turtle near the garbage container, the baby squirrel I fed out of my hand. It was during this time that Eric first revealed his secret to me—a wide-eyed fascination and love for animals. Over the years, it became one of our closest bonds.

We lived in that apartment for almost three years. Then Eric went into the Air Force, and we left for

Texas. He was slightly glum when we departed. He was excited to be moving forward and getting a shot at flying a fighter, but we were leaving behind a part of our lives we would never recapture. As we pulled out of the driveway for the last time, Eric sighed loudly. "I wonder if we'll ever have cows in our backyard again."

We never did.

*   *   *

Dr. Natarajan arrived shortly after the shift change started. Coming out to the waiting room, he smiled and spoke kind words.

I went back to Eric's room and stopped abruptly in the doorway. I noticed it immediately. Eric was back on the circle bed; Knight's orders, according to the day nurse Caitlin.

I flew into the bathroom and locked the door.

Russell and Lewis arrived to do the bronch. I'd forgotten it was Sunday and Knight was off. He switched Eric to the circle bed and then ran off so he wouldn't have to face me.

Russell reported that Eric had had some difficulty with his blood pressure overnight. Her tone sounded ominous. If they had medicine to lower blood pressure, couldn't they give him some to raise it? She hurried off before I could ask.

Orderlies flipped Eric to his tummy. Damn that circle bed. As I sat next to him, I noticed immediately that his back was a bright red color along the right side and onto his once-gorgeous behind. It was strange looking, almost artificial. I asked Caitlin about it, and she explained. "It's a red dye that's used in medicine to stimulate cell proliferation and help the wounds heal. It's called scarlet red."

I was reading Eric an article out of *Audubon* magazine when David showed up. He got in my face and began to scold me like a child. Was he trying to intimidate me? I tuned him out. Blah blah blah. I don't hear you, I silently repeated.

Some of David's words were registering. What did he say? Did he ask my permission to video-tape? Yes, there it was again. He wanted to go in Eric's room and film bandage changes. He thought Eric would want to know what happened. As David turned to why I should leave the hospital, I thought, *stop. Now.*

"I'm going home tomorrow," I practically shouted at him. "I'm going to the counselor tomorrow too. What else do you want from me?"

"I'm sorry if I seem harsh," David replied in a monotone. "But you've got to take care of those kids. Tia particularly."

He pulled up a chair and sat down. During the next ten minutes, he asked me many questions about Eric, what he'd been doing the past few years, his biking, our travels. He was trying to be caring, sort of.

"I've been telling you stories," I said. "Now it's your turn. I want to hear about Eric as a kid."

David looked thoughtful as he sat back in his chair. "Like all brothers, we had a mixed relationship. There was the time he saved me from dropping off the cliff into the icy stream when we were sledding. The cliff was only about six feet high"—he held his hand above his head—"and we were on the course Eric designed and knew extremely well. He grabbed the back of my sled and held me over the precipice, making me swear all kinds of allegiances to him before he pulled me back. To this day, I'm sure he pushed me over the edge before he saved me.

"I'm sure you know Eric is sensitive. He's a hopeless romantic. As a teenager, way before it was cool, Eric's favorite movies were the old Errol Flynn, Humphrey Bogart, and Fred Astaire flicks. I believe I even saw him shed a tear over some of those schmaltzy stories. His all-time favorite was *Peter Pan* because Eric never wanted to grow up.

"You know, of course, Eric used to paint in high school. He also took up photography. He had a great eye and a real touch with his photographs. He wasn't satisfied with just taking pictures, though; he had to develop them himself. He built a darkroom in our parents' basement when we were in high school."

"I know." I tried to smile. "We still have all his darkroom equipment. We've lugged it all around the world with us. Eric can't bring himself to part with it."

"That sounds like Eric." David paused and looked down at his hands. I thought I saw a tear in his eye.

"I'm sorry, David. I know you're in pain too."

He didn't say a word, just continued to look at his hands.

Patty was back. I felt myself exhale, my tight muscles relaxing slightly, when I saw her.

She told me Tim had asked her earlier if she'd be willing to go to Bombardier to speak. "They probably want me because I'm a doctor and can tell them about Eric's condition. But I think I ought to have your permission."

I gave it.

Patty and I spent the rest of the evening talking, telling stories, reading to Eric, and fielding phone calls and visitors. It was late when we walked back to the hotel. The talk turned to our undergraduate years.

"Patty, did I ever tell you about the Dean's Beans?"

"Is this going to be a boring story about soybeans?" she asked.

"Hardly. It's sort of a secret, though."

* * *

Everyone called it the Dean's Beans. No one seemed to know if Parks College owned the field or rented it from a farmer. The field had a small grass runway down the middle, and every fall the school hosted a fly-in. The Dean's Beans came alive with airplanes, roaring engines, laughter, flushed faces. Eric wasn't the only one there with a childhood dream to fly high and fast. You could see the exhilaration in faces; hear it in voices: "Isn't she a beauty?" "Wow, I've always wanted to see a Pitts." "Did you see that bird? There's only three in the whole world." Parks Air College could give a student the best aviation education possible, but they couldn't make a pilot. Like Eric, many of these people were born to fly.

All of us students were in agreement—the annual fly-in at the Dean's Beans was the best time, a magical time, to be at Parks. During the remainder of the year, the field was planted with soybeans or corn, except for the grass strip. It was right behind the girls' dormitory, and if your room happened to face that direction, you had a great view from the third floor.

One Saturday night, out of money and with no car, we decided to walk down the grass strip, cornstalks on all sides. Without a moon, it was totally dark. There were no streetlights, and I clutched at Eric's arm as I stumbled. He caught me and whispered in my ear, "I'll never let you fall."

We sat on the blanket he'd brought, and he put his arm around me. He pointed up at the stars and began to name them. The sky was perfectly clear, and the stars were brighter than I'd ever remembered seeing them. Had they always been that incredible? I felt for a moment that we were alone in the universe and we would always be this happy. I smelled the freshly mown grass, felt the warm breeze on my face, and listened to the crickets serenading us. As Eric continued his commentary on the stars, he noticed I was looking at him. He leaned over and kissed me. "Of all the guys in the universe, I'm the luckiest because you're my girl."

"I've never been lucky. I feel like if I'm too happy, something bad will happen."

"You can't live like that, Carol. You have to ride every opportunity life throws your way because sometimes shit happens. We're a team. We'll take on the world, hell, the whole universe, you and me. There's nothing we can't do together."

He hugged me in that warm and gentle way of his. I wanted to feel like this forever, under the stars, just the two of us. Looking up at the sky, I asked, "Do you think there's anybody else out there?"

"Sure there is. But we'll never know. There's no way to communicate with them; they're too far away. The laws of physics don't allow it. So in reality we are alone."

"That's sad."

"Not if you think about it. If they came, it wouldn't be in peace." He sounded serious.

We sat in silence for several minutes, staring up at the stars. He reached over, ran his hand through my hair, and drew me close.

"Eric, do you believe in fate?" I leaned on his shoulder and inhaled the smell of the Aramis cologne he always wore.

"I think we each control our own destiny. We make our own choices, and nobody but us is responsible for them. There's no God directing our actions. I'm an existentialist."

"I mean finding you. Do you think that somehow in the whole universe, we were meant to be together? That maybe some force brought us together?"

"Of course we were meant to be together, but I don't think there was a force involved." His hands were wandering.

"Maybe love is a force."

"I've never seen an equation for that." His lips were on my neck.

"I have."

"Really, what is it?"

"Carol plus Eric plus stars plus a grass strip plus a big, soft blanket yields love to the power of infinity."

He threw his head back and laughed. "You are so adorable. Did you know that?"

I looked at him coyly, batting my lashes. It always worked with him. "Yes I did, as a matter of fact. I thought maybe you hadn't noticed."

"I did notice. I have the most incredible, adorable girl in the whole universe. You're my little redheaded girl."

Then he kissed me, repeatedly, as we tumbled down to the blanket. The sound of zippers echoed as everything became sensation: the feel of his hands on my body, his lips tracing a line down my neck, the startling hardness of him as we shed our clothes and there was only us, as close as two people could be, under the stars in the darkness that now seemed full of light.

Day 21
Monday, October 30, 2000

*"When people tell me they have the best
mom in the world, I laugh.
No mom is better than mine.
No dad either."*
– Eric

After David joined the bandage change, video recorder in hand, I spoke with Mom and thanked her for all she'd done. I was extremely grateful, though I'd done a poor job of showing it. I'd always felt lucky to have such a kind and generous mother-in-law.

A short while later, David hugged Patty, then stiffly hugged me. Looking at me sternly, he said, "I'll be in touch with Dr. Natarajan. He should be doing the tissue transplant soon. You're still going to the counselor today, aren't you?"

"Yeah," I mumbled.

"Did you thank my mother?"

"Of course I did."

Patty frowned as he followed his mother through the double doors. "That man—" She stopped abruptly and shook her head.

Sandy and Marjorie arrived early that afternoon. "Are you ready to go to the counselor?" Sandy asked. "I'm going to drive you."

"Go ahead," Patty said. "Marjorie and I will stay and watch everything. You have your phone, and I'll call if anything happens. I checked us out of the hotel while you were reading to Eric. Our stuff is under the counter at the main nurse's station. Bombardier picked up the check. Go to the counselor."

"But why does it have to be the Catholic place?"

"Doesn't matter," Patty countered. "You and Eric went to a Catholic university, didn't you? Anyway, it'll keep David off your case."

There was no getting out of this. What a colossal waste of time.

The office on Oak Street tried to look homey, with figurines, cute wall hangings, and the standard Catholic-issue religious trappings. I fidgeted and looked at my watch, angry that David and Jennifer had forced me to be here.

The counselor, Irene, had a slight accent. She was a striking woman—dark skin and hair. She asked standard textbook questions: How do you feel? You have a right to be angry. It's all so sad. I'm sorry.

I was back at the hospital quickly, and Patty gave me an update. "Knight said nothing new. They took Eric off the paralyzing drug, but Russell says not to expect a response; he's still weak. I spoke with Alec, and he'll get Eric's paycheck switched to that new bank he liked so much."

"Eric liked it because it was a pretty redbrick bank with a popcorn machine in the lobby. He said every bank should have popcorn."

"That sounds like something he'd say. Do they have cows out back?"

"What?" I paused. "Oh…no, but Eric would have been excited about cows."

Patty wiggled a finger at me. "I saw you smile. Don't pretend you didn't."

"OK," I admitted. "Maybe I did a little."

"I spoke with that woman at the travel agency. Looks like you might lose the money for the Greece trip. It sucks. I argued with her about it."

Why wasn't I surprised?

Sandy interrupted us briefly. "Whenever you get home, that's jolly good. Marjorie and I are going back. We'll get the girls from school, help with homework, get them a snack, read books. Bob's your uncle."

"I love her accent," Patty said after they left.

"She's the best. Robin adores her; she's always at their house."

Caitlin entered Eric's room with a woman I didn't recognize. "I was in the trauma unit when your husband was brought in. I wondered how he was doing."

"Oh my God. Did he say anything? Did Eric say anything?" I could feel my heart pounding. "I've been trying to find out."

I knew someone would eventually come forward.

"Yes. He said 'I can't breathe' a couple of times. He was in bad shape; I've never seen anyone so badly burned. I've been having nightmares about it, and—"

Caitlin quickly interrupted. "I don't think Mrs. Fiore needs to hear that."

"Oh...of course, I'm sorry. It's only that—"

"Did he say anything else?" I asked. "Did my husband say anything else? Did he say 'I can't see'?"

She tapped at her bottom lip. "No. I'm sure he didn't. He said 'I can't breathe,' but I mean his eyes were—"

Caitlin coughed loudly. "Thank. You." A forced smile on her face, Caitlin quickly ushered the confused-looking woman out the door.

Patty and I prepared to head to the house. This was my first night home. I was terrified something would happen to Eric and I wouldn't make it back in time.

Never a granny driver, Patty made it to the house in record time. Marjorie and two excited children greeted us. They'd prepared a dinner, and there were welcome home signs all over the house. Marjorie left for the airport almost immediately.

I pretended to be famished as I forced down the girls' spaghetti supper. Every bite was painful, not because the food wasn't tasty but because my entire body seemed to be in some sort of mutiny.

It was late when we finished, and I sent them off to bed. As I tucked Robin in, she hugged me tightly. "Are you going to be home now, Mommy? Will you be here when I wake up? Will you walk me to the bus?"

"Yes, honey. I'll be here and take you to the bus."

I went downstairs to kiss Tia. "Mommy, I guess we're not going to carve pumpkins tomorrow for Halloween, are we? Daddy always carves four pumpkins. One for each of us. Remember? Your pumpkin has a crooked smile, and Robin's is the littlest."

"Not this year, honey. Next year. OK?"

"It's OK. I love you. Daddy loves you too." She hugged me. Her eyes were dry, and she didn't look quite so angry.

Day 22
Tuesday, October 31, 2000
Halloween

"Don't cheat kids out of good candy on the best holiday of the year."
– Eric

"**M**ommy, please come home tonight for trick-or-treating," Robin had implored, clutching me tightly before leaving for school.

Tia said one word as she hugged me. "Please."

Halloween was Eric's favorite holiday. He liked it more than Christmas. Every year he dressed up, usually in the Robin Hood costume he'd made himself. He bought the green velvet fabric, and without a pattern, he cut it out and used our portable sewing machine to stitch it all together with dark-brown thread. He pulled the stitches out and redid it several times, but the finished product was truly amazing. He completed the outfit with a hat he purchased at Sherwood Forest and a bow and arrows he bought in a toy store. I even sewed a Maid Marian costume for myself.

Almost every year at Halloween, starting in 1991, he'd don that outfit and greet kids at the door in a loud, booming voice: "Welcome to Sherwood Forest."

Last year, Tia, being in sixth grade and feeling she was grown up and sophisticated, was mortified to think her daddy was going to dress up yet again and embarrass her. He laughed when she suggested he not do it.

"I love Halloween," he'd reminded her. "I always dress up as Robin Hood, and anyway, that's why parents have kids—so they can embarrass them."

Eric took the whole candy aspect of Halloween seriously, insisting on buying good candy to distribute, exclaiming, "Kids don't want apples and pencils. I threw those away when I was a kid. And don't buy gum and sticky candy. Buy chocolate bars. That's the stuff kids like."

In the early days of our marriage, I'd argue we couldn't afford those candies. "Can't we buy something cheaper?"

"You'd cheat kids on the best holiday of the year?" He'd clutched his chest in mock horror. "Shame on you."

So chocolate bars it was. Eric distributed them at the door, greeting and admiring each child: "Hey, Spider-Man. How's it hanging?" "I'm not that old; I know you three are the Spice Girls." "Hi there, Dorothy. Those red shoes are great. Where's Toto?"

He eagerly answered every ring of the doorbell. Before he left to take Tia and Robin trick-or-treating, he reminded me to compliment everybody on their costumes.

Halloween evening was a production complete with a large meal, which always included pumpkin pie and pumpkin bread. Eric carved jack-o'-lanterns a few days before and saved the seeds to roast on Halloween night. He always carved four pumpkins. One was made to look like each kid and one for him and me. Robin's was the smallest, Eric's had the biggest nose, mine had a crooked smile, and Tia's had almond-shaped eyes.

We bought our pumpkins at a local Wichita farm called Pumpkin Junction, which Robin had discovered on a kindergarten field trip.

"Is it a sincere pumpkin patch?" Eric had inquired of her quite seriously.

"Oh yes, Daddy," Robin insisted. "I'm sure it is because they take you in a wagon to pick out pumpkins in a really big field."

The word of a six-year-old could not be wrong when it came to sincerity.

I sat beside Eric's bed on his favorite holiday. He would not be wearing his Robin Hood costume, and he would not be greeting the neighborhood kids with cries of "Welcome to Sherwood Forest." He couldn't hold his bow and arrows because he had no fingers to grasp them. The kids would have been terrified of my kind, sweet Eric. How could they know that inside was a gentle man who adored Halloween and delighted in admiring their costumes?

"There will be more Halloweens, Eric. I had someone buy good chocolate bars, like you always did."

That morning, Knight informed Patty and me that he was starting to see good pink tissue in Eric's lungs. He even smiled. Patty nodded and shot me a thumbs-up. Maybe it was going to be a better day.

Russell said there was mold around Eric's neck and the lab was running tests to see if he had an infection. He could beat that with antibiotics, I reasoned. But despite Knight's earlier smile, something didn't seem right. Was it Russell's body language when she told me? A twitch of her lip? Patty's silence?

I couldn't identify it, so I tried to ignore it. Eric was getting better, wasn't he? An infection was nothing compared to everything else he faced, right? It felt as though there were two people in my head, in a vehement debate. I wanted desperately to believe the optimist.

Patty and I were sitting in the hall when she spotted Father Luke. Pointing at the priest, she said, in a serious tone, "They have to take a special course at the seminary. It's a required class, and they absolutely have to pass or they don't get their holy badges. It's called

Face 101. They learn how to make that sad face of concern they give every time they see you."

It felt strangely odd to laugh. I didn't recognize the sound.

Patty grinned. "That young priest is an expert at 'the face.' I'll bet he got the highest grade in the class. Maybe he even teaches it."

There was that strange laugh again, coming from my body.

"I've seen those nuns too. They're required to take Face training at the convent. Maybe that young priest taught them."

He came toward us. Patty whispered, "Watch and learn while I do the Face."

The priest came over, the Face in perfect place, and stopped in front of us. His pale skin contrasted with his black hair, making him look even more tragic. His forehead wrinkled, and the sides of his mouth drooped as he inched toward us.

I scooted my chair back as Patty coughed loudly. She put on her own face, the serious, all-business doctor face, straightening up in her chair, lowering her voice, nodding seriously. She explained to him that Eric seemed a bit better and his lungs were now an encouraging pink color. The priest nodded gravely. After wishing us a good day and telling me once again how he was praying for us, he left, head bowed. His steps were completely silent as he walked down the tiled hallway.

Patty looked at me. I looked at Patty. She covered her mouth. I covered mine. The giggles escaped in spite of it.

The occupational therapist came by, rotated Eric's wrists and shoulders, scribbled notes on a pad. I watched her silently and shrugged at Patty.

"Because they're here, it means they think he's going to make it," Patty said.

I tried to smile—he was going to make it. Russell would take care of those other problems. I banished the pessimist from my head.

Knight wandered down the hall, peered in at Eric, then turned to me. I looked around for Patty, but she was gone. "Mrs. Fiore. There are certain rumors circulating about his condition. You may want to give the press a statement. They continue to call us."

I didn't want to know what the rumors were. "I'm not giving a statement."

"And your brother-in-law has asked me for pictures of your husband. Do you know about this?"

"Yes. He needs them for plastic surgeons. I told him it was OK."

"Fine. If that's what you want," Knight said stiffly.

As he turned to go, he glanced back and casually remarked, "The lungs look better."

When Patty reappeared, I told her what had happened, and she gave me another thumbs-up.

"Where'd you disappear to?" I asked her.

"I was looking at the pictures."

"What pictures?"

"The ones of Eric the nurses took yesterday," she said quietly.

"Well?" I asked.

"It's bad. But I think you know that. He'll deal with it. He's Eric, after all." She was trying to sound emotionless, matter-of-fact, but her voice had cracked slightly. She chewed at her lip and avoided my eyes.

I was cold again and wrapped my arms tightly around my chest, pretending for a moment they were Eric's arms. The pessimist had returned.

Early that afternoon the respiratory therapist was practically doing a jig. The vent settings were being turned way down. Patty made several calls to spread the good news.

"It's looking better today," I nearly shouted to one of the occupational people, forgetting Patty's earlier expression.

If I said it enough, it would come true. That pessimist could go fuck herself. I told Eric he was getting better. I told everyone who walked by. I told myself.

It was early evening when Patty and I climbed into the Jeep for the ride home. I didn't want to leave the hospital, but there were two girls at home who needed their mother. "Please," they'd said.

By the time we arrived, Robin was wearing her '50s girl costume: pink felt skirt with the required poodle (I'd made it last year), black saddle shoes, a white blouse with a scarf, and her hair in a high pony-tail. Tia had decided she was much too old to go out, but she'd dressed up in my mermaid costume and was prepared to hand out chocolate bars—the good ones, the ones kids like. The long, purple, sequined skirt and bright-green top looked better on Tia than it had ever looked on me.

"You two are gorgeous," I said, hugging them.

"Are you ready to get some candy?" Patty asked Robin.

"Bring me some," Tia called after her sister.

I stared out the window into the dark night. Candles flickered in the neighbors' pumpkins. They had carved big grins on the three pumpkins lining their porch. I thought of our pumpkins. The four that looked like us.

My stomach lurched and I ran for the bathroom.

Day 23
Wednesday, November 1, 2000

"No good ever came from treating people badly."
- Eric

P atty tucked Eric's shirt, slightly too big, into her jeans and adjusted the collar. "Do you think this looks OK?"

I nodded. "That's one of Eric's favorite Bombardier shirts."

We stood in the generous walk-in closet of the master bedroom. Patty pointed out that I had a ridiculous number of fancy gowns. Eric and I had gone to lots of formal parties while he was in the Air Force; I had been an officer's wife, after all. I'd taken over most of the space with all my clothing, relegating Eric's things to a small corner. He teased me about it, saying, "Why do you need so many clothes? And what's up with all the shoes? Really, Carol, someone might think you were Imelda Marcos."

I touched my favorite gown—the emerald-green one with the puffy sleeves and bows on the hem. Eric had bought it for me in a boutique on Regent Street in London. "I'll probably never wear this again…"

Patty bustled me out of the closet. "OK then. I'll wear this shirt. I hope I don't screw up my speech today. I don't like speaking in front of groups."

"You'll be great."

The dressing change was already in progress when we arrived at the hospital. Lydia, the nurse on duty, appeared to view taking care of me as part of her job. Today she wore a bright, purple-flowered headband, which matched her purple scrub top. Taking my hands in hers, she looked into my eyes, listening intently to me, giving me her undivided attention until Dr. Russell arrived.

"Eric had low blood pressure problems again last night," Russell said. "He had an EKG, and it showed tachycardia. We're sure he's septic, so we've started him on several meds: Primaxin, Vancomycin, Bactrim, and Tobramycin. His left hand and left forearm aren't looking good."

Why all those drugs? What were they? I understood nothing of what she'd said. Tachy-what? She asked me whether I had questions, but for once I decided to let her go without my usual outburst. I could tell she was busy. Patty would explain what she'd said.

The pessimist in my head began to scream about the infection, about Eric's hand and arm. I tried not to listen, instead asking Patty what a tachy-thing was. And what the hell did septic mean?

"Tachycardia means a fast heart rate, usually over one hundred," Patty explained. "It's the pulse, or 'P,' on the vital signs sheet. Russell told me they're watching it closely. It's probably related to the infection and all the meds. Septic means he has an infection."

Patty excused herself to make a phone call. She didn't want me to ask about Eric's hand and arm. She left a short time later for Bombardier.

I was glad I wasn't going. I couldn't bear to see so many people, not right now. Patty was in for a shock, though. She seemed to think there would be "a few friends." There would be hundreds; I was sure.

My university friend Linda stopped by the waiting room and dropped off a tape recorder for the girls to record messages to Eric. She also handed me e-mails that had come to the website she'd set up. I picked up the stack of papers and thumbed through them, but I was too tired to read.

Late that afternoon, Patty returned to the hospital.

"How did your speech go?" I asked her.

"I think it went well. I thought I was meeting with a few friends, but there were several hundred."

No surprise there. Everyone wanted to know what was going on. I had no doubt they cared, but there was also a morbid curiosity, like the proverbial train wreck. "You didn't tell…you know…details of his injuries, did you?"

"No, of course not," Patty said, sounding offended. "What happened?"

"First, let me say, I thought this was going to be some casual thing. You know, chatting with a couple people. I didn't prepare a formal speech, just some notes. I figured I'd answer a few questions, say hello, and that would be all. I thought everyone out there would be working, so I'd be fairly unobtrusive."

"And?"

"On the way out it occurred to me that I might have made more of an effort with my appearance. I haven't slept much, and you saw me: messy hair, no makeup."

I rolled my eyes. "You never wear makeup."

"OK fine. So that's true, but I suppose I could have worn something other than a T-shirt and ripped jeans."

I looked at her, feigning indignation. "That's Eric's Bombardier shirt. And I don't see a rip in your jeans."

"That's because these aren't the jeans I was wearing when I left the hospital. As usual I left too early, and while I was wondering how I ought to kill some time, I saw a jeans outlet store on the corner. I went in and bought the first pair I found in my size."

I grinned as she continued with her story. It was such a Patty thing.

"It was strange to meet some of the people I've been talking to every day for weeks on the phone. It was weird that everyone seemed to know exactly who I was."

"We do look alike," I said.

"Tim and Alec and I went into the boardroom. There were about thirty people in there, already sitting down. The place has impressive woodwork, fancy tables, paintings, and everyone was wearing suits. It was obvious these were the important people at the company. Tim is obviously one of these important people."

"Did you just figure that out? That's why Eric called him Mr. Ryan."

"OK fine, I'm slow. Anyway, I was glad I wasn't wearing old, torn jeans."

"Me too. I mean, oh my God."

Patty laughed. We'd always joked around with each other, and I think she saw it as a good sign that I was kidding with her again.

"Anyway, to get on with the story. Tim introduced me and asked if I'd give a summary of Eric's condition. So I did. You know, the same sentences I've been repeating to everyone who calls and everyone who comes to the waiting room. I think I've repeated it all a hundred times. I asked if anyone had questions. The first question was how you were holding up."

"What did you tell them?"

"I said you guys know Eric, right? Anybody who can actually live with Eric has to be tough, don't you think? I told them everyone thinks you're frail because you're so skinny, but they shouldn't be fooled by that. You can't live with Eric for twenty years and not have a backbone. Think about it."

"You said that?" I practically shouted.

"It's true, isn't it? Anyway, they all laughed."

"It was twenty-three years."

"Yes, I know, but I wasn't going to tell them you lived with the guy before you married him. This *is* Kansas." She smiled. "They asked a lot of questions about Eric's condition, especially his hands and his eyes."

"What did you tell them?"

"The truth. I said he'd lost some fingers and one eye was probably gone. That Eric loves his job and he'd want to come back to work when he was better. I told them the safety equipment he did have on worked, like the flight suit and the restraint. It was the stuff he didn't have on that was the problem."

"His helmet and gloves—"

"That's what I told them," she said. "They weren't required; otherwise, he'd have had them on. We all know Eric is a nut about safety stuff. I also told them the medical care was excellent, and no, they didn't need to send him to another hospital. I said you and the girls were holding up, but it was best if I gave Tim and Alec daily updates and they passed them along. I told them Eric couldn't communicate."

"Did you tell them he doesn't have a brain injury, that he's still Eric?"

"Yes, I did. I made it clear that the real problematic injuries were the burns and the lung inhalation. When we were done, Tim asked me if I'd mind talking to a couple of 'the guys.' I took that to mean the nonexecutive types, like the mechanics. I said yeah, that would be fine.

"I went to a hangar. It was huge. There was a platform set up, a microphone, enormous speakers, and at least several hundred people, all waiting quietly for me. Clearly these were the worker bees of the company. They had on overalls and safety stuff. I probably could have worn the torn jeans here."

"You ought to give the torn jeans thing a rest."

"Fine. Tim introduced me again and I gave the same tired speech about Eric's condition, but their questions were tougher, more to the point. They weren't subtle. They came right out and said stuff like 'Is he going to make it?' I said we think so, but he's extremely sick. Someone asked, 'Is it true his hands were amputated?' I said no, but a few fingers were. Someone else asked if he could talk, so I explained about the sedation and respirator. Rumors spread fast because someone asked about his eyes."

I felt a sudden jolt in my stomach as a sickening wave spread over me. "You said he wasn't blind, right?"

"Of course. They seemed great; everyone was worried. It felt sort of like talking to a big family. You won't believe the huge banner they all signed for Eric. I left it in your Jeep."

"Maybe we could hang it in the hallway when we get back to the house tonight."

"I told them you'd say that. Tim showed me the plane Eric was working on—the R-something."

"The RJ. It stands for Regional Jet."

"That was it. A cool plane. I think I'll check on Eric. I want to tell him I'm impressed with him. You know, I always was, but I was too stubborn to tell him."

She tried to turn her head to the side, away from me, but she wasn't fast enough.

I saw the tears.

Day 24
Thursday, November 2, 2000

"Nothing can drag me away from my little redheaded girl."
- Eric

"I spoke with David this morning," Russell began. "Dr. Natarajan will be doing the amniotic tissue transplant on Saturday. I believe the plastic surgeon he's working with will be by sometime today. Also, some of the grafts are not taking. Dr. Knight will be discussing a future surgery date with you, but his lungs do seem to be slowly improving."

She paused. There was something else. I felt myself tighten up as she continued. "Eric has an infection; the lab results came back this morning. He's on a heavy round of antibiotics, and we'll increase the Bactrim to assist in fighting it. We'll be trying to wean him off the Dopamine a bit."

"Will that help his blood pressure problem?" I asked her.

"Hopefully."

"What is the name of the infection?" Patty asked.

"*Stenotrophomonas xanthomonas maltophilia*." Russell said it slowly and clearly. I could tell from Patty's expression that she'd never heard of it.

I had a horrible feeling that it was my fault. Maybe someone with a cold or infection had been in Eric's room. My only job was to monitor visitors and be a watchdog. I couldn't do one simple job. "How did… how…I mean, did he catch it from someone?"

"No, of course not. This is an infection only seen in burn patients. He couldn't catch it from someone."

"You're giving him lots of antibiotics. That will kill it. Right?" I asked.

"Yes, we expect it will." There was something in her voice, and in her expression, that wasn't convincing. I couldn't say exactly what it was, but her hopefulness seemed forced.

After Russell left, I noticed Patty had a briefcase in her lap. "What's that?"

"Alec was here, but he had to leave. He'll be back to drive me to the airport. He wanted me to give you this." She handed me the briefcase.

"It's Eric's computer," Patty continued. "Alec says they deleted all the proprietary stuff, and it's yours to keep. He thinks you can look up information to help Eric."

I unzipped the briefcase and pulled out Eric's Toshiba laptop. I felt a crumbled collection of papers and pulled them out. It was a thick color brochure from De Drie Fleschjes. Eric must have gone there on his Amsterdam trip before the accident.

* * *

De Drie Fleschjes is a tiny pub at Gravenstraat 18 in Amsterdam. It is so small that there are no chairs or tables, only a few seats at the bar. It looks like many of the other tall, skinny, gable-roofed buildings situated along Amsterdam's numerous canals.

When we lived in the Netherlands in the mid-1980s, we used to go there frequently to see what was in the barrel. Eric had a key to the barrel, and we could drink as much as we liked, anytime we liked, because his squadron dues covered the cost. The problem was that you never knew what was in there, and often it was vile. Maybe that was part of the fun and the attraction of the whole thing.

Our barrel was no different from the other round wooden kegs lining the walls in De Drie Fleschjes, except for one thing. It had a plaque on it that read "32nd Tactical Fighter Squadron Camp New Amsterdam Wolfhounds." When you poured a drink from that keg, everyone in the pub knew you were a fighter pilot. The Thirty-Second was famous all over Holland.

Many of the Dutch thought being an F-15 jock was extremely cool. There were always people wanting to strike up a conversation, buy us proper drinks, or ask questions. Eric was in his element, flying his hands, telling tall tales while surrounded by admiring fans. He gave them what they wanted: stories to take home or tell at work. One could almost hear them say, "I got to meet a real live fighter pilot..." Eric said the only people impressed with fighter pilots were little boys and other fighter pilots, but I didn't believe it one bit, not here in De Drie Fleschjes anyway.

Sometimes we'd go with other couples to Amsterdam on the weekend. The pub was always the first stop, followed by dinner and a stroll around the infamous red light district. Generally Eric was too engrossed in conversation with the other pilots to notice the sights. With his hands flying and passion about the mission pouring from him, he would remark, "Oh... did we already do the traditional red-light walk?"

We would walk back to the train station for the thirty-minute ride to the rail station near our house, and then to our car for the short ride home. The last train left a few minutes before midnight, and anyone who wasn't on it had to spend the night in Amsterdam. Although this never happened to us, a few of the pilots seemed to be consistently stuck overnight. Monday morning briefings in the squadron usually included some mention of weekend romps in A'Dam. Eric liked to give the impression that he was a party animal, but truthfully, he was not.

With only a few exceptions, Eric rarely partied to excess. When he drank, it was in moderation. He was quite capable of acting wild and silly without drinking, and he was careful not to do anything that would jeopardize his flying or his career. Eric had no patience for people who drank excessively or used drugs. He was fond of saying that he was perfectly capable of getting high without the assistance of foreign substances: he went flying. Last month he'd pointed out a poster of the Blue Angels flight team to Tia, sternly saying, "You can't do that on drugs."

*   *   *

"I have to catch my flight," Patty said. "I'll call every day and speak with the medical people." Like Russell a few hours earlier, her cheerfulness sounded forced.

I hugged her tightly. *Please don't go. I need you.* But when I opened my mouth, those were not the words that came out. "Thanks for everything. I'll be OK. I'm in for the long haul, like you told them at Bombardier yesterday. Eric would be grateful to you." Now I was the one forcing cheerfulness from my voice.

Then she was gone.

Dr. Schmidt, the plastic surgeon, showed up to view the records and look in on Eric. He was one more faceless doctor, explaining the situation quickly, barely looking up from the chart. "I've come by at the request of Dr. Natarajan, who I understand will be performing a procedure on Saturday to try to protect the eyes.

I'm here to assess the situation with the lids. There is some lid retraction, and the lids are necrotic. I'll be investigating how best to reconstruct them. Without eyelids to protect the globes, the possibility of vision is compromised."

Why did everyone have to use that word: necrotic? Maybe it sounded more scientific. Maybe he couldn't say Eric's lids were dead.

"I...I...never thought about...you know...I guess you have to have eyelids."

"Indeed. I will be discussing with Natarajan how best to achieve this." His voice was flat and emotionless. Like Knight, he'd done all this before.

I asked quickly, "Will Eric be able to see?"

He looked up from the chart but avoided a direct look. "Mrs. Fiore, we're going to do everything in our power to ensure that he does."

Then he was gone too.

I returned to the stack of e-mails Linda had dropped off. I read several aloud to Eric. One was from a childhood friend. She talked about growing up with Eric, remarking that he was energetic, witty, and humorous. He had a big smile. She remembered his kindness to animals, his love for his collie. She ended the e-mail with the sentence "Whenever a military jet streaks overhead, we think of Eric and thank him and you for having worked to make our world a safer place."

I moved on to the next e-mail. "You're going to like this one, Eric. It's from your protégé Stephan. I think he's one of your biggest fans."

Eric,
    I heard about this e-mail address today, so I am writing to say hello.
    I flew from Los Angeles to Pittsburgh early this morning, and now I am at my "crash pad" here in Pittsburgh.
    Things sometimes don't seem fair. Of all the pilots I have ever flown with, you are the one who always stressed safety the most. You made me begrudgingly get rid of my metal clipboard and also made me wear my gloves when I flew with you. I will always be very grateful for everything you taught me about flying and flight testing.
    I cannot even imagine the hell you are going through now, but one thing is for sure. You have incredible energy, fighting spirit, and willpower. Not one day passes when I don't think about how you are doing, and every night I pray for you and your family. I never got to know your wife, just heard all the stories about the zoo, the evil cats, and all the discussions you and she had about driving the Miata. By the way, I think you should let her drive the Miata while you are in the hospital.
    Take care, Eric, and I will write again later.

"This next one is from a Parks friend. Remember when we used to fly out of Bi-State Airport in Cahokia when we were students?"

I read the e-mail. I remembered the incident the friend described. Eric had wanted to check out a plane at the airport, but the owner had a grudge against him. Determined to keep Eric from taking the plane out, the owner said there was a problem, and an A&P would have to check the plane first.

Eric whipped out his license and said, "I am an A&P, so consider it checked off." The owner's jaw dropped. He didn't know Eric had his license. Eric was still laughing when he took off.

Late that night back at the house, I looked for the Rolling Stones music. Where was it? I searched frantically. Then it occurred to me. I went out in the garage, slid the cover on Eric's Miata aside, and reached into the glove compartment. There it was, *Hot Rocks*, Eric's favorite. I took it back in the house and listened to "Wild Horses." It had always been our song since that first time we'd made love with it playing in the background. It now seemed to take on a special meaning. He'd always said nothing could drag him away from me.

Day 25
Friday, November 3, 2000

*"Hey, Carol. Look at the beautiful sunset
I baked for you."*
- Eric

"Eric's platelets are up to thirty-one. They were eleven yesterday," said Dr. Russell, smiling.

Patty had told me the platelets were supposed to be between 150,000 and 400,000, with the units in thousands usually left off. Russell's report of 31 was actually 31,000, but was still extremely low.

"Does he still have that bad infection?" I asked her. "What was it? Steno-something?"

"*Stenotrophomonas.* Yes, I'm afraid so. The culture came back positive again this morning, so he's still on the Bactrim, but we're keeping a close watch."

Eric's best friend called, and we talked about the eye surgery. RB's southern accent seemed thicker today.

Maybe he was tired. He told me once again about the pilot friend with one eye, but it didn't help. Eric was never going to fly again. He was never going to be an astronaut. He'd never fulfill his dream of going up in space.

"It's OK to be angry," RB said quietly.

"You've said that before. Maybe it's OK for some people, but it's not for me. I won't be able to help Eric if I go down the angry road. I may never be able to find my way out."

I was almost finished with the first Harry Potter book. The second had the section about the phoenix, the bird that rose up from the ashes, and it reminded me of the newsletter Jennifer had given me earlier. I pulled it out from between the pages of the book as I stood over Eric.

"Eric, there's this organization called the Phoenix Society. It's a support group for burn patients. I know you hate support groups and you'll say you don't need it, but…"

His eyes were still stitched shut. I looked at his hands, at the bandages on his face. I knew what was under them.

Rod, the day nurse, came in to take some readings, and he smiled as he wrote something on Eric's chart. "His numbers are better when you're reading to him. See, his blood pressure is up to 87/41. Better." He flashed brilliantly perfect teeth.

"Then I'll keep reading."

When I couldn't read anymore, I took Linda's tape recorder from my bag and played the song for Eric. Our song. Could he hear it? His mouth seemed to open a bit as I played "Wild Horses" the second time.

I spent about an hour in the medical library researching prosthetics. I found an artificial hand for a bicyclist and the name of a top surgeon in New York City that specialized in facial reconstruction after severe burns. I called his office and left a message.

Late that afternoon, I threatened Eric that I'd let Rod drive his Miata unless he got his blood pressure up. Russell had warned me that if it got too low, Knight would cancel the eye surgery. The eyes couldn't wait. We'd already waited too long.

A half hour later, Eric's blood pressure was up and Rod was congratulating me on my tactics to rile up Eric. A short time later Knight popped his head in and said he'd decided to skip the bronch today. He paused and said, "He really is a fighter."

His remark, said in the same flat voice he always used, caught me by surprise. His expression and demeanor were the same as before. Only the words were different. I could feel my mouth hanging open. Had he really said that? Rod smiled, his enthusiasm reaching all the way up to his azure eyes.

I looked out Eric's hospital room window. The sun was beginning to set. The sky was a reddish-yellow color, and the clouds cast an enchanting glow over the ground. I bent down and whispered to Eric, using the words he'd said to me so many times over the years. "I baked you a beautiful sunset."

It was late when I got home. The girls had been worried, they told me, and asked with fear in their voices if Daddy was all right. Robin clutched me tightly as Tia stared off in the distance, pretending nothing was wrong. But she was shaking ever so slightly.

"He's about the same," I told them. "There was a nurse named Rod who let Daddy get cold. I was mad."

Robin looked at me strangely. "Can't you take some of Daddy's sweaters to the hospital? He likes the blue one with the white stripes."

I hugged them both, a bit too tightly. The phone rang. It was a confident-sounding Dr. Natarajan, calling to see whether I had any questions about tomorrow's surgery. I thanked him and assured him I would be there.

After hanging up, I explained the eye stuff to the girls. Robin asked in a quiet voice, "Is Daddy blind?"

"Of course not, pumpkin," I answered, trying my best to sound convincing. "That's why the eye doctor is coming tomorrow. Uncle Dr. David found him and said he's the best doctor in the whole country."

"But Mommy," Robin insisted, "a boy at school said Daddy was blind. They said his hands got cut off too."

I looked at her, horrified. "It's not nice to say such things, is it?"

Robin and Tia both shook their heads no. Tia folded her arms across her chest and looked at me, a serious expression on her face. "Mommy, are you going to make the Christmas gingerbread cookies this year? They're Daddy's favorite. Maybe it would help him get better if you made them."

Robin nodded in agreement.

"No, it takes about three days to make them, and I'll be with Daddy in the hospital."

Tia and Robin looked at each other but didn't say anything.

"I'll tell you what," I continued. "I promise to make the cookies when Daddy can eat them. Right now, he's still getting his food from a tube, but when he's better, I know he'll want some of his favorite cookies. I'll make them no matter what time of the year it is. Will that be OK?"

They looked disappointed but nodded their agreement. Robin snuggled next to me. "We'll wait. We want to eat them with Daddy anyway."

*   *   *

As the years went by, I'd started to hate those cookies. I'd been thrilled when Eric's grandmother initially entrusted me with the secret fifty-year-old family recipe. That was twelve years ago, and I was tired of the laborious three-day job. I had to make the dough from scratch and roll it paper thin. Rolling the dough took hours and hours, and it always seemed to stick to the counter no matter how much flour I used. Then I'd have to reroll about half of it before using the cookie cutters. The baking was a delicate process, and the temperature and timing had to be perfect or the result was broken cookies. If I failed to grease the sheets properly, the cookies would stick. If I failed to take the cookies, carefully, off the sheets after exactly thirty seconds, they would break into tiny bits. The whole thing was a pain. However, the rolling and baking were nothing compared to the decorating.

The decorating process took an entire day. Each of the dozen different-shaped cookies had its own color guidelines. Eric insisted I decorate with fine paintbrushes, and I couldn't smear the colors or paint the cookies contrary to the exact specifications of his grandmother Nana. He loved her tremendously and took the rules seriously. He felt it was a way of honoring her, but his comments to me were endless: "Carol, the stars are supposed to be blue, not red. This is not Russia." "No, no, no. This is not the correct color for the gingerbread men." "Which brush did you use on these trees? The ornaments are too big."

On several occasions, I almost threw the cookies at him. He always apologized later, but the next year it would be the same. He never seemed to remember.

Every year I said the same thing. "I hate these cookies. I am *never* making them again."

Then I would see his silly pouting lip, fake tragic expression, and the sad faces of Tia and Robin. Against my better judgment, I'd do it. I wanted to be creative and try something new, but Eric was adamantly opposed.

One year I cut out ducks and colored them yellow. Eric refused to eat them. "What do ducks have to do with Christmas?" he fumed.

Another year I was tired, and instead of painting the tiny holly leaves, I poured sprinkles on them. He was furious. One year I accidentally broke the leg off one of the gingerbread men and then painted the stump with red frosting. Eric was not amused and declared the whole episode to be "rather sick." The next year I painted mad faces on some of the gingerbread men. He insisted I redo them and refused to stop fussing until I did. Eventually I gave up trying to do something new and resigned myself to the same old cookies.

* * *

After I explained to the girls that I had to leave early tomorrow for Daddy's surgery, I went in my room and took my good-luck charm out of the jewelry box. It had been a present from my mother-in-law when I started back to school four years ago. I carefully laid it next to my keys so I wouldn't forget to wear it tomorrow. It was my lucky silver necklace with a miniature bird feeder loaded with tiny birds. I'd worn it for all the important exams at Wichita State University when I was a graduate student.

It had never failed me.

Day 26
Saturday, November 4, 2000

"Always give people a chance to do the right thing."
- Eric

Clutching the lucky necklace hanging around my neck, I knew my motions were nervous, halting, compulsive. Nobody understood. How could they? I'd lived with Eric for over twenty years and witnessed the phobia he had about his eyes. I was so terrified I could barely function. All my ranting, all my pleading, all David's hard work, had brought us to this day.

If Eric were blind, there would be nothing I could do—this was what I wanted to shout at Dr. Knight. All you've done to save Eric will be for nothing if he can't see. Perhaps David was the only one besides me who knew that. Even Patty seemed to think that, in typical Eric fashion, he would deal with it.

He would not.

Dr. Natarajan walked in. I clutched the side of Eric's bed as tiny white stars danced around the room.

"We will be getting ready for the surgery now. Mrs. Fiore? Are you in need of assistance?"

I tried to regain my composure while he introduced his associate. The man shook my hand. He had a ruggedly handsome face and a pleasant voice.

At 7:45 a.m., the surgery team started to get Eric ready. Dr. Russell told me the culture came back positive, once again, for the bad steno-infection-thing. The heavy-duty antibiotics would continue. She explained the surgery was risky because Eric's blood pressure was low. Was there a choice? Time was running out for his eyes.

At 8:15 a.m., the anesthesiologist arrived with the transport team, and they started to unhook and transfer bags and lines. I stood far off to the side. About ten minutes later Dr. Natarajan returned, fully suited for surgery. I followed the team a short way down the hall, quietly, and watched as the bed with Eric on it disappeared.

I walked slowly back to his room to gather my purse and journal. Jan gave my arm a squeeze. "You did well this time, Carol." She ran a hand through her wavy black hair. "You did well," she repeated.

I sat in the hallway, writing in my journal. There were several visitors in the waiting room, but I didn't want to go out there. Not yet.

An hour later, I felt ready to face visitors. Sandy and Phil and Alec and Tim were already there—all the regulars, as Patty referred to them. There was the inevitable small talk, but nobody felt like conversing. The overhead television droned on while the dripping sound of coffee brewing and the clang of cups echoed from the small kitchenette.

I shifted nervously in my chair, still clutching the necklace. Patty and David called. Mom called. Lisa called. RB called. Linda called. I looked at my watch. I drank too much coffee. I waited.

At exactly 11:10 a.m., Natarajan and his associate came out to the waiting room. Dr. Natarajan began. "We have covered the right eye, and I am quite hopeful."

I leaped from my chair. "Thank you, Dr. Natarajan. Thank you so much."

He sat down in a chair across from me, motioning for me to sit. He proceeded to give me the medical details, but I found it difficult to concentrate on his words, nodding enthusiastically anyway as he continued.

"The amniotic membrane was well positioned and nicely secure over the cornea and the conjunctiva…no amniotic membrane grafting was done on the left…"

Dr. Natarajan leaned toward me. "Inspection of the left eye showed complete avulsion of the lids and complete opacification and keratinization. No further treatment was possible due to the severe damage of the lids and end stage of the cornea of the left eye."

I didn't move. I'd known all along. No one would say it, but I knew.

Looking at both doctors, I asked quietly, "Did I get this right? The right eye isn't as bad as we thought, and Eric still has a good chance for sight. He has a scratched lens that maybe you can fix, and you rebuilt his eyelid. And…and…his left eye…it's gone, and that's why you didn't do the membrane transplant thing on it?"

Natarajan and his associate looked at each other and nodded. Natarajan was the one who spoke. "Yes, Mrs. Fiore."

"He's not blind then?" I gripped my lucky necklace.

"No, Mrs. Fiore. We have hopes for the right eye. We have sutured it shut and left orders for erythromycin ointment to be applied to the lid fissure six times a day."

Why was I so stunned? I'd known about the left eye, so why did I feel as though someone had kicked me in the gut?

The room itself seemed to exhale in a noisy collective breath. The slumped posture of the visitors became straight, their faces smiling and nodding, then speaking in loud voices about the "good news" before leaving.

David called again. A huge lump was building in my throat. I tried not to cry because I didn't want David telling me I needed medication. I'd been fighting the feeling, trying not to think about the left eye, trying to be grateful for the right one.

"He said…he said…the left—"

"I know, Carol. Eric's left eye is gone. But you already knew that, didn't you?"

After I hung up, I put my head down on the desk at the nurse's station and sobbed. I was thankful for the operation and thankful to David. Was I asking for too much to have secretly hoped the doctors could save his left eye? Shouldn't I be grateful he still had the right one? I twirled the lucky necklace around my fingers. The more I thought about it, the more I cried.

An infectious disease specialist came to see Eric. He was a compact man, a bit taller than I, with no distinguishing traits, just another in the steady parade of medical workers. Dr. Russell introduced him without any pleasantries or small talk.

"As you know, he has a nasty infection," the new doctor said. "Burn patients are at high risk for these sorts of things. I'll be getting some labs; we'll try to stay on it."

He followed Russell into Eric's room and shut the door. A few minutes later, he came out, shook my hand, and assured me he would keep me informed. He and Russell walked down the hall, and though I strained to hear their conversation, their voices were too low. The infectious disease doctor had his hands stuffed tightly into the front pockets of his lab coat.

A few hours later Knight gave me his bronch report. As he turned to go, he looked back and gave a slight smile. "I heard the eye surgery went well."

Day 27
Sunday, November 5, 2000

"Never trust someone who hates dogs."
– Eric

I stared down at the stitches holding Eric's right eye shut. His left eye was open slightly and I glimpsed the cloudy gray of his once-gorgeous brown eye. Dead.

I walked out to the waiting room where I'd left Robin. I'd gone home late last night, and she wanted to spend the day with me because, as she'd pointed out several times, she didn't get to see me anymore. She'd made herself comfortable on one of the big couches, spreading out her books and games. I'd warned her to bring lots to do: we were going to be here all day. Tia had refused to come, claiming to have homework. Robin whispered to me that Tia slept and ate all day, and she had food stashed all over her bedroom.

"What page are you on?" Robin asked me. "You're reading it, aren't you? Like you said?"

"Yes, honey. I'm almost to chapter eleven. I've got a great idea, Robbie," I continued. "Why don't you go in and read some of Harry Potter to Daddy?"

She shook her head.

I put my arm around her. "What if I put my chair in the doorway of Daddy's room? Remember? We did it before. It's probably better if you stay outside the room so we can keep germs away. How would that be, pumpkin?"

"OK, Mommy."

About an hour later, Robin was still reading when Brenna and Caitlin began to give Eric his second unit of blood. Robin read steadily, without pausing, barely taking breaths. Her blond ponytail bobbed as she emphasized parts of the book she considered important, changing the inflection in her voice as she read the lines of different characters. There was an actor inside her, crying out.

Caitlin and Brenna weren't the only ones listening to Robin read. Everyone who came in seemed to pause, taking in Robin's words, her tiny face hunched over the big book.

"Robin, are you getting tired?" I asked.

The corners of her mouth fell slightly. "Can I stop now?"

Back in the waiting room, we found Tim sitting in a corner. Handing me a piece of paper, he said, "I'd like to ask your permission to use an article Eric wrote. We're starting a Flight Test newsletter, and he wrote an article about the icing deployment in South America. It's well written, as are all Eric's reports. I'd like to print it on the first page of the newsletter, but I thought I should ask your permission."

"Yes, of course. I think Eric would want you to print it. I used to tell people my husband chased ice for a living."

Tim smiled slightly. I looked down at the article I'd proofed for Eric a few weeks ago. I skipped to the last paragraph.

> Despite the many challenges, the 10002 icing team successfully and safely completed 37 flights for 107 flight hours in South America. Over 90 percent of the natural icing test conditions were performed, including evaluations by Transport Canada. Successfully conducting natural icing tests during July and August proves that the Bombardier Aerospace Flight Test team will literally "go to the ends of the earth" to get the job done.

"What is it, Mommy?" Robin asked.

"It's a story Daddy wrote about ice. Do you want to read it?"

Robin shook her head. "Maybe I should tell Tim a story about Daddy."

"I liked the rocket story you told me, Robin," said Tim. "I'd like to hear another one." He moved over to the couch next to Robin, rubbing his forehead.

Robin put her fingers on her bottom lip, tapping it. She looked at the ceiling. A big smile played across her face. "Mommy, I could tell Tim about Polly."

I had no idea what she was talking about.

"Oh, Mommy. You know. Polly. Polly Opossum. Don't you remember?"

Tim smiled. He was still rubbing his forehead. "Robin, tell me about this Polly."

"Well," said Robin with an authoritative air, flipping her ponytail, "Mommy found a dead opossum when she was running and it had a baby and Daddy saved it and we named it Polly and Mommy gave it to her professor."

"That's a wonderful story, Robin. Definitely more interesting than ice."

After Tim left, Robin asked, "Can Daddy move yet?"

"No, honey. He's back on that medicine I told you about. It paralyzes him so he won't fuss."

"Is he always going to be on that medicine?" she asked quietly.

"No. They tried to take him off it last week, but you know that old Daddy. He started fidgeting, so they had to put him back on it. Dr. Russell told me this morning they might try again in a few days to take him off it."

"That would be good."

An hour later Robin read Harry Potter to Eric as I took a call from Patty. "I spoke with Russell," she began. "She says things are about the same with Eric. I heard there's a lot of activity on the burn unit."

"A couple kids came in over the weekend. They were in a house fire. There's a woman who must be close to eighty who's been sleeping in the waiting room every night; her husband is a patient. I heard they're poor and live out of town. It's sad here. There's also a Hispanic guy with a big family, and that young girl is still in the room to the left of Eric's—the one who tried to kill herself."

"How are Tia and Robin doing?"

"Tia's angry, and Robin's sad. That's basically it."

"Are you taking them to the counselor you've been seeing?"

"I'm taking them on Tuesday." I paused. "Robin was up last night with nightmares. I let her sleep with me. But I'm worried about Tia. She's—"

"Tia will be fine," Patty interrupted. "Is she still eating everything in sight?"

"That's what people are telling me. I don't know what to do."

"There's nothing you can do. Worry about Eric. Let someone else worry about Tia's weight. It's not a critical issue right now."

I needed to be with Eric, but as the evening wore on, I knew my responsibility was to my two girls. And I knew there was an angry one at home, trying to drown her hurt with food.

Day 28
Monday, November 6, 2000

"I owe much of what I am to Parks Air College."
- Eric

I was furious.

Eric's temperature was down to ninety-seven, and the person responsible insisted it was fine. Bailey was a tiny, dark-haired nurse with small brown eyes and nervous, jerky movements. I had seen her before. Other medical people shook their heads as she passed. So far, Eric hadn't had her as his nurse, but perhaps with all the new patients who'd come in, someone in charge felt she could handle Eric. She couldn't. Fortunately for Bailey, Dr. Russell appeared as I was about to yell.

I knew my voice was shrill. "Eric's temperature is down to ninety-seven, and Bailey over there seems to think that's what it's supposed to be. Even I know it's supposed to stay over one hundred. Dr. Russell, could you please talk to her?"

"I saw Eric about an hour ago, and he's stable." She said it firmly.

"Could you check on him and have a word with Bailey? Why hasn't she turned up the heat?"

Russell nodded, her eyes focusing on the ceiling for a brief moment. Going into Eric's room, she motioned for Bailey to follow her. The door closed, and I fumed in the hallway. Why, of all the nurses, did Eric have to get her? I adored the nurses (except Rochelle); they were supremely competent. Eric had been fortunate up to this point. I felt myself slide quickly from anger to helplessness.

Russell came out of the room. "I'm making a note in Eric's record. It won't happen again."

Bailey was still in Eric's room, pretending to be useful. I heard the heat kick on. "Aren't you going to put blankets on Eric?" I asked her, aware of the ice in my voice.

"I've turned the heat up. It'll be fine," she said, looking at something out the window.

"You know what?" I continued. "The other nurses always put blankets on my husband when his temperature gets low. If you don't want to get some, I will."

I was being a bitch, and I didn't care. Eric hated incompetence above everything else, and I was not going to let this girl put his life in even more danger.

"Fine, Mrs. Fiore. I'll get blankets."

"Thank. You." I said it loudly, enunciating each word.

When Bailey returned with blankets, Jan was with her. "Bailey needs a little help with the dialysis," Jan said, trying too hard to sound as though things were fine. "That machine is a bit temperamental, as you know." She forced a slight laugh.

I watched Bailey cover Eric with blankets as Jan inspected the machine. She explained the machine to Bailey, her voice almost a whisper, and although I didn't understand what she was saying, I could tell from Bailey's vacant expression that she probably didn't either.

It was going to be a long day.

The room was getting hot, and I stepped out into the hallway. A few minutes later, I was on the phone with David telling him about Bailey. Irritation in his voice, he snapped, "Stop interfering with the medical people."

"David, you don't get it. She's incompetent. She could hurt Eric." Did he think I was so stupid I couldn't tell when someone was clueless?

Midmorning, one of Eric's friends from Cessna dropped off an oversized white T-shirt that said "Never Give Up" in big bright letters across the front. The more I stared at the shirt, the madder I became. I stuffed it in a bag so I wouldn't have to look at it. I couldn't let myself get angry.

The angry road led to broken promises.

Excited voices of the bandage team rang out. The door flew open, and Bailey rushed over to Russell. "He has a bleeder on his left hand," she said.

Covering the phone receiver, Russell said, "Put pressure on it. I'll be there in a minute."

Russell continued her conversation as Bailey went back in the room. I could hear animated voices, and once again Bailey came out and went over to Russell.

Covering the receiver, Russell asked, "What is it?"

"He's still bleeding," said Bailey, a bit louder this time.

"Did you put pressure on it like I told you?" Impatience tinged Russell's voice.

"Yes, but…"

I dropped my journal and quickly stood. What the hell was going on? I stared at Russell, still on the phone, and Bailey scurrying around. As I was about to say something, Russell hung up and went in the room with Bailey, shutting the door behind her.

Damn those bandage people. They weren't being careful again.

I was still standing in front of the door when, after what seemed like a long time, Russell came out. "Nothing to worry about, Carol. Only a small bleeder on his left hand. We may need to do another surgery, possibly this Saturday." She walked over to the cubicle next to Eric's room and picked up his chart.

They were going to cut something else off; I could feel it. "I don't want Bailey to be Eric's nurse any—"

"I'm not in charge of that." She dropped Eric's metal-bound chart with a clang on the desk. "You'll have to talk to Rochelle."

I stared after her as she walked away. She was tired of me. Could I blame her?

When Jan returned to help Bailey, I quickly escaped down to the coffee shop. I heard a song float quietly over the speakers and paused to listen.

I wanted to remember a time when life was better, as the song said, instead of the horror I was living through. The music reminded me of so many things. I knew the singer; there was no mistaking the wonderful voice of Harry Belafonte. It was one of the happy sounds from my childhood. My father, who was frequently crabby and often scary, would always seem less irritated when he played that music. Perhaps he put the record on when he was feeling upbeat, and that was why we liked it.

Harry Belafonte sang of September's beauty, and I thought of last month, of the September just passed and of how wonderful it had been. I thought of how much I loved Eric and how my life had seemed to be turning around for the better—my zoo job, publishing my research results, our trip to Greece, Eric not yelling. I stood in the hallway and listened to the song because I wanted to go back to September and keep reliving it and not feel as if someone had wrenched my insides out. I didn't want to lose Eric. I cried because I knew I could never go back, and I wondered if the birds would ever sing for me again.

I bought a bottle of juice and tucked it in my purse, returned to the burn unit and my vigil outside Eric's room, and as I'd done for so many days and weeks, I waited.

That evening when Knight came out of Eric's room, he smiled and said, "He's coming right along."

I stared after him.

Then I heard it. It had started up. Again. I wanted to put duct tape over her mouth. Why couldn't she shut up? What did she expect? She pours lighter fluid on herself in a vain attempt to commit suicide, and then wails and moans night and day when there are people here who want to live. If she wanted to kill herself, I could think of less painful ways to do it. What about taking a bunch of pills?

The moaning came closer. I looked up to see her coming down the hall in her fuzzy blue slippers and bathrobe. She had a bandage on her face, her hands completely wrapped. As she passed me, she let out a loud moan, no doubt intended to elicit my sympathy. I avoided her eyes. I'd lost my patience with her, and I didn't want Eric to have to listen to that. I assumed, as I always had, he could hear everything. Should I have been more compassionate?

Of course.

It was late when I turned down the street to our house. I stopped at the mailbox. There were many cards, as usual. I recognized the gold return address label on one long white envelope. It was from Patty, and she'd addressed it "Carol Fiore, wife of a hero."

After getting the girls to bed, I sat down with the mail, opening Patty's letter first.

> Dear Eric,
>
> Carol asked me to write you a letter about things.
>
> I went to Bombardier yesterday to talk to a "few friends" about your medical condition. First, I spoke to the big wheels in the mahogany boardroom. It was full. Then I spoke to some friends in the airplane garage. There were hundreds of people there. They were all worried about you, Carol, and the kids. They told me many stories about you, and they're anxious to have you back at work.
>
> You'll probably want to know that your company has been great. They've done everything possible to take care of things and help. Alec and Tim especially take care of Carol and have taken care of all paper and financial concerns so Carol only has to worry about you.
>
> You would be very proud of Carol. People think she's so fragile (because she's so thin), but we know better. She has been dignified and

tells everyone how you love to fly and how you love your job. She did NOT do the whiny wife thing you so despise. She has been there for you every second: talking to you, reading books, and keeping a close eye on everything the medical people say and do.

Carol is worried about how you will handle your injuries when you wake up. RB says you will be OK. He says after you get done being pissed (so are we) and depressed (so are we), you will move on and continue your inquisitive, productive life. Carol is very worried about how you'll react, but she's in for the long haul. She's never loved anybody but you. So when you get mad and disgusted and depressed and everything else, remember how she is there for you. It took us three weeks to get her to leave the hospital at all.

There are hundreds of people calling and sending e-mails. We have the Air Force people, Fairchild, Cessna, Montreal, Learjet, tons of them. Of course, there's the Parks College crowd too.

I told Carol my long-term predictions the first day, so I'll tell you too. I predicted you were too stubborn to die. I also think you'll be back at work in about a year. I base this partly on medical facts, but mostly on the force of will you possess. The doctors in the ER gave you

basically no chance to make it even through the
first night. When they called me, I couldn't even
get them to clearly say you were still alive. But
I was sure you'd make it. I went to my house
to grab some things before I went to DIA, but
I did not bring clothes for a funeral, despite
what the nurse told me on the phone. I knew you
wouldn't die. And you won't die now. You can't.
There are lots of people pulling for you. They
didn't let you or Carol down, and I know you
won't let them down. This is hard for me to say,
but after all I've seen it does make me want to
respect you a little.

Love, Patty

Day 29
Tuesday, November 7, 2000

*"Any of us could be the victim
of a bird strike."*
- Eric

Today was the presidential election. I wanted Al Gore to win, but because Eric was a fan of Daddy Bush, he thought the son would be as good. I'm a Democrat; Eric is a Republican. We usually canceled each other's votes.

One of the respiratory therapists told me if Eric could nod, someone from the election department would come to the hospital to take his vote.

It wasn't going to happen.

I rattled on and on to Eric, but there was no response, even though he was off the Norcuron. When I ran out of things to say, I pulled out Harry Potter and read.

Later Knight remarked, "He's going in the right direction. The blood pressure needs to go up some more, but he's going in the right direction."

"I told him I'd vote for Gore if he didn't get his blood pressure up," I replied.

Knight grinned and disappeared down the hall. Maybe that man wasn't so terrible after all. Maybe one of these days he would even refer to Eric by his name instead of always "him" or "the patient." Maybe when he did, it would mean Eric was going to live. The more I thought about it, the more sense it made. Maybe Knight couldn't see his patients as people unless he knew they were going to make it. Maybe Knight had seen a lot of people die.

During the bandage change, I watched Bailey wander aimlessly through the halls. I was glad she wasn't Eric's nurse today.

Dr. Russell stopped by to look in on the dressing change. She was coughing in a way that instantly made me frown, but I didn't see any other outward signs of sickness.

She squatted beside my chair. "Dr. Knight and I discussed the debridement. The surgery will be next week, either Monday or Tuesday. There is black tissue on the hands and left forearm." She paused, lowering her voice. "I think you realize Eric may need distal forearm amputation."

I didn't say a word. I didn't want to think about the surgery.

"His blood pressure is still low, probably due to the *Stenotrophomonas* infection." She stood up and straightened her white lab coat. "Dr. Natarajan was here this morning. It sounds like he has the situation under control. Also, I'll be gone for a few days at Thanksgiving, but of course someone else will be here."

Eric needed her. How could she leave? The more I thought about it, the worse I felt—not about her vacation, but about my behavior. I was being so selfish. She worked long hours, and here I was feeling resentful because she wanted to take time off for a holiday.

I hated the person I was becoming.

Leaving the hospital early that evening, I calculated I'd have enough time to go to the polls at the Catholic church down the street from the house, get the kids a quick dinner, and drive back to see Irene the counselor. Today was Tuesday, appointment day.

I walked quietly, my head bowed, hiding behind sunglasses, into the polling place. As soon as I gave my name at the front table, the woman volunteer stood up and hugged me. She was praying for Eric, she said, as she pointed to the long line, at least fifty people. Maybe I shouldn't do this after all.

I stood in line, fidgeting, looking at my watch. A woman who lived down the street, now near the front of the line, noticed me. She came rushing back to me, grabbed my arm, and hauled me to the front of the line, saying loudly, "You take my place, Carol. I know you probably need to get back to your husband. We're all praying for you."

It was a kind gesture, but I wanted to scream *no more with the praying*.

Several people in line overheard and exclaimed, "You go first."

I was quickly at the voting booth. I stared hard at the ballot. The two names for president stared back at me. Being an environmentalist, I reached for the lever with Gore's name. Of course I was voting for him. I was liberal. I was a Democrat. I believed in a graduated tax structure.

For months, Eric had yapped on and on about the serious issues facing the country. I couldn't believe he was voting for Bush. He liked Texas. He was conservative. He was a Republican. He believed in a flat tax.

Eric was never going to convince me. Once I was in that booth I was voting Democrat, and nothing Eric said was going to change my mind.

CLICK.

I looked at the lever I'd just pulled. I had voted for Bush.

As I turned to go, the line fell silent. Whispers floated after me as I hurried out.

I rushed the girls through dinner and whisked them into the car. Irene saw each of them separately, and then spoke briefly to me about her observations. "They're as well as can be expected under the circumstances. Tia is lost; she tells me she was always a daddy's girl, and Robin needs you right now. I'll work on getting them to cooperate with each other."

I hoped everything would be in order when we arrived at the hospital that evening so I could get them home to bed. Tia began to fuss almost immediately. "I want to go. I have homework…I'm tired…" She poked at Robin and whined louder.

We didn't stay at the hospital long.

"Mommy?"

I looked up from the bed where I'd been reading a stack of mail. "Tia, honey. It's late. Do you want to sit with me and talk about Daddy?" I patted the bed beside me.

"No."

"What is it?"

"I need a new backpack." She folded her arms across her chest. "Mine is ruined."

I got out of bed. "Let me see it."

She took me into her bathroom and pointed down at the backpack in the tub.

I shrugged.

"Don't you see it? Right there. A bird pooped on it!"

I smiled. "That can be washed, honey. Really. Would you like to use my backpack tomorrow?"

"OK, but what if another dirty birdie poops it? What if it gets me?"

"It's only poop." I took her by the hand and guided her back into my bedroom. I pointed up at the wall. "Did I ever tell you about that mask?"

"It's a Mardi Gras mask."

"It's not. Your daddy bought it for me in Venice. Would you like to know why?"

* * *

It wasn't the ordinary public water fountains that confused us; it was the people holding their heads under the spigot. Oh well, we reasoned, this is Venice, must be some crazy Italian thing. The more we looked, the more it appeared the people with wet heads were tourists. When it happened to me, the "why" of it became clear.

We'd had a wonderful day, walking through the streets of Venice, holding hands, eating gelato, and taking in the sights. I wore a sleeveless pink dress. My long red hair, usually pulled back in a braid, was down, pulled to the side with a flowered barrette. I wanted to be pretty for my handsome guy. Then it hit me. Literally.

There were pigeons everywhere, but I never saw the one that let loose on me. I'd never seen so much poop in my life. It hit me right on the top of my head and slid down my streaming hair onto my delicate dress. I did not look pretty anymore. Eric stared at me with a horrified expression. "Oh…gross…"

I was mortified. I thought of the time I'd laughed at Eric when a bird had hit him at the airport. Perhaps this was my punishment for chuckling at him. He smiled, took me by the hand, and led me out to the square. "Stick your head under the fountain. Now we know what they're for."

Venice is famous for its porcelain masks, and Eric bought me a beauty. About six inches tall, the mask was painted white. Gold glitter decorated the hairline. The female face wore eye shadow and coral-red lipstick. A single tear, outlined in gold and filled in with lime-green sequins, fell from the left eye. On the top of the head was a large circle filled in with bright pink glitter.

Eric grinned when he presented it to me. "Look, it has a big poop spot on the head."

Day 30
Wednesday, November 8, 2000

*"I like birds, but elephants are my
favorite because they're big."*
- Eric

"Hope is the thing with feathers." Isn't that what the poet Emily Dickinson wrote? I stared out the kitchen window at the two sparrow-sized birds, gray and white: dark-eyed juncos. The harbingers of winter. Whenever I saw them, I knew winter was on its way, and likewise, I knew winter was never over until the last one left. Did they signal hope or the coming of a cold, lifeless season?

The days were starting to run together, but with each passing hour, I became more hopeful. Dr. Knight still wouldn't say Eric was going to live, but I tried to believe he wouldn't die now. I steeled myself for years of rehab and therapy and made plans for the future. I thought about the inspirational speeches Eric would give at the World Burn Congress and the stories he would write for the

Phoenix Society's newsletter. I surfed the web for devices for his hands, special computer keyboards, and handlebars for his bicycle. I investigated ways to equip our home with handicap devices, and I called a friend who rescued and trained dogs for people with special needs.

Each day after I sent the girls off to school, I rushed to the hospital. I was home in time to tuck them into bed, and then I would wake up and do it all over again. My admiration for nurses increased. My respect for burn nurses, in particular, soared.

Dr. Russell was always there with a kind word, and Dr. Knight started to loosen up a bit, though he still didn't call Eric by name. He even stopped a few times to listen to an Eric story. I continued to complain to Dr. Pierce about the many breakdowns of the Prisma, and he continued to be kind and understanding.

Visitors came less frequently; even Candice didn't stop by as much. They had their own lives.

There were subtle indications things were not right: the failure of many grafts, continued low blood pressure, and various infections that continued to surface. Eric's lungs were improving, though. He had lived this long, he wouldn't leave me now, I told myself.

I stopped asking what had caused the accident or why it had happened. I knew I would never sue, nor would Eric. I would keep my promise, and I would not bring down aviation and "his" company. Instead, I tried to think of Eric's recovery, of how much he loved me, and of his promise never to leave me.

Day 31
Thursday, November 9, 2000

"Every animal has an important role, even mice."
- Eric

"David's leaving for Cancun today. His wife is going with him. I think her parents are watching their two little boys."

"How can he sit on the beach when his brother is in the hospital?" Patty was loud at the other end of the phone line.

"He has to go to a medical conference."

"No, he doesn't. I canceled mine. Nobody makes you go, especially now." There was disgust in her voice.

"I assume he'll call every day and check on things." I wasn't upset. I was sure David was confident of Eric's progress or he wouldn't leave the country. It was actually a good sign.

Patty made another sound of disgust.

"Knight's in Boston, so Lewis is here," I said, resting my head on one hand, the phone receiver held tightly in the other hand. "The damn Prisma clotted again."

"Probably because of the decrease in the heparin."

"But he'll bleed again if they don't decrease it. The nurses said it's probably his stomach lining that's bleeding. Doesn't aspirin make your stomach bleed? Eric popped tons of it because of those terrible headaches."

"He was probably killing his stomach, and of course he's too stubborn to see a doctor."

"He hates doctors." I exhaled loudly. "That's why this is all so tough for me."

"Doctors are saving his life right now."

"I know. Maybe he'll change his mind. Or maybe he'll hate them more."

"Russell has talked to you about Eric's left forearm, right?" Patty asked gently.

"I don't want to talk about it."

"Fair enough."

"Pierce went in Eric's room. I've got to go, Patty."

I was standing outside Eric's door when Pierce came out. "Clotted again. We have someone working on it now. The bleeding has stopped, so I'm going to increase the heparin, but I'll be monitoring it carefully."

"What if he starts bleeding again?" I asked.

"That's why I'm monitoring it carefully." He snapped the top of the metal chart down sharply.

I stared after him as he walked down the hall. Every time one doctor tried to do something to help Eric, it had repercussions on something else.

Then I saw them: the teacher with the three young nursing students, and I knew they were going to enter Eric's room. I realized, of course, students become competent by assisting in hands-on training in real situations, and I hadn't objected to the presence of a student in Eric's room; there had been several. But now there were three of them. At once.

I felt my whole body tense up as they started to go in Eric's room. Jumping up from my chair, I addressed the teacher. "Excuse me. Who are these people?"

"They're nursing students, Mrs. Fiore. I'm sure you won't mind if we go in for a few minutes to do some instruction." The teacher stood with her shoulders back, arms at her sides. She was so stiff I almost expected her to salute. Her tight bun perched atop her head like a silly gift bow. The three young, pretty girls seemed tired and a bit bored, their loose posture in direct contrast to their teacher's. One girl was chewing gum.

"I do mind," I said. "Why don't they have gowns on? I limit visitors to my husband's room for obvious reasons. I'm sure you understand why."

I struggled to hold back my anger. Patty and David had warned me about pissing people off.

"Ladies, the gloves and gowns are around the corner," the teacher said loudly, stiffly, enunciating each word.

The three fell in line behind their teacher, reminding me of baby chicks following a hen. I called after them, "Please wash your hands."

Sitting in my chair outside Eric's room, I glanced up at the open door. The dialysis nurse was staring at me but pretending not to, looking up, trying not to catch my eye, then quickly looking back down at the instruments. The instructor and students returned with gloves and gowns on and paraded into Eric's room, shutting the door.

I peered in the window; curtains were usually only drawn during procedures, like the bandage change. They were standing next to the dialysis machine and listening to the nurse. One of the students, the gum chewer, stared at Eric with a frightened expression. I flew down the hall to Jennifer's office.

"Why do they have to be in Eric's room? There are three of them now. I haven't objected when there was only one, but now there are three, and they didn't even have gowns and gloves on and—"

"Please slow down," Jennifer interrupted. She dropped a sandwich on her desk and nearly upset a can of soda. "Are you referring to the nursing students? I believe they're with their instructor, aren't they?"

"Yes, but my husband's injuries are not some show for the benefit of these students. I haven't objected before, but I don't want all these people in his room. Eric could get another infection. I've limited visitors for that reason, and now they're traipsing in there without even washing their hands. I have a right to say no, don't I?"

"Yes, you do. You've been good about letting students go in. I agree that staff should have consulted you, and yes, you do have a right to say no. Let's take care of this right now."

I sat in my chair while Jennifer stood, waiting for them to come out. She paced back and forth in front of the closed door, occasionally peering in the window. She patted me on the shoulder during one pass, smiled at me during another.

Ten minutes later, the door opened and they filed out. Jennifer took the instructor down the hall. Though Jennifer had her back toward me, I could see the instructor's expression. She was clearly mad, arms folded tightly across her chest, lips clenched together. The instructor shot me a hard glance as her students followed her down the hall.

When they disappeared from sight, Jennifer said, "I'm sorry for all that. I've told the instructor only one student at a time can enter." She patted me on the shoulder.

"Thank you, Jennifer." I forced a smile.

Linda dropped off a pile of e-mails but couldn't stay. I sat in Eric's room and read aloud to him from the sizeable stack. There were notes from all over the country.

Carol,

The most interesting situation I can remember with regard to Eric was when he was stationed in Roswell for some off-site flight testing (I think it was the Cessna Excel). He and a group of mechanics and other pilots were bunking in an old military building, and the place had an irritating population of mice.

Everyone but Eric set about trying to eradicate the mice. Eric, believing mousetraps to be barbaric and cruel, set about methodically tripping the traps so the mice would not get hurt. It was my impression that this became a source of heated discourse.

What will always stick in my mind is what a genuinely funny storyteller Eric could be. This guy could have you in stitches at a moment's notice. The dour lack of humor among the military brass, his descriptions of the idiosyncrasies of various Cessna managers, or observations of everyday basic human nature. I enjoy his laugh and his ceaseless (but realistic) optimism.

—Mark

Eric was such a gentle man. I knew because we'd had our own fuzzy problem.

* * *

"They're adorable," Eric said. "Look at the way they groom their tails. They're actually clean animals. I don't know why people are afraid of them."

He peered closer at the contents of the three mayonnaise-sized glass jars sitting on the counter. "Hello, *tupelenos*," he called loudly.

When I'd asked him months earlier why he called them *tupelenos*, he told me it was the Italian name for mice. I'd never heard that word and told him I thought he'd made it up.

He giggled as he held his cappuccino mug, gazing at the tiny house mice—each in its separate jar with sunflower seeds and hay. "Do you think they have enough to eat? You're going to let them go later, aren't you?"

"Of course I'll let them go, but if Sandy sees me, she'll go nuts. She's terrified of them. Do you want me to keep catching them in live traps? They're all over the garage. I suppose you'd be upset if I put poison out."

Eric put a hand over his heart and clutched at his chest. "You wouldn't poison innocent *tupelenos*, would you?"

Tia overheard and ran to her daddy. "Don't let Mommy kill the *tupelenos*."

Eric put his arm around her. They pouted dramatically.

"Of course I won't poison them," I said. "But it takes some finesse to transfer them from the traps into those jars so you two can watch them."

Tia looked at her daddy, and they both laughed.

"You're just mad about the *tupeleno* that jumped down your jammies, Mommy," Tia squealed.

Eric high-fived her, and the two of them laughed so hard Eric fell off his stool.

"I don't think it was that funny. And please, Eric, don't ask me again if it was tickly."

Eric whispered in Tia's ear, and the two of them erupted in giggles. I tried not to smile, but it had been rather funny. When the laughing stopped, Eric looked at me, a serious expression on his face. "Hey, Carol. Was it tickly?"

* * *

I picked up the next e-mail.

Carol,
   Hope you get this. This is Wayne. I admire Eric out of all the people I've met and who have influenced my life. Eric is one of the outstanding ones.
   I don't know if he ever told you this, but when it was time for Cessna to promote a new test pilot during the Citation X program, Eric, Brad, and I were the candidates. I got the promotion, based on who knows what, and Eric was upset. I imagine he told you, maybe not. Anyway, he fumed for weeks.
   I felt bad because I liked him and thought maybe this whole thing could damage our friendship, but I said nothing. One day passing in the hallway, he stopped me and said, "Wayne, I'd like to apologize." I asked him what he needed to apologize for and he said he'd been acting like

a jerk for the last few weeks and was sorry for it. He asked my forgiveness. No kidding; I almost fainted. I said there was nothing to forgive, I would have been just as upset, and made a joke about how he could get away with a worse attitude than I could. We laughed, shook hands, and parted with him telling me I was a better man than he was. That day has always stuck with me as a demonstration of his inner moral code.

I appreciate his endurance, his honesty, sincerity, humor (he was always cracking me up and I think he sometimes came to my desk to see me laugh). Most of all I appreciate his friendship.

The last time I saw Eric was at Semolina's restaurant; I think it was in August. I know he'd ridden his bike to my house not too long ago and had waited around for a while in the driveway for me to get home before he left. I will be forever sorry I missed him that day.

—Wayne

Hey Carol,

My husband and I were talking about Eric tonight, and I was reminiscing about Robin's birthday party. I remember Eric going to McDonald's to buy the happy meals, dressing up in the outfit, and then becoming scarce because there was way too much estrogen in that place.

One of the best memories I have of Eric is from Robin's party. He was in the kitchen sipping coffee (or cappuccino?) and he was listening to all the girls giggle. I said something about what an imaginative party Carol puts on and all the hard work, and he had the biggest, loving, proudest grin, and he was nodding in agreement. His eyes were glowing with happiness as he lifted the cup to taste his coffee. He was leaning against the kitchen sink soaking up the whole atmosphere. He somehow seemed so fulfilled with life at that moment, listening to all the giggles float around the air like musical notes. I got an overwhelming feeling from him of pure love for his family.

I thought I'd put this in with the other e-mails. I wanted to share that with you.
—Linda

It was kind of Linda to write that. I missed how the two of us used to hang out at school, working on labs, laughing about some of the undergraduates. I missed the life I'd had before it caught fire.

I left the hospital early. My girls needed me. I needed them. Maybe David was right. I needed to be a better mother.

As usual, I couldn't sleep. I checked on the girls, both asleep. Then I wandered into the living room and watched Flutter sleeping peacefully, her head under one wing. Dusty, my sweet Dutch bunny, was awake, so I let her out of her cage to run around. We shared a carrot.

I trudged back up to the bedroom and began a search for Eric's notes. I found one he'd written to me this past summer, when I got the education job at the zoo. He'd signed it with his trademark heart face.

Dear Carol,
Congratulations on your job offer.
I know the pay isn't half of what you're worth,
but it's good to know other people realize
you're the best person for the job.
Love,

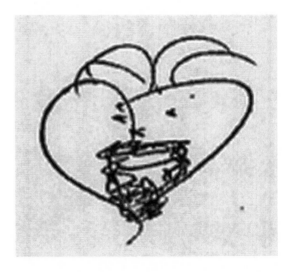

I found a postcard with a picture of three wolves in a forest.

This is a picture of Alaska. These wolves are trying to eat me.

I have a bad toothache. What if these wolves had a toothache?

I bet they'd eat the dentist.

I miss you. Maybe that's why I have a toothache.

Love,

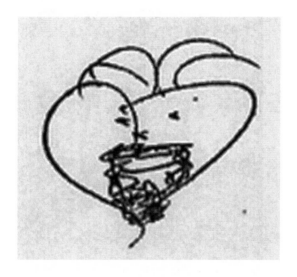

Day 32
Friday, November 10, 2000

"Never trust management theories with catchy bullshit phrases."
- Eric

K night was still in Boston, so Lewis performed the bronch, reporting that Eric's lungs were showing a definite improvement. Russell should have sounded more cheerful, but she repeated twice that his blood pressure had been showing wild fluctuations. How serious it was, she wouldn't say.

At noon, Candice showed up. I tried to be kind, but even though I hadn't seen her in several days, I had no tolerance for her. I forced a smile as she yapped on and on about trivial dumb stuff. I wasn't listening to most of what she said.

"I can arrange for someone to bring Thanksgiving dinner. Are you going to be here, or are you going to go home that day?"

"I don't know. Thanksgiving is still a way off," I replied in a monotone.

"You know how fast holidays come up. I was saying to one of my friends…" I was too distracted to listen as she droned on. I caught snippets about her family holidays, her neighbors, her in-laws. Yak yak yak.

"Should I have someone arrange for Thanksgiving?" She tapped her foot.

"Oh…sorry. Can you ask me in another week or two?"

"Of course," she replied, her smile wide, her perkiness on overload.

I retreated to my chair outside Eric's room.

Later in the day I began to fret about how much Eric was suffering, and I couldn't stop thinking about it. Images of him trying to cry out drifted through my mind.

"I was in there for a good part of the bandage change," Rod the day nurse said, "and he didn't show signs of discomfort, like increased heart rate or over-breathing the vent. He's on some heavy medication." Rod wasn't looking at me when he spoke, and I wondered if I could trust his words.

Eric's blood pressure was still extremely low. I told him about the ongoing craziness with the presidential election, about the squabbling and the blaming. I thought it would get him mad enough to raise his blood pressure—it didn't. When I couldn't think of anything else to say, I read Harry Potter. I was almost finished with the first book, and Robin had insisted I read the second. It had a phoenix in it.

By that evening, Eric's blood pressure was up a bit. Then I noticed it. So did Rod. Eric's right eye was definitely coming open. The sutures were pulling apart, and I could see a tiny bit of the globe. Rod suggested I call Dr. Natarajan.

"I don't know how to reach him. David is handling this." Why was I the only one who'd noticed the eye? Or didn't anyone besides me think it was important anymore?

David.

It occurred to me that he hadn't called. I phoned Patty, but she hadn't heard from him either. I called New York. Dad suggested I call David's home and speak with his in-laws. They would know how to get him. I called. No answer. I left a panicked "call me immediately" message.

I got a sickening feeling, suddenly, urgently. I ran to the bathroom and fell to the floor over the toilet seat. Heaving as though my gut were being squeezed through a juicer, I brought up only coffee.

Something was terribly wrong.

Day 33
Saturday, November 11, 2000

*"People who aren't afraid to live
aren't afraid to die."*
– Eric

Damn that David.

I listened to his answering machine again. Why hadn't he called? The stitches in Eric's right eye were becoming longer and longer. Feeling rage for the first time at the thought of David lying on the beach, I slammed the phone down. Why had David gone? I'd assumed it was because he thought Eric was better, but now I wasn't sure. Was he running away from the pain? Like Dad? Like I wanted to?

"I…I…can't get a hold of David," I said to Russell. "He's been in Cancun for two days, and nobody knows how to reach him. Eric's eye…it…it's coming apart…" I pulled a wad of tissues from my pocket and blew my nose.

"Why is he in Cancun?" she asked.

"Some medical conference...but...his wife went."
As soon as the words left my mouth, I knew I hadn't
said them nicely.

There was an awkward pause. "I left a message for
Natarajan. Hopefully he'll return your call shortly."

Fifteen minutes later Natarajan was on line one.
Grabbing the phone quickly, I explained the situation. He seemed distressed at the news I gave him,
promising to discuss it with Russell. Why hadn't
someone told him earlier? Had I really been the
first to notice it? Were things worse than I thought?
Is that why no one cared about the eye, because it
didn't matter?

Natarajan promised to call the oculoplastic surgeon
right away and then call me back. He suspected Eric
would have to go back to surgery. I told him Knight had
scheduled Eric for surgery on Monday. Could someone
fix it then? Natarajan asked to speak with David.

"David's in Cancun. No one can get a hold of him,"
I said, trying not to sound too angry. David hadn't told
Natarajan either.

"I will call you back, Mrs. Fiore, and let you know
how we are going to proceed." He was formal, as usual.

I locked myself in the bathroom and sat on the
floor, rocking back and forth. Something was changing. I couldn't explain what, but things around me
seemed to be odd, out of place and time. Superman
couldn't be blind! Superman couldn't die! How could
the world exist without him?

Dr. Russell told me Eric had ARDS, or acute respiratory distress syndrome. His white blood count was down to 2.8, and his platelets were only 23. Down and down. The numbers continued their awful spiral.

Lewis performed the bronch. The lungs were looking better. Nothing else was. I spoke with Pierce's partner, but he didn't have much to say. He acted as though the Prisma didn't matter, that the machine breaking was unimportant. Down and down.

Dr. Natarajan came in while I was reading Harry Potter. I watched from the corner while he examined Eric's eye. There was no expression on his face as he turned to me. "Mrs. Fiore, there is some lid retraction, and that is what you are seeing. The amniotic tissue is still in place. I will be leaving orders for an ointment to be applied around the clock. It is paramount that this is done to protect the eye. He will need to be back in surgery to repair the lid. I will be speaking with Dr. Russell about the timing of the surgery. We will do everything possible for your husband, Mrs. Fiore."

Were people telling me what I wanted to hear so I wouldn't cry? Things weren't going well, and I wanted to yell at people, especially David.

I called David's house again. Still no answer. I didn't want to call Patty because I knew I'd get hysterical if I tried to tell her everything that had happened. After all she'd done, I didn't think it was fair. She'd get on the next plane if she heard me. I didn't know what else to do, so I walked up and down the hall, back and forth, back to my chair, up, down the hall, back again.

Eric's nurse Anna appeared to be in her early thirties, with a short auburn ponytail. Before it was even noon, I wanted to strangle her. She was gruff and definitely had her own way of doing things. Even her voice was rough, not at all the clear voice of Caitlin.

I was used to the way the other nurses did things, even Rochelle, who, despite her personality, was an extremely competent nurse. Anna's way was different, and I didn't like it.

She had turned Eric onto his tummy, and I noticed his respiratory tube was caught underneath him. Several respiratory therapists had told me a twisted or kinked tube was a bad thing, so I told Anna.

"Excuse me, but I do know what I'm doing."

"It's not supposed to be twisted under him," I shouted.

Anna stood completely still and stared at me, her mouth slightly open.

I stomped out of the room and marched over to the nurse's station. Rochelle was there, but I didn't care. "Would you please call a respiratory therapist right away?"

Before she could say anything, I saw one of the RT people coming down the hall. Recognizing him, I ran over and said, "Can you please come in Eric's room?"

He followed me without a word. Glancing back, I saw Rochelle shake her head and look skyward.

Entering the room, I pointed to the twisted trachea tube. The RT guy looked at Anna and said, "Please assist me so I can fix this. Mrs. Fiore is quite correct. The tube should not be positioned in this manner."

It took only a few minutes to reposition the tube. The young man rechecked all the equipment carefully as Anna stared down at Eric's chart, roughly turning pages, her face flushed.

Anna went about her duties in the room, completely ignoring me, refusing to look in my direction. It reminded me of the childish way my mother acted when I was a kid. I knew I had made an enemy in Anna, but what else could I have done?

I continued to read and talk to Eric while getting nasty looks from Anna. She'd pretend not to look, but I'd see her out of the corner of my eye. I almost expected her to stick her tongue out at me.

Anna seemed competent except for the twisted tube incident, but she had a major attitude. Who appointed her Queen Bee of the burn unit? Perhaps if I pissed her off enough, she wouldn't ask for Eric again. I wasn't sure how much of a choice there was for the nurses, but maybe she'd say, "I refuse to have that patient because his wife is a bitch."

I was OK with that.

Then Eric could have Jan, and Caitlin with her melodic voice, athletic, brilliant Brenna, and Lydia,

who worried about me too. There was entertaining
Rod, and at night, Amanda with her big voice and big
heart, and Laurel—my favorite nurse. I cared about
people's feelings, but compared to Eric's health, they
were irrelevant.

I continued to call David's house with no success.
At first I'd felt confused about his trip, then concerned.
Now I was angry. Why was no one answering?

I called New York. Mom answered the phone this
time, and I explained the situation in the calmest voice
I could. "I have to speak with David. I've called his
house several times, but no one answers. Aren't his in-
laws there taking care of the boys?"

"The boys are in California with them." She didn't
ask what was wrong.

"They are? Why didn't Dad tell me? Do you have
the number?"

Less than thirty seconds later, David's mother-
in-law picked up the phone. I explained the situation: it was critical, and I had to get a hold of David
immediately.

"I'm sorry. David can't be reached," she told me.

"But there must be a number where I can call him."

"No. I'm sorry. He can't be reached. Those are the
instructions he left. I'll tell him you called when he
phones here."

I hung up and immediately dialed Patty. She was
disgusted. "You can't tell me that with two small boys,
they didn't leave a phone number. Cancun isn't in some

third-world country with no phones. He should be calling you every day."

Back in Eric's room, I opened Harry Potter to the
last chapter.

The infectious disease specialist spent a considerable
amount of time in Eric's room, looking at the chart,
speaking with Anna and Russell, and looking at lab
results. While he was writing at the cubicle desk next
to Eric's room, I asked, "Why is my husband's blood
pressure so low?"

He wheeled around in the chair and leaned back.
His two index fingers under his chin, he eyed me for
a moment. His beige-brown eyes stared through me. I
felt uncomfortable. "Your husband has a serious infection," he said.

"That Steno-thing?"

"*Stenotrophomonas.* It's not responding to the
Bactrim."

"Can't you use another antibiotic?" I pleaded.

"There's nothing else. Bactrim is the only drug we
have at this time. Perhaps years down the road another
drug will be developed, but right now this is all we
have."

"So his blood pressure is low because of the
infection?"

"Yes. His body doesn't seem to be able to mount a
defense." He turned back to the desk, pausing over a
page in Eric's massive chart. Tapping his finger on it,

he turned around. "His white blood count and platelets continue to drop. If his pressures aren't up in two to three days, he's going to die."

He might have been addressing a medical school class, explaining quite matter-of-factly the fate of someone he'd never met. Someone unimportant. Someone ordinary. Someone clearly *not* Eric.

I stared at him, feeling my mouth fall open.

"I'm sorry, Mrs. Fiore," he said, as though I were a student in his class. "If his pressures don't come up, if his body is not able to mount a bicarbonate response to the acidotic condition I am seeing, if his white count doesn't come up, he's going to die in a few days."

"But…what…what is the white count supposed to be?"

"The normal range is 4.3 to 10.8 if you leave the thousands off." He looked over his shoulder at Eric's chart. "His count is well below 4.3."

I was underwater. I couldn't get to the surface, couldn't get a breath. "Can't you give him a blood transfusion?" I felt myself choking.

"Only for red blood cells. White blood cells are made in the bone marrow. He has to do that himself."

"What if he can't?" Now I was wailing.

He stared at me.

"Why are the white blood cells so low?" The voice that came out of my mouth was a squeak.

"The Bactrim is chewing them up."

"What?" I began coughing. "Then stop the Bactrim!" I was screaming now.

"If we do, the infection will kill him. And as I said, there is no other drug available."

"Are you sure?" The voice was not mine.

"Quite."

"Then why do you give Bactrim if it destroys the white blood cells?"

"Normally the patient can produce more. Your husband has serious injuries." His beige-brown eyes were ripping my skin off. I was burning, my insides boiling, fire melting my lungs.

My reply was loud. Too loud. "Dr. Knight didn't think he'd make it. Dr. Knight thought he would die, but he didn't. My husband won't die. He didn't live this long to die now. You don't know him."

He shut the chart. "I'll be back later. Please call if you have questions."

I furiously wiped at the tears. He was worse than Knight. I ran to the waiting room. I felt frantic, pulling at my hair, clenching and unclenching my fists. The regular group of visitors was there: Alec, Tim, Phil.

Trapped in a deep pit, I tried to tell them. Nobody understood. "Would you like some coffee?" Alec asked.

Coffee? Was he serious? How about not sending Eric on that flight in the first place? Could he get me that?

Tim tried to pat me on the shoulder. "Eric won't give up the fight, Carol."

I moved into the far corner. Everyone was always touching me, putting his or her arm around me, hugging me, patting me as though I were a child.

I'd had enough.

Day 34
Sunday, November 12, 2000

"Flexibility is the key to airpower and almost everything else."
- Eric

I followed Russell into the conference room. Sitting down next to me, she took a deep breath. "We need to talk about decisions."

"What decisions?"

"How aggressive should our treatment be? Eric's blood pressure remains low, and his platelets and white blood count continue to drop. He could code."

"You mean…you mean…" Lights danced in front of my eyes.

"If his heart stops, what do you want us to do? You're his wife."

It took me a few moments to understand what she'd said. I didn't want to believe it. I wouldn't believe it. "I want you to get it started again," I croaked out, "with that machine. I've seen it on TV."

"Of course. If that's what you want."

"Are you giving up on Eric? I mean are you going to—"

"Carol." Russell looked at me intently. "We'll do everything in our power for Eric. We still plan to take him to surgery tomorrow, and I know Dr. Natarajan is trying to get someone in here. We're not giving up, but we must know how to proceed."

Suddenly I was up, walking in fast, tight circles around the conference room. I started counting them: one...two...three... My nails dug into my arm: four... five... Round and round I went.

I felt Russell's arms around me, and then I was sobbing, heaving. She guided me to a chair and handed me a box of tissues. "He said he'd want every chance to live if something ever happened. I'm giving him that. Please. Eric won't die."

I thought about my last sentence and knew it wasn't true. Maybe I'd known for some time now. No one thought he'd make it. Wanting something, even as desperately as I did, didn't make it so.

Someone was squeezing my fingers, then holding my head. The strange voice came again, cracking and shrill. It was me. "I had a dream last night. It was the first good dream I've had about Eric since the accident. I dreamed he was walking and talking and writing a book. He had scars and a patch over his left eye, but he wasn't blind. He was smiling."

Russell walked with me to Eric's room. Dr. Lewis arrived, followed by a tech pushing the bronchoscopy machine. About twenty minutes later, the door opened and Lewis gave his report. His voice was quiet, almost a whisper. "And his platelets are extremely low."

When Patty called, I could only force out a few words. "I don't want him to die."

The voice at the other end was calm, but the tone was distant, unsure. "I'll call Russell," was all she said.

Sandy came by to drop off the second Harry Potter book. She also handed me a container of chocolate cake. "Robin helped me make this. She thought you'd fancy it." She knew things were bad; I could see it in her eyes.

Opening the book, I forced my eyes to focus. Robin wanted me to get to the part about the phoenix, and I felt a great urgency to read quickly. When I grew tired of reading, I pulled out Linda's tape recorder and played "Wild Horses" over and over.

I called David's in-laws that afternoon. They still hadn't heard from David. Why hadn't he called? The only answer I received was that they'd give him the message.

As the afternoon wore on, I felt myself slipping. Things occurred around me, but they felt like a dream. My entire body was numb, my senses suppressed. It was like listening to people underwater. My eyes refused to focus.

Visitors were in the waiting room, and I staggered out to see them. I bumped into two walls but couldn't feel it. The visitors didn't stay long. I didn't know them. I didn't care. I tried to be congenial, but every time I opened my mouth to speak, it felt as if someone else were talking. I listened to the words and wondered how they were coming out of my mouth.

Late in the afternoon, Dr. Natarajan called. His associate, who'd assisted him before, was out of town, and he was trying to get Dr. Schmidt to fix Eric's lids during tomorrow's surgery. He was unsure if Schmidt could come tomorrow, but he thought he might be able to come on Tuesday.

"But Dr. Natarajan, the surgery is tomorrow. I know Dr. Knight won't let Eric go to surgery two days in a row. His blood pressure is already too low."

"Perhaps it will be possible to reschedule the surgery for Tuesday."

He agreed to speak with Knight and to continue trying to get Schmidt. What was I supposed to do now? What was Knight going to say? And where was David?

Day 35
Monday, November 13, 2000

"Life is too short to drink bad coffee."
- Eric

We were in the conference room: Knight, Russell, and I. Knight had returned from Boston, and he was taking Eric to surgery today. He said it in a rather odd way, as though if he found something better to do with his time he would do that instead. He didn't say he was doing the surgery as though it were an order, a command from God-Knight, the way he always did. He shrugged and said he guessed the patient would go to surgery.

I'd spoken with Dr. Natarajan on the phone earlier. Dr. Schmidt couldn't get here until tomorrow to fix Eric's eye. I had to make a decision, and I knew what it had to be, not what I wanted, or what Knight wanted.

I stood up, and the words came out of my mouth. I looked at Knight when I said them, and for the first time in all these many long days, my voice did not crack. "No. You're not taking him to surgery. Dr. Schmidt can't come until tomorrow. You have to wait. Eric would want me to take care of his eye."

Dr. Knight leaned back in his chair. He took his glasses off and wiped them on the corner of his shirt. After a long pause, he looked at me. "We need to do the debridement. He has several areas of blackened necrotic tissue, especially on his left forearm, and—"

"I know." Did I actually interrupt Knight? "I signed the authorization. It said 'debridement, possible split thickness skin grafting, possible left hand or forearm amputation.' I read it several times. I added 'left' next to forearm amputation. I didn't want there to be any misunderstanding about which arm it is."

Russell shifted uncomfortably in her seat and ran a hand through her long ponytail. Knight didn't say a word, just continued to look at me with no expression at all. I was taking charge. I hoped Eric would be proud of me.

The room was completely silent as I continued. "So...I'm sorry. The surgery will have to wait until tomorrow. You could have done it last week if there was such a hurry."

Knight leaned back even farther and continued to stare. No, I thought, I will not cry. Hands at my sides, I looked straight ahead and willed myself to stay in control as I spoke. "If Eric's eye isn't saved, then everything you've done to help him will have been for nothing. If he can't see, he will die."

I was breathing hard. My voice was beginning to crack. I looked out, over their heads, because if I looked directly at Knight, I might start crying.

Knight stood up. "I'll cancel the surgery."

He left.

Why had Knight let me have my way? He never had before. He was good about ignoring my outbursts, such as about the circle bed. "I'll do what I think is best for the patient" was his motto. He didn't give a damn what I said. Why now?

I called Patty and told her what had happened. She found Knight's behavior out of character too. "Maybe he's realized how important the eye is." She seemed to think I had won a victory against a god, even congratulating me.

Jan and Brenna stopped talking when I went back into Eric's room. Opening the second Harry Potter book, I read, occasionally peering at them from behind the book.

I shut the book. "The eye doc couldn't come today, so I had to cancel the surgery. Eric would have wanted me to. I'm sure of it."

The two nurses gave each other a quick glance. Without a word, Brenna went back to Eric's chart. Jan said, in barely a whisper, "I hope you know what you're doing."

Knight arrived with a tech and the bronchoscopy equipment. His report was brief. "We've stopped the Bactrim, and he's on Leucovorin therapy and GCSF."

What was GCSF? I didn't feel like asking. Knight paused to write something in Eric's chart, and as he was leaving he turned back to me. "I've rescheduled the surgery for tomorrow at two o'clock. Have your brother-in-law call Natarajan."

Knight didn't sound mad. He sounded...sad. There was a quick flicker in his eyes, a slight downturn of his mouth, and then it was gone.

"Thank you for rescheduling, Dr. Knight," I said. "David's in Cancun. I still haven't heard from him. I have Dr. Natarajan's number, so I'll call and tell him."

Knight raised one eyebrow but didn't say anything.

I spoke with Natarajan's office. My message was firm. Schmidt had to be here by two o'clock. I wouldn't be able to stop the surgery tomorrow. If I didn't hear something in a few hours, I'd call again.

Russell was back. Jan handed her lab results, which she read to me in a voice that was professional and formal. She'd never read me lab results before. "Eric's pH is critical at 7.13. His white blood count is one thousand, and his platelets are critical at five thousand." She paused and then repeated, "His platelets are critical."

She'd told me earlier Eric was off the Bactrim. That meant the drug wasn't chewing up his white blood cells. Now his body would have a chance to make new ones. Those platelets would go right up. My guy would show them all.

But by early evening, Eric's blood pressure dropped farther. I wondered if there was some sort of damage occurring inside his body because of the continued low blood pressure. I was afraid to ask.

Before the shift change, Jan came in the room to tell me David was on line two.

I ran to the phone. "David, I've been trying to get you for four days!"

"What is it, Carol? My in-laws said you left a message to call." He sounded exasperated, as though I were interrupting him for no reason at all.

"Yeah. I left a message. Lots of them. Days ago." I took a deep breath. "Eric's eye came open, and I couldn't get you, and he was supposed to go to surgery today, but I had to cancel it because the eye doctor couldn't come. I told Knight myself. I've been calling Natarajan. Eric's blood pressure is really low, and he's off the Bactrim and—"

"I'll call Natarajan."

"Too late, David. He's left his office already."

David spoke in a calm but quiet voice. "I have his pager number. Is Russell there? I'd like to speak with her."

He should have talked to her days ago. What *was* his problem? I spotted Russell chatting with one of the respiratory people. "Just a minute," I said angrily.

Russell saw me walking toward her. "Yes, Carol?"

"David's on the phone. He wants to talk to you. Shall I tell him you're busy?"

She exhaled loudly. "No, I'll be right there."

Day 36
Tuesday, November 14, 2000

"What's the use of a life without passion?"
- Eric

———————————————

I spun around quickly as the container of Vaseline dropped from my hands, hitting the floor with a dull thud. I thought I'd heard Eric's voice.

I froze.

Then I felt it. In that instant, I knew. Eric was going to leave me.

"No!"

Jan rushed in, looking quickly at the monitors. I stood in the middle of the room, face wet with tears, hands shaking, staring down at the container.

The bronch seemed to take forever as I fidgeted in my chair in the hallway. The door opened, and Knight put his hand on my shoulder. He'd never done that before. "There were lots of clots. He's also acidotic. He's unable to maintain his blood pressure, white blood count, and platelets. Overall he is declining quickly."

My words spewed forth in a hoarse yell. "His name is Eric!"

Knight squatted down, moving within inches of my face. "I've canceled the surgery. His condition is too unstable."

I looked down at the ugly white tile floor. He still couldn't say his name. Then I looked back up at him. "You canceled the surgery?"

"Yes. His condition is critical. If I took him in now, he'd die on the table."

After Knight left, Russell said gently, "He does care, Carol."

"No, he doesn't!"

I ran into Eric's room and threw open Harry Potter. I had to get to the part about the phoenix.

I signed the authorization for bedside eye surgery, and at 1:50 p.m., Dr. Schmidt arrived with his assistant. Knight asked me to come to the conference room. I followed him down the hall. Jennifer and Russell were already there. Looking at their faces, I knew. "I...I don't want to hear this..."

Jennifer stood up and took me by the arm. She guided me to a chair and whispered that Dr. Knight had to speak with me and I needed to listen.

"But...the eye surgery...and..."

Dr. Russell stopped me. "Dr. Schmidt will not leave before he speaks with you."

Knight cleared his throat. "Some decisions need to be made. It's pointless to continue treatment. I've seen this happen many times. The patient has started down a road from which there is no return. His systems are starting to fail one by one. But protocol demands we are clear about the course you want us to take."

Jennifer put her hand on mine. "What Dr. Knight is trying to say—"

"I KNOW WHAT HE'S TRYING TO SAY. I'VE GOT TWO FUCKING MASTER'S DEGREES!"

No one spoke. The room was silent except for sobbing—life shattering, the-world-is-over-Superman-is-going-to-die sobs. They were coming from me.

I felt a sharp, stabbing pain in my chest. "*I killed him*! Oh my God, I killed him! Because I wouldn't let you take him to surgery. It's my fault. It's all my fault."

Knight and Russell shook their heads no. Knight spoke first. "Of course you didn't kill him. Don't be ridiculous. I was glad you stopped the surgery yesterday. If I'd taken him in the condition he was in, he most likely would have died on the table." His voice was calm, the words spoken clearly, with conviction.

Dr. Russell whispered to me, "Why do you think he gave in so easily?"

"Mrs. Fiore. What course of action should we take?" Knight folded his arms across his chest.

"I want you to do everything you can to save him. If his heart stops, I want you to restart it. OK? OK? SAY YOU WILL!"

Knight let out an audible sigh, and although he shook his head in a manner that indicated he was displeased, only one word came out of his mouth. The word was yes.

I returned to my post outside Eric's door. Schmidt came out and shook my hand. "I've done everything I can. I'm afraid the amniotic membrane sloughed off. I'll get the complete report to you if you wish."

"But…but…what are you going to do now?"

He looked at me sadly. "Let's wait and see what happens. Dr. Knight feels the outlook for your husband's survival is slim."

He thought Eric was going to die too. The eyes didn't matter anymore because he was going to die. That's what everyone thought.

"Carol," Dr. Russell said softly, "I think it might be time to get Eric's parents out here."

"Right away?"

"Yes, right away. May I call your sister?"

By the time Patty arrived around midnight, Eric's white blood count was 0.5 and his platelets were 1,000. I grabbed her tightly. "Did Eric have a good life, Patty? Did he? Did he have a good life?"

"You know damn well he did." The words were choked.

"Patty," I stammered, "did…did…you bring black clothes this time?"

Tears flowed down her cheeks. "Yes, Carol."

The Last Day
Wednesday, November 15, 2000

"When I die, have a party in my honor, and tell stories about my exploits. Don't forget the beer."
– Eric

7:10 a.m.

Through a haze, I saw Knight come into the room and look at Eric. Russell leaned over the chair I'd sat in all night. "Dr. Knight would like to speak with you in the conference room."

I followed them down the hall. I couldn't feel my legs as my footsteps fell clumsily on the tiled floor. I stumbled through the doorway and fell into a chair.

Dr. Knight rubbed at his forehead. "I'm sorry, there's not much more to offer."

I sat there knowing what was going to happen and wondering how I was going to get through it. "I'm going back to Eric. I have to get to the part about the phoenix."

I shuffled back to Eric's room. Jan and the respiratory therapist finished quickly and shut the door as they left. There was no sense in being brave anymore, or in hiding my tears. It was time to tell Eric the truth. "My love, remember when I told you about the bacterial infection you got because your skin isn't protecting you the way it should? They gave you medicine, the only stuff in the world that kills it, but it chews up your white blood cells. You've been having blood and plasma transfusions, but they can't give you white blood cells. Only your body can make them. You're too weak to make more, and your body is giving up. You fought so long and hard, Eric. Nobody thought you would make it out of surgery that first night, but you did. You said to the whole world that Eric Fiore could fight harder than anyone. I keep watching your white blood count go down. I keep watching your blood pressure go down. Soon your organs won't be able to work anymore. They'll start to die, and...and..."

Opening the Harry Potter book, I said to Eric, "I'm going to read to you all day. We'll get to the part about the phoenix."

I read. With all the strength I had, I read.

Late Morning

A thin reddish fluid oozed from his head bandages; thick yellow tissue dotted his chest; his left eye protruded through the bandages; blood flowed from his G-tube. Eric was dying. I was dying. We had fought so hard, all these days, and it had been for nothing. I was in a cloud of exhaustion as I heard various reports in and around Eric's room. His blood pressure was falling; his white blood count was down to 0.2; his platelets were at 4.

Everything was falling.

I continued to read, as best I could. RB arrived, and Patty once again commandeered the conference room for the family.

Early Afternoon

David finally arrived. He'd spoken with several plastic surgeons, and he had plans: Eric was going to be flown to a special hospital for facial reconstruction when he was better. David was back from Cancun and full of ideas, his face glowing with encouraging possibilities for Eric's recovery. Perhaps David had been in more denial than I had been, or maybe he'd believed me at last: Eric would not die.

In the conference room, I listened to David for over five minutes without saying a word. I felt as though I was looking at the real him for the first time. His deep brown eyes, so like Eric's, were filled with emotion, and what I saw confused me. He was not the arrogant, controlling man I'd thought he was, but a vulnerable being desperately trying to believe his big brother hero would not die. He was lost, so terribly lost, and his love for Eric had driven his interactions with me, with Knight.

In that instant, I knew I had misjudged David. We were the same, both wanting the man we adored to live. The difference was that I knew the truth, and David did not.

Midafternoon

"How is he?" RB asked Knight.

"He's going to be dead before this time tomorrow." Knight flung the words across the room. He appeared almost…angry. RB didn't say a word.

Motioning for him to stay with Eric, I plodded down the hall to the conference room. Patty and Sandy were speaking in low whispers. Seeing me, they stopped.

"I'm going to get some coffee," I told them.

Stepping outside the door, I heard them resume their conversation. Something made me hesitate. I paused and listened out of view.

"…can't believe he said…"

Patty was telling Sandy about an earlier meeting. I hadn't been present. "…me, and David, and RB… Russell was there too with Knight."

I moved closer to the door.

"… only lasted about ten minutes. David came in on his shiny white horse ready to save the day. Apparently he'd talked to a couple plastic surgeons about Eric's face: one in San Fran and the other in New York, I think."

Sandy sounded confused. "What are they going to do with his face?"

"That's where a lot of the infection is coming from. You have to debride the area aggressively or you have all sorts of problems. If Eric had worn his helmet and gloves, he would be walking out of here in a month or two."

"Really?" I heard Sandy ask.

"Yes. That part's hard to take. I think the infection came from his head, and it wouldn't have happened if he'd been wearing his helmet."

There was a long pause before Patty continued. "Anyway, David was telling Knight in an animated way how the debridement was going to be done. You met Knight. He doesn't like to be told what's going to be done. I think David felt guilty about going to Cancun when his brother was in the hospital. Carol couldn't get a hold of him for four days, and Eric's eye started to open up. David's the one handling the eye stuff."

"What did Knight say?"

"Nothing at first. He let David go on and on. He never even cleared his throat. He sat there, legs crossed toward the door, his chin in his hand, and never said a word. Russell never even looked up, and of course RB and I didn't say a word."

I stepped closer to the door.

"When David was finished, Knight leaned back in his chair and said—and I'll never forget his words as long as I live—'I'm going to tell you something. He's going to be dead in forty-eight hours no matter what we do or don't do. He's rotting from the inside out. Do you understand what I'm telling you? He'll be dead in forty-eight hours or less, no matter what.' There was absolute silence. I've never seen a person deflate the way David did. He said nothing. I don't think he could talk at this point. Anyway, Knight left, just got up and walked out of the room. We all sat there somewhat stunned. Nobody said anything, and—"

Sandy interrupted, "How's Carol doing with this?"

"She knows. She told me Eric was dying, and for the first time…"

I walked back to Eric's room. The thought of coffee made me feel ill, and I didn't want to hear anything else.

Eric was going to die.

Today.

Approximately 3:00 p.m.

Knight called a conference with all of us: David, Patty, Russell, Brenna, Jennifer, me. RB was on Harry Potter duty. Knight spoke slowly. "Nothing we do or don't do is going to make a difference. I suggest we think about taking some of the devices off-line."

I stood up. "You'll do everything you can to keep him alive. I won't give you permission to unplug him." I sank to the floor. "*Please.* If his heart stops, restart it."

Knight's body was rigid as he leaned forward in his chair. His eyes narrowed at me. "Mrs. Fiore. You're the wife. The decision is yours, but I do not want people jumping on your husband's chest. You do not realize how traumatic that would be for everyone involved. And why would we be resuscitating him? All his systems are failing. Let Eric die with dignity."

I stared up at Knight. He said Eric. He said his name.

"I…I…can't make that decision. I give my permission to Patty and David to make it. They're the doctors." I flew down the hall to Eric's room.

Patty came in minutes later. She put her hand on my shoulder. "David and I are taking care of it. Knight is right."

Late Afternoon

The conference room was full of people: Patty, RB, David, Sandy and Phil, Tia and Robin, Linda, Tim and his wife, Alec and his wife, and even Candice. Various people from Cessna, Raytheon, Boeing, and Bombardier had been stopping by all day. Word had traveled fast. Several people took turns reading Harry Potter, and every half hour Robin would demand to know what page we were on. Tia sat sullenly in a chair with her arms crossed and refused to talk to anyone.

I asked Dr. Russell if she would talk to the girls. Everyone else went out to the main waiting room. Taking the hand of each girl, Russell said, "I'm so sorry. We've done everything we can and your daddy has fought bravely, but he's going to die."

Robin immediately burst into tears, pulled back her hand as though it were on fire, and clutched me tightly.

Tia stood up and screamed at Russell, "What do you know? You don't know my daddy. You're a stupid doctor. You're not God. You don't know."

Russell tried to explain that there was nothing left to do; they'd done everything possible to save him.

Tia screamed even louder. "You better not unplug those things. You better not kill my daddy!"

I could see the pain in Russell's eyes as she winced at the words.

Later Tia insisted to everyone in the room that she hated Russell. Patty shook her head sadly but didn't say a word.

Eric's blood pressure continued on a downward spiral. He had regular treatments, blood products, bandage changes, and labs. But we all knew. Russell checked on us throughout the day, and Robin continued to ask, in a frantic voice, what page we were on.

Early Evening

Sandy had taken the girls for a walk around the hospital when Tim, Alec, and Patty sat down with me in the conference room. David and RB were with Eric.

"Tim and Alec need to know what you want in the way of a service," Patty began. "They'll make it happen. Think about it and let us know."

"But...but he's not..."

Patty took my hand. "You don't have to do it now. I thought it might be easier if you did. Maybe tell us what you're thinking. Did Eric ever tell you what he wanted?"

Not specifics, but he'd given me a direction. "He wanted a military funeral." I heard the words fall from my lips, but I didn't recognize the voice. "He was proud to…" I began to sob. "…to be in the Air Force."

This was a dream, a terrible nightmare. I was going to wake up any minute. Eric had promised he'd never leave me. He always kept his promises.

Tim wrote in a red notebook.

Getting up, I pointed toward Eric's room. I staggered down the hallway. David and RB left when they saw me. I stood over Eric, holding his bandaged hand. Words weren't necessary. I knew what he wanted.

A few minutes later, I was back in the conference room. "Eric wants an F-15 flyover."

Tim and Alec gave each other a look that said it was not going to happen. I heard Patty whisper to Tim, "Try, OK?"

No one moved, no one coughed.

"I want it in a hangar," the Carol-caught-in-the-nightmare continued. "I want everyone to wear their flight suits."

Tim began writing in his notebook again.

"I want people to tell flying stories about Eric. I don't want prayers or priests or any of that bullshit."

Patty shifted uncomfortably in her seat.

"I want them to play 'Wild Horses.'"

Tim continued writing. I started to say something, then pointed, once again, toward Eric's room. I ran down the hall. RB was still reading aloud. I grabbed the Harry Potter book from his hands.

Patty peered in the room. "Robin wants to read to her daddy."

I handed the book to Robin, and Patty set up a chair in the doorway for her. My innocent ten-year-old slumped over the book and read in a quiet voice, full of fear, full of confusion, as silent tears fell on the pages.

I thought about raising her and Tia alone.

Lisa arrived. She looked so much like Eric with the same thick, dark eyebrows, the same deep-brown eyes, the same gorgeous dark hair. Her first words to me were, "You have to tell him to let go."

I needed Eric. I would die without him. How could I let him go?

A short time later, while Lisa was in with Eric, I went up to Brenna and blurted, "Can I see Eric's medical record?"

She looked at me, surprise on her face. "Of course." She pointed to the thick chart on the cubicle desk.

I sat down and opened it. I knew exactly what I was looking for, and it didn't take long to find it. The heading said "Operative Report," and the date of the operation was yesterday. The doctor was Schmidt. I skimmed the three-page report. I had to know. Was Eric's right eye gone?

"The patient's left globe was protruding and partially necrotic…"

I knew that. His left eye was gone. I kept reading.

"The previously placed amniotic membrane was loose and sloughed off the central cornea…given that the amniotic membrane was no longer serving a useful purpose…the membrane was removed and discarded…"

I felt tears fill my eyes as I tried to read on through the film of water. I knew what it was going to say.

"Prognosis for normal lid function is grim. It is expected that given the nearly complete avascular nature of the lids, that there will not be normal sensation or motor function. Furthermore, if the patient survives…"

My chest hurt as violent heaves threatened to tear me apart.

"…if the patient survives, I anticipate that there will be severe continued contraction of what appeared to be essentially avascular lids. The prognosis of the globe given a central corneal ulcer is also poor…"

I shut the record.

He was blind.

Approximately 7:00 p.m.

I put my arm around Robin's shoulders. "I think you better skip ahead to the part about the phoenix."

Robin looked up from the chair in Eric's doorway. "I already did, Mommy."

There was nothing I could do. "Keep reading, honey. Then if you get to it, you can read it to him again."

"I already read it twice. Just in case," she replied, looking down at the book clutched to her chest.

Approximately 8:00 p.m.

"We're leaving now, Carol." Serious Brenna, always professional, was crying.

Jan clutched me in a tight hug. "I'll never forget Eric. It's been a privilege to have cared for such an incredible man."

Brenna hugged me. I squeezed her in return and didn't want to let go. She whispered, "It has been an honor to know you."

Then they were gone.

The night nurse introduced herself. I'd never seen her. Was she competent? It didn't matter. "I'll be checking on things as the night progresses, but we'll try to stay out of your way. I'm very sorry, and if there's anything you need, please ask."

"Eric's parents?" I asked Patty as she walked in.

"They'll be here soon."

I looked at her helplessly. Putting her hand on my shoulder, she asked, "Can people come in?"

I nodded. There was no point in restricting visitors anymore, no point in protecting Eric from germs. My role as watchdog was over. I felt my hands nervously wiping at my face, twisting my hair. "Patty, please…I can't…please, Patty…"

"Remember what Lisa told you. You have to let him go. He has to know."

How could I survive this night? How long was it going to take? I didn't want Eric to die, but I wanted it to be over. I felt awful thinking it, wanting it to be over. I felt as if something were standing on me and I couldn't breathe. People started to come into the room. First Lisa and then David. Tia and Robin came with Sandy and Phil. Then Tim and his wife, along with Alec and his wife. RB was there too. I was glad the priest wasn't there.

Everything was blurry as I babbled to Eric. I had a strong feeling he needed to hear my voice. I told him about everyone who was in the room. I told him how we all loved him. I told him he was a hero.

Everyone was quiet. I couldn't see them; I could only see Eric as I continued rubbing his bandaged arm. I heard David say he had to leave to get his parents. Then Patty told David he should stay, she would go to the airport. Alec offered to drive.

I continued talking to Eric, reminding him of the adventures we'd had together. I tried to laugh about the house in Woudenberg with no bathroom. I couldn't. All the time the horrible monitors kept inching down. His blood pressure was falling, heart rate, everything, all slowly falling. I knew there wasn't much time. I turned on Linda's tape recorder. I played our song. I played it again.

While the tape was playing, Sandy whispered to me, "I'm going to take Tia and Robin outside for a bit."

I looked over at them, near Eric's bedside. Robin was at the foot, barely inside the room. She was crying, her head in her hands, refusing to look at Eric. Tia was angry, arms folded, defiantly staring straight ahead. Should I let them be here, at the end? It wasn't my decision. Tia said she'd never forgive me if I made her leave.

RB spoke, telling Eric he'd never had a friend so amazing. Then Alec's wife talked about how much Alec had loved to fly with him. Phil told Eric we were the best neighbors they'd ever had and he and Sandy would take care of the girls and me. Tim tried twice to talk, but couldn't.

I looked down at Eric. "Tim is here. You know how you always said you thought you were Tim's favorite test pilot? I know you are."

Lisa told him he'd fought hard. "It's all right to let go." She looked at me as she said the words.

I shook my head no, his parents weren't here, he couldn't let go. Then I saw what Lisa had seen in the hallway. Eric's parents were here. They'd made it. Patty bustled into the room, looked up at the monitors, and said, "They're here, Carol. Eric's parents are here. You can tell him now."

Mom and Dad gathered around Eric, along with Alec and Patty. Sandy and the girls had come back in the room. "Your parents are here, Eric. Everybody is here. We're all with you."

To lose a child...I loved Mom and Dad *so* much. I was afraid to look at them. I was filled with so much pain that if I took in even a small amount of theirs, I would break.

Tim hugged me. "We're going to leave. We think it should just be the family." He paused. "You're right. I told Eric earlier today that he was my favorite test pilot."

One by one, people said good-bye. Tim and his wife, then Alec and his wife, and then Sandy and Phil. RB asked, "May I stay, Carol?"

I nodded.

Mom said abruptly, a bit too shrilly, "Dad and I would like to speak to Eric alone, please."

I didn't want to leave. Patty whispered, "Let's sit in the hallway. I'm watching the monitors carefully. I'll tell you."

My feet seemed attached to the floor, but I knew I needed to go. I picked them up slowly and let Patty guide me out the door. I sat down in my chair, the one I would soon never sit in again, and stared into Eric's room. Mom shut the door.

The door opened, and Mom came out. Dad was still in the room. When he came out, I started to get up. RB looked down at me. "May I, Carol?"

I nodded. Then it was Lisa's turn, then David's. They were quick. I looked at the clock. It was almost 11:00 p.m. The monitors were going down faster now. The nurse continued checking, unplugging things. The respirator was still on. They wouldn't take that off, Patty said. Just dialysis, stuff like that.

"I'm going to take the girls down to the cafeteria," Lisa said to Patty. "Tia says she's hungry."

"Be fast. It could be any time now," Patty whispered.

I was beyond the point of being able to talk to Eric, so I continued to play our song. Dad sat in the hall and looked in the room. Medical people came and went. And still the monitors crept downward. I wondered if anyone else had the same awful thought I did: make it be over.

I thought of all the adventures I'd had with Eric. I was back at Parks, and he was handing me the tool bit he made for me. We were in Vienna, and he was buying me the long-promised pastry. We were flying, and I was laughing. We were having picnics, and traveling, and he was pretending to be Robin Hood. We were making love, and making babies, and watching our children grow up. We were walking around the zoo, my zoo, and I was telling him about the animals, and he was telling me it is better to have found one's passion at thirty-six years old than never to have found it. And I was asking him how he'd always known he wanted to be a pilot. And he was telling me pilots are born, not made.

Above it all was the promise he'd secured from me so many times—to honor aviation and never bring down the thing he loved. I'd vowed to tell the world about him.

Patty squeezed my arm and pointed up at one of the monitors. It had started straight down, rapidly. "Tia and Robin…" I moaned.

"Don't worry, I'll find them," she said as she raced out of the room.

The monitor was going straight down. I grabbed Eric's arm desperately. "I love you, Eric. I'll make you proud, Eric...I'll never forget my promise...and..."

A strange noise sputtered from one of the machines. A stream of liquid trickled out of the corner of Eric's mouth and ran down the side of his face. I quickly took a corner of the bed sheet and wiped it off.

The lines on the machine...down and down...

Patty ran into the room; Lisa was behind her, followed by Tia and Robin. They gathered around the bedside. Tia and Robin were both crying and telling their daddy how much they loved him.

Robin held his bandaged hand.

All the lights in my world started to flicker and go out. Darker and darker until only one small light was left. I could barely see, barely breathe.

I started to say something and looked at Patty. She was staring at the monitor, and then everything went dark.

Patty whispered to me, her voice shaking, "Carol, he's gone."

After the Funeral
Monday, November 27, 2000

*"If anything ever happens to me,
you'll be OK, Carol.
You're stronger than you think."*
- Eric

I t was a chilly fall day in Wichita, windy, over-
cast. Eric was buried, everyone was gone, and I
was home—back to the house we had picked out
together, with the wallpaper Eric had put up, the book-
shelves he had built.

His shoes were by the door, his beloved sports
car in the garage, his bicycle in its same spot with his
helmet hanging from the handlebars. For a moment, I
thought I smelled the familiar scent of cappuccino in
the air.

The house was silent. The kids had gone back to
school, and I was alone.

I looked out of the kitchen into the living room.
Dead flowers draped their once-graceful heads over

vases and baskets. Pictures of Eric stood in frames, gazing, smiling. I thought of our trip to Greece and I wondered if I would ever go. I looked down at my wedding ring, and I was sure I would never take it off.

I knew something else. I couldn't live without him. I fell to the cold linoleum floor. I knew what I had to do. It was a coward's way out of the pain, but I didn't see any other choice. I hoped everyone would forgive me.

Sitting on the kitchen floor, I gripped Eric's ring on the cord around my neck. I don't know how long I sat there. Minutes? Hours?

I felt something near me. I looked out the window above the kitchen sink. Sitting on the railing, a foot from the window, a sparrow-sized, gray-and-white bird with a black forehead peered in at me with inky eyes. His perky gray crest ruffled in the breeze. He cocked his head.

I stared.

I stared again.

It couldn't be.

Eric always asked me why we didn't have this familiar New York bird in the scruffy stand of trees behind our house. I'd answered that "our woods" weren't the right habitat for it. Yes, there were some in Wichita, but never in our woods. I was positive because I'd been documenting the birds in our backyard for the Cornell Lab of Ornithology for years, so I'd have known.

The bird came closer. There was no mistaking it. It was a tufted titmouse—the bird Eric had pestered me about for years. It was the bird of his youth, the one we'd never ever seen in our woods.

Eric sent it.

I didn't believe in God, but I'd always believed in my connection to Eric. So why hadn't I felt anything when the crash happened? I didn't know until Sandy came to tell me, and I'd been confused about it for all these many weeks. I'd lived with Eric for almost twenty-three years, loved him, followed him around the world, had his children. He was a part of me. Wasn't he?

Eric sent it.

If I wasn't connected to Eric, then how could I go on? Who was I now? Who would I become without him? How could I raise two little girls without him?

Eric sent it.

For a minute, maybe two, I was convinced. But how could he have sent it? He was dead. He wasn't coming back. I was alone. But if he could have sent it, he would have. He'd have known that of all the things he could have done, I would understand this bird.

I wanted desperately to believe Eric had sent it. I fought to believe it against the rational, scientific atheist I'd always been. I needed that connection with him to be real because without it I wouldn't know who I was. I would truly be alone.

Could I find myself? Or would I have to make a new me, one without Eric?

I stared out the window long after the bird flew away. In the end, I couldn't believe Eric had sent it. I'd have given anything to see him, just once more.

But.

I would not be delusional or spend my life looking for signs in everyday occurrences or in coincidences. I would learn to handle grief in other ways because now, somehow, I knew I couldn't take the easy way out. It was going to be excruciating—knowing I would never see Eric again—but I would not believe a religious fantasy I'd rejected my whole life. I vowed, right there, to honor Eric with memorials and scholarships and to keep my promise to him.

I knew I would be going on a long journey.

As I grabbed the trashcan from under the sink, preparing to clean up the dead flowers, I glanced once more out the window. My friend had returned. It would be the last time I would see a tufted titmouse in my yard. I blew him a kiss as he flew away. In the end, did it matter how the bird got there?

It was there—a tiny gray ball of feathered hope.

Almost Thirteen Years Later
Monday, July 8, 2013

"When I die, I want the world to know about me.
Maybe someone will write a book."
– Eric

"I think you're making a mistake to list the book as fiction." Kate leaned against my kitchen counter. "It will sell better if you market it as creative nonfiction."

"I know, but I can't," I replied. "You read the introduction. If every word isn't completely accurate, including all the descriptions and all the dialogue, then technically it's fiction."

Kate shrugged and crossed her thin arms over her brown T-shirt. "I don't think other writers would agree."

"It would be ironic if I were sued over a book that's about not suing." I paused to take a drink of water. "I didn't write it to make money. I'm giving a lot of it to charity anyway. I've been working on it for a decade; I need to be done. I keep reliving Eric's death every time I edit. I can't do it anymore."

"It's beautifully done," Kate said sincerely.

"Really?"

She nodded. I'd first met her in a writing workshop about four years ago and had been relying on her excellent editing abilities ever since. She had also been helping me with a teen fiction trilogy full of environmental themes. I'd been having great fun with my characters, and it was a chance to use my ecology background. It was a much-needed break from years of writing about grief.

"There are some problems," Kate continued. "Read my comments, and we'll have lunch next week to talk about it." She walked over to the kitchen table, opened the large white folder containing the manuscript, and flipped to the last pages. "Here."

"The epilogue?"

"Why does it take place five years after the accident? It's been thirteen. No one wants to know what you were doing eight years ago."

I'd worked diligently writing that section. The setting was perfect—a Rolling Stones concert with the girls. Members of writing groups over the years had insisted on the epilogue, which showed the girls being normal: arguing, bantering in the car, enjoying something together. I'd used lots of description. I'd brought in memories of our song, "Wild Horses." The Stones didn't sing it that night, but I managed to make the story work anyway.

I hadn't thought it would take thirteen years to publish the book, so an epilogue that occurred five years after the accident might have worked. Then there were scores of rejections, and the NYC literary agent who didn't do much with the book for two years. I'd had to start the publishing process all over again. It had been the most frustrating experience of my life.

"What should I write about in the epilogue?" I asked Kate.

"You."

"Me? I'm a geek who writes and exercises. No one wants to read about that."

Kate made an exaggerated sigh. "Your readers want to know who you are now. The accident changed you. It's a difficult question, but who do you think you might be now if the accident hadn't happened?"

"Maybe I'd be a zoo education curator."

Kate took a sip of her wine. "Now you're a writer instead."

"My kids would have a father," I countered. "And life wouldn't be so hard."

"You've become strong because your life has been hard."

The kitchen was silent except for the noisy snoring of my old Maltese dog—a gift from Patty to the girls right after the accident.

I considered Kate's words. "You're right. I should rewrite it, but what else will people want to know?"

Kate threw her hands up. "That Robin finally persuaded you to go to Greece with her last year. That you still have *that* car. That you were able to return to Russia and Tia went with you because she's as fascinated as you are with the country. That you set up scholarships in Eric's memory." She gave me a pointed stare. "That you don't date."

"I tried that once. It didn't work." I glanced over at Sydney, my Moluccan cockatoo, sleeping in the next room. She'd been my buddy for twelve years. "He didn't like Sydney."

"I think it's more than that."

I twirled my wedding ring. I was about to be brutally honest with myself. Kate had been my friend for years; I was sure she already knew.

"For years it was because no one could ever be Eric," I admitted. "But I guess it's more than that now. When you love someone, a part of your identity is bound to that person. When Eric died, I didn't know who I was anymore. Writing the book has been painful, but I learned a lot about myself: who I was then, who I want to be now. I like relying on myself and making my own decisions, even though it's hard sometimes. Eric would have made it easier for me. Patty tried to do the same; she didn't understand when I couldn't let her take care of me anymore. Maybe another man might make things easier too, but I refuse to relinquish control of my life to anyone. You read the manuscript; you know Eric was a bit controlling."

"A bit?" Kate practically shouted. "He was the cookie Nazi."

"I still make those cookies at Christmas. Robin helps me decorate them. She made Harry Potter characters out of the gingerbread men three years ago. Then she made vampires. Last year it was *Avengers*. I don't hate the cookies anymore. Robin makes it fun."

"See? You're strong; you're in control of your life. And what about the speeches you give at Skeptics conferences? You've come a long way since you threw that priest out of Eric's room."

I sat down at the kitchen table. "It was scary coming out of the atheist closet, but when my article was published on Richard Dawkins's website, I couldn't hide anymore."

Kate spread her hands out wide in a see-there gesture. "I'll repeat it again: you're stronger. You've worked hard to become a writer. Rewrite the epilogue, make the changes I suggested, and we'll talk. You're almost there."

She was right. I'd gone back to school years ago, taken formal writing classes, joined writing groups and workshops, and practiced the craft almost every day. I read boring grammar books. I'd worked for over a decade learning to write so I could tell the world about Eric. The book had consumed my life, and I wasn't giving up now. I was, after all, a Parks College graduate. That means you never quit.

"By the way, Kate," I said, changing the subject. "My mother-in-law is coming in September. She hasn't seen the girls in a couple years. I'd love to have you meet her. Maybe we could all go out for lunch."

"What about your father-in-law?"

He'd hardly left the house in years. Eric's death had broken him into pieces that could never be put back together. Even spending time with the girls and me seemed painful for him. A counselor had told me the three of us were a constant reminder of Eric.

"Dad's not coming; just Mom."

* * *

At 3:00 a.m. I am still awake. Kate stayed several hours, and our conversation lingers. Leaving, she'd said, "I don't think I've ever told you how sorry I am for what you went through."

No one has said those words to me in years.

Frustrated with my insomnia, I turn the light on and try, unsuccessfully, to read a news magazine, but I finally throw it across the room. Pictures of Eric look out at me from every available space in my bedroom. It seems much longer than thirteen years since he's been gone.

It was difficult for the girls, moving and leaving their friends a year after Eric's death, but now they agree—Colorado is a good place to live. People are more open-minded and liberal here. The scenery is spectacular.

Are the girls all right? People frequently ask. There was much counseling in the early years after the accident, and most of it was a waste of time. Tia manipulated the counselors; Robin ignored them.

Robin is an anthropology graduate student. I'm proud she's dedicating her life to making the world a better place, and I enjoy hearing her speak endlessly and passionately about her volunteer work. She doesn't talk about the accident, and she doesn't tell people about her father. She says the tragedy doesn't define her and she's OK. But I saw her grow up quickly after the accident, losing the rest of her childhood. Perhaps that's why I enjoy taking her to one of her favorite places—Harry Potter World at Universal Studios in Orlando. I see her radiant smile and hear the laughter, so much like Eric's. She has his fast, cheerful walk as we traipse around Universal. I wear my Harry Potter shirt often—the one with the phoenix on it.

For five summers in a row, Tia attended a camp in the New York Adirondacks for kids with eating disorders and weight problems. She finally admitted she has a food binging problem, one she must deal with her entire life. She turned it into a strength, becoming a manager for a store that sells fashionable clothing for curvy gals. She enjoys helping women feel good about themselves—whatever their size.

I was dismayed when Tia dropped out of college after less than two years, but I've come to realize she is her own woman. She's an excellent salesperson, winning several awards and even a cruise. She has Eric's wicked sense of humor and often makes me laugh when no one else can. Tia talks about the accident and her father frequently. She lives with her boyfriend, a caring man who spoils her and treats her with respect. He's even half-Italian. Tia worries constantly that he'll get in an accident, and nothing I say eases her fears.

One of my greatest regrets since Eric's death has been in allowing certain family members—surprisingly not David—to persuade me to take antidepressants. I was on them for almost three years, becoming something of a zombie, devoid of passion or goals. I made bad decisions, permitted people to take advantage of me, became a fraud victim, and allowed Tia to get away with inappropriate behavior while in high school. My painful experience with antidepressants prompted me to write my second published article.[*] The success of that piece encouraged me to continue writing magazine articles; I've published seven to date.

Even after so many years, I continue to relive Eric's service in the Bombardier hangar. Many of the pilots wore flight suits and told stories about Eric—just as he wanted. The Air Force gave him military honors, but I never learned the identity of the pilot in the low-flying jet that streaked by as the hangar doors opened for the firing of the guns. Bombardier folks said they had not arranged it, and the Air Force didn't do it.

---

[*] Fiore, Carol. "Grief Without Pills," *Grief Digest*, October 2008 Volume 6, Issue #2

The girls and I want to thank the pilot.

A few years ago, I spoke to a pilot who'd been in Argentina with Eric during the summer right before the accident. I told him how Eric had changed when he returned, even letting me drive the Miata. He'd smiled sadly and related a long conversation he'd had one evening with Eric. They'd been talking and drinking for hours while Eric confided to him about some of the problems we'd been having. Eric said he wanted to be a better husband. The friend had finally said, "So stop talking about it and do it." He claims Eric sat there, alone, long after everyone else had left.

I think of Eric every single day. I miss his gentleness, his sense of humor, his brilliance, his playfulness. He was a complicated man, but as I often joked with him, never a boring one. But thinking about Eric doesn't always keep me from thinking about other things.

The burns. Sometimes the thoughts are so debilitating, I turn the radio or television up to deafening levels in an attempt to block the thoughts. It doesn't always work, and there are days when I can't stop thinking about them. I'm terrified of fires. I've lined the electrical outlets of my house with smoke and carbon monoxide detectors.

Maybe I shouldn't live so close to the fire-prone Rocky Mountains, but it's peaceful and has an abundance of wildlife, especially birds. I have two acres and many pets, including a domestic duck I rescued six

years ago while working at the local wildlife shelter.
She makes me laugh. There was no laughter for many
years after the accident, especially during the time I
waited for *the* answer.

It took three and a half years—long, painful years of
flinching every time the phone rang—to get the NTSB
report. I remember the exact date it came: April 13,
2004. I rummage through my box of papers and reread
excerpts from the NTSB document titled "Accident
Number CHI01MA006; NTSB AAB-04/01."*

*The copilot (Eric) was performing the radio com-
munication and other related pilot-not-flying
duties...*

*The accident flight was also a training and orien-
tation flight for the copilot...*

*Bombardier's operation of its flight test program
was deficient because the preflight briefing was
inadequate, because a relatively inexperienced
flight test pilot was chosen for a flight that involved
a complex maneuver he had never flown (and in
an aft c.g. configuration greater than he had ever
flown), because a build-up for the accident flight
was not considered, and because the company*

---

* All excerpts are courtesy of the National Transportation Safety Board. The
complete report is available online at http://www.ntsb.gov/doclib/reports/2004/
AAB0401.pdf

failed to identify a history of the pilot's practice of high rotation takeoffs...

The NTSB determines that the probable cause of this accident was the pilot's excessive takeoff rotation, during an aft center of gravity (c.g.) takeoff, a rearward migration of fuel during acceleration and takeoff and consequent shift in the airplane's aft c.g. to aft of the aft c.g. limit, which caused the airplane to stall at an altitude too low for recovery. Contributing to the accident were Bombardier's inadequate flight planning procedures for the Challenger flight test program and the lack of direct, on-site operational oversight by Transport Canada and the Federal Aviation Administration...

I never sued any person or entity because of the accident, though attorneys pursued me. When one lawyer told me my children would hate me if I didn't sue, I told him to fuck off. Tia and Robin told me I rocked. So did Eric's parents. David and Lisa approved too.

I never publicly blamed anyone, and when the press called for a statement about the content of the report, I said, "No comment." Keeping my promise to Eric has been, and still is, difficult. Every day I work at not being angry. I try not to whine. I refuse to be a victim because honoring Eric's memory has become a driving force in my life. Not only did we love each other, we loved aviation.

I continue to look up when a plane flies overhead. Sometimes I smile as I pause and think of our adventures, especially our first date. I started flying gliders again, but it didn't last long. The cockpit was lonely without Eric. I still haven't flown powered planes. They have engines that can catch on fire. I'm not afraid to die, but I'm afraid of burns. I doubt I will ever fly powered planes again, though I have no problems as a passenger on commercial airlines.

I read the written transcript of the voice recorder again. I don't need to. I can recite almost every word of the 31:01-minute recording. The last minutes are the worst.

Time: 1449:48.82
Eric: rotate.
Bryan: OK, we're flying.
Eric: V two.
Cockpit area microphone (CAM): [sound similar to stick shaker sounds for 2.2 seconds]
Bryan: whew.
Dave: what are you doing?
Aircraft mechanical voice (AMV): bank angle...
CAM: [sound similar to stall aural warning sounds for 1.1 seconds]
AMV: bank angle...
Eric: [sound similar to heavy breathing starts]
AMV: ...bank angle...
CAM: [sound similar to stick shaker for 0.15 seconds]

AMV: ...bank angle...
CAM: [sound similar to stick shaker for 0.22 seconds]
Bryan: hang on.
CAM: [sound similar to stick shaker for 0.3 seconds]
Dave: what are you doing?
CAM: [sound similar to stall aural warning sounds for 0.82 seconds]
Eric: [sound similar to grunting]
AMV: bank angle...
Bryan: hang on.
Eric: we're not [unintelligible word]...
1450:00.79
CAM: [sound of impact]

The part of the report that is the most difficult to accept, to live with, is what it says about Eric's slow extrication from the aircraft.

There were not sufficient ARFF personnel equipped with protective gear in the immediate response to fight the fires and perform a rescue... The firefighters stated that they could hear the pilots calling for help...Firefighters stated that additional personnel during the initial response would have allowed them to suppress the cockpit fire more quickly...

The copilot was extricated from the cockpit about 20 minutes after ARFF units arrived...

The Safety Board addressed ARFF staffing concerns when it issued Safety Recommendation A-01-65 to the FAA. Safety Recommendation A-01-65 asked the FAA to "amend 14 Code of Federal Regulations 139.319(j) to require a minimum Aircraft Rescue and Fire Fighting staffing level that would allow exterior firefighting and rapid entry into an airplane to perform interior firefighting and rescue of passengers and crewmembers...

What I'd heard in the hospital was true after all. This—not Dr. Knight, as I had thought—is what has tormented my dreams all these years.

* * *

In July 2004, I saw Dr. Knight for the first time since that meeting in the conference room on Eric's last day. He was with his wife, and they attended a speech I delivered at a softball tournament to benefit burn patients. As I was preparing to return to Colorado, he gently cautioned me to "drive carefully." He looked older, heavier, sadder.

Then later, that October, the girls and I were asked to give a speech in Wichita at a foundation dinner to benefit Saint Cornelius Medical Center. Dr. Knight and his wife made our hotel reservations, picked us up for the dinner, secured a helicopter ride for us, and drove us back to the hotel. During my speech, I glanced at Dr. Knight. My voice cracked as I stared in disbelief. Tears were streaming down his face, and he was sobbing.

I struggled to remain focused on my words as confusion seeped through me. After the ceremony, I found Knight, alone, in the hallway.

"Dr. Knight?"

He looked up at me with bloodshot eyes. "That was a wonderful speech," he said, his voice barely a whisper.

I hugged him. "I know you did everything you could to save Eric." I paused. "And I know you really truly cared."

Are you a nonbeliever looking for grief help?

A Grief Workbook for Skeptics
by
Carol Fiore

Available in 2014

**Flying Kea
Press**

Made in the USA
Middletown, DE
12 August 2015